Only Rakes Need Apply

Books by Kate Pearce

The House of Pleasure Series
SIMPLY SEXUAL
SIMPLY SINFUL
SIMPLY SHAMELESS
SIMPLY WICKED
SIMPLY INSATIABLE
SIMPLY FORBIDDEN
SIMPLY CARNAL
SIMPLY VORACIOUS
SIMPLY SCANDALOUS
SIMPLY PLEASURE (e-novella)
SIMPLY IRRESISTIBLE (e-novella)

The Sinners Club Series
THE SINNERS CLUB
TEMPTING A SINNER
MASTERING A SINNER
THE FIRST SINNERS (e-novella)

Single Titles
RAW DESIRE
ONLY RAKES NEED APPLY

The Morgan Brothers Ranch
THE RELUCTANT COWBOY
THE MAVERICK COWBOY
THE LAST GOOD COWBOY
THE BAD BOY COWBOY
THE BILLIONAIRE BULL RIDER
THE RANCHER

The Millers of Morgan Valley
THE SECOND CHANCE RANCHER
THE RANCHER'S REDEMPTION
THE REBELLIOUS RANCHER
THE RANCHER MEETS HIS MATCH
SWEET TALKING RANCHER
ROMANCING THE RANCHER

Three Cowboys
THREE COWBOYS AND A BABY
THREE COWBOYS AND A PUPPY
THREE COWBOYS AND A BRIDE

Anthologies
SOME LIKE IT ROUGH
LORDS OF PASSION
HAPPY IS THE BRIDE
A SEASON TO CELEBRATE
MARRYING MY COWBOY
CHRISTMAS KISSES WITH MY COWBOY
LONE WOLF

Published by Kensington Publishing Corp.

Kate Pearce

kensingtonbooks.com

KENSINGTON BOOKS are published by
Kensington Publishing Corp.
900 Third Avenue
New York, NY 10022

Copyright © 2025 by Kate Pearce

All rights reserved. No part of this book may be reproduced in any form or by any means without the prior written consent of the Publisher, excepting brief quotes used in reviews.

Without limiting the author's and publisher's exclusive rights, any unauthorized use of this publication to train generative artificial intelligence (AI) technologies is expressly prohibited.

All Kensington titles, imprints, and distributed lines are available at special quantity discounts for bulk purchases for sales promotion, premiums, fund-raising, educational, or institutional use.

This book is a work of fiction. Names, characters, businesses, organizations, places, events, and incidents either are the product of the author's imagination or are used fictitiously. Any resemblance to actual persons, living or dead, events, or locales is entirely coincidental.

To the extent that the image or images on the cover of this book depict a person or persons, such person or persons are merely models, and are not intended to portray any character or characters featured in the book.

Special book excerpts or customized printings can also be created to fit specific needs. For details, write or phone the office of the Kensington Sales Manager: Kensington Publishing Corp., 900 Third Avenue, New York, NY 10022. Attn. Sales Department. Phone: 1-800-221-2647.

Kensington and the K logo Reg. U.S. Pat. & TM Off.

ISBN: 978-1-4967-5515-5 (ebook)

ISBN: 978-1-4967-5514-8

First Kensington Trade Paperback Printing: November 2025

10 9 8 7 6 5 4 3 2 1

Printed in the United States of America

The authorized representative in the EU for product safety and compliance is eucomply OU, Parnu mnt 139b-14, Apt 123
Tallinn, Berlin 11317, hello@eucompliancepartner.com

Only Rakes Need Apply

Chapter 1

Tavistock Square, London 1819

Lady Carenza Smythe-Harding put down her teacup and sighed. "There is *one* thing I miss about being married."

Her sister, Allegra, looked up from her embroidery. She sat close to the large window overlooking Tavistock Square to take advantage of the light. "Having someone to reach those high shelves for you and murder the occasional spider?"

"Those things are very useful," Carenza acknowledged. "But I was thinking about something rather more . . . intimate."

There was a snort from the other side of the fireplace, where their friend Olivia Sheraton sat, her slippers propped up on the fender in a very unladylike manner. "Like what exactly?"

"The . . . marriage act."

"You miss Hector's cock?"

"Olivia!" Allegra exclaimed. "How . . . crude!"

Olivia raised an eyebrow. "You know how long it takes Carenza to get to the point. I just thought I'd move the conversation along at a more interesting pace." She took off her spectacles. "I can imagine that lacking an effective male member after being in an intimate relationship might be difficult."

"And, for all his faults, Hector was very good at it," Carenza admitted.

"He was a terrible womanizer, sister. He learned all those skills at your expense!" Allegra frowned. "You're lucky he didn't give you the pox!"

Olivia nodded. "She's right about that, but if he gave you pleasure in your marriage bed, you were lucky." She shuddered slightly. "I can't say I enjoyed a second of Albert's attentions. Not that he was able to perform very often, being so elderly and infirm."

Allegra raised her hand. "Have you both forgotten I am a spinster? This is not a topic of conversation I am qualified to participate in."

"Then perhaps you should listen carefully," Olivia said. "It will help you not to make the same mistakes we did."

"I don't consider Hector a 'mistake,'" Carenza objected. "I was delighted to marry him."

"Because he charmed you and your parents into believing he was a gentleman of honor, when, in fact, he was a horse-mad, gambling man whore." Olivia had always been a plain speaker. "Who shot himself in the head when his gambling debts outweighed what was left of his fortune, leaving you reliant on your father to give you a home."

"Yes," Carenza said. "Thank you for reminding me."

"I'm sorry." Olivia made a face. "I've done it again, haven't I? Been too blunt. No wonder no gentleman wants to marry me."

"Even with your substantial fortune," Allegra said helpfully.

Silence fell as Carenza poured them all more tea. She was currently living in her father's town house in London. He much preferred his estate in Norfolk and rarely came to the city. He'd been happy to let his younger daughter, Allegra, reside in the town house with Carenza as chaperone, claiming it kept the staff on their toes and the place less likely to be robbed.

Olivia was the first to start speaking again. "My experience of being a widow has been that many well-meaning gentlemen have offered to 'console' me. Has that not happened to you?"

"Married gentlemen, yes." Carenza sighed. "I had to pour a glass of red wine down Lord Stratford's coat last week to make him understand that I was not interested, and his wife is a *friend* of mine." She frowned. "I just want a man in my bed."

"You have staff," Olivia pointed out.

"And I live in my father's house, where most of the staff have known me since I was a child. I can hardly jump into bed with any of them."

"They'd probably tell Father, too," Allegra added. "He'd be extremely annoyed if he had to fire any of his old retainers."

Carenza fought a smile. "He'd probably care more about that than about what I was up to."

"What you need is the kind of man Hector was, but without the entanglement of being his wife," Olivia said thoughtfully. "A rake, in fact. He will need to be discreet, free of disease, not demand payment—because then you would be veering into paid-companion territory—and not be after your name, notoriety, and, most important, your money."

Carenza nodded. "Yes, and he can't be married, engaged, or publicly courting another woman. He must be content with a few hours of my time at my convenience and nothing else."

"A few hours?" Allegra frowned. "I thought a physical union took only seconds."

"Maybe if you are a stallion or a pig," Olivia said. "But humans can do far better than that." She winked at Carenza. "One good thing is that Hector set your standards *very* high."

The door into the drawing room opened to admit Maude Cooper, the fourth member of their enduring circle of friends and Hector's sister. She took off her bonnet, revealing hair the same auburn color as her deceased brother's, and sparkling blue eyes.

"Hector had high standards? For what exactly?" She set down her bonnet and gloves on the sideboard and helped herself to tea. "Why have you all suddenly gone quiet? Were you talking about me?"

"We were talking about being widowed—something that has not happened to you," Carenza said.

"I might as well be widowed," Maude said as she sat down. "It feels as if Gerald will never come back from France. The war ended years ago, but apparently he still needs to be there to soothe foreigners' brows and reassure them that such a man as Napoleon will never terrorize France again."

"Napoleon wasn't a monster," Olivia objected. "He initiated some excellent policies in his day."

"Before he proclaimed himself emperor and crowned himself at his coronation?" Maude asked. "He ended up being just as awful as the previous monarchy."

"That is somewhat debatable," Allegra submitted. "The Bourbon dynasty were *far* worse. In fact—"

"Be that as it may." Carenza hastened to intervene before the discussion turned into an argument. "We were discussing the limitations of being a widow."

"Carenza is missing her husband's intimate attentions," Olivia said.

Maude made a face. "Ew."

"We were discussing ways she could find someone to replace him in a somewhat more limited fashion," Olivia explained.

"It's a shame we aren't in France," Maude said. "The French are very accommodating about such matters and consider lovers an important addition to any long-term liaison. When I resided there, I was propositioned quite openly, often in Gerald's presence."

"We're in London. There have to be some gentlemen to fit

the bill." Allegra rose and went across to the desk. "Shall we make a list?"

"And do what with it?" Carenza inquired. "Pin it to the door and wait for them to come knocking?"

"That probably wouldn't be a good idea." Allegra frowned. "Is there anyone we could ask? Papa, maybe. Or Dorian?"

All the Musgrove children had been blessed with interesting names by their somewhat eccentric parents.

"I don't think our father or oldest brother would wish to be party to such a thing." Carenza shuddered. "If I did involve them, Papa will assume I want to be married again, and that is far from the truth."

"I suspect it will take you years to get over Hector's unfortunate death," Maude said. "And you are only a year out of half mourning."

"Papa has been asking about both of us marrying," Allegra said apologetically. "He said that two years is quite long enough to mourn such a noddlecock."

"Allegra!" Carenza shook her head.

Maude started to chuckle. "It's all right, Carenza. I loved my brother very much, but he wasn't the most reliable of men. He's been dead for over two years, and you deserve to have some fun."

Allegra held up her pen. "How about putting an advertisement in the newspaper? We could do that anonymously and have the newspaper's office collect the replies."

"That's not a bad idea," Olivia said. "Write this down, Allegra. 'Titled lady seeks experienced, unmarried rake for afternoon dalliance. Please reply to this advertisement with precise measurements including height, age, length and girth of male member, and current financial statements. Interviews will be conducted before the end of the month.'"

"I was only teasing." Allegra set down her pen. "I cannot write such an invitation to licentiousness."

"Then pass the paper to me." Olivia held out her hand.

"I'll wager we'll get plenty of applicants to interview if we word it like that." She glanced over at Carenza. "I'll even pay for the damned advertisement and help you make the final decision."

"How kind of you," Carenza said.

"You aren't really thinking of doing this, are you, sister?" Allegra asked, her expression concerned. "Father would not be happy with you at all."

"He won't know anything about it unless you tell him," Carenza said. "And I'm sure you wouldn't do that. Neither of us want to be dragged back to Musgrove Hall in deepest Norfolk, do we?"

Allegra looked thoughtful. "I'd prefer to stay in London, but if I don't tell him, I would prefer to be kept in ignorance of the entire proceedings."

"I promise I won't say a word about it," Carenza assured her. "In truth, I doubt we'll get any replies at all."

Olivia walked over to the desk, dipped her pen in the inkwell, and started writing. "I'll get my maid, and we'll walk around to the newspaper offices on the Strand. I'll send her in with the advertisement and the money, and make sure that no one recognizes me at all."

Struck by a sudden qualm, Carenza addressed her friend. "There is no need for such haste. Perhaps I ought to consider the matter before I come to a decision."

"It takes you an hour to pick which gown to wear every single day," Olivia objected. "And that was when you were wearing unrelieved black. If I wait for you to make up your mind, we'll both be another year older, and you'll be turning into one of those bitter dried-up widows we used to laugh at when we were debutantes."

"That's rather harsh," Carenza tried to protest. She looked over at Maude, who was listening with a smile on her face. "What do you think I should do?"

"If you are careful, I cannot see any harm to it," Maude

said. "You are a widow, and there is nothing wrong in having a little fun now and again."

"Allegra?" Carenza turned to her sister, who was looking rather dignified.

"I have already expressed my thoughts on this matter. I request not to be involved in the slightest."

Carenza looked out of the window and attempted to gather her thoughts. She did miss being bedded. If she could find an unexceptionable man to give her his all, why shouldn't she?

"All right. I'll do it."

Olivia clapped her hands. "Excellent news. I'll just call for my maid, and we can stop at the Strand on our way home." She winked at Carenza. "If things go according to plan, you'll be well bedded in a week!"

The Honorable Julian Laurent made his leisurely way through the entrance hall at White's, pausing only when his progress was impeded by a crowd gathered around the infamous betting book.

"What on earth is causing such a hubbub?" he murmured to the overexcitable heir to a dukedom who happened to be standing next to him. "Has Prinny died?"

"God forbid." The hapless youth grinned sunnily at him. "This is far more exciting."

"Somehow, I doubt that."

"There's a bet been placed about the identity of the so-called 'lady' who paid for the advertisement!"

Julian raised an eyebrow. "How thrilling. Please excuse me."

He eased past the excited throng and made his way into the dining room, where he was due to meet his younger brother. He smiled slightly as Anton rose to greet him.

"You're early," Julian said.

"You're always late," Anton replied as they shook hands. He was sporting a rather fine and luxuriant mustache in the style of many cavalry officers. "And the military has made me very punctual."

As Julian joined his brother at the table, he noted that he looked well in his new uniform. Julian would never tell him so, but he was proud of his brother. After their widowed mother had applied to Julian for funds, he'd happily bought Anton his new commission.

The waiter took their order, and Julian set his napkin on his lap. "When are you off?"

"Three days." Anton grimaced. "I'm not looking forward to the journey."

"It's a long way to India," Julian acknowledged. "But you wanted this advancement, yes?"

"Of course. It's the only way for a man to get ahead now that the war with France has ended." Anton frowned. "Don't you approve?"

"I'd rather you were closer to home," Julian said easily. "But that's mainly because, as her second-favorite son, our dear mother worries about you so much."

"Which means she'll be directing all her attention at you." Anton grinned. "You'll constantly be at her beck and call, which will leave you no time for dalliance."

"Oh, I suspect I'll manage somehow, and we both know she far prefers the company of Aragon. As the heir, he is the only son who truly matters." Julian poured them both some wine. "Just promise me that you will write to her on a regular basis, and all will be well."

"I'll do my best. It's the least I can do." Anton held up his glass. "Thank you for everything you have done for me."

"I can hardly take credit for everything."

"Mother couldn't afford to buy me a commission, Julian. I know it was you."

"What else is one to do when one is a veritable Croesus?" Julian shrugged. "I never expected to inherit a fortune from my dearly departed godmother—God bless her eccentric little heart."

"The Walcott family still hate your guts for that." Anton topped up his glass. "Percival absolutely radiates with fury every time your name is mentioned."

"Percival should have spent less time mocking his great-aunt and more time listening to her incredibly outrageous stories about the court fifty years ago. I learned a lot and gained a whole new level of disdain for the aristocracy who rule us."

"Of which you are now one," Anton pointed out.

"I have no title," Julian returned. "Only 'the honorable' from our father, as I'm the second son."

"Poor Aragon might have Father's title, but he has only a tenth of your wealth."

"Which is why our mother cordially dislikes me." Julian smiled at his younger brother. "And Aragon constantly asks to borrow money."

He would miss Anton's breezy presence in more ways than one. Not only had Anton provided their mother with someone to dote on, but he'd been a jovial barrier between his two older brothers. With no Anton to joke with, how would he and Aragon negotiate their somewhat delicate relationship?

"Excuse me, sir."

He sat back to allow the waiter to set his plate in front of him.

Anton picked up his knife. "The beef looks excellent, as always."

"Indeed."

Another burst of noise filtered in from the crowded lobby as one of the diners exited.

"What's this nonsense about a bet?" Julian asked, watching Anton begin to eat his dinner with remarkable speed.

"The mysterious lady?" Anton chuckled. "If I were staying in London, I wouldn't mind having a pop at that."

"Pop at what exactly?"

"You haven't heard? Apparently, a lady put an advertisement in one of the newspapers asking for applications for a lover with a very specific set of requirements."

"One has to doubt a lady would stoop to such behavior," Julian remarked. "And wonder why the gentlemen in the hallway care so much."

"I suspect it has something to do with the frankness of the advertisement." Anton waved down a waiter. "Can you provide me with a copy of today's *Times*?"

"Of course, Captain."

Within two minutes, the man was back with a well-ironed copy of the newspaper.

"Thank you." Anton looked over at his brother. "Excuse me for a moment while I locate the specific advertisement."

Julian continued to eat his dinner as his brother went through the long list of personal columns.

"Ah! Here it is." Anton cleared his throat. "'Titled lady seeks experienced, unmarried rake for afternoon dalliance. Please reply to this advertisement with precise measurements including height, age, length of male member, and current financial statements. Interviews will be conducted before the end of the month.'"

"Good Lord," Julian said.

Anton refolded the paper and grinned at him. "I know. It must be a joke. Someone wants to see who'll take the bait and will record the names of all these fools being interviewed by some madam and publish them to much ridicule."

"That sounds highly likely."

"I mean, if a lady wants a lover, there are better ways to find one."

"Through her husband, perhaps?"

"You've had your share of married lovers, brother."

"Only when both parties understand the terms of the . . . liaison, and hopefully no one gets hurt."

He tried not to think about his recent experience with Lady Brenton, when his blithe confidence in their arrangement had been sadly mistaken. It had almost put him off fornication for life.

"Well, whoever she is, I wish her luck." Anton set the newspaper on the tablecloth. "Do we have time for pudding? We're not due at Musgrove House until three."

Julian followed Anton into the drawing room of Musgrove House, where they found not only their two hostesses but their friend Mrs. Sheraton. As his brother was busy charming the Musgrove sisters, he went over to pay his respects to the rather eccentric widow. She had a classic oval face, dark hair and blue eyes, and a perfect rosebud mouth. She was brutally honest, happy to send any gentlemen who offended her running for the hills, and had the acid wit of a cynic. He enjoyed her company immensely.

"Mrs. Sheraton." He kissed her proffered hand. "How lovely to see you."

"Always a pleasure, sir." She smiled at him. "Carenza tells me that Anton is on his way overseas."

"Yes, he sails in three days."

"Allegra will be devastated."

Julian turned slightly so that he could see the grouping around the fire. Anton's face was alight with excitement as he described something vividly with his hands. Lady Carenza was smiling and nodding, but her sister seemed somewhat distraught.

"I never realized she had a tendre for him." Julian spoke more to himself than to his companion.

"Neither did she, until she heard he was leaving," Olivia murmured back. "I suppose as you all grew up on neighboring estates, she just assumed he would always be there."

"A terrible mistake to make." Julian's thoughtful gaze fell on Carenza.

"I'm sure she will write to him," Olivia said.

"I hope she will. Whether he'll reply is another matter. He is not the most reliable of fellows."

"You are one of the very few gentlemen of my acquaintance who are capable of being objective about your family."

Julian bowed. "I am a realist, Mrs. Sheraton. It seems I cannot help myself."

Carenza came toward him, her hands outstretched. "It is always a pleasure to see you, sir."

He smiled down into her hazel eyes. Her honey-blond hair was gathered in a high topknot with a single curl resting on her throat. She wore a modest lace fichu knotted over the bodice of her gown. She wasn't an acknowledged beauty, having been dubbed too countrified on her debut by one of the unkinder patronesses at Almack's, but Julian had always admired her.

"Anton insisted that he had to say his farewells to you and your sister in person."

"And that is the only reason you came to visit us?"

"You know I enjoy your company, Carenza," Julian said as she offered him a seat. "We have much in common."

She went to ring the bell for refreshments. "Including my late husband," Carenza said lightly as she returned to sit opposite him. "Although even you were unable to contain his excesses in the end."

"I did my best, but Hector was . . ."

Mrs. Sheraton spoke over his shoulder as she came to join them. "An inconsiderate and amoral reprobate?"

"He had his demons, as most of us do," Julian admitted.

"He had more than most, and they killed him in the end," Mrs. Sheraton said as she sat down and spread out her skirts. "How you two were ever friends is a puzzle to me."

"We met at Harrow when we were seven." Julian shrugged. "We formed a bond to fight off all the bigger bullies."

"Hector was never a bully, Olivia. You can at least give him credit for that," Carenza said.

Mrs. Sheraton sniffed. "When one sets such a low standard, surely even Hector can crawl under it."

Anton tried and failed to conceal a snort.

"Your new gown is very fetching," Julian said.

"Thank you." She smoothed her skirt's folds. "After two years of mourning dresses I was convinced that in light pink I looked like one of the madams seeking customers in Covent Garden."

"You look delightful." Julian smiled at her.

Her cheeks blushed to compete with the rose of her dress. "I appreciate the opinion of one of the best-dressed men in London."

"My brother is rather fine, is he not?" Anton agreed. "Even in my dress uniform, he threatens to outshine me."

"Hardly," Allegra Musgrove said, her earnest gaze fixed on Anton's oblivious face. "You look wonderful."

The door opened to admit the butler with the tea tray.

"How is your father?" Julian asked.

"As hale and hearty as ever," Carenza replied as she poured him some tea.

"And apparently keen to marry both his daughters off as soon as possible," Mrs. Sheraton chimed in as she claimed her own cup of tea. "Perhaps he wants his town house back."

"As he dislikes London immensely, I doubt it," Carenza said. "He just wishes us to be happy."

"As all fathers do," Julian said gently, aware that Hector had proven to be a terrible husband for Carenza, and that he'd been responsible for introducing them to each other—something he bitterly regretted.

"I think Carenza will find her own way to happiness." Mrs. Sheraton winked.

"As I'm sure will you, my dear Olivia." Carenza sipped

her tea, her smile serene. "But I am in no rush to be married again."

"I am well aware of that," Olivia said.

Julian couldn't help but notice the pointed glare Carenza gave Mrs. Sheraton when she thought he wasn't looking. Allegra's expression appeared guilty, and he had no idea why. Was it possible that Carenza had already found a gentleman she wished to marry? The idea made him vaguely uneasy.

Anton, who was always good at defusing tension, introduced a new topic of conversation. "Are you aware of the latest scandal regarding the unknown lady seeking to interview her lovers through an advertisement in *The Times*?"

Allegra spluttered into her tea and hastily put down her cup. "I do beg your pardon. I have to go and speak to Cook about the lack of refreshments." She hurried out of the room.

Mrs. Sheraton assumed an expression of great interest and replied to Anton. "It sounds quite delightful! Is this woman interviewing the whole of the ton?"

Anton chuckled. "Apparently, she wants only the scoundrels. And she requires *all* their measurements!"

Beside him, Carenza shifted in her seat. "Olivia . . ."

"But this is fascinating, Carenza! I wish I'd thought to do such a thing before my father forced me to marry a seventy-year-old man who was barely able to perform his marital duties." Mrs. Sheraton fluttered her eyelashes at Julian. "Will you be applying, sir? It is well-known that you are an accomplished flirt and presumably skilled in bed."

"I suspect it is all a scheme to embarrass and expose any man stupid enough to reply to a newspaper advertisement from a so-called lady," Julian said lightly. "All a woman with such 'standards' will get is the dregs of society."

"That seems harsh, brother," Anton said. "There were plenty of gentlemen at our club today who seemed eager to either participate or place a bet on the outcome."

"At your club?" Carenza repeated faintly.

Julian glanced sharply at her.

"Yes." Anton chuckled. "Someone opened a bet about how many men will turn up when the lady starts her interviews."

Mrs. Sheraton stood up. "I do apologize, gentlemen, but I must be on my way. My singing teacher is coming at four to take me through my scales."

She kissed Carenza on the cheek and smiled as Julian and Anton rose to their feet. "I wish you all the best in India, Anton. I'm sure you'll be a great success."

Anton offered her his arm. "I'd be delighted to walk you to your carriage, ma'am."

"Thank you." Mrs. Sheraton placed her hand on his sleeve. "I'll speak to you tomorrow, Carenza, darling."

Julian waited until their voices died down before resuming his seat beside his hostess. "Is something troubling you?" he asked as she stared into space.

She wouldn't look at him, and he possessed himself of her hand. "I would not normally presume to ask about something so personal, but we are old friends." He paused. "Is it possible that . . . Mrs. Sheraton is the person who posted that advertisement for a lover?"

"Not exactly."

She turned to look at him, and he went still.

"Olivia did pay for the advertisement, but . . ."

"But—" Julian prompted, as she seemed unable to continue.

"But she did it for me."

The silence after she'd blurted out the truth went on for so long that Carenza grew dizzy from holding her breath.

"I . . . beg your pardon?" Julian's faint smile disappeared as he released her hand.

"I asked her to place the advertisement on my behalf."

"What in God's name possessed you to do such a remarkably stupid and reckless thing?"

"I don't believe I have to explain myself to you, sir." Carenza raised her chin. "I am a grown woman who is perfectly capable of making her own decisions."

"Obviously not." His tone was biting and his eyes a frosty blue. "Does your father know about this?"

Anger stirred beneath her embarrassment. "Of course he doesn't. And if you run off to Norfolk to tell tales on me, I will think very poorly of you, indeed."

His incredulous expression hardened into something else entirely. "If it gets out that it's you—and it will—your reputation will be ruined."

"I think Hector already accomplished that feat for me, Julian," she snapped. "If I am to be an object of pity and derision, at least this time I'll have earned it for myself."

He stared at her for a long moment and then drew in a ragged breath. "Will you at least stop and think about this properly?"

"Why? So you can lecture me again?" She rose to her feet and took a hasty turn around the room. "I didn't expect this from you. Of all my friends, you know how Hector treated me during our marriage."

"Then find someone better!" He stood up and faced her.

"What if I am deceived again?" Carenza asked. "I thought I was making a good choice the first time and look what happened!"

He was standing so close that she could smell the bergamot on his skin. Hurt by his unexpected reaction, she gathered her resources and met his incredulous gaze.

"The only thing I miss about marriage is sex," she said. "The only thing I *require* from a man is that and nothing else."

"You're determined to make a fool of yourself and ruin

your reputation just for a tussle in the sheets with some man who won't *value* you?"

Carenza shrugged. "Hector didn't value me, but he was an excellent lover."

A muscle ticked in his jaw as he regarded her. "I don't approve of this, Carenza." He stepped away from her and picked up his hat and gloves. "And when everything goes awry, don't expect me to restore your reputation."

"I won't." Carenza fought a desire to brain him with a candlestick. "You never did a thing to stop Hector behaving as if he were still single. Why should you assist me now?"

"That's not true, I—" Julian abruptly stopped speaking. After a moment, he bowed. "I wish you good day, my lady."

Carenza inclined her head an icy inch. "Good afternoon, sir."

He walked out and shut the door with a definite click, leaving Carenza unsure whether to scream or cry. She walked over to the window and watched the brothers drive off in Julian's curricle. If Julian thought to bully her into giving up her scheme, he would be disappointed. All he'd done was make her realize that even he—her oldest friend—had double standards. It made her angry enough to ignore society's opinion of her.

Olivia was correct. What right did any man have to dictate how she behaved during her widowhood? Her gaze followed the carriage as it turned the corner. She'd expected better from Julian. They'd grown up on neighboring estates, and he'd always been her ally. His disapproval hurt. She sat back in her chair with something of a flounce. She refused to be cowed. Having her name bandied around in the gentlemen's clubs was nothing new. Hector had even bet on her himself when his finances were particularly low.

But how to manage the matter now that every gentleman in town was aware of the advertisement? She walked over to her desk and took out a sheet of paper. As Olivia had gotten her into this mess, her friend was honor bound to find a way to make things work as planned.

Allegra came into the drawing room, a plate of cakes in her hand.

"Oh! Where has everyone gone?"

"Anton escorted Olivia to her carriage. I think she had him convinced that she'd been the one to place that advertisement. Julian stayed behind to advise me to stop her from doing anything further."

Allegra set down the plate. "Anton didn't even come and find me to say goodbye."

"He's always had a horrendous crush on Olivia, you know." Carenza tried to be gentle.

"Hasn't every man? Even Hector—" Allegra stopped speaking.

"Flirted with her on every occasion they met?" Carenza finished her sister's sentence for her. "I was quite aware of that, but Olivia would never betray me."

"Yet she happily monopolized Anton's time when she knows how I feel about him." Allegra ate a cake and then another one. "She isn't always nice, Carenza."

"I know, and if you wish me to chastise her, I'd be happy to do so." She indicated the letter she was writing. "I am halfway through composing a note to her demanding she sort out the mess she has created. I can always add an extra paragraph on your behalf."

"I'm not sure there's any point." Allegra was obviously reluctant to let the subject of Anton go. "She'll just want to know why I didn't tell Anton how I feel about him and claim that anything she did was to make me jealous enough to stand up for myself. And she'd be right."

"Unfortunately, she often is." Carenza blotted the letter. "I should have insisted on reading the advertisement before she took it to the newspaper. I didn't realize she intended to include *everything* we joked about."

"You should have known she would." Allegra offered her a cake. "What did you tell Julian when he asked you to intervene?"

"I told him it was none of his business."

"Does he know her family?" Allegra asked. "I do hope he won't tell tales on her."

"As she can honestly deny that the advertisement concerns her, she has nothing to worry about, does she?" Carenza selected a cake and bit into the jammy center. She had no intention of telling Allegra that Julian knew the truth about who the advert was for and wasn't at all pleased with her. "I am the one risking my reputation."

"Then perhaps this is a sign that you should not proceed," Allegra said. "The idea that they are betting on you at White's is insufferable."

"But why should men be allowed to get away with such behavior when women are not?" Carenza asked.

"Women are allowed, *ladies* are not."

"Unless they are married or consort with other married men. It is most unfair." Carenza ate the rest of her cake, as she pictured the revolted expression on Julian's face when she'd told him the truth. "If Olivia can come up with a suitable way for our scheme to go ahead without drawing any more attention on ourselves, I am still willing to proceed."

Allegra shook her head. "I believe you are making a mistake, sister."

"Then I will do everything in my power to make sure that if things do go awry, you are not held accountable in any way." Carenza met her sister's worried gaze. "The last thing I want is to damage your reputation."

"What reputation?" Allegra raised her eyebrows. "I'm Hector's sister-in-law, and our father married an opera singer who isn't received in society." She smiled. "And as Anton has left for India, my heart is already broken."

"You can do far better than Anton, my love."

"We shall see about that." Allegra offered Carenza the plate of cakes again. "As our visitors have all deserted us, why don't we finish the refreshments ourselves? I can't bear to see Cook's good work go to waste."

Chapter 2

"Carenza . . ." Julian glanced over at his companion's obstinate face as she steadfastly ignored him.

She was pretending to listen to the Italian opera singer serenading the party.

"You have to talk to me at some point and give up on this foolish scheme."

"Why?" She answered without looking at him. "You are neither my father, nor my husband, and have no authority over me."

"But I am your friend," Julian said softly. "I care about you and your reputation."

She didn't bother to answer him, and he felt an unusual stirring of irritation. "They are still betting on you at White's," he told her.

She shrugged one shoulder, which vexed him even more.

"Olivia believes she has a foolproof method to ensure that our identities are not revealed."

"That hardly reassures me," he murmured as the song finished and everyone clapped. He rose to his feet. "May I escort you in to supper?"

She met his gaze. Her hazel eyes were shining in the candlelight, which also brought out the glints of silver in her fair hair. She wore a patterned muslin gown with gold lace at the bodice and a tall feather in her coiffure.

"If you wish." She stood and placed her gloved hand on his sleeve. "I wonder where Allegra is."

"She is just ahead of us," Julian said. "She's talking to Viscount Chartwell."

"He would do very well for her as a husband," Carenza commented. "He loves music, he prefers to live in the countryside, and he is a widower with no children."

"I would have to agree," Julian said, glad to have a conversation that didn't involve an argument. He wasn't used to being on Carenza's wrong side, and he found it unsettling. "I don't know anything unsavory about him."

Carenza used her fan. "Then I will invite him to call on us and bring his sister to dine. Allegra deserves to be happy."

"As do you," Julian reminded her as they joined the line heading into the supper room.

"Then why are you so determined to stop me from enjoying myself?"

Julian barely repressed a sigh. "Back to that, are we?" He looked down at her. "Can we call a truce while we eat? I have a very delicate constitution."

She turned away to look around the room. "Of course. Shall we sit with Allegra?"

"Yes. Why don't you join her while I get us both something to eat?" Julian suggested.

"Thank you." She smiled and walked away, the soft skirts of her muslin dress flowing gently around her.

His fingers flexed with a sudden desire to tip her over his knee and spank her well-rounded arse until she begged for mercy. He half smiled. From what Hector had let slip in his more drunken moments, she'd probably enjoy it.

"Mr. Laurent?"

He turned to see his secretary, Simon Benson, at his elbow.

"I am sorry to disturb you, sir, but I knew you would want this information at the earliest opportunity."

"Thank you, Simon." He quickly read the note and looked over at his secretary. "Well done."

"Thank you, sir." Simon blushed. "I assume you'll want me to handle this matter myself?"

"I think we need to discuss our tactics before noon tomorrow, but I suspect we will both be necessary to implement my plan." Julian smiled.

The information Simon had obtained suggested why Mrs. Sheraton was not present at this evening's entertainment.

"I recommend that you forget about work for the rest of the evening. I know you appreciate opera."

"Are you quite certain, sir?" Simon cast a longing glance back at the drawing room. "I do have plenty of tasks to keep me occupied in my office."

"They can wait until tomorrow," Julian said firmly. "Now, get yourself something to eat and go and enjoy yourself for once."

Julian collected two plates of food and made his way over to where Carenza sat with her sister and Viscount Chartwell.

"I do apologize for the delay, my lady." He sat down and took two glasses of wine from the tray of a passing waiter. "I had a business matter to deal with."

"We managed to entertain ourselves during your absence, sir." Carenza smiled at him. "Viscount Chartwell was just telling us about the restoration work he is doing on his music room at his town house."

"How interesting." Julian turned to the viscount. "I do hope your decor is less extravagant than that in Brighton?"

The viscount chuckled. "Rest assured I have no aspirations to achieve the dizzy heights of His Royal Highness's pavilion, if that's what you mean, sir."

"Thank God for that." Julian was glad to see the viscount had a sense of humor. "I would be delighted to attend a musical evening when you are ready to show off your new music room to the world, Chartwell."

"I would be honored, Mr. Laurent. You are known as a great patron of the arts." Viscount Chartwell looked at the sisters. "And, of course, I include the ladies in my invitation."

"As you should." Julian nodded. "Lady Allegra lives up to her name and is an excellent musician."

Allegra blushed. "I consider myself . . . competent, and I am always willing to improve."

"My sister is being modest, my lord," Carenza said. "She is an exceptionally fine vocalist and pianist."

Viscount Chartwell bowed his head to Allegra. "Then I shall be imploring you to lend your talents to my first concert, my lady."

Julian met Carenza's gaze over her sister's head and winked. It was pleasant to share a moment of unity when their present relationship was so uncertain. Who would've anticipated that? Julian had never experienced a moment's anxiety about his best friend's widow. She had always appeared to be the perfect woman to him.

"Would you care to take a turn around the room, Lady Allegra?" Viscount Chartwell stood and offered his arm. "We can ask our hostess what pleasures await us in the second half of the program."

"I would be delighted." Allegra rose, too, the blush on her cheeks matching the color of her gown. She placed her gloved hand on his sleeve, and they walked away.

"He is definitely interested in her," Julian murmured into Carenza's ear. "Would you like me to find out more about his family and finances?"

"That would be most kind of you," Carenza said. "If my father bestirs himself to come to town and finds out Allegra has a beau, he will expect a full report on his suitability."

"Are you expecting your father?" Julian asked.

"Why would you wish to know that?"

He raised his eyebrows at her sudden change of tone. "Not to tell tales, I can assure you."

She fiddled with the lace on her shawl. "I suppose you expect me to be grateful for your forbearance."

"I expect—" He bit back what he had intended to say and shrugged instead. "I expect you to do as you wish."

She raised her chin. "I intend to."

"Have you finalized your list of acceptable scoundrels yet?" he asked idly after a long, rather uncomfortable silence.

"I'm hardly going to tell you if I have, am I?"

So much for the cessation of hostilities. It appeared they were at war again.

"I suppose not." He reached for her plate. "May I tempt you to some dessert?"

"No, thank you."

"Then shall we return to the music room?"

She rose to her feet and looked down at him. "Of course."

Julian peered out from behind the corner of the Wheatsheaf public house on Charing Cross Road and saw Simon coming toward him. It was a chilly day with a hint of rain in the air, but there was more than a hint of excitement in the crowd milling around in the stable yard ahead of him. He recognized several of the most depraved individuals in society, who were only tolerated because of their family connections or wealth. There was also a scattering of the press.

There was no sign of Mrs. Sheraton or, thank God, Carenza. If they were ensconced in the inn, he hadn't seen them enter, and he'd been there for at least an hour planning the best way to execute his plan to save his friend from herself.

"Mr. Laurent." Simon came up to him. "I think I've discovered why they chose this particular venue."

Julian trusted his secretary implicitly, but even so, he'd struggled to confide in him and expose Carenza to further censure. It was only when he realized he couldn't be seen openly meddling that he'd consulted with Simon and come up with what he hoped was a workable plan. Simon had applied to the advertisement posing as an applicant and had received further instructions by letter as to where he should meet the lady for his interview.

"Mrs. Sheraton's dresser is related to the landlord, Mr. Cox, who has a second house right next door to the inn where his family resides."

"Ah, so the two buildings are connected." Julian nodded.

"Exactly, sir. Anyone could enter the house on the street behind this one and not be seen coming into the pub." Simon took off the leather purse strung over his shoulder. "I have the coin here, sir, and the stable boys are ready and waiting at the corner."

"Excellent. I think a judicious mix of the fear of ridicule in the press and some generous bribes should change most people's minds."

Simon glanced across the street, his expression doubtful. "I hope you are right, Mr. Laurent."

"Make sure Roger and Mac have plenty of the smaller coins," Julian said. "Their job will be to get rid of the onlookers while you focus on anyone who looks like a serious candidate. Remember, our aim is to make them all believe this is a gigantic joke to expose them all to the gutter press. I will stay here and emerge only if necessary."

"Yes, sir." Simon settled his hat more firmly on his head. "Wish me luck."

Julian watched as his stable boys and secretary began their work. Soon, the crowd grew noticeably smaller, and within twenty minutes, most of the press had left as well. Finally, only three stubborn fools remained, obviously refusing to listen to Simon's entreaties. Julian recognized all three of them and strolled toward the inn. The men didn't notice him, as they were immersed in an argument about who would enter the inn first.

"What in God's name is going on here?" Julian's calm voice rose above the fray. He raised an eyebrow as one of the young bucks turned toward him. "Is that you, Calloway?" Julian asked. "Why the devil are you hanging around in the middle of a stable yard?"

"No one asked for your opinion, Laurent," Calloway said. "Just toddle off and leave us alone."

"You didn't fall for that advertisement, did you?" Julian allowed a small chuckle to escape his lips. "Good Lord."

"What's it to you?" Calloway demanded.

"Just that I would've thought that a gentleman of your current . . . means would not want his face lampooned in the newspapers." Julian looked at Calloway's companions. "It will be a pity when your allowances are cut off after your families disown you in embarrassment."

"I say, Laurent, you can't—"

"No woman of means would be seen dead in this place." Julian looked around the stable yard. "Admit it. You have been set up, gentlemen."

"Maybe you want us to leave so that you can go in there yourself," one of the men muttered.

"Hardly." Julian met his gaze. "I need neither money nor approval from any woman. But please, go ahead." He waved them toward the door. "Embarrass yourselves while I watch. I'll be dining out on this story for years."

Calloway made a rude gesture and strode toward the inn.

Julian looked over at the other two men who were muttering between themselves. "Do you intend to accompany him?" Julian asked. "If so, I am more than willing to make sure that your names are spelled correctly for the gentlemen of the press over there."

Julian smiled as the men retreated. He turned to look up at the inn. It was likely that some of the men would find their courage and return, but he'd done his best to chase them off.

Perhaps it would be good for Carenza to deal with a few of her "applicants" just to see how truly awful her idea had been.

Julian walked back onto the street. He had no intention of going through the same door Calloway had just entered. If Simon was correct, there was a far easier route to his misguided friend Lady Carenza, and he intended to make full use of it.

Olivia, clad in a black dress and a veil that was so thick she could barely see through it, was currently perched on the window seat trying to look down into the courtyard of the inn.

"Where did they all disappear to? Half an hour ago there were at least twenty gentlemen out there, and now there appear to be none."

Carenza, who was similarly attired and sitting at the table, a notepad and pen in front of her, sighed. "I told you this was a ridiculous idea."

"You did not." Olivia came to join her. "You know full well that I wouldn't have placed the ad if you hadn't secretly wanted me to."

There was a knock at the door, and Olivia hastily lowered her veil. "Yes?" she called out.

Bernadette, her maid, looked in. "There's a gentleman to see you, ma'am."

"Please send him in."

Olivia nudged Carenza, who opened her inkwell and dipped her pen in expectantly.

A blond man, whom she immediately recognized as Jeremy Calloway, the younger son of an impoverished but politically powerful earl, came striding into the room and bowed extravagantly.

"Ladies." His smile was condescending. "Which one of you is in need of my . . . attentions?"

"That is not something you need to know at this point, sir." Olivia answered him with a fake-sounding French accent. "We are here on behalf of our client. She will decide which candidate she favors at the appropriate time."

"Ah! French, is she? That would explain a lot." He gave them a lascivious wink. "Well known for their enthusiasm in that area."

Carenza pressed a gloved finger to her brow. She already had a headache, and it was still early.

"What makes you believe you are the ideal candidate for this role?" Olivia inquired.

Carenza wanted to laugh, because Olivia sounded like she was interviewing him for the role of secretary and not a lover.

"I'm young, fit, and lauded for my exploits between the sheets." He pointed at his groin. "Ask any of the whores at Madame DeVane's. They'll tell you how good I am at pleasuring the ladies."

Olivia looked down at her notes. "If you frequently consort with prostitutes, sir, have you ever contacted the pox?"

"How dare you!" Calloway's mouth dropped open, and his face turned an alarming shade of puce. "Has someone been gossiping about me?"

"You do understand that my mistress would require you to visit a doctor of her own choosing to establish the veracity of your claim to be pox-free, sir?" Olivia continued.

"I will do no such thing!" Calloway blustered. "Good day to you both!" He left the room, slamming the door behind him.

Olivia scratched a line through his name. "He definitely has the pox."

Carenza nodded.

Bernadette returned. "Do you want the next one, ma'am?"

"Yes, please." Olivia smiled encouragingly at Carenza. "There can't be anyone worse than that, can there?"

There was.

In quick succession, they dealt with a pastor who loudly lectured them about immorality and the certainty that they were destined for hell, a callow youth who'd written a poem for his mystery lady and simply wanted to read it aloud, and an elderly gentleman who was so drunk he could barely stand, let alone state his case.

Carenza's headache intensified. "Olivia, this is madness."

"I'm quite enjoying it." Olivia grinned at her. "It's like watching a terrible pantomime at the theater."

"It's certainly a farce," Carenza agreed.

"Let's see one more gentleman, and then we'll pause to reconsider our tactics," Olivia suggested.

"Fine." Carenza lowered her veil.

"This is the last one, ma'am," Bernadette announced from the door. "The others seem to have left."

"Thank God," Carenza murmured, and Olivia elbowed her in the side.

A tall, well-dressed man came into the room and bowed low. Upon straightening, he dropped his breeches to reveal himself in all his glory. He pointed at his erect member and smiled proudly at them.

Carenza felt a giggle well up in her throat. When Olivia started shaking beside her, she wasn't sure how either of them would find the ability to speak.

"Very nice, sir," Olivia said in a stifled voice. "Perhaps you might give us your name?"

At this point, Carenza shrieked with laughter, and the man pulled up his breeches and left without saying a single word.

They collapsed, laughing and holding each other until Carenza was able to stop.

"No more," she pleaded.

Olivia wiped tears from her eyes and nodded. "I'll go and tell Mr. Cox that we're done for the day and send Bernadette to fetch the carriage. I'll ask that they wait for us at the end of the lane."

After Olivia left the room, Carenza ripped up the sheet of paper she'd written on and recorked her ink bottle. She was wiping her pen clean when she heard the door open again.

"You were quick," she said.

When there was no response, she raised her head. Julian leaned against the door, regarding her with his infuriatingly cool gaze. All desire to laugh deserted her.

"Why on earth are you here, and where is Olivia?" Carenza asked.

"I suggested she should take her maid and go home before someone recognized her." He paused. "As you might imagine, she wasn't prepared to abandon you until I reassured her that I would see you safely back to Musgrove House."

Carenza got to her feet, went over to the fire, and dropped the ripped paper on it. She watched it burn and then viciously prodded the ashes with the poker until they were no more.

Behind her, Julian sighed. "I do wish you'd put down that poker."

"Why?" She turned toward him with it still in her hand. "I didn't ask you to come and interfere."

"There were several members of the press hanging around. I was concerned that you and Mrs. Sheraton would be followed. The simplest solution seemed to be to warn her and take you home myself."

For some reason, his calm logic wasn't making her feel any less aggrieved. "I don't appreciate being managed, Julian. I'm perfectly capable."

"I, of all people, know that."

Carenza put down the poker and went to the table to collect her belongings. "Then kindly leave. Unless you wish to apply for the position I'm advertising for?"

There was a long silence.

"What if I do?" he asked.

Her breath caught, and she stared at him for a long moment. "Don't be ridiculous."

He shrugged. "If offering my sexual services saves you from an unsavory affair with another man, then yes, I am willing to be your lover."

He strolled toward her, and she tensed. Despite his larger-than-life presence, he wasn't the tallest man of her acquaintance, which meant she could look directly at him without craning her neck.

His eyebrow shot up. "You can't possibly think I'm going to take advantage of you right now."

"After the day I've had, nothing seems impossible."

He opened his mouth, and she held up a finger.

"Please don't lecture me."

"What makes you think I would do that?" Julian asked. "As you've pointed out, I'm neither your father nor your brother. You're perfectly capable of drawing your own conclusions about this fiasco without any help from me."

"Exactly." She stuffed everything into her reticule and turned to the door. "Which also means that I am perfectly capable of finding my own way back to Tavistock Square."

He stood by the door, his expression hard to read. "I am taking you home."

She marched right up to him, but he refused to yield. "Julian, I am not in the best of moods. Please stand aside."

He met her gaze, his blue eyes determined. "I'm more than happy to move when we have established that I am going to escort you home whether you like it or not."

Carenza hesitated. She was alone in a part of London she didn't know well. Mr. Cox would ensure that she came to no harm, but if Julian was correct, and there were members of the press hanging around, she should accept his offer and stop being stubborn about nothing.

"Carenza . . ."

She let out a breath and lowered her veil. "Fine. You win." She set her gloved hand on his proffered arm. "We can leave through the back entrance of Mr. Cox's residence next door."

"That was clever of you," Julian commented as they exited the room. He allowed her to lead him toward the back of the building, where a second set of stairs took them into the other dwelling.

Mr. Cox, who was sitting by the fire reading a printed tract, stood up when they entered. "Mrs. Sheraton said to offer you her apologies for leaving, my lady, but that she knew you'd be safe with his lordship, here."

Julian had asked Mr. Cox not to mention their prior financial arrangement, which had given him access to the inn through this very kitchen.

"Thank you. I'll take good care of her, Mr. Cox," Julian said, and received a wink in return.

He reckoned the landlord must have done well over the course of the day, what with all the bribes and the increased custom in the public bar. He only hoped the man had the sense to keep his mouth shut if anyone came looking for information. He'd have to ask Simon to keep an eye on him.

"Shall we?" He offered his arm to Carenza, who hadn't spoken a single word. "My carriage is at the Golden Dove, which is a short walk from here."

After making sure nobody was watching, he escorted her from the building and walked her through a series of lanes to the stable yard of the Golden Dove. He usually preferred to drive himself, but on this occasion, he'd brought his closed carriage and coachman in case he needed them.

In the carriage, Carenza took the seat opposite him and waited until the door closed behind him before raising her veil. Julian risked a smile at her and was met with a glare.

He sat back against the seat and regarded her. "How many men turned up?"

"Enough."

"Did any of them come up to scratch?"

"That's my business."

He allowed a considerable silence to develop between them before he spoke again.

"I doubt any of them can offer you what I can. Discretion, reliability, all my own teeth, good health, expertise." He ticked the list off on his fingers.

"You consider yourself an expert in bed?" Carenza asked.

"I've never had any complaints."

"You do know that women lie about such things."

"Not about me." He smiled because he had a strange desire to annoy her, and he was enjoying himself.

"Perhaps I should ask my acquaintances." Carenza crossed her arms. "I'm sure someone has some interesting things to say about your rakish ways."

"Please do. Although, I pride myself on my discretion, and I choose my partners for the same reason."

"You mean married women who wouldn't want to risk their position in society."

"Yes," Julian agreed. "Mostly, but not always."

She sniffed. "Widows, then?"

"Absolutely." He smiled again. "Come on, Carenza, admit it. You wanted a rake. I'm the perfect lover for you."

"You're almost as conceited as Hector," she retorted.

"But is it conceit, when I know I'm an expert in pleasuring women?" He raised an eyebrow. "Perhaps a demonstration is in order."

The carriage came to a stop, and she held up her hand, her expression flustered.

"No! I mean, I have to get on. Allegra will be worrying about me."

He fought to contain his amusement as she lowered her veil, flung open the door, and almost tripped on her gown as she stepped down. He came around the carriage at a more leisurely pace and followed her to her front door.

"I am yours to command, my lady. Send me a note and I will come to you immediately." He took her hand and kissed it.

He thought he heard a growl from behind her veil.

"Go *away*, Julian."

He descended the steps, blew her a kiss, and returned to his carriage, well satisfied with his morning's work. He'd scuppered her plans to find a lover and had made his own case as a superior candidate. As he settled into his seat, his smile disappeared. He'd never seen Carenza so flustered. She sailed through life with the grace of a swan. Her ability to rise above Hector's crassness and infidelities had always impressed him.

What had started as a simple attempt to save her reputation was fast becoming a personal challenge. Carenza had unwittingly aroused all his competitive instincts. He never liked to lose, and taming Carenza Musgrove was a contest he was excited to take on.

Chapter 3

"Whatever is the matter, Carenza?" Allegra set down her embroidery. "You've been pacing and muttering ever since you came in."

Maude, who was sitting opposite Allegra in the drawing room, nodded. "Is something wrong? You haven't told us anything about how your event went yet."

Carenza took a deep breath. "The men who answered the advertisement were . . . unsuitable."

"What a surprise," Allegra said.

Maude grimaced. "That is a shame. Perhaps you'll have to find a lover the old-fashioned way and attend lots of balls in a succession of daring gowns that simply shout out that you're looking for a paramour."

"You read too many novels," Allegra said.

"And you don't?" Maude grinned at Allegra.

Carenza finally sat down. "To be honest, I wasn't expecting much interest in my advertisement. But after finding out it had been discussed at White's, I did assume I might see a better class of gentlemen."

"From what I understand, most gentlemen thought it was a ploy by the newspapers to make the men look bad," Maude said. "No one enjoys being ridiculed in the press."

"It will be interesting to see whether the morning papers

even mention it," Allegra said. "One can only hope the news doesn't reach Father in Norfolk."

"I doubt it will," Carenza said. "Unless someone who knows exactly who we are decides to tell him."

"Olivia might enjoy a good joke, sister, but I don't think she'd betray you," Allegra hastened to reassure Carenza.

"I wasn't thinking of her."

"Then who? Surely you can't imagine Maude or I would—"

"Of course not." Carenza shook her head. "I was thinking of Julian."

Both women blinked at her.

Maude was the first to recover. "Julian Laurent?"

Carenza nodded. "As you might imagine, when he discovered my scheme he was shocked that I was contemplating such a step and attempted to dissuade me. When I refused to listen, he turned up at the inn and insisted on taking me home."

"What did Olivia have to say about that?" Maude asked.

"Before he spoke with me, he sent her home with her maid," Carenza said.

"And she went willingly?" Allegra looked at Maude.

"He told her the press were outside and that it would be better if we left separately. She apparently agreed."

"Then it was a good thing that you did let Julian accompany you home," Allegra said. "Think of your reputation!"

"Did he lecture you all the way back?" Maude asked. "That might account for your current agitation."

"He—" Carenza stopped speaking. She was not ready to admit that Julian had offered to be her paramour. "He *was* rather annoyed with me."

Allegra gave an exaggerated shudder. "I've seen him give other people a set-down, and it is never pleasant. He has such a cold way about him."

Carenza had never thought of Julian as cold, but she'd certainly underestimated the steely determination beneath his languid exterior. His unexpected offer had made her blush and stammer like an untried debutante. But she couldn't deny that she was intrigued. Could she begin to think of Julian as a possible lover as opposed to her deceased husband's best friend?

That was the issue at hand and not his ability to be discreet. She already knew his discretion was a given.

"I suppose Mr. Laurent still feels somewhat responsible for you, Carenza," Maude said. "He and Hector were very close."

"I suspect you are right," Carenza agreed. "There is no point in being annoyed with him for looking out for my best interests."

"How did he find out in the first place?" Allegra asked.

Carenza looked over at her sister. "That was my fault. He suspected it was Olivia who was advertising for a lover, and I felt obliged to set him straight."

"Not that," Allegra said. "How did he know you'd be at the Wheatsheaf today?"

"I'm not sure." Carenza frowned.

"I mean, it's not as if he'd be likely to be passing by such an establishment," Allegra pointed out. "He only leaves his house to visit his club, see his mother, and attend to his social duties."

"Then I assume he must have read the advertisement," Carenza said.

"Which only asked for interested applicants to apply."

Maude chuckled. "Are you suggesting that the extremely rich and available Mr. Laurent stooped to replying to an advertisement to find a lover? I find that extremely unlikely."

"Once he knew it was me, he probably pretended to be someone else, or got his secretary to apply for him," Carenza said, vaguely unsettled. "And why we are wasting so much energy discussing this matter is beyond me."

Maude exchanged a glance with Allegra and rose to her feet. "I should be going. I'm expecting a letter from Gerald today."

"Is he coming home?" Carenza asked.

Maude's expression tightened. "Your guess is as good as mine. I've grown so used to being disappointed that I hardly dare hope anymore."

Carenza got up and embraced Maude. "He'll come home. He has to."

"At some point there will be nothing left for him to do," Allegra agreed. "Napoleon is safely on Saint Helena, and the continent is beginning to settle down."

"One can only hope." Maude kissed them both and left.

Allegra looked over at Carenza. "I can't believe Gerald is so oblivious to his own wife's misery."

"It is not uncommon in a marriage, sister," Carenza said.

"I know Hector led you a merry dance."

"It wasn't particularly merry," Carenza confessed. "I cried myself to sleep on many occasions."

"And yet in public, you always looked so serene," Allegra said. "Father was always so proud of you."

The butler came in and bowed. "Mrs. Sheraton has called, my lady. Do you wish to receive her and her companions?"

Carenza glanced at the clock. It was rather late, but there was no reason to be uncivil. Visitors might take her mind off the dilemma of Julian, and she desperately needed to speak to Olivia anyway.

"Please send them up and bring some refreshments." She rose to her feet to greet the three people who came into the drawing room. "Good afternoon, Olivia, Lady Brenton, Mr. Walcott."

Olivia came over to kiss her. "I do apologize for my lateness, but I met Mr. Walcott and Lady Brenton in the park, and we were so busy comparing notes on the opera singer we heard yesterday evening that I quite forgot the time."

Mr. Walcott bowed low. "Lady Smythe-Harding, Lady Allegra."

"Good afternoon." Carenza offered him her hand. She knew very little of him apart from the fact that he was vaguely related to Julian.

"I believe you are acquainted with Lady Brenton?" Mr. Walcott asked.

"Yes, of course." Carenza curtsied to the lady in question.

Lady Brenton was an exquisite dark-haired beauty who always made Carenza feel like a cart horse.

"We share many of the same interests."

Mr. Walcott tittered. "One of them being Julian Laurent."

Carenza went still. Had Julian's intervention in her affairs gotten out? Or, even worse, had he revealed to others that he was bringing her to heel?

She quickly became aware that everyone was looking at her and tried to regain her usual calm. "How so?" she asked politely.

Lady Brenton didn't look amused. "Mr. Walcott is jesting."

"Hardly, my dear," Mr. Walcott said. "All I meant was that Julian was best friends with Hector Smythe-Harding and that you are also a good friend of Julian's."

"Please excuse Mr. Walcott, Carenza," Olivia intervened. "He is not an admirer of Mr. Laurent, as Julian was left a fortune by his godmother that Mr. Walcott believes should have come to him."

Mr. Walcott attempted a tight smile. "Even if what you say is correct, Mrs. Sheraton, it is hardly the place to discuss it. I can assure you that I am still pursuing this matter through the courts."

"I thought they recently ruled against you again," Olivia said sweetly. "And that there were no longer any grounds for further appeal."

Carenza tried not to smile as Mr. Walcott's jaw worked

and he struggled to speak. "As I said, ma'am, such matters are better left to those who have a greater understanding of the law and are not merely regurgitating rumors read in the press."

If Mr. Walcott thought his remarks would cow Olivia, he was soon disappointed.

"Regurgitate?" Olivia's eyebrows rose. "That's an interesting word. I will have to share your opinion of *The Times* journalism with those I know who work there."

"I merely meant that a particular reader such as yourself, ma'am, might not have a complete understanding of the topic."

"Ah, yes, because women cannot be expected to understand such weighty matters," Olivia said.

Mr. Walcott looked relieved. "Exactly, ma'am."

The parlormaid arrived with the tea tray and they all sat down. Carenza took the opportunity to steer the conversation into less stormy waters. Lady Brenton said little, her attention busy cataloging the contents of the drawing room.

Her gaze lingered on the portrait of Carenza's family over the mantelpiece. "Your mother doesn't like to come up to town?" she asked Carenza.

"No, she prefers life in the countryside, as does my father."

"I suppose that is for the best." Lady Brenton set down her barely touched tea. "Considering."

Carenza was beginning to wish she hadn't chosen to receive her callers, what with Mr. Walcott fencing with Olivia, and Lady Brenton's avid curiosity about her parents.

"Our parents are very happy together," Carenza said. "Aren't they, Allegra?"

"Indeed," Allegra valiantly backed her up. "They have been married for thirty-five years and are still blissfully in love."

Lady Brenton shuddered slightly. "I assume your brother intends to marry at some point?"

"I should imagine so," Carenza said.

"One can only hope that his peers can overlook the . . . deficiencies in his parentage and allow one of their daughters to marry him."

"I don't think that will be a problem. He is a handsome man with a large fortune and several thriving estates." Carenza was getting tired of Lady Brenton looking down her perfect nose at her.

"But the *connection* . . ."

Carenza was done being polite. "To what, ma'am?"

"Your mother was an opera singer, yes?"

"A very successful one."

"But still—forgive me—not of your father's class."

"Surely that was for him to decide?" Carenza raised her eyebrows.

"But society—"

"Society may think what it likes, Lady Brenton," Carenza said firmly. "May I offer you more tea?"

The clock on the mantelpiece chimed the quarter hour, and Mr. Walcott rose to his feet.

"We must take our leave, Lady Smythe-Harding. Are you attending the Ross ball tonight?"

"I haven't decided yet," Carenza said as she set down her cup and also stood up.

Lady Brenton curtsied and took Mr. Walcott's arm. "Thank you for the tea, my lady."

"You are most welcome." Carenza smiled.

Olivia, who hadn't bothered to get up, waved her farewells from her chair. Allegra followed the visitors out, claiming that she wished to speak to the cook, and Carenza returned to her seat.

"I apologize for bringing them with me," Olivia said. Like Carenza, she was no longer wearing black, instead wearing something summery. "They were impossible to shake off."

"Perhaps they wished to come here." Carenza regarded her friend. "They were certainly curious enough."

Olivia winced. "Lady Brenton was incredibly rude."

"We are fairly used to having to defend our parents, Olivia. It's not the end of the world. They don't come to town very often for that reason. My father can't stand watching my mother being treated with disdain." Carenza gathered the cups and set them on the tray. "I thought you handled Mr. Walcott very well."

"He literally quivers with fury every time someone mentions Julian's name."

"I suppose he feels justified in doing so when Julian was only related to his family through his godmother. It must have come as something of a shock to be disinherited like that."

"Dear Percival and the rest of his family made no effort to visit Lady Beryl in her declining years. Julian was the only one who made sure she kept her house and her health, and so he deserves every penny of her fortune."

"I'm not disagreeing with you, Olivia," Carenza said. "I am, however, quite cross with you for leaving without me earlier today."

Olivia grinned at her. "But Julian was positively *insistent* that I allow him to take the matter into his hands."

"Still . . ."

"In fact," Olivia continued as if she hadn't heard the reprimand, "he's highly protective of you, and one has to wonder why." Her gaze returned to Carenza's face. "You're blushing. What's afoot?"

"It's simply because I'm still angry with both of you."

"And that is unlike you." Olivia sighed. "I do apologize if I've truly offended you, but I did think Julian had a point about us leaving separately, and I knew he'd take good care of you." She paused. "Which reminds me, how did he find out in the first place?"

Carenza sat down and fussed around with the tea tray. "Find out what?"

"Your involvement with the advertisement."

"He thought you had placed the ad, and I felt obliged to tell him the truth."

"Hence his interest in preserving not my good name but yours." Olivia sat down as well. "I've never seen him quite so animated on someone else's behalf. He always struck me as an observer rather than a participator in chaos."

"I can assure you that he participated with an extreme lack of humor and a ruthlessness to get his own way that bordered on insulting."

"Did he?"

Carenza didn't like the way Olivia was looking at her. "Please don't read anything into it. He and I are old friends."

"Like brother and sister?"

"Hardly." Carenza didn't even want to think about that—especially after what Julian had proposed. "Although we do squabble rather a lot."

Olivia finished her tea and rose to her feet. "I must be off. I just wanted to reassure myself that you got home safely."

Carenza smiled at her friend. "Hopefully no one will ever know that it was us, and the whole thing will die down when the next scandal occurs in the ton."

"You don't wish to continue the scheme?" Olivia looked surprised.

"You saw the quality of the applicants. I'm not that desperate." Carenza followed Olivia to the door. "I'll have to resign myself to finding a paramour in the usual fashion."

"Or ask Julian." Olivia kissed her cheek. "I'm sure he'd be delighted to assist you."

As she got ready for the Ross ball later that evening, Carenza was still considering exactly what Olivia had meant by her parting remark. Carenza had chosen a gown in pink that flattered her skin and had her maid dress her hair in elaborate coils on the top of her head to support the Smythe-Harding tiara.

She added diamond eardrops and a necklace left to her by her grandmother that Hector had been unable to pawn. Long white gloves, kid slippers, and a fine shawl completed her outfit to her satisfaction. Anyone who saw her at the ball would never believe she'd spent the earlier part of the day interviewing candidates for the position of her lover.

Except Julian—he would know.

She went down to the hall to await Allegra and make sure the carriage was ready at the front of the house. Her sister was always punctual, and she appeared at the top of the stairs dressed in her favorite blue.

"You look rather fine this evening, Carenza," Allegra said. "Are we expecting royalty at this ball?"

"Not that I know of. I just felt like making an effort." Carenza got into the carriage, and Allegra followed her.

"I'm not surprised after this morning's fiasco." Allegra folded her hands together on her lap. "One can only hope that you are done with such nonsense now. I did try to warn you."

Was there anything more annoying than a sanctimonious younger sister? Carenza simply ignored her and looked out of the window. Would Julian be at the ball? And if so, how did she intend to deal with him? She'd recently discovered she did not have the face for subterfuge, and pretending everything was fine might be a challenge. The problem was that Julian knew her better than almost anyone outside her family.

She'd have to avoid him. Perhaps if she filled her dance card very quickly, she wouldn't have a moment to spare. Carenza relaxed back against the seat. Dancing would be a good opportunity to meet a gentleman who might give her what she needed without her having to deal with Julian's provocative offer at all.

Chapter 4

After their earlier adventures, Julian hadn't been sure if Carenza would attend the Ross ball, so he was quite surprised to see her descending the steps with Allegra at her side. She looked well in a pink gown that showed off her remarkable bosom and slender neck. Diamonds glinted around her throat and in her ears, and he smiled despite himself. She'd come ready for battle, but with him, or with every other available man in the vicinity, he wasn't quite sure.

Later in the evening, when he'd been unable to get near enough to Carenza to speak to her, his older brother, Aragon, came up beside him. He was tall and dark like Anton and bore little resemblance to Julian.

"Is that Carenza Smythe-Harding over there?"

"Yes, I believe it is." Julian eased away from his brother.

"She looks well." Aragon studied her intently. "I'd like to see her mounted on a strapping stallion."

For a moment Julian could only blink. And then he remembered his brother was horse-mad and thus was probably not making some crude sexual joke.

"She'd look wonderful on Apollonia," Aragon continued. "Will you come with me and ask her if she'd like a ride in the park?"

"You're perfectly capable of asking her without my assistance, brother," Julian pointed out. He had no intention of helping Aragon make advances to the woman he was currently pursuing himself.

"But you're so much better at all that useless social chitchat than I am," Aragon complained.

"Then it's high time you learned to do it for yourself." Julian gave his brother a shove in the right direction and stood back to observe the fun.

Carenza was already surrounded by a bevy of men and appeared to be having a very pleasant evening indeed. By the time Aragon reached her side, she was already being led away on the arm of her next dance partner, the very eligible Lord Atworth, newly widowed and definitely on the hunt for a second wife who'd be willing to bring up his four children. In truth, a perfect match for Carenza, and one Julian would approve of if it wasn't for his inconvenient desire to possess her himself.

Aragon returned, his expression doleful. "Some lucky stud took her off before I could even say hello and present my credentials."

"You'll have to be quicker next time," Julian said.

"Or I could write her a note and invite her out for a ride without having to deal with all this nonsense." Aragon brightened considerably as he waved his hand at the assembled guests. "That might work."

"I think that's an excellent idea," Julian agreed.

"You do?"

Julian raised an eyebrow. "Yes."

"You're not making fun of me?"

"Not at all."

Aragon nodded. "Good, then no need for me to stay at this ball any longer. Tell Mama I'm off to my club."

"Tell her yourself," Julian said. "She won't take it well from me."

Aragon grinned. "I do love it when she tells you off. Makes up for a lot of the other stuff—like you inheriting a fortune and putting me quite in the shade."

"She adores you."

"I know, which is why she'll forgive me." Aragon winked. "I'll compose a letter to Lady Carenza and have it delivered tomorrow."

Inwardly, Julian sighed. Then he made his way through the crowds to where his mother sat with the other dowagers and ladies who didn't like to dance. Julian had inherited her looks and inscrutability, but little else. For some reason, she preferred both Aragon and Anton to him. After years of trying to gain her approval without success, Julian had learned to simulate her indifference and gave her nothing more than she offered him.

He bowed in front of her. "Mother, Aragon asked me to offer his apologies. He has left for his club. I will ensure that you get home safely in his stead."

Her perfect brow creased. "Did he leave because of you?"

"Not at all."

"Because you can be quite cutting," his mother said. "And he is still upset over your inheritance."

Julian smiled. "I believe he had a letter he wished to write, Mother."

"If you say so."

Julian inclined his head. "As soon as you wish to leave, just ask someone to find me and I will be instantly at your disposal."

He heard her sigh as he turned away and ignored it. He would never understand why he was such a disappointment to her, but he refused to let it dictate his choices in life. He was so eager to get away from his mother that he almost bumped into Carenza and had to take her elbow to steady her.

"I do beg your pardon, my lady. I was woolgathering."

She blushed to match her gown, and he found himself smiling.

"Julian, how nice to see you." She looked desperately over his shoulder. "I was looking for Lieutenant Greenwood. I'm supposed to be dancing with him."

"I think I saw him heading toward the cardroom." Julian kept hold of her elbow and gently steered her toward the wall, where they wouldn't be in the way. "Would you like me to go and find him for you?"

"If you would."

"Of course." He bowed. "Please excuse me."

He walked as far as the door of the cardroom and saw Lieutenant Greenwood striding toward him. He wore his dress uniform, which bristled with medals from the recent conflict with the French.

"May I speak to you for a moment?" Julian asked.

"I'm a little busy, sir." Lieutenant Greenwood looked down from his superior height. "There's a lady expecting me for a dance."

"Unfortunately, Lady Smythe-Harding has ripped the hem of her gown and has gone upstairs to have it fixed. She sends her apologies."

"Hmph." Lieutenant Greenwood frowned, his moustache bristling. "Damned shame. Excellent woman."

"I'm sure she'll come about, sir, and will be ready to dance with you at the next available opportunity," Julian said smoothly.

"Jolly good." The lieutenant disappeared back into the smoke-filled cardroom.

Julian returned to Carenza, who looked hopefully up at him.

"Alas, the lieutenant was occupied, my lady. Perhaps I might take his place?" He offered her a charming smile and his arm.

She didn't move an inch. "What have you done?"

"Me? I merely did as you requested."

"You put him off, didn't you?" Carenza held his gaze.

"Why would I do that?"

"Because . . ." She hesitated. "You *know* why."

"Because I am still waiting for an answer to my offer and you have spent all evening deliberately avoiding me?" Julian asked. "If you wish to say no, don't be a coward—just say it."

Her eyes flashed. "I am not a coward."

"Then let's find somewhere quieter to talk, and you can tell me exactly why you are finding it so difficult to give me an answer."

He took her hand and led her back into the main hall, down a corridor, and into the library.

"How did you know this was here?" Carenza asked suspiciously.

"I went to school with Callum Ross. I stayed here once when my parents were abroad."

He took a moment to bank up the fire and light more candles so that he could see her properly. He stood up, dusted off his hands, and turned to face her. She'd gathered her shawl around her shoulders and held it tightly over her bosom. Her expression was hard to read.

"Well?" he said.

She sighed. "If you want the truth. I don't know what to say to you."

Her honesty was disarming.

"Why not?" Julian asked. "We are still friends. You can speak freely to me."

"That's just the point. I am intrigued by your suggestion, but it is difficult to think of you in terms of being my lover when we *are* friends."

"Surely that should help?"

"But what if we end up hating each other?"

"I could never hate you, Carenza." Julian smiled. "You might drive me to madness, but never that."

"I value your friendship. There were times when Hector—"

He held up his hand. "That is all in the past. What you are asking for now is simply physical satisfaction, yes? I can provide you with that."

She raised her chin. "If we do go ahead, I have some conditions."

"I'm glad to hear it." He nodded. "What are they?"

She began to pace the room, her expression intent. "Firstly, that we are discreet. No one must know what we are doing."

"Agreed, although how you will prevent your sister and your close friends from finding out is beyond me."

"I am aware that I don't have the face for intrigue. I might have to tell them, but I will swear them to secrecy."

"Fair enough, what else?"

"*I* decide when we meet and what we do while we're together." She met his gaze. "I don't want to be possessed, or coerced, or—"

"I'm not the kind of man to force a woman to do anything she doesn't wish to," Julian said evenly. "I would hope you'd know that."

She rolled her eyes. "And here you go, taking offense when none is meant. I simply wish to make decisions about my own body. Hector didn't listen, and I was too infatuated to know how to make him pay attention to my needs as well as his own."

"I'm not interested in what Hector—"

"But I am." It was her turn to speak over him. "I was married to the man, and in my opinion, he is relevant to this discussion because I do not wish to deal with his like again."

"I can assure you that I am nothing like Hector in bed." Having seen his friend in close quarters with several women, Julian could have elaborated, but the last thing he wanted to do was humiliate Carenza with tales of her husband's numerous infidelities. "Anything else?" Julian asked.

"That as soon as one of us wishes to end our liaison, the

other will accept their decision and we can go back to being friends."

"Agreed." Julian held out his hand. "Shall we shake on it like gentlemen?"

A smile curved her lips. "Don't you have any conditions of your own?"

"Nothing I can think of at the moment." He advanced toward her, and she went still. "Perhaps we might follow the handshake with a kiss to see if we are compatible?"

"That is a good idea." Despite her agreement, she sounded uncertain as he took her hand and firmly shook it. "Because if we don't enjoy that, then we certainly won't want the rest of it."

Carenza was aware that she might be babbling as Julian brought her hand to his lips and kissed it. She couldn't ever remember being so close to him. His eyes were a very light blue, almost silver, with a broad brown band near the edge . . .

"Carenza." There was a note of command in his voice that made her continue to look at him. "There's no need to be afraid. I promise I won't bite."

"I am slightly out of practice at this," she admitted. "You might have to be patient with me."

"Don't worry." He leaned in and kissed her bare shoulder, his touch as light as thistledown. "I intend to take my time."

He feathered kisses up the column of her neck until he reached her jaw and gently set his teeth on her earlobe. An unexpected wave of lust shot through Carenza, and she grabbed hold of his sleeve.

"You like that," Julian murmured, his voice so close to her ear that she shivered.

He nuzzled her earlobe again, a little harder, his hand cupping her chin while his thumb caressed her lower lip. She expected him to kiss her, but he moved on, his mouth and fingers trailing over her collarbones, the curve of her bosom, and down the other side.

His scent surrounded her, a hint of bergamot, the warmth of brandy, and a lingering curl of smoke from the cardroom. She wanted to turn her face into the curve of his throat and simply breathe him in.

"I thought you were going to kiss me." She was almost shocked to hear her own voice making such a demand.

He chuckled. When she looked him in the eye, he said, "I believe you wished to be in charge of such matters, my lady. I am merely awaiting instructions."

She set her hands on his shoulders, went on tiptoe, and kissed him firmly on the mouth. She waited for a moment to see if the universe objected and then did it again, this time running the tip of her tongue along the seam of his lips.

His arm came around her waist like a vise, and he jerked her hard against him. "I do apologize," he said. "It appears that I am not very good at doing as I'm told . . ."

She wasn't listening anymore, her body demanding she pay attention to the needs she'd suppressed for so long. She slid one hand behind his neck and urged his head down until his mouth met hers in a fiery clash. He kissed her properly then, and she responded, all the frustrated heat inside her bursting forth into one long, lascivious kiss that made her moan his name.

He backed her against the wall, their mouths still attached, his hand curving around her bottom and making her aware that he was fully aroused. She rolled her hips, and he groaned and slammed his other hand on the wall above her head, his breath harsh as he looked down at her.

"I thought you said you were out of practice."

Carenza froze. "I . . . have offended you."

"*What?*"

"With my enthusiasm. Hector said it was unladylike."

"Hector was a fool," Julian said. "Do I look like I am offended?"

Carenza studied him carefully. "No."

"Then pray continue."

Suddenly aware that they were in someone else's house and that there were other people around who would like nothing more than to discover her with a paramour, Carenza took a deep breath. "Perhaps we should stop."

He looked down at her, his expression hard to read, and took a step back. "As you wish."

"I don't wish, but I am reluctant to be discovered with my legs wrapped around your waist as you pleasure me against this wall."

"I wish you hadn't said that." His breath caught. "I can't tell you how much I want to lock the doors and take you at your word."

She licked her lips, and he cupped her chin and leaned in close.

"Are you wet enough to take me?"

"I believe so."

His eyes briefly closed. "I wouldn't be gentle."

"I wouldn't want you to be."

He groaned and leaned in to kiss her. "You are not making it easy to walk away when it would be much more satisfying to push up your skirts, unbutton my breeches, and fill you with my cock."

Her body throbbed with temptation to agree that was exactly what he should do, but sanity prevailed. She'd lost her head when Hector had overwhelmed her with his physical desires, and she wasn't willing to lose herself again. The whole point of this current experiment was that she should be the one in charge.

"Luckily, we agreed only to a kiss," Carenza reminded him.

"I could kiss you wherever you need me—use my fingers and tongue to bring you to a climax."

Carenza's knees went weak. Good Lord, no wonder Julian was so successful with women. Even his voice was a seduction. She stiffened her spine and very carefully didn't look at his breeches.

"I need to find Allegra. She will be wondering where I am."

"Of course." He nodded and moved away, his expression composed. "May I ask if you have concluded that we suit?"

"I think so." She strived to copy his conversational tone. "Do you?"

"I think I've proved my worth." He went over to the fire and extinguished the candles on the mantelpiece. "Perhaps you should leave first. We are all about discretion."

"Yes, thank you." She studied her reflection in the mirror, aware of him watching her in the glass. "Do I look disheveled?"

"Only a little—as if you have enjoyed an energetic dance." He smiled. "Only those who know you well might wonder what you've really been up to."

"Then I should go home alone, because Allegra and Maude are here."

"You can hardly leave your sister behind," Julian objected.

Carenza wished she hadn't attempted to make a joke and tried to match his nonchalance. "How practical you are."

"It is my besetting sin." He inclined his head, his attention on the fire. "I won't approach you again this evening."

"Oh." Carenza, who had reached the door, paused. "As you wish. Good night, Julian."

"Good night, Carenza."

She opened the door and looked back at him, but he didn't acknowledge her, which was slightly discouraging. He'd said he'd enjoyed kissing her—had he been telling the truth? He'd never been the kind of gentleman to mince words, and if she hadn't performed to his satisfaction, surely he would have mentioned it?

Carenza stopped walking as she entered the main hall, took a steadying breath, and reminded herself that taking a lover was her choice and that if Julian didn't wish to claim the honor, she would find someone who would.

"Lady Smythe-Harding."

She looked up to see Lieutenant Greenwood bearing down on her, a determined expression on his face as he pointed at the hem of her gown. "Fixed your skirt?"

For a moment Carenza had no idea what he was talking about and then she nodded. "It's fine now, sir. I do apologize for missing our dance."

"No matter." He offered her his arm. "Shall we go into supper together? If we hurry, we can be first in line. Lady Ross always offers an excellent supper table."

"Yes, of course." Carenza set her hand on his arm. "That would be delightful."

Chapter 5

Julian sat up in bed as Proctor, his valet, set a breakfast tray on his knees and proceeded to open the curtains. After receiving his unexpected inheritance, Julian had bought one of the new town houses springing up in the city and had enjoyed decorating it and choosing all the furniture without interference from his family. His mother had been offended both by his decision to leave the family home, which she insisted reflected badly on her, and Julian's resolve not to ask for her help with any aspect of the house.

"It's a beautiful morning, sir. What do you have planned?" Proctor asked as Julian sipped his coffee.

"I have some business to attend to in the East End and then I might take my phaeton out to the park this afternoon."

Proctor made a face. "May I suggest one of your older coats for your morning activities, sir? Last time you came home from that place you were covered in jam and other unknown substances. It took me all day to restore your coat to a wearable condition."

"Whatever you think best." Julian grinned at him. "I trust your judgment implicitly, Proctor."

"I always like to see you turned out well, sir." His valet bowed. "Do you wish to have a bath this morning? Or should that wait until your return?"

"I'll bathe when I return. That'll wash off the jam."

"And the other unmentionables." Proctor shuddered and turned to leave. "I'm surprised you haven't caught fleas."

Julian ate his breakfast in a leisurely fashion and was just perusing the morning papers when his brother burst into the room.

"Morning, Julian."

Julian lowered the newspaper. "Did you forget where you live again, Aragon? It's deuced early to be disturbing a man."

Aragon sat on the side of the bed and eyed the contents of Julian's breakfast tray like a hopeful dog. "Anything left for me?"

Julian sighed and handed over the tray. "I was just about to get up, anyway."

"No need to rush on my account," his brother mumbled through a mouthful of toast. "I wrote that note to Lady Carenza. Took me hours. Had to ask the waiter at White's how to spell her name properly."

"Good for you." Julian stripped off his nightshirt, poured hot water from the jug his valet had left him into the matching bowl, and vigorously washed his face and upper torso. "Did she respond?"

"Not yet. It is still early." Aragon started on the remains of the eggs. "It occurred to me that you know her quite well."

"I knew her deceased husband. We were at school together." Julian put on his shirt and stepped into his breeches. "My acquaintance with the lady herself is of no consequence."

"You'll still come with me, though, when I take her riding." Aragon looked up at him. A sizable amount of toast crumbs adhered to his mustache. "You're very accomplished at this chitchat nonsense."

"As I mentioned yesterday, you just need practice, brother. Hiding behind me will not further your suit with the lady in question."

Aragon drank the remains of Julian's coffee and then added more to the cup from the pot. "Mother said you'd say that."

"And yet again, she was correct."

"She said you wouldn't choose to oblige me because you lack"—Aragon paused as if trying to recollect her exact words—"filial obligations."

"As I recently paid for Anton's promotion, she has a very short memory." Julian turned to the mirror and tried to concentrate on the arrangement of his cravat. "When are you supposed to go riding with Lady Carenza?"

"*I* don't know." His brother's mirrored reflection shrugged. "She hasn't responded yet, and you know what ladies are like. Their social engagements are legion."

"When she does respond, send me a note, and if I am free, I will accompany you."

"Excellent." Aragon stood up, dusted down his waistcoat, and strode toward the door. "I knew you'd do the right thing in the end."

Julian pinned his cravat in place and picked up the black coat Proctor had left out for him. It had occurred to him that assisting his brother with his current flirtation with Carenza worked in his favor. It would give him a perfectly legitimate reason to call more regularly on her, and as his mother would never dream of letting Aragon marry anyone for at least the next ten years, no harm would be done to all concerned.

He put on his rings, stowed his watch and purse in his pockets, and went down the stairs, filled with unusual optimism. From the odd hint Hector had dropped about Carenza, Julian had assumed she'd tolerated her husband's advances with the usual lack of enthusiasm of most society wives. The single kiss Julian had shared with her had dispelled that notion in an instant.

Her response also explained her decision to look for a new bed partner. He was intrigued by the idea of having a lover who told him what to do. He'd never been very biddable. Only time would tell if he would succeed in following Carenza's orders.

He made his way to the mews behind his house, where his groom had his horse ready to go.

"Thank you, Bert." Julian mounted his horse and headed out.

It was a clear spring morning, which he was grateful for as he made the familiar ride into an area where the buildings were close enough together to block out the sunlight, and the population increased until he was surrounded by a multitude of people. He was always relieved that his destination was directly on the London Road and not down one of the infamous back alleys from which some unfortunates never returned.

He reined in his horse at the front of an austere, stone-faced building, and the porter who managed the courtyard gate recognized Julian and let him in with a nod and a smile. There was a small stable yard to the side of the building where he was able to leave his horse in relative comfort and with the knowledge that it would still be there when he returned.

He approached the open kitchen door, through which the smell of porridge scented the steamy air. Someone was shouting—someone was always shouting here—and he recognized the voice of the cook and fought a smile.

Mrs. Bellingham was a tall woman who commanded her kitchen staff as though she were the Duke of Wellington. Everyone was terrified of her, but they also knew she had a kind heart and would protect the orphans with everything in her power.

"Come 'ere, you little rascal, I—" She paused midtirade, her soup ladle in the air, as she saw Julian. "Morning, sir."

"Good morning, Mrs. Bellingham. Is Miss Cartwright in?"

"Where else would she be at this time in the morning?" Mrs. Bellingham gave him a bemused look. "Some of us have jobs to do."

"Yeah, we're not toffs like you," the small boy who had

raised the housekeeper's ire piped up. "Swanning around all fancy like."

"You keep your mouth shut, Tommy, and have some respect in front of Mr. Laurent," Mrs. Bellingham said. "And get out of my kitchen, you thieving little devil."

"Where is he supposed to be, ma'am?" Julian asked. "I can escort him back, if you like."

"In the hall with the other boys having his breakfast." Mrs. Bellingham glared at the boy. "Not in 'ere under me feet."

"Come along." Julian put his hand on the boy's shoulder. "Let's leave Mrs. Bellingham in peace."

Tommy sighed and allowed Julian to escort him out of the kitchen. "I was just a bit hungry."

"Then go and have your breakfast."

Julian braced himself for the noise and sight of twenty boys sitting in long rows eating. It reminded him of his days at Harrow, except these boys wouldn't be regularly beaten, at least not while he was on the orphanage's board of trustees. His gaze fell upon Miss Cartwright, who was managing the cauldron of porridge. She looked flushed, her brown hair coming down to create soft curls around her face.

Julian had met Miss Cartwright and her brother Martin through an acquaintance, and after visiting their establishment, he had offered his financial support.

"Mr. Laurent!" Miss Cartwright smiled at him. "How lovely to see you." She hesitated, glancing at the line of boys in front of her. "If you don't mind, I'll finish feeding the boys, and then I'll attend to you."

"Shall I wait in the office?" Julian offered as he gently maneuvered Tommy toward the back of the line.

"Yes, please." She returned to her task.

Julian held out his hand to Tommy and lowered his voice so Miss Cartwright couldn't hear him. "Give it back."

"What?"

Julian raised his eyebrows. "You know the rules."

After a lot of complaining, Tommy returned Julian's purse and pocket watch.

"Is that it?" Julian asked.

With a martyred sigh, Tommy produced Julian's handkerchief.

"Thank you."

Julian left the hall and went into the office Miss Cartwright shared with her brother. It was a tidy, if somewhat spartan, space due to the orphans' predilection for stealing things. Most of them had survived by thieving and had been brought in off the streets. Teaching them more honest trades and how to read and write took a considerable amount of time and energy. The Cartwrights didn't always succeed, but the boys who did stay on benefited from their kind but firm direction and moved on to better lives.

While he waited, Julian used the time to do his monthly audit of the accounts and was reading the daily record when Miss Cartwright came in. Julian rose to his feet.

"Is something wrong?" she asked as she closed the door.

"Not at all. Just my usual monthly visit." He pointed at the book. "Things seem to be going well."

"They are, which is why I was surprised to see you." She sat down heavily at her desk. "I must confess I'd forgotten which day it was."

Julian, who wasn't used to being forgotten, smiled. "Is everything all right? You seem rather tired."

"We took in four new boys last night, and they didn't settle well. I spent the whole night trying to prevent them leaving."

"Then I hope you get some rest today." He winced when she gave him a look. "Yes, I know your budget doesn't allow for such matters, but perhaps it should."

"Are you satisfied with our accounting?" Miss Cartwright asked, her gaze drifting to the clock behind him.

"Yes, of course." He nodded. "I can see that you are anxious to resume your duties, so I will leave you in peace."

"Thank you." She rose to her feet and headed for the door, her relief at his pronouncement evident. "I'll expect you next month."

Julian bowed as she swept past him. He took his time walking back through the kitchen and yard, making sure everything was as it should be. He took his responsibilities as a trustee seriously and dropped in regularly. He had to admit that Miss Cartwright was also part of the attraction. Her refusal to see him as an eligible man was both refreshing and amusing. And, as Carenza was learning, he'd always loved a challenge.

Thoughts of Carenza had him directing his horse toward her current home. She'd left the Smythe-Harding town house after Hector's death and returned to her father's London home, which her father rarely used. There had been some delay in locating the new heir to Hector's title, but the new earl had recently moved into Carenza's old home with his wife and mother.

Julian left his horse in the capable hands of Carenza's groom and made his way to the front of the house, where he offered the butler his card. He was instantly shown up the stairs to the drawing room and went in to discover a room full of ladies.

Mrs. Sheraton hailed him from the couch. "Just the gentleman we need!" She gave him a wicked smile. "We're trying to pick a new lover for Carenza."

"I'm fairly certain she doesn't need my help for that." Julian went over to kiss Mrs. Sheraton's hand and then turned to Carenza, who had risen to greet him. He smiled deep into her hazel eyes and was rewarded by a flash of annoyance. "She has impeccable taste."

"Not in men," Mrs. Sheraton pointed out.

"Hector wasn't all bad," Carenza said somewhat tartly.

"So you mentioned." Olivia winked at her.

"I wonder if I might speak to you in private for a moment, Lady Carenza?" Julian asked.

"Why?"

Julian fought a smile. "It is a family matter."

"You don't like your family," Mrs. Sheraton, who was not above eavesdropping, commented.

"Unfortunately, that doesn't mean they don't require my attention," Julian countered. "And this is a very particular matter concerning my brother."

Carenza ignored her friend and addressed her guests. "If you will please excuse me for a moment?"

She left the room, and Julian followed her through to a small, private sitting room beside her bedroom suite. He shut the door behind them and leaned against it. She turned to look at him, and he simply looked back.

"*Is* there something you want?" Carenza asked. "Or do you merely wish to stare at me with that rather annoying smile on your face?"

"I was thinking about you last night." He loved the way the color instantly rose in her cheeks. "I was imagining undressing you."

He advanced toward her, and she held her ground, looking up into his face as he cupped her chin.

"I took a very long time exposing every inch of your delicious skin with my mouth, my hands, and used all my senses to arouse you." He slid his fingers down her neck and ran them along the lace bodice of her dress, enjoying the way her breath hitched.

"Julian, I have guests . . ."

"Mmm . . ."

"I have to get back." She sighed as his fingertip grazed her nipple. "This is most unfair."

"Did you think of me at all?" he inquired. "Did you imagine commanding me to undress for your pleasure?"

"I might have."

Her admission made him want to throw caution to the winds, pin her to the wall, and have his way with her, but he reminded himself of their agreement.

"And what would you have done to me in your dreams?"

She met his gaze quite fearlessly. "Anything I wanted to."

"Such as?"

She smiled at him. "Oh, I don't have time to explain everything. We'd be here for hours, and Allegra would come and find me."

"What about a more practical demonstration?" he suggested. "I am yours to command."

She considered him carefully. "I've always wanted a man to . . ." She paused. "I feel foolish even suggesting such a thing."

"Don't be," Julian said. "What is your desire?"

She took a deep breath. "When you asked to speak to me alone, I thought you might bring me in here, and . . ."

"Ravish you?" Julian offered.

"Not quite all the way. That would take too long. I was thinking it would be more of a signal of intent." She looked up at him. "If that makes sense."

"Ah. You'd like a man to make you look forward to what he's going to do to you later."

"Exactly."

He took her hand and led her toward the writing desk. "May I?"

She glanced at the clock. "Whatever you do, it will have to be quick. We've been here for quite a while already."

He put his hands around her waist and sat her on the side of the desk. "Pull up your skirts and petticoats."

"What are you going to do?" she asked as she pulled up her skirt to expose her naked thighs and tied stockings.

"This." He went down on his knees, spread her thighs wide, and used his mouth on her most sensitive parts. To his satisfaction, she was already wet, her clit begging for his attention as he tongued it, making her quiver and roll her hips toward him.

Aware of the need for haste, he thrust two fingers inside her and scissored them wide as he continued to flick his tongue hard over her now-throbbing clit. She was wet enough for him to add another finger, and he circled his thumb roughly over the aroused flesh he'd already kissed.

With a throaty moan, she climaxed, her fingers gripping his scalp as waves of clenching need ran through her. Julian gently disengaged her hand from his hair and stood up. He found his handkerchief and wiped his mouth, staring at Carenza. She was breathing hard, her cheeks flushed, and her eyes wild.

He raised an eyebrow. "I'd offer you my handkerchief, but I want you to go back to your guests just as you are." He stepped closer and kissed her with all the wild savagery he'd repressed while he'd pleasured her. "Will your friends notice that you've been pleasured, Carenza?" he murmured into her mouth. "Will they see it in your eyes, on your flushed cheeks? I wish I had time to attend to you properly and send you back in there well satisfied."

She placed both hands on his chest and gently pushed him away. "We have to stop."

"As you wish." He bowed. "Let me set you to rights." He helped her down and rearranged her skirts and bodice to his satisfaction. "There. You look your usual calm self."

"I heartily doubt it." She looked up at him. "Thank you."

He bowed. "You're very welcome. Shall we return to the drawing room?"

"Was there anything you wished to talk to me about? I can hardly tell Olivia and Allegra that we spent ten minutes alone and spoke of nothing."

"Then tell them that I came to warn you that my older brother is intent on courting you."

"Don't be ridiculous."

"It's the truth. He wants to take you riding in the park. He thinks you look splendid on a horse."

"He did send me a note about that. I was going to ask you whether I should go."

"I'd accept his kind invitation," Julian advised. "He wants me to come with him, which gives us the opportunity to be together without comment."

He opened the door for her, and they walked back toward the drawing room. To his relief, most of the guests had departed and only Allegra and Mrs. Sheraton remained. Yet again, he was slightly chagrined at how quickly Carenza had regained her composure. He began making plans about how and when he would disrupt her again.

"I don't want to give Aragon false hope," Carenza said as he escorted her to her seat.

"Don't worry, my mother will never let him get married until she picks him a bride." Julian stepped back with a smile. "You'll be quite safe, I assure you."

Carenza resumed her seat, aware that her body was now fizzing with the sultry, slow pulse of release. Olivia was looking very closely at her, which didn't bode well for Carenza's chances of getting away with allowing a gentleman to pleasure her during calling hours. Allegra was chatting away to Julian without a care in the world and seemed oblivious to her sister's appearance.

The butler came in. "Lord Tobias and Lady Harriet Smythe-Harding, my lady."

Carenza stood up to greet the new heir to her late husband's title. She was surprised, because after an initial formal visit, the earl and his wife had made little effort to socialize with her since coming to town. Tobias was Hector's second cousin, the oldest son of Hector's first cousin.

"How very kind of you to call," Carenza said. "May I offer you some refreshments?"

"No, thank you." Tobias seemed somewhat ill at ease. "There is a matter I wish to discuss with you."

Carenza raised her eyebrows, inviting him to continue.

It was his wife who spoke up. "You need to give it back."

"I beg your pardon?" Carenza asked.

"The tiara," Lady Harriet said. "It's mine now."

Carenza suddenly realized why they'd come. "Oh, my goodness, of course. I quite forgot the tiara belonged to Hector's side of the family."

"You should not have been wearing it at a public ball. It made it look as if you still consider yourself to be the countess." Lady Harriet's face was flushed and angry.

"My sister is still the dowager countess," Allegra pointed out. "That's a fact."

"It was a genuine mistake," Carenza said evenly. "I have no desire to be the countess. I will have it fetched for you immediately."

Tobias bowed. "That is most kind of you."

His wife spoke over him. "And what about the other things?"

"What things?" Carenza stared at her.

"I believe my wife is referring to the rest of the jewelry that belongs to the estate." Apparently emboldened by the rudeness of his wife, the earl found his tongue. "There are several pieces missing."

"And you think I have them?"

Lady Harriet glared at her. "You have the tiara."

Carenza tamped down her instant desire to defend herself and rang the bell. When the butler appeared, she said, "Ask Agnes to bring down my jewelry box, will you? And anything else of that nature that I have in my possession."

Carenza was too annoyed both with herself and with the couple in front of her to have time to make small talk. She'd genuinely forgotten that the tiara was a Smythe-Harding piece and would never have worn it if she'd remembered.

When Agnes came into the room with the jewelry boxes, Carenza unlocked them, retrieved the tiara, and gestured to the new earl and countess. "Perhaps you'd like to look through all my jewelry and make sure I haven't taken anything else?"

"That's hardly necessary," the earl said, as if he'd finally realized how rude he was being.

His countess had no such scruples. She rummaged in her reticule and brought out a list. "I'll do it."

Julian met Carenza's gaze and raised his eyebrows, obviously offering his help.

Carenza didn't need it.

After a thorough inspection, the countess appeared somewhat annoyed. "There is nothing that matches the descriptions on my list. What have you done with the other pieces?"

Carenza turned to the earl, who was now bright red. "I suspect Hector pawned the other items to pay his debts."

"I'm quite certain Lady Carenza is correct," Julian spoke up. "As the late earl's best friend, I can vouch for his propensity to gamble to excess, leading to an inability to pay his bills." He studied the earl. "And if I might offer a little bit of advice? Next time you have a family dispute, perhaps you should ask your solicitors to manage matters for you, rather than barging into a lady's house during visiting hours and calling her a thief."

Lady Harrier raised her chin. "She wore *my* tiara."

"Considering your appalling manners, I'm surprised you didn't rip it off her head at the ball." Julian's voice dripped with contempt. "Lady Carenza is well respected in society. Your behavior toward her has been noted, and will do you no favors."

"I quite agree." Olivia came to stand beside Carenza. "Even Hector wouldn't have behaved so badly." She looked down at

Lady Harriet. "I hope you enjoy your tiara, my lady, because if this story gets out, I doubt you'll find anyone who'll invite you to a social event where you can display it."

"That is grossly unfair." The earl cleared his throat. "My wife is a passionate woman who believes in being honest. The fault is clearly Lady Carenza's."

Julian walked over to the door and held it open. "May I suggest you leave before I kick you out?"

"You have no authority in this house, sir," Lady Harriet said as she turned to the door.

"You gave me all the license I need by revealing a family matter in front of Lady Carenza's guests," Julian snapped. "If you didn't wish your appalling behavior to be known, you should have conducted yourself more honorably."

Lady Harrier visibly bristled. "Don't you worry about this story getting out, sir. I'll be telling everyone I know *exactly* what happened!"

"Be my guest. If you wish to look more a fool than you already do." Julian bowed as she swept past him, the red-faced earl following.

Julian shut the door and looked over at Carenza. "Please don't worry about such nonentities."

"But I was at fault. I completely forgot about that silly tiara."

"That may be true, but the new earl and his wife handled the matter badly," Julian said. "A simple letter to your man of business would have solved the problem without causing you such distress in your own home. They were both ill-mannered and undignified."

Carenza sighed as she sat down. "She'll tell everyone, won't she?"

"Of course she will." Olivia patted her hand. "But she knows no one of any consequence. You can remain silent while Julian and I make sure that everything she says is treated with the contempt it deserves."

Julian nodded as he took the seat next to Olivia.

"You don't have to do anything at all," Carenza said. "The last thing I need is a war with my deceased husband's family."

"A war they started and brought into your drawing room," Olivia said firmly. "As I said, leave it to us. I can assure you that your reputation will remain intact."

Olivia stood up, came over to Carenza, and kissed her cheek. "I have to go. My dressmaker is due at my house within the hour." She stared down at her friend. "Please don't worry."

Julian escorted Olivia down to the hall and then came back up into the silent drawing room. "She's right, you know," he said.

"Who? Olivia or Lady Harriet?" Carenza asked.

"Olivia, of course." Julian sat opposite her, crossing one elegant, booted foot over the other. "No one will take any notice of Lady Harriet's shrill accusations."

"If only I hadn't tried to dress up last night to impress . . . people. I would've left the bloody tiara in its box."

Julian's eyebrows shot up. "It's not like you to curse, my dear."

"Maybe I am not used to being at fault."

"No one is perfect."

"You have no idea what it is like to be the daughter of a woman who is considered socially unacceptable," Carenza said. "Allegra and I are not allowed to be wrong-footed. Someone might suggest it is because of our inferior breeding."

Julian studied her carefully and then nodded. "Actually, it explains a lot."

"How so?"

"Why you put up with Hector for so long, for one. You never appeared to care, even when he was behaving outrageously." He paused. "I always admired your inability to be shocked or hurt by him."

"I couldn't afford to behave in any other way," Carenza said simply. "Imagine if I'd thrown a tantrum at a ball when Hector danced right by me with one of his mistresses? I'd have been the one scorned, and you can guarantee that my mother's name would have figured prominently in the condemnations of my common behavior."

"Not by me."

"Thank you. You might be a great arbitrator of fashionable society, but even you couldn't have changed the tide in my favor."

"I would've done my best."

It was unusual to see Julian without his usual slightly mocking smile, but Carenza appreciated his sincere address of the topic.

"Anyway." His smile returned. "This isn't about me. I do think Olivia is right and that you should carry on as if nothing has happened. Let Lady Harriet vent her spleen to her little friends, and I doubt we'll hear any more about it." He stood and came toward her.

"I hope you're right." Carenza rose to her feet.

He cupped her chin. "You'll be fine."

"If you say so."

He kissed her gently on the lips. "I do. And as your official lover, I suggest you turn your mind to more enticing thoughts. Like when I'm going to bed you."

"We're official now?"

"Oh yes." He kissed her again more roughly and released her. "Goodbye, my dear."

He turned to the door only to find that it was already open, and Allegra was standing there staring at both of them.

Carenza froze, but Julian wished Allegra a good day as he walked past her and went off down the stairs.

"Well," Allegra said as she stared at Carenza. "I take a stroll around the park and miss all the excitement. What on earth has been going on?"

Chapter 6

"Jolly good seat, eh?" Aragon spoke so loudly that half of Hyde Park, including Carenza, must have heard him clearly. "Told you she'd look capital on one of my horses."

"You were quite correct, brother," Julian murmured as Carenza's ears went red.

"Nice seat, good wide hips." Aragon nodded approvingly. "Ripe for breeding."

Carenza was wearing a dark blue riding habit cut in the military style and a tall black hat with an ostrich plume that made her look rather like a hussar. She was an excellent rider, with or without Aragon's horse under her. Julian was a competent horseman, but riding was not something he chose to excel at. He left that to the more sporting gentlemen. He was quite happy parading up and down Hyde Park, but he rarely hunted.

They had already progressed to the end of Rotten Row and were due to ride back. Julian glanced over at Carenza as she capably shortened her reins and made the turn.

"Are you enjoying yourself, my lady?" he asked as she drew up beside him.

"Surprisingly, yes." Her smile confirmed her words. "I miss a good gallop."

"Good Lord." Julian shuddered slightly. "I don't."

"Well, we can't all enjoy the same things," Carenza said. "That would make life very dull, indeed."

He was glad to see that she'd regained her composure after the confrontation with Hector's cousins the day before. He'd heard nothing further about the matter. He had begun to hope that the new countess had heeded the wisdom of his words and kept her indignation to herself.

Aragon came up along Carenza's other side. "Care for a race, my lady?"

"Of course!"

"Count us down, brother," Aragon requested.

Julian obliged and then watched in some satisfaction as Carenza beat Aragon by half a length. He took his time riding toward them and was amused to see that his brother looked rather put out.

He smiled at them both. "Shall we stroll for a while? The grooms can hold the horses."

"That would be very pleasant," Carenza said.

After dismounting, Julian walked over and lifted her off the horse, holding her scandalously close to his chest as he let her down. She raised an eyebrow.

He shrugged. "I did say I'd take every opportunity offered to get close to you, my dear."

"But not in front of your brother." Carenza stepped away and gathered her long riding skirt, sliding the end loop around her wrist.

"Aragon wouldn't notice if I stripped you bare and ravished you right in front of him."

"I hardly think that's fair."

"Trust me." Julian patted her hand. "He's too busy wondering how you beat him in a race and whether you really are the right woman for him after all."

"Hardly, brother." Aragon came toward them and offered Carenza his arm. "With respect, I was doing the gentlemanly thing and letting the lady win."

Julian felt Carenza stiffen and hastened to conceal a smile.

"Please don't hold back on my account, sir," Carenza said tartly. "I'm quite happy to beat you on your terms."

"I say, that's hardly..." As Aragon spluttered, Julian placed Carenza's gloved hand on his arm and walked into the shade of the trees. "Now, hold on a minute."

Julian ignored him, and they continued on the path, Aragon sulking behind them. It was getting busier, and there was no room for them to walk three abreast. Julian acknowledged his acquaintances but didn't stop to chat, his attention all on Carenza, who appeared her usual serene self. Aragon paused to speak to a horse-mad duke, and they continued on without him.

"Mr. Laurent."

Julian stopped only because Lady Brenton was blocking the path, her expression determined. He bowed and recognized her companion at the last minute.

"My lady, Mr. Walcott, how delightful." He wasn't entirely happy to see his old mistress and his godmother's grandson together, but there was little he could do about it. "Are you enjoying the sun?"

"It is very pleasant," Lady Brenton said. She glanced up at Julian through her eyelashes. "We were just talking about you."

"I'm impressed that I merited a moment of your time, my lady," Julian said. "One might think you had far better things to gossip about."

"Lady Brenton was expressing her sympathy as to the flagrant stealing of my inheritance," Percival said. "She said she was not surprised at a certain person's moral ambiguity, as she had experienced it herself."

Julian met Percival's gaze. "Be very careful what you say next, sir, because, as you already know to your cost, I am a strong believer in taking liars to court."

"I mentioned no names, sir," Percival said. "Perhaps it

is your guilty conscience that makes you see an accusation when none is meant."

"I think we all know exactly to whom you were referring, Mr. Walcott," Carenza spoke up. "And I, for one, am more than willing to stand up in court and say so."

Lady Brenton tittered. "I see that you've found yourself a new defender, Julian."

Carenza raised her chin. "As far as I am aware, there has yet to be an occasion when Mr. Laurent has had to defend anything, ma'am, because the courts know his inheritance was completely legitimate. That 'honor' belongs to Mr. Walcott, who is prone to making accusations and he has lost every case."

She inclined her head, and started walking again, her hand still on Julian's arm. Lady Brenton had the sense to move to one side.

"Good morning," Carenza said over the sound of Percival's spluttering. She smiled. "I do hope you both have a splendid day."

Julian waited until Lady Brenton and Percival were a good distance away before he spoke again. "You didn't need to defend me."

"Why not? You are my friend."

"I am quite capable—"

"I'm well aware of that." She stopped and looked up at him. "You always stand up for me. Why should I not do the same for you?"

He studied her indignant face. "This might sound ungrateful, but I've been attempting to distance myself from Percival's accusations, and your defense of me in public might rile him up."

"Oh dear." Carenza bit her lip. "I didn't think of that."

He hastened to reassure her. "I doubt he'll have the nerve to try the courts again, but seeing him today with Lady

Brenton—someone who appears to sympathize with him and egg him on—wasn't helpful."

"Did I mention that they called on me?"

"Together?" Julian frowned.

"Yes, Olivia said she met them in the park and felt obliged to bring them with her when she called on me. But their appearance at my home felt more deliberate than that." Carenza took a deep breath. "Olivia said Lady Brenton is your mistress."

"Was."

"Was what?"

"Lady Brenton *was* my mistress for a short and extremely volatile period before her irate husband tried to kill me."

"I thought you never bedded happily married women?"

"She said she was a widow, and, as the esteemed Lord Brenton was never seen in society, I made the mistake of taking her at her word."

"Until he returned from the dead and tried to murder you for seducing his wife."

Julian stared down at Carenza. "Are you laughing at me?"

"Laughing at the great Julian Laurent? Never." Carenza grinned at him. "You must admit that it is rather amusing."

"Not when you're in the middle of . . . a certain act, and a man bursts in brandishing a pistol and threatens to shoot off your most prized possession."

Carenza was laughing so hard that Julian was able to draw her off the path and into the shade of a group of trees before she realized it. He turned her so that they were hidden from view and her back was against a tree.

She looked up at him. "I'm sorry, but I have to know. How did you get away?"

"I threw Lady Brenton into her husband's arms, causing him to drop the pistol. While he dealt with her hysterics, I gathered my clothing and left."

"And he didn't come after you?"

"He did turn up at my house at some point," Julian acknowledged. "He had a notion of challenging me to a duel."

Carenza considered him. "And did he?"

"Not after I'd invited him to watch me shoot." Julian paused. "In truth, once we'd had a drink together, he was quite amenable to forgetting the whole thing."

"I find that rather unlikely."

"Then you underestimate my powers of persuasion, my dear," Julian said. "He was well aware of his wife's predilections and normally tolerated them because he is not in good health and the marriage was not a love match. He was more annoyed that she had brought a man into his house—which she'd promised not to do—than the fact she was having an affair."

"How lucky for you."

"I am always the luckiest of men." Julian sounded as if he were mocking himself. "Ask my mother or Percival Walcott."

"My father always says we create our own luck," Carenza said. "Perhaps you should take more credit for your actions than you think."

He studied her for a long moment before leaning in close. "May I kiss you?"

He had an uncanny knack of deflecting the conversation away from himself. Not for the first time, Carenza wondered why. "In a public park, with your brother bearing down on us?"

"Yes." His gaze grew more intent. "You're buttoned into a tightly cut riding habit that covers you from your neck to your toes. Your mouth is the only part I *can* kiss."

Carenza pretended to sigh. "With such unassailable logic, how can I deny you?"

His kiss, in contrast to the lightness of his tone, was surprisingly direct and intimate. Carenza responded immediately, her tongue clashing with his as he sought mastery of her mouth. She brought her hand up to his neck.

"Tallyho!" Aragon's loud voice came from the path close to their hiding place.

Julian released her. "As usual, my brother has impeccable timing." He offered her his hand. "Shall we go and find him? Hopefully he's gotten over his chagrin about being beaten by a woman and will prove more agreeable company on the way back."

As soon as Carenza stepped back on the path, Julian let go of her hand.

Aragon offered her his arm. "Shall we walk back together, my lady? I'm sure you've had enough of Julian's nonsense. He's all very good in a drawing room charming the ladies, but his equine knowledge is sadly lacking."

By the time they reached their horses, Carenza had worked out that Aragon was horse-mad and very little other than that mattered to him. She'd barely had to speak as he'd enumerated on the breeding of the mare he'd lent her to ride, the pedigree lines of all the horse's immediate ancestors, and the prospects Aragon was considering as studs.

As her groom approached, Aragon finished his monologue with, "Jolly good show, Lady Smythe-Harding. You're just the kind of filly I like to mount."

Carenza thought she heard the groom give a quiet snort. She smiled at Aragon. "Thank you for the chance to ride your beautiful mare, sir. It was a privilege."

Aragon looked ridiculously pleased with himself. "Next time we'll go out without my annoying little brother, eh? We can have a proper gallop."

"And another race?" Carenza asked.

He laughed and bowed. "Only one when I let you win again, my lady."

"I'd much prefer to beat you fair and square," Carenza said. "I mean, if you are so sure you'll win, it wouldn't hurt to prove your point, would it?"

Aragon considered her. "But you'll cry, and I don't know

how to deal with crying ladies." He turned to Julian, who had come up alongside them. "Tell Lady Carenza that I'm not one of those poetic types."

"Poetic types?" Julian raised an eyebrow.

"One of those poets who write love sonnets for ladies."

"Like Shakespeare?"

"That's the chap." Aragon slapped his thigh. "Met him at Eton. Such a bore. I'd much rather talk to my horse."

With that, he bowed again and went to speak to his groom, leaving Carenza staring up at Julian.

"Your brother . . ."

"Yes, I know," Julian said. "He's delightfully single-minded. Horses are his passion, and he doesn't care who knows it."

"He is very nice, though," Carenza added, to be fair. "But not the sort of man I wish to marry."

"Don't worry. My mother will decide whom Aragon marries, and he'll oblige her. As long as the lady likes horses and doesn't mind being referred to as his favorite filly, his wife will be remarkably happy."

"You like him, don't you?" Carenza said.

"He's my brother. Of course I like him." He paused. "Despite my mother's attempts to keep him away from me."

"Have you ever asked your mother why she treats you as she does?" Carenza asked.

"No, why would I?" He smiled at her. "We're not the sort of family who indulge in that kind of emotional nonsense."

"I think if I were you, I'd like to know." Carenza held his gaze.

"Well, I do not," he said firmly. "What if I'm illegitimate or something? Why on earth would I wish to know that? May we speak of something else?"

"Of course."

"I've found a safe place for us to meet." He took a card

from his pocket and handed it to her. "Direct your coachman, or the hackney cab if you're being discreet, to drive around to the back of the establishment. Come to the kitchen door and ask for Mrs. Mountjoy."

"And who might she be?"

"I promise I'll tell you all about her when we meet. Would tomorrow at eleven be convenient?"

"I'll have to check my appointment diary," Carenza said. "I'll send you a note."

Julian bowed. "Excellent." He glanced over his shoulder. "My brother is glowering at me. I suppose we should mount up and go home."

After Carenza changed into a morning dress, she went down to the drawing room and found Allegra with Olivia. One look at her sister's face told her that Allegra had been talking far too freely with their friend.

"You're bedding Julian Laurent," Olivia said.

Carenza looked at Allegra, who went red. "I'm sorry! It just slipped out."

Carenza sat down. "While Olivia was torturing you?"

"She didn't need to do that. My shock over seeing *that man* kissing you was too big to contain within my person," Allegra vigorously defended herself. "And Olivia said she'd guessed anyway."

"Of course she did." Carenza sighed. "Goodness me, Allegra, you are worse at keeping a secret than I am."

"That wouldn't be hard," Olivia commented. "And I did guess. You were very flustered when you came back into the drawing room after your little chat. If the monstrous Smythe-Hardings hadn't turned up and started demanding you turn out your pockets, I would've said something at the time."

"They were rather horrible, weren't they?" Carenza, who was far more willing to discuss Hector's relatives than her relationship with Julian, carried on. "I don't think Hector would've liked them at all. I know I was at fault for not returning the tiara, but I'd grown so used to hiding it from Hector that I'd almost forgotten it belonged to his family."

"They were completely at fault," Olivia stated firmly. "Now, tell me everything about Julian Laurent."

"There isn't much to tell. He simply offered to be my lover."

"Just like that?"

"Well, obviously, he was annoyed about the advertisement, and he said that if I was determined to take a lover, it had better be him because at least he'd be discreet."

"That's hardly romantic," Olivia objected.

"I'm not looking for love or romance," Carenza reminded her friend. "Just a lover."

"I've heard he's very good." Olivia winked. "From reliable sources. Can you confirm that?"

Carenza gave her friend a pointed look. "I am not going to reply to that, Olivia."

"After all my help to bring him to such a point?" Olivia looked pained. "If it hadn't been for the advertisement—"

"I wouldn't have ended up in danger of losing my reputation," Carenza reminded her friend. "What possessed you to use the exact wording of our made-up advertisement?"

"I thought it would draw a larger crowd," Olivia said. "And when I say larger, I mean—"

Allegra loudly cleared her throat. "At least no one suspects Carenza of being that particular lady. That is good."

"Did I mention that Mr. Cox is still getting letters from aspiring applicants?" Olivia said. "I am enjoying reading them."

"Please don't share them with me." Carenza shuddered.

"Why would I? You've already found the perfect man for the job." Olivia nodded. "In truth, it has turned out very well indeed for you."

"I hope you are right," Carenza said. "I like Julian."

"It is possible to remain friends with your lovers, Carenza," Olivia said. "You just have to remember not to have feelings for them. It makes it so much easier to let them go. I've never found it a problem."

"That's because you don't have feelings." Allegra winced. "I'm sorry. That was rude of me."

"Rude, perhaps, but still true," Olivia said. "I trained myself not to feel during my marriage and succeeded beyond my wildest imagination."

Carenza hated the derisory note in her friend's voice. "Someone will show you how to love again, Olivia. You just haven't met him yet."

"And I hope I never will," Olivia responded. "Life is far simpler when I can be selfish and think only of myself." She rose to her feet. "Speaking of which, I'm meeting a delicious naval officer for dinner this evening."

"Did he reply to the advertisement?" Allegra asked.

"No, but I have seen some intriguing candidates who wish to be considered." Olivia winked at Carenza. "If Julian doesn't come up to scratch, let me know."

Allegra waited until Olivia left before she spoke again. "I'm sorry. I shouldn't have told her about you and Julian."

"If you hadn't told her, I would probably have blurted it out myself," Carenza said. "But please don't mention it to anyone else."

"Even Maude?"

"If Maude asks, you may tell her," Carenza conceded. "But that's it. The last thing I want is Father coming up to town and insisting I marry Julian."

"Father would approve of him," Allegra said. "He told me once that he'd always thought Julian would be a better match for you than Hector."

"I wish he'd mentioned it at the time," Carenza muttered. "It would have been most helpful."

"You were very adamant that it was Hector or no one."

"Don't remind me," Carenza said.

"Are you really happy about Julian becoming your lover, sister?" Allegra asked, a note of concern in her voice.

"Yes, I believe I am." Carenza smiled at her sister. "At least he'll be discreet."

Chapter 7

The address Julian had given her was just behind Grosvenor Square in Mount Street, which was a row of far less grand dwellings than the square. Carenza directed the hackney cab to pull up behind the house and got down, the veil over her bonnet already lowered to conceal her face. To her relief, the back gates of the houses had numbers, and she easily located the right one.

She walked up the neat garden path and knocked on the back door. A young girl opened it and curtsied with a smile. "How can I help you, miss?"

"I'm here to see Mrs. Mountjoy."

"Come in, then, and I'll tell her you're here." The girl looked at Carenza appraisingly before leading her down the corridor. They bypassed the kitchen and went through another door into a hallway. "You after new staff or what?"

"Bridget, that's none of your business," a clear voice called out.

Carenza looked up to see a middle-aged woman descending the stairs. Despite her reprimand, she smiled at the girl.

"Sorry, ma'am." Bridget curtsied to Carenza. "I was just excited."

"That's quite understandable, but let me speak to our guest before you make any assumptions, and please bring us some tea."

"Yes, ma'am." Bridget grinned and hurried back toward the kitchen.

The woman turned to Carenza and held out her hand. Her voice had the same upper-class ring as Carenza's, but her dress was far less fashionable. "I'm Mrs. Mountjoy. You must be Mrs. Smythe. Mr. Laurent said you might be passing by. Please follow me."

Not without some trepidation, Carenza followed Mrs. Mountjoy into a pleasant sitting room at the front of the house. It was furnished with considerable charm in rich colors that appealed to Carenza's tastes.

"What a very pleasant room," Carenza commented, her gaze drawn to a remarkably fine portrait in pride of place over the fireplace.

"I managed to purloin some of my favorite pieces before I left my family home for good," Mrs. Mountjoy said. "The rest of the house is not quite so elegant."

Carenza sat down and stared at her hostess. "Forgive me, but you look remarkably familiar. Have we met before?"

Mrs. Mountjoy considered her. "It's possible that we attended the same events at some point. We are of similar age."

"Then how . . ."

"How did I end up here and not presiding over a mansion in Grosvenor Square?" Mrs. Mountjoy smiled. "It's a perfectly reasonable question."

"But none of my business," Carenza said quickly. "I can only apologize for my rudeness."

"I chose to marry a doctor—a man without vast financial means—and my family, who were counting on me making a brilliant match, disowned me," Mrs. Mountjoy explained. "Frederick died three years ago, and I've continued his work as he would've wished."

"His work?"

"I help young women who find themselves in distressed circumstances."

Carenza considered her next words carefully. "That is an admirable thing to do."

"I think so." Mrs. Mountjoy nodded. "You might think it strange that I no longer miss the life I once had, but I don't." She paused. "I never quite fitted in."

The door opened, and Bridget came through with a tray that she set down in front of Mrs. Mountjoy.

"Look! I didn't spill a drop this time," Bridget said.

"Well done," her employer complimented her. "Perhaps you might go and fetch the sugar bowl? It seems to be missing."

"Oh." Bridget frowned. "Bloody hell." She left in some haste.

Mrs. Mountjoy smiled. "She is something of a work in progress, but in time, I think she'll make an excellent parlormaid."

"Perhaps you might let me know when she is ready," Carenza offered. "Our current parlormaid is getting married this summer, and we will need a replacement."

Mrs. Mountjoy offered her a nod of approval as she poured them both some tea. "Julian said I'd like you, and he was correct."

"He often is," Carenza agreed. "Which is remarkably annoying."

"I can't argue with you on that." Mrs. Mountjoy made a face. "You must be wondering how I met him and why he considered this house a safe place for you to meet."

Carenza sipped her tea.

"I met Julian when I married my husband. I'm not sure how they became acquainted, but they were already good friends." Mrs. Mountjoy paused. "When Frederick died, Julian helped me with the funeral arrangements and stood by my side when my parents tried to force me to go back home."

"That sounds very like him," Carenza said. She was probably one of the very few people in society who knew that beneath Julian's charming exterior there was a far more complex man. Even so, he still occasionally surprised her.

"We've never been lovers," Mrs. Mountjoy continued, and Carenza tried not to blush. "I would consider him a valued friend in his own right. When he told me about you, I, of course, offered my help."

Carenza wasn't quite sure how she felt about Julian discussing her with a stranger, but Mrs. Mountjoy's matter-of-fact manner was slightly reassuring.

Her hostess took two labeled keys off the ring at her waist. "The top two floors of this house are used as living accommodation for me and for rental purposes. One of the apartments is vacant, and I offered it to Julian so that you could meet." She handed Carenza the keys. "This one allows you entrance through the kitchen door, and that one with the yellow ribbon unlocks the apartment on the left upstairs."

"Thank you."

"You can use the backstairs to enter and leave the house. There is no need to seek me out." Mrs. Mountjoy smiled. "It is nice to be able to do something for Julian instead of always being on the receiving end." She set down her cup. "Would you like to see the apartment?"

"Yes, please." Carenza hurriedly finished her tea and stood up.

Mrs. Mountjoy opened the door and was met by Bridget, who was breathing hard and carrying the sugar bowl.

"Sorry, ma'am, I had to break some bits off the block, and then Cook made me clean up all the mess."

"Please set the bowl on the tray, Bridget," Mrs. Mountjoy said. "And thank you for your efforts."

"But what about your tea?" Bridget asked as they went past her.

"We will return to it shortly, my dear. There is no need to clear away." Mrs. Mountjoy started up the stairs, Carenza at her heels. "You may go back to the kitchen."

"Yes, ma'am." Bridget's martyred sigh was loud enough to be heard at the top of the stairs.

"She still has a lot to learn, but at thirteen, she's young enough to want to change," Mrs. Mountjoy said as she continued up the second flight of stairs. "She was working in a brothel and ran away when the owner told her it was time to earn her keep." She paused outside a door with the number four on it. "Here we are. It's just across the hall from my suite of rooms."

She gestured for Carenza to unlock the door and invited her in. Carenza entered with some trepidation but found a charming space with a large double bed, a sitting area, and a separate dressing room.

"The necessary is outside," Mrs. Mountjoy said. "But I doubt you'll be needing it unless you stay the night."

"Thank you," Carenza said.

Her hostess nodded, turned to the door, and then paused. "I do hope you are adequately 'protected' for this liaison, Mrs. Smythe."

"Adequately protected?" Carenza frowned. "Oh! You mean against conception?"

"As I mentioned, my husband was a doctor. He had a very specific interest in women's health, and I feel it is important to carry on his work. Protection should also be used against sexual diseases."

"I assume Julian doesn't have any of those," Carenza said quickly.

"You'd be surprised." Mrs. Mountjoy glanced at the watch pinned to her bodice. "I'd better let you explore the apartment. Julian will be here in a few minutes."

She walked out, leaving Carenza with the strong urge to follow her, run out of the house, and keep going. She retreated to the window and gazed out over the street. What on earth had she been thinking? This whole affair had become far too public—what with the advertisement, Julian's unexpected offer, and now a whole household of people who'd seen her creeping up the backstairs and knew exactly what she was doing.

She glanced longingly at the door. Should she go? Or did

she at least owe Julian an explanation before she fled back to her comfortable life in Tavistock Square?

The door opened, and Julian stood there, his calm gaze moving over her as he came into the room.

"Having second thoughts?"

"Second, third, and fourth thoughts," Carenza said. "Why on earth did you tell Mrs. Mountjoy all about me?"

He raised an eyebrow. "Because I required her help, and I knew Anna wouldn't begrudge another woman the chance to have a lover if she wished to do so."

"How . . . remarkable of her."

"There is no need to be jealous of Mrs. Mountjoy, Carenza. She—"

"I am not jealous. She told me that you aren't lovers, although I don't know why, as she is very handsome and obviously doesn't care about social niceties."

"She is also the widow of a good friend of mine," Julian said evenly.

"As am I." Carenza faced him.

"You're . . . different." He held her gaze. "I want to bed you."

There was something in his voice that made her knees go weak. She resolutely straightened her spine and faced him.

He tilted his head to one side and observed her, which made her feel uncomfortably warm.

"May I kiss you?" Julian asked.

"In the mood I'm in, I might bite."

"Good." He strolled toward her, his blue gaze intent. "I am more than happy to indulge your temper."

She glared at him, annoyed by the hint of a smile on his lips—a smile she wanted gone. He cupped her chin with the delicacy of a man trying to tame a tiger and looked down at her, a question in his eyes.

"Kiss me," he commanded.

She needed no further invitation and promptly bit his lip.

He groaned into her mouth and met her temper with equal fire, turning the kiss into something of a battle. His arm came around her waist and he sat her on the window seat and leaned in as they fought for dominance.

She ripped her mouth clear of his. "Take your coat off."

"Just my coat?"

Gripped by a fiery recklessness she'd never felt before, Carenza tugged at his waistcoat. "All of it."

He undressed with a grace and speed that spoke of practice and an assurance Carenza had never had. And, oh God, he was beautiful. Lean but well-muscled, his chest just hairy enough, and his stomach flat. He was also fully aroused.

She met his gaze. "I want you."

"Tell me how."

She swallowed hard. "Hard and fast, and right now."

One eyebrow rose. "Just as you are?"

"Yes." She nodded. "I want to feel *everything*."

Julian took a moment to consider his options. His cock was one hundred percent in favor of doing exactly what Carenza had asked for, but—

"I can make you ready," Julian's better half offered.

"No." Carenza was pulling up her skirts to expose the soft curve of her thighs and above. "Just do it."

He smoothed a hand over his already wet and straining cock. "I don't want to hurt you."

"I don't care." Carenza looked at him.

"You might be sore tomorrow."

"I'd like that."

Julian desperately tried to remember that he was a gentleman and a renowned lover, but his instinct was roaring at him to take what she offered and make her his.

"As you wish." He picked her up again and placed her on the side of the bed, spreading her thighs wide. "This is a better height."

She set one of her heels on the bed, exposing her most secret places to Julian's lust-addled brain. He wanted to drop to his knees and feast on her, but she'd asked for his cock, and he was in no mood to deny her. He pulled her as close to the edge of the bed as he dared and lined his cock up with her entrance. She watched his every move, and it made him even more excited.

"If you change your mind," he murmured. "Just—"

"Just do it, *please*." She hooked one foot around his arse and kicked him like a horse.

He pressed forward, aware that she was wet but that she was tight, so very tight, that he would have to work to get fully inside her. He rocked his hips and eased forward, gaining a little each time as her reluctant flesh yielded to the stiff unrelenting pressure of his shaft. It was the hardest he'd ever had to work for a fuck, and he gloried in every minute of it as she gasped his name and strained to take all of him. Eventually, he could go no farther, and he looked up at her.

To his surprise, she was looking down at where their bodies were almost perfectly joined.

"Hard enough for you?" he asked.

She bit her lip and rocked her hips slightly forward, allowing him to gain another inch. "God, yes."

He met her with another thrust of his own, and she gripped his arm so hard her nails went into his skin. He kissed her very gently.

"Shall I slow down now?"

"No!" She was back to scowling.

"But I want you to climax," Julian said, his breathing as uneven as hers.

"Then make sure that I do."

Her fierce demands were both unexpected and incredibly arousing.

"As you wish."

He slid his middle finger between her lips to make it wet and then moved his hand down to cup her mound, his finger placed firmly on the throbbing center of her bud. His hips came forward, thrusting his cock as deep as he could go, and she growled his name and met him with a twist of her own. He forgot about being a gentleman, about making sure of her pleasure, and simply fucked like a man possessed until he felt her come, and then he joined her with a roar and a final thrust that made her fall backward onto the bed with him on top of her.

It took him a few minutes to gather enough breath to ease his cock free and stand. She remained on the bed looking up at him, her gaze sultry, satisfied, and so alluring that his cock twitched again. He climbed up beside her and began to remove her clothes.

"What are you doing?" she asked.

"Getting you naked for our next bout."

She smiled at him. "That was exactly what I wanted. Thank you."

"We'll see whether you're still thanking me tomorrow when you'll be sore," Julian said as he unlaced her stays to reveal the glorious mounds of her breasts. "I suspect you'll be cursing me every time you sit down."

"I'll certainly be thinking about you," Carenza said. "Isn't that what you wanted?"

Julian knelt to kiss her exposed nipples and felt her shudder as he sucked on them and then groan when he grazed them with his teeth. He hadn't expected her to be so . . . demanding. He'd always been the dominant party in bed, and he still wasn't sure how he felt about being ordered around.

"You might think about me, Carenza, but if I came around and demanded to fuck you again, I suspect you'd tell me to wait for a few days."

"Would I?" There was a faraway look in Carenza's eyes

that made everything male in Julian spring to attention. "Or would it be even sweeter?"

His cock had hardened again, and all thoughts of a leisurely session of lovemaking flew from his mind in a tide of possessiveness. He used his knee to spread her thighs wide and simply thrust himself home again. Carenza made a sound of deep appreciation as he began to move, her feet sliding up his thighs to rest on his arse as she took every onslaught and gave it back to him.

He curved his arm under her buttocks, lifting her higher into his shorter thrusts, his groin grinding against her sensitive flesh until she came again. This time he didn't come with her and wrenched another climax out of her before he had nothing left to give. He rolled off her and stared up at the ceiling wondering what on earth had happened to his polished bedside manner.

A disturbing thought crept into his head. "Carenza . . ."

"Mmm?"

"We should have discussed this before we began, but if you are pregnant, I will marry you."

She came up on one elbow. Her thick, fair hair had escaped almost all its pins and hung over her shoulder. "I can see why you and Mrs. Mountjoy are such good friends. She warned me not to engage in sexual congress with *any* man, including you."

"This isn't a cause for levity. I was remiss. I should have taken better precautions."

"I can't have children," Carenza said. "And even if I could, I don't regret what we just did together."

Julian looked at her composed face. It was a personal subject that he was loath to probe, but he should have discussed such matters with her earlier, and he was furious with himself for putting her in such a position.

He opened his mouth to speak, and she placed her fingers over his lips. "I do not wish to talk about this right now.

Rest assured, I will not be presenting you with a child at any point."

He held her gaze. "Are you quite certain?"

"Yes." She smiled at him. "Now, will you help me get dressed? If I don't return soon, Allegra will be sending for the Bow Street Runners."

He did as she asked, again amazed at her ability to shut that demanding sexual part of herself away so easily and return to the even-tempered, calm creature everyone knew.

Downstairs, he sent one of the kitchen maids to call a hackney cab for her. A few minutes later, he watched Carenza leave from the back door, her head held high, and a becoming flush on her cheeks.

After waving her off, he turned to see Anna watching him.

"Would you like some tea?" she asked.

"Yes, please." He followed her back into the deserted kitchen and sat at the table.

"I know who your mystery woman is," Anna said as she brought the teapot over. "We did our curtsies to the Queen in the same year. It's Lady Carenza Musgrove, isn't it?"

"I'm sure I don't have to ask you not to mention her name again, ma'am," Julian said somewhat stiffly.

"Like that, is it?" She shot him an amused glance. "Is there a husband in the vicinity?"

"No, he's dead."

"Well, thank goodness for that. After Lady Brenton, you'd be wise to be careful."

"Don't worry. I am." Julian sipped his tea, his thoughts still with Carenza and her unexpected effect on him. He liked the snap of her temper, her urgency, her *need* for him to satisfy her on her own terms.

"I found a place for Mary O'Leary," Anna said.

"Excellent news."

"Ask the Cartwrights to keep an eye out for another candidate for me."

"I will."

She laughed. "You seem somewhat distracted. I wonder why."

Julian finished his tea and set the cup back on the tray before rising to his feet. "I should go. Thank you for your help."

"I was intrigued that you actually asked me for something." Anna looked up at him. "Now I think I know why."

Julian shrugged. "Affairs are commonplace, ma'am. Having seen the consequences of such liaisons, you, of all people, know that."

She regarded him for far longer than he was comfortable with. Finally, he broke the silence.

"Please don't worry about Carenza. I will make sure she suffers no ill effects from this."

"I'm not worried about her, Julian. All my concern is for you."

He nodded and left the room, pausing only to pick up his hat and cane before departing through the front door and heading toward Grosvenor Square. He had no idea why anyone should worry about him. He rarely made mistakes and prided himself on his social relationships, especially with women. If there was an art to being an excellent lover who would never embarrass a lady in public and end an affair with a smile and the promise of friendship, he was the master of it.

Once he and Carenza were done, they'd return to being friends, with no hard feelings on either side. He paused before he crossed the street and instinctively brushed his tongue over his slightly swollen lip where she'd bitten him.

At least, he hoped she would. Carenza in a rage would be something to behold.

Chapter 8

"Good morning, ma'am." Julian bowed to his mother in the drawing room of his old home. "You asked to see me."

"Yes." She didn't invite him to sit, or offer him tea, and her expression of cool dislike was her standard response to him. She wore a plain morning gown in dark green and a matching lace bonnet and fichu in white. "Are you quite sure that color suits you? You look rather washed-out."

"My pallor is probably due to my extravagant life, ma'am." Julian pretended to sigh. "A bachelor around town has to keep up appearances and remain fashionable."

"I wanted to speak to you about your brother."

"Which one?" Julian asked.

"Aragon, of course. Anton is safely away from your influence and on his way to India."

"My influence on Anton is one of the things I am most proud of in my life." Julian allowed a hint of ice to permeate his reply. "He is a credit to the whole family. I am glad to have funded his advancement in his career."

Julian rarely let his mother rile him, but his steady relationship with his younger brother was something he cherished.

She made a face. "I suppose you expect me to be eternally grateful for that small kindness, don't you?"

"Grateful? You haven't even thanked me," Julian reminded her.

"Such a peevish, needy little boy. I see nothing has changed." His mother sniffed. "One shouldn't have to thank someone for simply doing their duty to their family."

Julian took out his watch and glanced at it. "Is there a reason you asked me to call, ma'am, or shall I be on my way?"

"Sit down."

Reluctantly, Julian did as she asked.

"I don't appreciate you filling Aragon's head with nonsense."

"As far as I am aware, all Aragon's thoughts are of horses, ma'am, and I'm fairly certain I had nothing to do with that. Now, if he'd suddenly developed an interest in fashion, or dancing—"

"He's developed an interest in a woman!" she spoke over him. "A woman you introduced him to."

"Hardly, Mother. If you recall, we grew up with the Musgroves as neighbors in the country."

"And I distinctly discouraged any fraternization with that immoral household."

"You might have discouraged it, but children will find a way to be friends despite adult disapproval," Julian countered.

"You should not have reintroduced her to him, then."

"He asked me to," Julian said. "I told him you wouldn't approve."

"On that we can agree. Carenza Musgrove is not a fitting bride for my son. Her family are not at all the thing."

"Aragon would never marry without your consent, ma'am. He adores you." Julian couldn't quite believe he was having to defend his older brother. "I also suspect Lady Carenza is not horse-mad enough for him."

"You will keep him away from her."

Julian raised an eyebrow. "He is a grown man capable of managing his own affairs, and you've made quite certain that he would never listen to me or take my advice over yours."

His mother's lips thinned, and she stared at him. "I see you intend to be as unhelpful as ever. I don't know why I bothered to ask."

He rose to his feet. "To be perfectly honest, ma'am, neither do I. But then, I've always been a disappointment to you, and I'm sure you'll feel vindicated that nothing has changed." He bowed. "I'll see myself out."

He went down the stairs, the familiar feeling of resentment and frustration settling in his chest. She didn't like him—her own child—and she never would. He rarely allowed her to rile him anymore, but sometimes . . .

He nodded his thanks to the butler as he opened the front door for him. Perhaps he should go to Jackson's and find someone to spar with, because his mood certainly wasn't presentable in polite company. He stepped up into his phaeton and took the reins back from his tiger.

In truth, he'd like to see Carenza and take her to bed. He took a few deep breaths, his unseeing gaze on the busy road in front of him. Eventually, his groom coughed.

"Horses don't like this standing about, guv."

"You're quite correct." He clicked to his lead horse and eased his way into the traffic between a brewery cart and a closed carriage. "Hang on."

It was one of the rare occasions when Carenza was by herself in the town house. Allegra had gone out with Maude to the dressmaker's, and Carenza had set herself the task of writing a letter to her parents—something that was long overdue. The last thing she wanted was for her father to grow anxious and decide to come to London. She was trying to think of how to detail her social timetable without mentioning that Julian had been her escort to almost every event of the past week.

Her father might not pick up on such things, but her mother would. Carenza didn't want to get into any discussion as to her current choices—choices that would horrify her father and probably amuse her mother. Even in the short week since Julian had first taken her to bed, she was behaving differently.

She put down her pen and stared out the small window that overlooked the garden. There was no denying it—she was aware of him in such a different way now. When he stood behind her, she smelled his skin and yearned to lean back and rub her face against his throat until he grabbed hold of her and . . .

"Mr. Julian Laurent, my lady."

"Oh!"

She stood up in something of a rush as Julian came into her private sitting room. As usual, he looked perfect, his cravat intricately knotted and fastened with a diamond pin, his breeches tightly fitted and tucked into tall, black riding boots. She went over to greet him, and the butler left the room.

"Am I disturbing you?" He bowed, his expression unreadable. "I did tell the butler that my visit was not expected."

"You are practically family, sir," Carenza said. "There is no need to stand on ceremony with me."

She studied his face. This was another new source of awareness. She now understood how much he concealed behind his exquisite exterior. Despite his apparent ease, one of his fists was clenched, and he was vibrating like a coiled spring.

"What's wrong?" she blurted.

He raised a perfect eyebrow. "What do you mean?"

She cupped his chin. "You're angry about something."

He turned his head so that her thumb brushed his lips, and he sucked it into his mouth.

"God . . ." Carenza grabbed hold of his shoulder.

He jerked her hard against his body and kissed her with a roughness that offered no compromise. She allowed him to back her against the door and fumbled to turn the key while he continued to ravish her mouth.

He kissed his way down her neck to her shoulder, thrusting one hand into the front of her bodice to cup her breast while the other hand rucked up her skirts. He wrenched his mouth away, his breathing as erratic as hers.

"Tell me to stop."

In reply, she attacked the buttons of his breeches and shoved them down to bare his muscled arse. He picked her up, drew her open thighs over his hips, and thrust home so hard that the door rattled in its frame. Carenza closed her eyes to enjoy the sensations, the intrusive pulsing of his cock, his harried breathing, and the growing excitement throbbing through her veins that seemed to match his own passion.

For several glorious moments she could think of nothing except his physical presence and her response to it. He groaned her name as they came together in one last fiery crash that left them both breathless and clinging to each other.

"Carenza?"

Very faintly through the door, Carenza heard Allegra calling her name. She met Julian's blue eyes and went still.

"Where *are* you?"

Holding her slightly panicked gaze, Julian slid one hand under her skirts to where they were still joined and set his finger over her already swollen and straining bud. Even as Allegra's voice grew louder, he flicked and rubbed Carenza into another climax that had her burying her face against his arm to stop herself from screaming. Impossibly, she felt his cock filling again as she clenched around his shaft.

He eased almost free and then slammed forward, filling her completely. She forgot all about Allegra in the instinctive need to fight him to completion. She came again, and then again until he finally joined her, his body pinning her to the door with the strength of his climax.

Someone knocked about an inch from Carenza's head, and she didn't even care.

"Carenza?" Allegra huffed as she rattled the latch. "I told

Jones this lock was faulty. I'll have to get him to take a look at it."

"Not now," Carenza breathed as she heard Allegra finally retreat. "Please don't ask him right now."

Julian buried his face in her shoulder, his whole body shaking.

Carenza stroked his hair. "What's wrong?"

He finally looked up, and she realized he was laughing. "I have thoroughly debauched you in your own home, which I promised not to do."

"I'm more worried about Jones discovering exactly what is preventing entry into this room than what we did together," Carenza said. "Can you put me down?"

"Of course."

He eased out of her, and she winced as he set her feet on the floor.

"Are you all right?" he asked as he rearranged his clothing.

Carenza just nodded, amazed at his ability to look so undisturbed when she probably looked a complete fright. A quick glance in the mirror confirmed that she was correct. She patted ineffectively at her hair, which was coming down.

"I should go up the back stairs to my bedroom and compose myself."

"An excellent idea," Julian said. "And I will open this door and take myself off." He paused to study her. "Do you require my assistance to get upstairs?"

"No, thank you. If I let you anywhere near my bed, I suspect I wouldn't let you leave."

His mouth quirked. "There you go again, making provocative statements when you know I have to go."

She stepped close to him. "You could stay. No one will come into my bedchamber without my permission."

He kissed her gently on the forehead. "And your father would quite rightly shoot me if he found out I'd been taking advantage of you in his own house."

She stiffened. "Taking advantage of me? Are you suggesting that using my bed is somehow different from fucking me against the door?"

His slight smile disappeared. "Don't start."

"And what does that mean?" Carenza raised her chin. "I am entitled to my opinion."

"Indeed, you are, and in any other circumstances I would be delighted to argue the point, but we are in something of a hurry right now, and we need to move." He unlocked the door, peered outside, and beckoned Carenza forward. "All's clear. You go, and I'll see myself out."

She stomped up the stairs to her bedchamber, which was empty, undressed without any help, and got into bed. She was very wet between her thighs and would request a bath before she dressed for dinner. She slid her hand between her legs and cupped her mound, which was still throbbing and sensitive from Julian's attentions. Should she have allowed him such liberties in the family home? From the moment she touched him, she'd forgotten all about propriety and simply existed in the physical realm.

She pressed her palm against her mound and felt an instant response. If he'd come upstairs with her, she would've taken him again. . . . She trembled as she set off another climax, one sadly lacking the expertise of Julian's tongue, cock, and fingers. But he hadn't been polished today, had he? He'd arrived in a state and one touch of her fingers had ignited his desire. There had been no pretty words or deliberate lovemaking, just an emotion that needed to be satisfied.

Carenza closed her eyes. Should she have behaved like that? Probably not in society's opinion. Did she care? Not particularly.

Everyone had always expected her to show her common ancestry. Perhaps she would oblige them in this.

* * *

Olivia and Maude joined the sisters for dinner and sat in the drawing room afterward, discussing Gerald's supposed return and Maude's ambivalence about his coming home.

"He can't expect you to simply fall into his arms as if nothing has happened," Olivia pointed out. "You've barely seen each other for two years."

"Men don't think like that," Maude said. "As far as Gerald is concerned, nothing has changed."

"She's right," Carenza said. "Men can be very difficult to understand sometimes."

"Don't tell me that Julian Laurent has . . . faults?" Olivia gasped. "But he's the perfect gentleman."

Carenza fought the blush she knew was rising on her cheeks as she remembered exactly how ungentlemanly Julian could be.

"No one is perfect," Allegra said firmly. "But we should all strive to do better."

Eager to divert the conversation away from her lover, Carenza turned to Olivia.

"How is your naval officer?"

"Gone." Olivia waved her hand dismissively. "And good riddance. He was remarkably stuffy. I already have someone else in mind."

"That's remarkably fast," Carenza said.

"Actually, it's one of your castoffs from the advertisement we placed in the newspaper. He wrote you a long and very well-thought-out letter stating all the reasons why he believed your behavior would ultimately reflect badly on you."

"How kind of him." Carenza rolled her eyes. "Did you write back?"

"Yes, and we have entered into an interesting correspondence about the rights of women." Olivia sat back. "I am looking forward to meeting him in person one day."

"I do hope you won't pretend to be me," Carenza said.

"I promise I won't sully your good name." Olivia looked unrepentant. "Although you should be aware that there are some rather unpleasant rumors going around about you."

Carenza frowned. "Not about Julian."

"No, about you blatantly stealing the Smythe-Harding tiara."

"I told you that woman would be unable to keep the matter to herself." Carenza sighed. "And I cannot refute what she says, because I was in the wrong."

"You don't need to say anything," Olivia said. "She is a nobody."

"You don't understand," Carenza retorted. "Because of our parentage, Allegra and I are held to impossibly high standards. If we fail to be less than perfect, we are instantly condemned."

Olivia raised her eyebrows. "That's rather melodramatic, dearest."

"It isn't," Allegra said. "You have no idea."

"Then your friends will do everything in their power to quash her little stories, and it will quickly be forgotten when the next scandal comes along," Olivia said firmly.

"I forgot to tell you that the new countess pointedly ignored me last time we were in the same company, Carenza," Allegra said. "She was with that woman who was Julian's mistress, and they seemed very close."

Carenza frowned. "You mean she's made friends with Lady Brenton? That can't be good. She'll be seeking out Percival Walcott next."

"Oh, she already knows him," Allegra said. "He was in the same party as Lady Brenton. But as no one knows about you and Julian, there aren't any connections or rumors to exploit, are there?"

"One would hope not," Carenza said. "I must warn Julian to be on his guard."

"I'm fairly sure he's already aware of any threats to his person or to yours," Olivia said. "One thing Julian Laurent is not, is a fool."

Julian sank lower into his bath, his gaze on the wavering light from the candlestick in front of the mirror in his dressing room. All was quiet around him. Proctor had finished laying out his nightclothes, they'd discussed his morning attire, and he had no immediate worries. But yet . . .

He tipped his head back and rested it on the edge of the tub. He'd been foolish, reckless, and downright stupid to make love to Carenza in her own house, where her family or servants might discover them. He wasn't a green, young sprig desperate to sow his oats. He was a disciplined man who thought before he acted and rarely made errors. After his meeting with his mother, he should've listened to his first instinct to take out his annoyance in the boxing salon and never gone near Carenza.

One touch of her fingers had set him off, and he'd taken her up against the door without caring for the consequences.

Not that she'd tried to stop him. He liked to think that if she had, he would've stepped back immediately and apologized. But she hadn't. In truth, she'd encouraged him.

It would not do.

He had to find a way to regain his composure and give her what she'd asked for—the sexual expertise of an accomplished rake. The kind of man who enjoyed performing and giving pleasure without engaging his own feelings. The next time they met, he wouldn't apologize, but he would reestablish the rules. He didn't like feeling out of control, and he suspected it was the same for Carenza.

Perhaps a reasonable conversation between two old friends would be enough to ensure that neither of them felt out of their depth again. Slightly reassured by this notion, Julian dunked his head under the water and came up blinking to discover someone looming over his bathtub.

"Thought you'd drowned for a minute," Aragon said cheerfully. "Was wondering whether I remembered that Dutch trick that was all the rage to pump the water out of your lungs."

"It's almost midnight," Julian said. "Why are you in my bedchamber and, more importantly, which one of my staff let you in?"

Aragon handed Julian a drying cloth. "No need to get on your high horse, brother. I came through the garden, went in the back door, and came up the servants' stairs."

"Well, if you intended to enter the house unannounced in order to murder me, you've missed the perfect opportunity." Julian dried off quickly and put on his silk banyan.

"Good Lord." Aragon frowned. "You're right! I could've held your head under the water until you drowned and just skipped off without anyone realizing I'd been here." He paused. "I am your heir, aren't I?"

"No, I've left everything to my favorite charities." Julian sat down beside the fire to dry his hair, and Aragon joined him.

"Blast it, Julian. You know I need the money more than some ill-nourished brats."

"But with my fortune, those children won't be starving, will they?" Julian answered. "And I'm shocked at your lack of Christian values."

"Mother says I just have to marry someone rich and all will be well," Aragon said. "But none of those women want to have anything to do with me. When I do succeed in dancing with them, all they do is ask questions about you."

"At least that gives you something interesting to talk about," Julian said. "I hate to be inhospitable, but is there something you wanted? I was about to go to bed."

"Oh! Yes." Aragon sat up straight. "Lady Carenza."

"I can't help you."

"Come on, Julian. You're a friend of hers."

"And I am under strict instructions from our mother to avoid the connection at all costs."

Aragon's color rose alarmingly. "I'm a grown man. Mother has no say in my personal life."

"Tell that to her," Julian advised. "Or else she'll continue to rule your life as she sees fit."

Aragon stared at him, slapped his thigh, and nodded. "You're right. I'll tell her what you said."

"Please don't, or else I'll be in trouble again," Julian said. "Form your own opinion on the matter and present it to her in your own words."

"But it's much more fun when she gets annoyed with you." Aragon stood up.

"Not for me." Julian met his brother's gaze. "Have you any idea how it feels to constantly be held responsible for all the sins of the family?"

Aragon looked surprised. "I suppose she does pick on you rather a lot."

"She's made me the scapegoat for as long as I remember," Julian said. "Why do you think I left home?"

Aragon stared fixedly at him as if trying to solve a mathematical equation.

Julian rose to his feet and headed for the door. "Good night, Aragon."

His brother strode toward him and then stopped. "Wait. I haven't told you what I came for yet."

Julian repressed a sigh. "If it has to do with Lady Carenza, I am not interested."

"I've invited her and her sister to a picnic in the park."

"I'm sure you'll have a delightful time."

"You have to come." Aragon looked pleadingly at him.

"Did you not listen to a single word I just said to you?" Julian demanded.

"Not really." Aragon shrugged. "Things go in one ear and out the other."

Julian opened the door. "Good night, Aragon."

His brother made the mistake of stepping to one side, which allowed Julian to close the door in his face. He had no regrets in doing so and hoped Aragon was finally beginning to understand that he refused to be a go-between who incurred everyone's wrath.

The peace and resolution he'd reached during his bath had deserted him. He'd been too honest with Aragon. He'd probably go home and tell their mother everything Julian had said, which never went well.

He returned to the bath and stuck a finger in the water. It was tepid. It was too late to expect his staff to lug more hot water up the stairs, so he might as well go to bed.

He wasn't sure what had possessed him to tell Aragon how he felt about being the unloved middle child. To his brother, it was just the way things were and thus not worth questioning. And why Aragon was still interested in Carenza, who had given him no encouragement, was a thing of mystery. Perhaps his brother really was beginning to chafe at their mother's leading strings.

He got into bed and blew out the candle. There was still some light from the streetlamp, but his house was relatively quiet for Mayfair. The scent of the burned-out candlewick drifted across him and he closed his eyes. Carenza would never entertain an offer of marriage from Aragon. Julian was certain about that. But his brother's courtship would prevent other men from pursuing her as well.

He opened his eyes. Even if Carenza currently believed she had no wish to marry again, should he be preventing her from exploring that option? She saw him as a dalliance to provide for her physical needs, but at some point, surely, she would want more. She wasn't the kind of woman who should remain alone for the rest of her life. Surely Hector hadn't done that much damage.

But if she couldn't have children, many gentlemen wouldn't want to marry her. However, someone like Lord Atworth already had several and would probably be content . . .

"Damn and blast it!" Julian, now fully awake again, swore into the darkness. "This cannot continue!"

He had plans—long-term plans, to be fair—that included the interesting Miss Cartwright. She was a woman he admired immensely and who, so far, seemed immune to his charms. But patience and persistence were part of his nature, and he had no doubt of his ability to win her over. At present, Miss Cartwright saw him as just another nobleman frittering away his time with a fashionable cause, but he would show her his worth and dedication if it took years.

Julian sat up and checked his pocket watch that sat beside his bed. It was barely twenty minutes since his brother had left, and all Julian's desire to sleep had gone with him. He'd never been the kind of man who failed to get a good night's rest, and he wasn't going to start now.

He resolutely lay down again and closed his eyes. He had a meeting with the board of supervisors for the orphans in two days' time. He was due to give a speech and would need his wits about him.

Work would give him an excuse to avoid Carenza for a few days, which would be good for him—and for her.

Chapter 9

"I've sorted this morning's post, sir." Simon placed several stacks of letters on Julian's desk. "But there is one letter that I'd like to bring to your immediate attention."

Julian held out his hand, but his secretary hesitated to pass the letter over. "Is it that bad?"

"I'm not sure. Shall I read it out to you?"

"If you must, but I am capable of reading my own correspondence. Who's it from?"

"Mr. Cox."

"Who?"

"The proprietor of the Wheatsheaf."

"And what the devil does he want?" Julian sat back so he could see Simon's face.

"That's why I wanted to read the letter to you, sir. I was concerned that I was picking up a . . . threatening nuance that wasn't there."

"I doubt it, but fire away."

Simon cleared his throat and began to read. "'My lord.'" He paused. "I've no idea why he thinks you're a peer, but—"

"No matter. Go on."

"'I wanted you to know that I have received several offers from interested parties'—that bit is underlined twice—'regarding the lady who placed the advertisement. As a poor'—also underlined—'but honest man, I was wondering if you might advise me what to do. I don't wish to reveal their identities, but needs must, and I'm sure they'd understand that I must make ends meet. Yours, respectfully, Reginald Cox.'"

"It's an out-and-out threat," Julian said.

Simon nodded. "That's what I thought, sir, but I wanted to make sure I wasn't overthinking it."

"I think we should pay him a visit." Julian stood up. "Get your coat."

"Shall I order the carriage, sir?"

"No, I don't want to draw attention to the blasted place. We'll hail a hackney cab at the corner of the street." Julian was already on the move. "I'll meet you back in the hall."

Fifteen minutes later, they were awaiting Mr. Cox in one of the private parlors in the inn. Julian had declined refreshments and stood by the fireplace while Simon sat on the windowsill overlooking the stable yard.

The door opened, and the proprietor came in. "Morning, your lordship. Good of you to call so quickly."

"I claim no right to a title, Mr. Cox. Plain Mr. Laurent will do," Julian said. "Now, perhaps you might be so kind to explain exactly who wants information from you."

"Oh, I don't know if I should do that." Mr. Cox looked uneasily over his shoulder. "They might come after me."

"I might not be a peer, sir, but I have far more power than the press in this country. Tell me which publications are hounding you, and I will ensure that they cease doing so immediately."

"It's not just the press, Mr. Laurent. It's the pamphlet printers and others who should know better."

To his credit, Mr. Cox did look more genuinely anxious than greedy, but Julian still wasn't convinced of his innocence.

Julian glanced at Simon. "Perhaps you could get Mr. Cox to write down a list of all those who are currently importuning him for information that he knows damn well he was paid to keep to himself."

"Now, hang on, sir." Mr. Cox stepped between them. "I did what I did as a favor to my daughter. I didn't ask for no money from her employer."

"But I suspect you received some anyway."

Mr. Cox had the grace to look ashamed, but it didn't last long. "I never expected all this attention, sir. My staff are threatening to leave if the press don't stop bothering them. They've even been round to my own house and upset the missus."

"If you provide me with a full and comprehensive list of everyone who has been a nuisance, I will endeavor to ensure that you are left in peace, Mr. Cox," Julian said firmly. "We cannot have you bothering the ladies."

Simon cleared his throat and stood up. "The sooner we have the list, the sooner we can make things right for you, sir. I'm more than willing to stay behind and get a start on that right now, Mr. Laurent."

Julian put a gold guinea in Mr. Cox's palm. "That's an excellent idea. Are you game, Mr. Cox?"

"Aye, I suppose so." The landlord sighed. "I wish I'd never gotten involved in this matter in the first place."

"You and me both, sir. But we must protect the reputations of the ladies, on that we must agree."

Mr. Cox nodded. "There's paper and pens in the desk behind you, Mr. Benson, if you'd care to help yourself."

"Excellent." Julian turned to the landlord. "As soon as Simon has that list, we'll get cracking, and we'll keep you informed."

As he left, Julian noted that Mr. Cox didn't look terribly happy with the outcome of the meeting but hadn't had the balls to say so. Julian stepped out into the stable yard and was immediately hailed by name. Not ideal.

"Morning, Laurent." Young Calloway was lounging in the shadows with one of the grooms. Was he one of the people Mr. Cox had alluded to? It seemed likely. "Strange to see you here again when you warned me off."

Julian looked at him. "Good morning. It seems my warnings to you were ignored. Rumor has it that the unknown ladies sent you packing and that you didn't take it well." He paused as a flush gathered on Calloway's face. "Are you back hoping for another glimpse of those females who afforded the press such amusement at your expense?"

"My business here has nothing to do with you," Calloway snapped.

"Nor does mine with you." Julian inclined his head a civil inch. "I'll wish you a good day."

He walked off into the street, aware of a strange sense of disquiet with the whole incident. Why was Calloway hanging around the inn? Had his rather public humiliation, which had featured heavily in the gutter press, made him angry enough to want revenge? Not for the first time, Julian cursed Olivia and Carenza for their stupid decision to place the advertisement in the first place. If it was Calloway who was pressuring Mr. Cox, how could Julian stop him without exposing himself and the woman he cared about to public scrutiny?

Calloway's father was an influential peer who had shielded his spoiled son from all the consequences of his actions. Julian had no acquaintance with the older man or any idea how to reach him, which didn't bode well if Calloway was determined to cause mischief. And being caught coming out of the inn himself was unfortunate. Julian could only imagine the conclusions Calloway was drawing. Julian hoped his social standing would ensure that any gossip emanating from Calloway would be treated with the contempt it deserved.

He hailed a cab and directed the driver to take him to Carenza's house. It would be prudent to warn her and Mrs. Sheraton about Mr. Cox's potential inclination to share his story with anyone who had the means to pay for it.

He gazed out of the dirty window as the hackney cab turned a corner. It would also give him the opportunity to subtly remind Carenza that their liaison was supposed to be a light dalliance and not a torrid affair.

Fifteen minutes later, after the cab had battled through the morning traffic, he arrived in Tavistock Square. He'd forgotten how early it was and was ushered into the dining room, where Carenza and her sister were enjoying their breakfast.

He bowed. "I do apologize for my unintentionally early arrival. I had a matter to deal with on the London Road and came straight on from that."

"Please join us." Carenza, who was looking very charming in a yellow sprigged-muslin dress, waved him to a chair. "Have you eaten, or would you prefer coffee?"

"Just coffee, please." Julian sat down and waited until the butler brought him a cup and a newly brewed pot of coffee. "Thank you."

Allegra had been eating her way steadily through a large plate of toast and marmalade while reading a periodical. She paused to look over her spectacles at him. "I met someone you are acquainted with last night."

"That's hardly surprising, Allegra," Carenza said. "We do move in the same social circles."

"This was at the board meeting for the London Foundling Society." Allegra crunched through another half piece of toast and drank some tea before continuing. "A Mr. and Miss Cartwright."

"Ah, yes." Julian nodded. "I'm surprised they were at that particular meeting because I don't believe they deal with newborns."

"Perhaps it's something they intend to pursue?" Allegra said. "This city is full of abandoned and unwanted children. A lot of those who take babies in do not do well with them."

"I'm well aware of that." Julian shuddered. "The Cartwrights currently house about twenty boys ranging in age from four to fourteen. They teach them to read and write, and when they are ready, they apprentice them to a trade."

"How excellent." Allegra nodded approvingly. "I'm surprised you know anyone so worthy."

Carenza frowned. "Allegra . . ."

"Well, come on, Carenza. Have you ever imagined our dear Mr. Laurent has a serious bone in his body? He's an excellent flirt, a great dancer, and knows how to navigate the niceties of society with aplomb, but anything beyond that—"

"I'd be happy to escort you to the Cartwrights if you wish to renew your acquaintance with Miss Cartwright," Julian said.

"I would love to visit their premises," Allegra said.

"There's no need." Carenza spoke at the same time as her sister.

"I've always maintained that education is the key to economic advancement." Allegra smiled at Julian as she rose from her seat. "Who would've imagined you had hidden depths?" She left the room with her small Pomeranian dog, Jester, trotting at her heels.

Julian drank his coffee as the staff cleared away the breakfast and left him alone with Carenza.

"I'm sorry about my sister."

"Because she is refreshingly honest?" Julian asked.

"That's one way of putting it." Carenza sighed. "She prides herself on her bluntness."

"She didn't say anything that wasn't true. Many people regard me as an overdressed, insufferable fop with a sharp tongue."

"No one who really knows you thinks that," Carenza said.

"Although I do wonder why you've gone to such pains to give that impression to the majority."

Julian shrugged and offered her his usual charming smile. "Perhaps it's easier to let people believe what they think than challenge their perceptions." He set down his cup. "I didn't come here to talk about me. There is trouble brewing elsewhere." He related his conversation with Mr. Cox earlier that day and his unfortunate encounter with Calloway, and Carenza grew very quiet.

"I could strangle Olivia," Carenza eventually said.

"You wrote the advertisement," Julian reminded her.

"I didn't. I merely made suggestions, and Olivia decided to put the original draft in the newspapers! I thought that was just for fun between friends."

"Perhaps Mrs. Sheraton isn't as good a friend to you as she should be."

Carenza looked at him. "Please don't involve yourself in the matter of my friendships."

"Am I not also your friend?"

"Yes, but this is a completely different conversation and you know it."

"I'm just warning you not to assume her values are the same as yours."

"And I'm asking you to stop talking." She glared at him. "And currently, you and I are not friends. We are lovers."

Julian raised an eyebrow. "Can we not be both?"

She blushed. "I don't do . . . *that* with my friends."

"Strip them naked and demand things? I'm glad to hear it." He paused. "There is no need for such intensity between us, Carenza. We are perfectly capable of carrying off a light affair *and* a friendship."

There was quite a long silence as Carenza folded her arms and sat back, her hazel eyes calm. "If you think what is happening between us is 'light,' then I cannot imagine what your other affairs have been like."

"That's exactly my point."

"You wish to end the relationship?"

He frowned. "I didn't say that. I just meant that such affairs are generally conducted with less intensity."

"I see. You're suggesting I'm too forward."

"That's not—"

"You're just like Hector." Her smile disappeared. "He didn't want an equal partner in bed, either. He wanted someone to applaud and admire him."

"I know what Hector was like, and I can assure you that—"

"Of course. You have intimate knowledge of my husband's rutting ways because you had a first-class view of them!" She breathed out hard through her nose.

"Carenza, will you please calm down and let me finish a sentence?" Julian snapped.

"Calm down?" She looked him right in the eye. "I think I've heard enough. You agreed to an affair on *my* terms. Perhaps Allegra was right and all you are fit for is—"

"Don't." He reached over and cupped her chin.

"What? Talk? Enjoy bedding you?" She tried to jerk out of his grip, but he pulled her close and kissed her hard.

She wrenched her mouth away. "That's not fair."

"Neither is deliberately maligning my character and offering me no right to reply," he growled. "If we were truly alone now, I'd turn you over my knee and spank you."

"You wouldn't dare," she breathed.

"Is there a lock on that door? Because if there is, you sorely tempt me to let you find out I am a man of my word." He kissed her until she stopped trying to bite him.

She responded with equal gusto. "And I can't believe you have reduced me to fighting with you over the breakfast table!"

He eased back, his breath as harsh as his inconvenient need for her. "This is what I'm talking about—this lack of discretion in both of us. Anyone could come through that door and we'd be scuppered. We *cannot* allow our passions to overrule our good sense."

She stared at him and slowly nodded. "You might have a point."

"Thank you for at least acknowledging that!"

"Perhaps we need to extinguish this fire between us in a different way," Carenza said.

"How so?"

"Feed it for a few days and let it die down naturally." She looked down at her hands. "I've been invited to a house party this week. I've been wondering whether I should go."

He regarded her closely. "I have a better idea."

She might have rolled her eyes. "Of course you do."

"I will arrange a party at my hunting lodge in Epping. I'll invite only those who either know about our affair or who would be willing to turn a blind eye to it," Julian said. "Would that suffice?"

"I suppose so."

He rose to his feet, aware that his body was aroused and that another trip to the boxing salon to work off his passions would be necessary. He almost groaned when Carenza leaned forward and kissed the prominent bulge in his buckskin breeches. He gave her a severe look.

"I do hope you are similarly inconvenienced."

"I might be, but I hide it far better." Her smile was wicked. "Perhaps you'd better put on your cloak before you advertise your condition to the entire world."

"Perhaps I should avail myself of your facilities and take a hand to myself." He glanced ruefully down at his groin. "It wouldn't take more than a few strokes to bring me off."

"Or I could—"

He stepped back to avoid Carenza's seeking hand and bowed. She pouted, and the urge to unbutton his breeches and slide his cock between her lips almost overwhelmed him.

This would never do. He needed to regain control of himself.

"I'll be in touch."

She nodded. "As you wish."

"Goodbye, Lady Carenza."

"Have a *lovely* day."

He left, careful to carry his cloak over the front of his breeches like some callow lad. On the way back to his house, he wanted to kick himself. He'd failed to convince Carenza there might still be repercussions from the advertisement and, even worse, he'd botched reducing their affair to a more conventional level and probably made things worse. Good Lord, no wonder his mother looked at him with disdain.

He reached home, intending to leave for the boxing salon immediately, only to be accosted by Simon in the hall.

"I have the list from Mr. Cox, sir."

"Thank you. You may leave it on my desk." Julian was already moving toward the stairs when Simon cleared his throat.

"You might want to read it now, sir." He handed Julian the note to peruse.

Julian scanned it quickly and raised his head. "Why on earth are Walcott and Lady Brenton on here?"

"I don't know, sir, but I might be willing to take a guess."

Chapter 10

Julian drank his third brandy and stared into the fire at his club. He had eaten at White's with a group of friends and politely declined their invitation to join them at a discreet brothel, which had caused some good-natured ribaldry. He had enough trouble managing one woman's needs without adding any other's.

He'd always imagined Carenza was the perfect wife for Hector. She appeared calm and in control. Hector's constant dalliances and appalling lack of judgment had never seemed to ruffle her composure in the slightest. Julian had thought, God help him, that bedding her would be easy. That she understood the game and would engage in a pleasant affair that meant nothing to either of them.

Except she wasn't willing to play by the rules and, as he'd foolishly allowed her to set them, he was heading rapidly toward hell alongside her. He'd been stupid to underestimate her. As a child, she'd shown great courage and a fierce determination to outdo all the boys on the estate next door. They'd often tried to dissuade her from tagging along with them, but she'd been dogged in her pursuit. He remembered her brother, Dorian, tying her hair ribbons to a tree once to stop her from following them.

He smiled as he remembered her indignation when she'd

finally caught up with them, sans hair ribbons and her hair down her back.

"What ho, brother."

Julian looked up as Aragon patted his shoulder and took the chair opposite him. A waiter paused by his side, and Aragon ordered two more brandies.

"You're looking very thoughtful, Julian."

"Just contemplating how the best-laid plans are certain to fail."

"Very true." Aragon nodded vigorously. "That's why I avoid 'em like the plague. Mother is far better at organizing my life than I'll ever be."

Julian fixed his brother with a patient stare. "And that is why you'll never find a lady willing to marry you."

Aragon studied him for a long moment, his brow creased in obvious thought. "Ah, you think I allow Mother too much control over my life."

"Yes."

"And if I take a wife, she won't like that, because she'll want to tell me what to do instead."

"Well done."

"There's no need to be sarcastic," Aragon said. "What if I made it clear they can *both* tell me what to do?" He looked hopefully at Julian.

"What if they ask you to do totally opposite things?"

Aragon frowned. "I didn't think of that."

"Can you imagine living in a house where our esteemed mother was at constant war with your wife?"

"Well, that's easy to solve. I just won't go home." Aragon sat back with a satisfied air. "Leave 'em to it."

Julian considered ending the conversation there, but some perverse desire to hear what Aragon would come up with next made him continue. "If you never go home, how will you sire an heir?"

The waiter returned with the brandies, and Aragon took

a moment to light a cigar and drain his glass before turning back to Julian. "That's easy." He paused to blow a smoke ring far too close to Julian's face. "I'll pack Mother off to the dower house."

Julian contemplated that scenario as he sipped his own brandy. "If you ever do that, will you invite me to watch?"

Aragon slapped his thigh and roared with laughter. "You're a very funny man."

"I'm quite serious," Julian said.

"Has Lady Carenza ever met Mother?"

"I would assume they've met in society at some point. Why?"

"I was thinking of inviting Lady Carenza to dine with us at home."

"With our mother, who has expressly forbidden you from courting her?"

"It's my house." Aragon looked mulish. "I can invite who I damned well please."

"I agree." Julian nodded.

"With me?" Aragon's eyebrows shot up. "That's a first."

"You should invite both the Musgrove sisters," Julian said. "And me."

"Naturally. It's still your home, brother, whatever Mother says."

Julian met his brother's gaze. "Thank you."

"I'll just inform the housekeeper, and she can tell Cook. Mother won't need to know anything about it until the guests are arriving," Aragon said happily.

"An excellent strategy," Julian said.

"Do you really think so?" Aragon smiled at him. "I'll send Lady Carenza a note, and as soon as I get her acceptance, I'll arrange everything."

"One thing before you go," Julian said. "I'm thinking of organizing a small house party at my place in the country, and I wondered if you would like to come?"

"Me?" Aragon looked absurdly pleased. "You've never considered me worthy enough to grace your country retreat before."

"Which was very remiss of me." Julian paused. "Will you come?"

"Yes, please, but don't tell Mother. She thinks you're a bad influence on me."

"I wouldn't dream of it," Julian assured his brother.

Aragon rose to his feet. "I must be off. I promised Cardew I'd visit a new gaming hell with him."

"Please be careful," Julian said.

"It's not me you have to worry about, brother. I'm only going with Cardew to stop him from wasting his money." He paused. "He's an old friend of mine, and I do try to look out for him."

"You're a good man." Julian looked up at his brother.

Aragon shrugged. "Least I can do. I've never enjoyed gambling. All those numbers make my head spin." With a wink he departed, leaving Julian alone again with the realization that without his mother standing between them, he was beginning to like his older brother far more than he had anticipated.

"Good evening, Laurent." Percival Walcott slid into the chair Aragon had just vacated.

"Walcott." Julian sat back and waited to see what Percival wanted.

"Was that your brother you were speaking to?"

"Yes."

"Last I heard, you two were estranged over your unexpected inheritance." Percival paused. "It must have been as galling for him to be overlooked as it was for me."

"Fortunately for me, he isn't the kind of man to hold a grudge."

"Yes, he's remarkably easygoing, isn't he?" Percival said

with a sneer. "Not a lot of sense, but that hardly matters when he's an earl."

"Is it difficult?" Julian asked.

Percival looked flummoxed. "What?"

"Constantly carrying that chip on your shoulder. Does your tailor have to account for it when he makes your coats? It would certainly explain the lack of fit." Julian stared at Percival. "Perhaps if you spent less time airing your grievances and more on bettering yourself, you'd be a happier man."

"I'd be happier if you hadn't used your charm to extract a fortune from my aunt."

Julian was in no mood to tolerate Percival's endless parade of accusations. He rose to his feet. "Was there something in particular you wanted to speak to me about?"

"Yes. Calloway's been gossiping about you and the mysterious lady who placed the advertisement."

"I never listen to gossip."

"But surely you'd like the opportunity to clear the air?" Percival asked.

"With you?" Julian raised an eyebrow. "Hardly."

"I was trying to give you a friendly warning that your name might be dragged through the press, but, as usual, you are too proud to take the hint." Percival took a hasty step back as Julian strolled past him, not bothering to answer.

Julian went into the entrance hall and asked for his hat and cloak. He'd rather his name was in the newspapers than Carenza's, and that was all there was to it. Percival could whine as much as he wanted, as long as Carenza's reputation remained unsullied.

Still, he didn't like the association between Calloway and Percival one bit. They both disliked him and would love to see him fall from society's graces. The worst thing was there was very little he could do until they showed their hands more openly. Why Percival couldn't let the matter of the inheritance go after two years of whining and losing several court cases, Julian couldn't fathom. Money, as his father had often mentioned, was the biggest bone of contention in all families, rich or poor.

He bade the porter good night and decided to walk back to his house. He'd agreed to take Carenza and her sister to meet the Cartwrights the following morning when he was due to give his speech. Miss Cartwright hadn't seemed very enthused by the notion of a visit, but her brother had reminded her that they needed the goodwill of those able to finance their efforts, and she'd reluctantly agreed.

Julian was fairly certain that both sisters would heartily approve of the Cartwrights' work and would be inclined to offer their assistance. As the treasurer and keeper of the books, Julian knew exactly how far Miss Cartwright squeezed every penny and admired her for it. He'd considered adding to his own financial contributions but didn't want Miss Cartwright to feel any kind of obligation to him that might make her think his genuine admiration for her was tied to his purse.

He rarely met women quite like Miss Cartwright and Anna Mountjoy—ladies by birth who chose to work for the good of others rather than further enriching their families by making the right marriages. Society women often took up "causes," but in his experience, they shied away from the reality of the actual work and quickly lost interest when something new came along.

But wasn't he guilty of the same? He nodded at the nightwatchman as he passed by and finally turned into his street off the King's Road. He'd rarely interested himself in such matters until Mrs. Mountjoy had introduced him to the Cartwrights and he'd entered a whole new world. He had no intention of giving up his post on the board now even if he never succeeded in engaging Miss Cartwright's interest. To be considered useful and to do something to help others was an eye-opening experience.

He paused to find his key and stared at his front door. He'd spent so many years cultivating the appearance of a man without a care in the world that he'd almost come to believe that was all he was. Carenza had reminded him that those who knew him well knew he was more than that—but was he?

The door opened, and his butler bowed to him.

"Good evening, Mr. Laurent."

"Good evening." He went into the hall and relinquished his hat and cloak. "I'm going straight to bed. Would you be so good as to send Proctor up to my rooms?"

"Yes, of course, sir."

Julian went up the stairs and into his bedroom. For the first time he pictured Carenza naked and waiting for him in his bed and groaned. She was not manageable at all; in fact, she was quite the opposite, and worse still, part of him was enjoying it immensely.

"Is everything all right, sir?" Proctor inquired as he came in through the dressing room door.

"Yes, thank you." Julian smothered a yawn. "I think I drank too much brandy."

"Then you'll sleep well tonight." Proctor helped him out of his tight-fitting coat. "Any instructions for tomorrow, sir?"

"Yes, make sure I'm up by eight. I'm visiting the Cartwrights."

Proctor bowed. "Then I'll make sure to press and put out your fourth-best coat."

"Perhaps you could make it my second best? I am giving a speech," Julian said as he untied his cravat. "And I promise I won't go near a single child."

The next morning, despite dressing as plainly as he could, it still took Julian a considerable amount of time to get ready. He arrived at Musgrove House to find Carenza and Allegra awaiting him in the drawing room. Neither of them was prone to dress extravagantly, but he was pleased to see that they both wore simple gowns that would withstand the inevitable stickiness of the institution.

He apologized for keeping them waiting and escorted them down to his carriage. Carenza took the seat opposite Allegra, and Julian sat next to her.

"I don't need to remind you to keep your wits about you, do I?" Julian said. "The only skill most of these boys excel at when they're taken in is pickpocketing."

"Don't worry, I left my diamonds at home," Carenza said. "And the Musgrove tiara."

"Not the Smythe-Harding one?" Allegra winked at her.

Carenza gave her a severe look. "I don't have the ability to find your jest amusing yet. That woman is still giving me the cut direct."

"And I don't see it affecting your social life, sister, so perhaps you did get the last laugh after all," Allegra commented as she looked out of the window. "Where exactly are we going, Julian?"

"The East End," Julian said.

"I am aware of that from the filth, but what is the address?"

"Whitechapel Road. The Cartwright Institution is quite close to the London Hospital. We'll be there in a minute."

Julian's coachman knew the way and required no direction. When the carriage drew to a stop, Julian stepped out to help down Carenza and Allegra.

"Oh." Allegra looked up at the house and the ten-foot-high wall that surrounded the front facing the road. "It is rather grim, isn't it?"

"But solid and well-maintained," Carenza said as they approached the side entrance. "And is that a garden at the rear? How nice for the children to have somewhere to play." She smiled up at Julian and took his arm. "I am so looking forward to meeting the Cartwrights."

The door opened, and Martin Cartwright beckoned them forward. He was a jovial man who had all the warmth his sister outwardly lacked.

"Come in! You are most welcome." He shook all their hands with great vigor and led them through to the office. "I'd offer you refreshments, but I'm not sure we have any."

"There's no need." Carenza smiled at Mr. Cartwright, who immediately looked smitten. "We're far more interested in seeing your facility than sitting around drinking tea."

Julian was once again struck by Carenza's immense kindness and her ability to always think of the right thing to say. Allegra was her complete opposite.

"We currently have twenty boys here, which means we're at full capacity," Mr. Cartwright said.

"You don't take girls?" Allegra asked.

"Not at the moment. If we do encounter young females, we take them to our friend Mrs. Mountjoy, who takes care of them in her establishment."

The door opened, and Miss Cartwright came in. She wore her usual gray dress and apron, and her hair was braided tightly to her head.

"Good morning," she said. "I apologize for my lateness, but the needs of my charges must always come first."

"Absolutely." Allegra nodded. "We quite understand and can only commend your dedication to your duty."

Miss Cartwright almost smiled.

"We won't take up too much of your time, Miss Cartwright," Julian reassured her. "We know you are busy preparing for the committee meeting. In fact, if you wish, I could conduct the tour myself."

"That's very kind of you to offer, sir, but my brother and I know the place best." Miss Cartwright turned to the ladies. "Would you like to follow me? We'll start upstairs in the dormitory and work our way down from there."

* * *

Later that afternoon, after Allegra and Carenza had returned home and had their lunch, Allegra took out her notebook and looked expectantly at her sister. "Shall we discuss the Cartwrights?"

Carenza, who had just got to an interesting part of her novel, groaned and set the book aside. "You took notes?"

"I always do." Allegra glanced down at her neat handwriting. "If I intend to devote my time and money to a charity, I like to do my research."

"I thought it was very well run and that the Cartwrights were realistic about their chances of success, but brave enough to try to help anyway."

Allegra frowned. "That was my initial conclusion, too. But I did have some reservations."

"Such as?"

"The size of their current premises. There is very little room for expansion."

"I suspect with just the two of them managing twenty boys, they have no desire to expand."

"But what about girls?"

"Mr. Cartwright did mention an organization they worked with who helped with that," Carenza said.

Allegra consulted her notes. "Oh yes, Mrs. Mountjoy. What do we know about her?"

Carenza aimed for a neutral tone. "Julian told me that despite family opposition, she married a friend of his who was a physician. Unfortunately, he died, but since his death, she has continued his good works."

"Who would've thought Julian knew such peculiar people?" Allegra marveled. "It seems very unlike him."

"I'm pleased to see him devoting his attention to worthy causes," Carenza said.

"Well, it's obvious why he picked that particular worthy cause, isn't it?" Allegra closed her notebook.

"I don't know what you mean."

"Miss Cartwright." Allegra raised her eyebrows. "Didn't you see the way he looked at her?"

Carenza considered their morning visit anew. Julian had shown a marked partiality for Miss Cartwright. However, Miss Cartwright had offered him only cool politeness.

"I thought she was far more interested in the welfare of the children in her care than in courting potential benefactors or flirting with Julian," Carenza said. "In truth, she was almost rude at times."

"She certainly grew impatient with my questions," Allegra said. "Which leads me nicely to my other concern. If we did agree to financially support the institution, how much say would we get in how the money would be used?"

"Probably none, if Miss Cartwright has her way. She bristled at the slightest hint that her standards weren't perfect."

"Julian didn't seem to mind," Allegra said slyly. "In fact, he rushed to agree with every word that came out of her mouth."

"She's not interested in him in the slightest," Carenza said.

"Are you jealous, sister?"

Carenza snorted. "Hardly. I have no claim on him, but they would not suit. She has no sense of humor at all."

"Mayhap he's tired of women who laugh at his jokes and seeks someone with a more serious frame of mind?" Allegra suggested. "I must admit, I cannot fault him for such a choice."

The butler came in and bowed to Carenza. "Mrs. Sheraton is inquiring whether you are receiving callers, my lady."

"Please ask her to come up and ask Cook to provide some refreshments," Carenza said. "Thank you, Jones."

Olivia came in looking very glamorous in a dark green walking dress and a bonnet with peacock feathers to match. She barely waited until the butler left the room before turning to Carenza. "I have some bad news."

"What has happened?"

"Mr. Cox has proved to be an unreliable keeper of secrets." Olivia shook her head. "He's now trying to blackmail me." She sat down heavily in the nearest chair. "I'm not sure what to do."

"Mr. Cox also approached Julian," Carenza said. "Julian came here the other day to warn me."

"And what does he intend to do about it?" Olivia asked.

"He said he had the matter in hand and that there was nothing for either of us to worry about."

"Obviously he was wrong," Olivia said.

"May I suggest you speak to Julian directly about the letter you received?" Carenza said. "I'm sure he'll be willing to help you."

"For a gentleman who claims to be only dallying with you, Carenza, Julian Laurent is being extremely protective of your reputation, but I doubt he gives a jot about mine."

"We grew up on neighboring estates," Carenza said. "We've been friends for far longer than we've been lovers."

"That's all well and good, but there must be more to it." Olivia snapped her fingers. "Of course! Mr. Laurent is annoyed because Percival is attempting to link him with the scandal and gossiping in the clubs."

"Julian didn't mention that." Carenza frowned. "But one has to wonder whether Mr. Calloway has shared his suspicions with Percival and made things worse."

"Calloway?" Allegra asked. "What does that rascal have to do with it?"

Carenza shared a grimace with Olivia. "He was one of the very few gentlemen who turned up at the inn to be interviewed. We sent him on his way when he refused to say whether he'd ever had the pox."

Allegra shuddered. "I'm fairly sure he has."

"I wouldn't be surprised," Olivia agreed. "I wonder when he encountered Julian?"

"I believe they met outside the inn," Carenza said cautiously. "But you'd have to ask Julian to be certain."

"Where is he?" Olivia looked around the room.

"Not here," Carenza said. "Unless he's hiding somewhere."

"Then we need to summon him to a conference," Olivia said. "I'll have a note sent to his house."

"He might be busy," Allegra said. "He is very involved in good works these days."

"Julian is?" Olivia looked surprised. "I suppose it's a better use for his money than gambling or drinking it away. Did he tell you he's invited me to a house party?"

Slightly unnerved by the rapid change of subject, Carenza blinked. "House party?"

"Yes, at his place in Epping Forest." Olivia went over to the desk and began writing a note to Julian. "He did invite you, didn't he?"

"Of course, I'd forgotten all about it," Carenza confessed.

"How romantic," Olivia said as she rose to her feet and headed for the door. "I'll take this down to the kitchen and get someone to deliver it immediately. By the time we sit down to dinner we should have heard from him."

She left the room, and Allegra stared at her sister. "Olivia's invited herself to dinner again."

"So she has," Carenza sighed. "I'd better have a word with Cook."

Chapter 11

They were halfway through dinner when Julian arrived. Olivia, obviously on edge, looked him up and down as he bowed in greeting and set her wineglass on the table with something of a thump. "I suppose it took you two hours to get ready to venture forth after receiving my urgent message."

Julian glanced at Carenza before he sat down. Then he turned to Olivia and said, "With respect, Mrs. Sheraton, I was dealing with estate matters at my solicitor's and didn't receive your note until I returned home."

Olivia sniffed. "I'll wager you still took the time to change before you came out again."

"I could hardly appear before you in my morning clothes. What would people think?" Julian said with an easy smile that Carenza guessed was a deliberate attempt to enrage Olivia.

"People?" Olivia looked around the room. "It's just us."

Knowing how her friend could keep an argument going for hours, Carenza hastened to intervene. "Perhaps you might care to explain to Julian why you thought it was so urgent for him to talk with us, Olivia."

"I'm being blackmailed by Mr. Cox," Olivia said.

"Ah." Julian sat back and regarded her. "I wondered whether he would try that."

"And you didn't think to mention it to me?"

"You assured me that he was an honest man who would never double-cross you. I chose to believe you and gave him the benefit of the doubt when he approached me with a similar offer."

"And what should I do?" Olivia asked, her fingers tapping.

"Nothing."

"That's hardly helpful."

Julian offered her a calm stare. "I will deal with Mr. Cox."

There was a note of steel in Julian's voice that Carenza had learned to recognize. She'd never seen him lose his temper, but he could be intimidating when he chose, which was why he was feared by a goodly portion of the ton.

"That's not good enough," Olivia said.

Carenza sighed. "Olivia . . ."

"Don't try to defend him, Carenza," Olivia snapped. "You are hardly unbiased."

"I've known Julian all my life," Carenza countered. "I trust him implicitly."

"And so do I," Allegra joined in. "If Julian says he will take care of the matter, he will."

"I suggest you write back to Mr. Cox, tell him you are considering his offer, and leave it at that, Mrs. Sheraton," Julian said. "I won't allow him to spread disinformation."

"The trouble is," Allegra said slowly, "he's not lying, is he? Carenza and Olivia truly were at his inn interviewing men for the position of Carenza's lover."

Everyone looked at her, and she shrugged. "I'm sorry, but it's the truth."

"He was paid to ensure that their identities remain secret," Julian said. "And he is attempting to renege on that promise, which means action must be taken against him."

"I didn't pay him." Olivia looked at Carenza. "Did you?"

"Well, you paid well over the going rate for the use of his parlor," Carenza said. "And I gave him a handsome bonus when I left, which, for all intents and purposes, was a bribe."

Olivia was still staring at Julian. "What I don't understand, Mr. Laurent, is how you came to be involved in this matter so deeply that Mr. Cox decided to blackmail you as well. Neither Carenza nor I asked for your help. In fact, you were dead set against the idea, so why is Mr. Cox asking you for money?"

"Perhaps because I attempted to protect the reputations of two ladies I am acquainted with."

Olivia's eyebrows shot up. "That's the worst excuse I've ever heard."

Carenza winced as Julian's expression turned frosty.

"With respect, I will remind you, ma'am, that if it hadn't been for you publishing such a provocative advertisement in the first place, there would be no scandal to address."

"There's no point looking down your nose at me, Mr. Laurent, it won't work," Olivia said. "And I'm not interested in what I did but how you became so involved in the matter. Did you speak to Mr. Cox before the event and offer him money to save our reputations?"

"I did not."

"Then why is he attempting to blackmail you?"

Carenza looked at Julian and said, "You escorted me out of the inn through Mr. Cox's house."

"That's correct."

"Then one might assume Mr. Cox recognized you, or found out who you were, and decided to blackmail you."

Olivia blew out a breath. "I suppose that makes sense, but I still don't like it."

"The issue at hand isn't dealing with the press or the scandal sheets," Julian said. "I can take care of them. My bigger concern is about those in society who have taken an interest in the matter. They are the people who can affect your standing in society."

"Such as Mr. Calloway," Carenza said. "Who didn't appreciate being sent away."

"I probably didn't help with that." Julian grimaced. "I admit to giving Calloway's name to the press. He featured prominently in their articles about the matter."

"That would certainly explain his animosity toward all of us, but he is hardly a powerful figure in society," Olivia countered.

"He might not be, but his father is," Julian said. "And for some reason, Calloway has suddenly become very good friends with Percival Walcott."

"Now I understand why you are so willing to help us, Mr. Laurent," Olivia said. "Self-preservation."

"If you choose to view it like that, I can't stop you." Julian shrugged. "I'd rather see it as a joint endeavor."

"That saves all our reputations?" Olivia asked.

"Yes," Julian told her. "Why not?"

Julian stayed after dinner and managed to outlast both Mrs. Sheraton and Allegra so that he could talk with Carenza alone in the drawing room. He hadn't enjoyed the confrontation with Mrs. Sheraton. She was extremely sharp and not averse to asking the most personal of questions. It was only thanks to Carenza that he'd avoided having to reveal his rather more involved participation in their scheme.

He sat back and sipped the brandy the butler had brought him while Carenza drank her tea. She wore a cream silk gown with a delicate lace trim around the edge of the bodice that framed her magnificent bosom rather well. He had the sudden urge to sink to his knees beside her chair, bury his face in her cleavage, and simply breathe her in.

"Julian."

"Yes?"

"How did you know the way out through Mr. Cox's house?"

Damnation. He should have known Carenza would pick up on that. "I beg your pardon?"

"You heard me. How did you know?" Carenza asked.

"I simply followed you?"

She gave him a severe look. "You practically dragged me out of that private parlor by the hair. I certainly wasn't leading the way. Were you lying to Olivia when you said you hadn't met Mr. Cox?"

He frowned. "I didn't lie. I said I hadn't met him before your 'event.'"

"Then when did you meet him?"

"When I worked out that neither you nor Mrs. Sheraton had entered the inn from the front. It seemed obvious that there was another entrance. I found it when I strolled around the corner."

"You found it."

"I am quite capable, my dear." He had no intention of telling her that Simon had provided him with all the necessary information before the event had even started. Instinct told him that she wouldn't appreciate that level of interference from him at all.

"Then I assume you gave Mr. Cox money to allow you to access the inn from his house?"

"Yes." That was a truth he was willing to give her.

"Which is the real reason why he is blackmailing you as well as Olivia." She set her cup back on the tray. "And because you interfered, Calloway and Percival Walcott are now interested in the matter and willing to use it to hurt you."

He didn't like her summary, but it was hard to dispute it. "That is the unfortunate case," he agreed.

"*Unfortunate?* I wish you'd kept out of it."

"And let you ruin yourself for a foolish whim?"

There was a pointed silence, and then she raised her chin. "Perhaps you should go."

"Why? Because I am right?"

"No, because I am not in charity with you, and if you stay

any longer and try and charm me when you are most definitely at fault, I might do something I regret." She rose to her feet. "In fact, I'll save you the trouble. Good night, Julian. Ask the butler to see you out when you're ready to leave."

Courtesy obliged him to stand up as well. "It's not like you to run away from a fight, Carenza."

"But you don't fight fair, do you? You undermine me with your charm and your body, and . . ." She waved her arms in the air before heading for the door. "After an evening of you and Olivia sniping at each other, I don't want a fight right now."

"Then what do you want?" Julian followed her.

"Honesty?" She half turned to stare at him.

"About what in particular?"

"See?" She shook her head. "You can't help yourself, can you?"

"I want you. Is that honest enough?" He took her hand.

"That's not what I mean, and you know it."

"I see. You want honesty on your terms and not on mine." He lightly kissed her fingers, and she curled them into a fist. "But obviously, I cannot argue with a lady."

"You are infuriating."

"As are you. We agreed to a physical relationship, and the only honesty you get to demand from me is for that." He released her hand and bowed. "Good night, my lady."

He left her standing in the doorway, her color high and her expression furious. He wanted to stride back up the stairs, take her in his arms and kiss her until she forgot everything except her need for him, because that was real—that was honest—and if she couldn't see that, then maybe there was nothing between them at all.

Carenza stomped upstairs to her room, her thoughts in a whirl. Julian was infuriating. She wished she'd never agreed to let him be her lover, because it complicated everything between them. She allowed her maid to assist her into bed and then sat there, the candles still burning and a book on her lap.

If she could have her way, Julian would be with her right now, and she'd . . . tie him up? Make him beg for mercy? The very thought made her want to smile. Despite his efforts to convince her that she was in charge of their relationship, she doubted his instincts would allow him to take the more subservient role for long. He'd already threatened to spank her. What else might he be prepared to do?

And why was she even thinking about him after he'd reprimanded her and left? He was the one who was at fault. She wanted to shake him so hard that he lost his damnable composure and met her on equal terms. He'd roused something in her that Hector had never appreciated and that she'd quickly learned to hide.

Hector's preferred method of marital relations had consisted of her lying as quietly as possible on the bed while he "performed" over her. He'd rebuffed her attempts to reciprocate in kind and made her feel foolish for having physical needs at all. She'd learned to deal with his gradual lack of interest by shutting down and pretending she was somewhere else until he'd complained that her dullness meant he was justified in seeking sexual excitement outside their marriage.

Looking back, she wished she'd had the courage to stand up to him, but like all women of her class, she'd been taught to put up with a faithless husband by ignoring the inevitable. She wished she'd taken a lover earlier, but Hector had made her feel useless enough not to even try.

And now Julian had brought all the suppressed physicality she'd hidden beneath the surface to sudden, shocking life, and she was somewhat afraid of whom she'd become. . . . She wanted him at the most inconvenient times, and a simple touch of his hand fired up her senses in a way she'd never imagined possible. She even relished fighting, because when he allowed his annoyance to show, she sensed she could provoke him even more.

She sighed so hard she almost blew out the candles. This was not helping her relax. She reached into the drawer beside her bed and retrieved the silk bag Olivia had given her on the first anniversary of Hector's death.

"Now that you've pretended to mourn him, Carenza, it's time to take care of yourself."

The bag contained a scandalously carved jade penis, which Carenza had come to appreciate immensely. She released the silk cords at the neck of the bag and let the dildo slide out onto her palm, where it lay heavy and cold. Her thumb caressed the intricately carved details of the tip, and she shivered with anticipation.

Her last thought, as she slid her hand beneath the covers and parted her thighs, was that Julian would enjoy watching her pleasure herself. With that picture firmly in mind, she closed her eyes and slid the solid weight home.

Chapter 12

"Good evening, ladies." Aragon beamed as he greeted Carenza and Allegra after they entered the drawing room. "I'm so glad that you could come."

Julian was standing beside his mother and had heard her sudden intake of breath when the Musgrove sisters had been announced. She was now realizing exactly whom her eldest son had invited to dinner. He wondered what she would do. Common courtesy dictated that she would act as if nothing was wrong, welcome her guests with decorum rather than warmth, and ensure that the evening went as well as could be expected.

"Is this your doing?" she murmured without turning her head.

"Nothing to do with me, Mother. It was all Aragon's idea."

"I doubt that. I'm aware that you are attempting to exert your influence over my son, and I do not appreciate it."

"One might think a mother would be pleased that both her sons are getting along so famously." Julian smiled at her. "In truth, I am glad to call Aragon a friend."

There was no time to say more, as Aragon brought Carenza and Allegra over to greet their hostess.

"Mother, you remember Lady Carenza and Lady Allegra, don't you?"

"Of course." She inclined her head an icy inch.

"Good evening, Lady Isobel." Carenza curtsied along with Allegra. "Thank you for the invitation."

"Wonderful!" As usual Aragon seemed oblivious to his mother's fury, which Julian enjoyed immensely. "I've been mounting Lady Carenza in the park."

"Your son has been very kind, Lady Isobel," Carenza said.

"Of course he has," their mother said with something of a snap. "I brought him up to be civil to people of all classes."

"Even lowly folk like us." Allegra entered the conversation, her chin raised at a dangerous angle. "I'm amazed that we aren't swooning at the great honor, Carenza."

Aragon laughed and lightly punched Julian on the arm. "Lady Allegra is quite the wit, isn't she?"

"Indeed," Julian murmured, aware that Carenza was giving him a rather pointed stare. "Who else have you invited to your dinner party, brother?"

"Well." Aragon looked at Carenza. "I didn't want you to feel that you didn't know anyone, so I took the liberty of inviting the new earl and his wife."

"The Smythe-Hardings?" Carenza asked.

"That's the ones." Aragon turned to the door. "They've just arrived. Come along, Mother, I'll introduce you to them."

He placed his mother's hand on his sleeve and went off, leaving Julian facing two accusing faces.

He held up his hands, aware of an unfortunate desire to laugh. "I swear I had no idea Aragon was going to do this."

"How on earth are we going to sit around a table together when they won't even acknowledge I exist?" Carenza demanded.

"I'm sure Aragon has thought of that," Julian said.

"And I'm fairly certain he hasn't," Carenza hissed at him.

The butler appeared to announce dinner, and Carenza managed to smile at Aragon when he offered to escort her into the dining room.

Julian offered his arm to Allegra. "This should be fun."

Allegra looked up at him as they approached the dining room. She was wearing her favorite shade of blue, which made her eyes sparkle. "Or it might be a complete disaster."

"Either way, my mother will hate it," Julian said. "And I know I can rely on you to help me soothe the stormy seas."

She threw him a challenging glance as they approached the table. He pulled out her chair and set her napkin on her lap. His mother sat at the top of the table, Aragon on her right and the new earl on her left, which meant Carenza was directly opposite Lady Harriet, the new countess. Julian was next to Lady Harriet and opposite the curate of the church his mother favored in London. There were two more couples whom he thought were distant relatives come to visit London who were suitably overawed by the present company and unlikely to utter a word.

Aragon smiled at everyone. "My first dinner party."

"Hardly, dear," his mother responded. "We've enjoyed hundreds of such events."

"Not ones that I've planned all by myself," Aragon said. "I set everything up with the housekeeper and cook. I didn't want you to be bothered with all the details."

"I'm sure you didn't." For once his mother sounded slightly annoyed with Aragon.

"Are you enjoying the Smythe-Harding town house?" Aragon asked Lady Harriet, oblivious to his mother's tone. "As far as I remember it is very conveniently situated."

"The house is in an excellent location," Lady Harriet, the new countess, agreed. "Unfortunately, the interior does not match the exterior. We've had to tear out all the decor and sell off most of the furniture." She paused and raised her voice. "Everything had been done in such bad taste we could barely manage to live there."

The gloves are off . . . Julian couldn't help but look at Carenza. Her face bore an expression of polite interest.

"Whoever decorated the house had no discernable elegance or style. In truth, it reminded me of some gaudy theater or something." Lady Harriet gave a little laugh. "The former occupant of the house might disagree with me, but—"

"Oh, no," Carenza said sweetly. "I didn't like the decor myself, but Hector's mother was responsible for it, and I didn't feel it would've been right to change a thing when his whole family loved it so much." She sipped her wine. "I'm sure you'll get some comments on your decision when you host the Christmas party this year."

"Christmas party?" The earl looked over at Carenza.

"It's a Smythe-Harding tradition." Carenza smiled at him. "Ask Mr. Hoskins. He'll know what to do, as he's been there for at least forty years."

"Mr. Hoskins has been fired without a reference." The earl glanced nervously at his wife. "He was too inclined to think he knew better than his employers."

"I found he usually did know what was best." Carenza's tone remained even, but Julian knew her well enough to see that she was angry at the new earl's apparent callousness. "But I'm sure your new staff will cope perfectly well."

The countess said, "We're not taking on new staff, and we have no intention of hosting such a party. I despise hangers-on."

"That's a shame," Aragon said. "I always enjoy a good Christmas gathering and Hector and Lady Carenza used to host a wonderful party." He turned to his mother. "I know! We'll have one here and invite everyone."

"I hardly think—"

Julian spoke over his mother. "What an excellent idea."

"Perhaps you might devote your attention to amusements at your own premises, Julian, and not make use of mine," his mother snapped.

"Hang on, Mother. This is still Julian's family home," Aragon said. "And, as the head of the household, I'll ensure he'll always be welcome here."

The look Julian's mother gave him should have turned him to stone, but he ignored her and smiled at his brother.

"Thank you, Aragon," Julian said.

Aragon nodded and turned to Carenza. "You'll come, won't you, Lady Carenza?"

"Of course I will."

"Then that's all I need to know." He finished his glass of wine and sat back to allow the footman to remove his soup plate.

Briefly, Julian wondered how many courses were left and what else might go wrong. He turned to Allegra and asked, "What did you think of the Cartwrights?"

"I was most impressed," Allegra said. "Miss Cartwright is a formidable woman."

"She certainly is."

"She mentioned her family are connected to the Devonshire Cartwrights," Allegra said. "I have an acquaintance with the current earl of that branch. I'll have to mention Miss Cartwright when I next write to him."

"I doubt her family approve of the work she does," Julian said.

"Then perhaps it would be better if I didn't mention her at all," Allegra replied.

"Who is this woman?" Aragon, who appeared to be enjoying his role as host rather too much, inquired. "A love interest at last, Julian?"

"Miss Cartwright and her brother run a charitable institution for orphaned boys," Allegra explained. "Mr. Laurent is on the board of trustees. Carenza and I might be joining him."

Lady Harriet sniffed. "Considering the state of the Smythe-Harding earldom, I am surprised the previous countess can afford to be charitable toward anything." She pointedly didn't look at Carenza. "Unless, of course, her settlement is the reason why the earldom was left in such financial disarray in the first place."

"I fear you have been misinformed, ma'am," Julian said. "I was one of the executors of Hector's will, and I can assure you that he took far more from his wife's finances than she ever got from him."

"It might surprise you to know, Lady Harriet, that Carenza and I are well provided for by our father and have no need of anyone else's money or their charity," Allegra said. "In truth, without Hector spending all Carenza's allowance, she is far better off than she was during her marriage."

Lady Harriet looked at her husband. "As you feared, it is obvious that the previous countess and her family are willing to introduce the most inappropriate discussions about money to the dining table."

"You started it," Allegra said, "by inferring that my sister had somehow diddled the earldom out of a fortune, when the truth is that Hector almost bankrupted *her*."

Lady Harriet turned to her hostess. "I can only apologize on behalf of my family, my lady, for the common nature of those who were once, unfortunately, linked to the Smythe-Harding name."

Carenza set down her fork. "Will you excuse me for a moment, ma'am?" She left the dining room with her usual calm demeanor.

Julian waited until the conversation changed to something less fractious and slipped out of the room, murmuring that he needed to speak to the butler. He found Carenza in one of the parlors, her back turned, her shoulders shaking as she stared out of the window. He shut the door behind him.

"My dear girl . . . you can't let that woman upset you." He reached her side and turned her around. He was both shocked and pleased to discover she was not crying but rather laughing like a maniac.

"This is ridiculous," she breathed. "I keep wanting to laugh because she cannot bear to be bested."

Julian chuckled as he gathered her into his arms and kissed the top of her head. "She's even shut up my mother. Inviting Lady Harriet was a masterstroke my brother doesn't even realize he created. I must remember to congratulate him." He slid his fingers under Carenza's chin so that she had to look up at him. "Are you really all right?"

"I am. There is nothing Lady Harriet could say that could hurt me more than Hector already has." Her gaze was clear.

He kissed her, and she kissed him back. The clock on the mantelpiece chimed the quarter hour, and he reluctantly drew back. "Will you meet me tomorrow at the usual place at twelve?" he asked.

"I thought we were done with all that."

He frowned. "Whatever gave you that idea?"

"*You* did."

"I merely suggested we needed to be careful. Mrs. Mountjoy's house is the epitome of discretion."

"You also suggested I expected too much of you."

"Everyone does." He smiled. "You should hear my mother on the subject."

She studied him for a long moment and then looked toward the door. "I should get back."

He took her hand. "How much will you wager me that Allegra and Lady Harriet are still at it?"

"I'm hoping your mother will regain control of the conversation and shut them both up," Carenza said.

"I'm not sure if that's possible. But I suspect she'll try."

They reentered the dining room separately as Julian needed to find the butler and resumed their seats. It quickly became obvious that his mother was pointedly ignoring her guests and speaking solely to Aragon, while Lady Harriet and Allegra glared at each other over their plates of lamb shanks in parsley sauce.

"Did I miss anything?" Julian whispered to Allegra as one of the footmen replenished all the wineglasses.

"Not particularly."

"It's a shame Mrs. Sheraton isn't here," Julian said.

"Only if you wanted to see pure carnage over the dinner table. Olivia would never allow Carenza to be insulted like that."

"You're doing a good job of defending her yourself, my lady."

"Thank you." Allegra frowned. "Carenza has a tendency to be too nice, but luckily I don't have the same restraint."

The lamb was removed and replaced by the fish course along with a change of wine. Aragon began loudly quizzing the new earl about his stables, which meant Lady Harriet had a chance to regroup and attack again. Carenza wasn't sure how she felt about the whole ridiculous evening. Instinct told her to leave and that to engage in further conversation with Lady Harriet would only make matters worse. But she couldn't abandon her sister, in case she destroyed her own social reputation along with Carenza's.

One part of her, the quiescent wife, the woman who had always looked the other way and smoothed things over, was desperate to make things right, while the new Carenza relished a fight where nothing was left unsaid and her enemies were destroyed in front of her eyes.

"Did you ever find the jewelry that was missing from the Smythe-Harding vault?" Lady Harriet asked Carenza.

"I can't say that I considered it my concern," Carenza replied, her desire to leave deserting her. "You've already been through my jewelry collection."

"I was trying to give you the benefit of the doubt," Lady Harriet said. "My husband said I should not have called you out in public for your thievery, but I won't apologize."

Carenza looked at Lady Harriet, aware that anything she

said wouldn't satisfy her inquisitor. The new countess had taken against her before they had even met.

"I suspect you are the kind of woman who rarely apologizes for anything, ma'am."

"That is because I am invariably proved right," Lady Harriet said.

"If you truly want to know where the rest of the jewelry is, you should inquire at the more upmarket pawnshops and work your way down to the less reputable shops." Carenza paused. "Of course, if you'd consulted Mr. Hoskins, he could probably have told you exactly where Hector had disposed of the jewelry. Hoskins was very close with Hector."

"I doubt your former husband was friends with a servant."

"Hector, for all his faults, was devoted to those he considered his friends. He grew up with Mr. Hoskins, and Hoskins remained loyal to him even during the worst of times. If Hector wanted to pawn something, he would've taken Mr. Hoskins along with him. Perhaps if you wrote to him, he might help you."

"I have no idea where the man is, and I doubt he could assist me, anyway."

Carenza frowned. "But Mr. Hoskins and his family had accommodation in one of the mews cottages behind the house. Did you evict them?"

"Of course I did."

Carenza stared at Lady Harriet. "Hoskins cared for his sick mother, and after his wife died, two of his daughters lived with him. One of them lost her husband at Waterloo."

"None of which is my concern." Lady Harriet poked her husband's shoulder as the footmen filled the table with desserts Carenza feared she'd be unable to eat. "She says she hasn't got any more of our jewelry."

The earl gave his wife a quick nod and tried to return to his conversation with his hostess, but Lady Harriet was having none of it. "She *says* Hector is responsible for the losses, but I doubt that."

"Hector?" Aragon joined the conversation. "That man would pawn anything if it gave him a few extra guineas at the gaming table." He laughed heartily. "I once saw him turn out his pockets, strip off his rings, and add his watch and chain just to win a bet on a card game. And he still lost." He turned to Carenza. "I don't know how you put up with him, ma'am."

Carenza smiled politely, but Aragon was in full flow.

"He wagered your favored mare on a race, didn't he?"

"Yes."

"And lost it, of course, because he was blind, reeling drunk at the time—begging your pardon, ladies—and shouldn't have been allowed near a gaming table or a racecourse."

"I'm sure he wasn't as bad as all that," the new earl said.

"Yes, he was." Aragon nodded. "An absolute wastrel."

Lady Harriet glanced pointedly at Carenza. "Perhaps he needed wiser guidance at home."

"No," Aragon said simply. "He was a bad man." He winked at Carenza. "That mare of mine you rode in the park the other day? I chose her specifically because she's descended from the same line as the one you lost."

"That was very kind of you, sir." Carenza smiled at him.

"It was nothing." Aragon looked embarrassed. "I just remember at the time thinking it wasn't right that Hector took away something you loved."

Lady Isobel cleared her throat. "Would the ladies like to join me in the drawing room and leave the gentlemen to their port?"

Carenza would much rather have stayed with the gentlemen, but she rose to her feet and dutifully followed the countess to the rather chilly drawing room. It was decorated in shades of the palest blue and cream, rather like a Wedgewood dish. Carenza wouldn't mention that bit of whimsy to her hostess. Lady Isobel's dislike of Carenza perhaps rivaled Lady Harriet's.

Carenza walked over to the window that overlooked the square. It was already dark, and a splattering of rain hit the square windowpanes and rattled the glass. She was tired of pretending that everything was fine and wished she could go home.

"Are you all right?" Allegra came to her side.

"I will be. I wish we hadn't come."

"I've quite enjoyed getting the best of Lady Harriet, and both of the Laurents have been resolute in their defense of you."

"Yes, they have."

"I know you cannot come to care for Aragon, but he is being remarkably sweet." Allegra lowered her voice. "Which hasn't gone down well with his mama. Brace yourself, sister. I suspect Lady Isobel has a few things to make clear to you as well."

Carenza squared her shoulders and went to join the other ladies, who were grouped around the fireplace.

Lady Isobel looked up as she approached. "Would you care for some tea, Lady Smythe-Harding?"

"Yes, please." Carenza took the tea and sat beside Allegra on the couch farthest away from the meager warmth of the fire.

"Surely that is my title now," Lady Harriet piped up.

"I suppose it is." Lady Isobel's expression indicated that she didn't seem enamored of the new countess, either. "I should have added the dowager part."

"There is no need," Carenza said. "In fact, I've reverted to using my maiden name and prefer Lady Carenza."

"That's rather modern of you," Lady Isobel commented. "Are you one of those women who think they are equal to men?"

"Equal?" Allegra raised her eyebrows. "In my opinion, women are far superior altogether!"

"I believe we all have different strengths that complement each other." Carenza attempted to diffuse her sister's inflammatory comment.

"I'm glad to hear it," Lady Isobel said. "One does wonder what values are shared in an unconventional family such as yours."

Carenza's head began to ache. Allegra cleared her throat, and Carenza kicked her in the ankle.

"Don't," Carenza murmured. "It's not worth it."

"As you wish." Allegra scowled at her and sipped her tea as Lady Isobel drew the other ladies into a discussion about their "good works."

Soon, Lady Harriet's gaze fastened on Carenza. "Are you sure those earrings are yours?"

Carenza repressed the desire to scream and concentrated on projecting calm as Lady Harriet sprang to her feet and stalked over to her.

She pointed her finger far too close to Carenza's face. "Take them off. I wish to examine them more closely."

Carenza rose to her feet. She was a good deal taller than the other woman and intended to use that height to her advantage. "I will do no such thing. These earrings were a present from my father on my twenty-first birthday."

"I doubt that."

Carenza locked gazes with the infuriated countess. "You are embarrassing yourself in front of your hostess, ma'am. You should apologize and resume your seat."

"Take them off!" She lunged at Carenza.

Allegra stepped between them and shoved Lady Harriet. The countess clutched at her chest and screeched so loudly Carenza had an urge to cover her ears.

"I've been assaulted! Help! Fetch the Watch!"

Lady Isobel approached, her stern gaze on Lady Harriet.

"You are hysterical. I will ask your husband to take you home." She paused. "And do not expect an invitation to this house ever again."

There was a clapping sound from the doorway. It appeared the gentlemen and the butler had been observing the scene.

Aragon strode forward. "I quite agree, Mother. Smythe-Harding? Please collect your wife. She is behaving appallingly."

Tobias rushed over to his wife and grabbed her arm. "Come along, dear."

"But she assaulted me!"

"I didn't see anything." Julian looked around the room. "Did anyone else?" Everyone shook their heads, and Julian smiled at Lady Harriet. "Perhaps you have imbibed too much wine, ma'am, and would do better to seek your bed at home. A letter of apology to my mother in the morning should suffice to cover your embarrassing behavior."

He stood back as Tobias escorted his still-protesting wife out of the room.

Julian went over to Allegra and bowed. "I almost wish you'd planted her a facer."

"I did consider it," Allegra allowed. "But I was trying to be polite."

"I would like to go home," Carenza said, aware that her voice was trembling. "Will you come with me, Allegra?"

"Yes." Allegra firmly linked their arms, and they walked over to their stony-faced hostess. "Thank you for an enjoyable evening, Lady Isobel." Allegra turned to Aragon. "And thank you for the invitation."

"It was great fun!" Aragon said. "We should do it again soon, don't you think, Mother?"

Chapter 13

The last thing Carenza wanted to do on the day after the dinner party was to traipse over to Mrs. Mountjoy's. Her inclination was to hide in her bed and not see anyone, but Allegra had other ideas. She marched into Carenza's bedchamber full of determination and unwilling to listen to excuses.

"You can't stay in bed. I've invited Miss Cartwright to visit us this morning."

"You're perfectly capable of dealing with her yourself," Carenza pointed out.

"But I need you to be there."

"Why?"

"Because your opinion is important to me."

Carenza groaned and flopped back onto her pillows, but Allegra didn't go away.

"Come on, Carenza, don't be such a wet blanket. We've faced far worse than that obnoxious Lady Harriet."

"Don't forget Lady Isobel."

"Yes, I got the distinct impression that she had no idea that her son had invited us to dinner."

"I suspect you're right."

Carenza's maid appeared in the door and smiled at her mistress. "Lady Allegra said you'd be wanting your bath, ma'am. It's all ready for you."

"Thank you." Carenza gave her sister a look of loathing as she got out of bed. "You are far too managing."

"Someone has to be." Allegra smiled triumphantly. "I'll see you in the small parlor at ten. Miss Cartwright can offer us only an hour of her extremely valuable time."

Carenza deliberately lingered over her breakfast and arrived at the parlor at five minutes past the hour to find Allegra already in conversation with Miss Cartwright. Her sister looked at the clock as Carenza came to shake Miss Cartwright's hand.

"Now we can get on." Allegra opened her notebook. "I hope you don't mind, Miss Cartwright, but I have a few questions about your charity."

"My brother is more knowledgeable about the financial standing of our endeavor, but I will do my best to answer you." Miss Cartwright clasped her hands together on her lap and sat up straight. She wore a plain black gown with no adornment apart from two silver buttons at the throat. Her bonnet was also black but had weathered in patches to a dull gray where it had no doubt been much exposed to the weather.

Carenza had yet to see her smile, but she had a calmness about her that spoke of a determination Carenza could only admire.

"Can you tell me where the initial funding for your charity came from?" Allegra asked.

"I'm not sure how that is relevant to our current discussion," Miss Cartwright said.

"How can it not be relevant?" Allegra raised her eyebrows. "A firm financial footing is essential for any foundation."

Miss Cartwright sighed. "My brother received an inheritance from a relative."

"And that was sufficient to buy your current premises and begin your work?"

"Not quite. I also received a payment in lieu of a dowry from my father."

"How on earth did you manage to persuade a man to do that?" Allegra asked.

A small smile flickered on Miss Cartwright's lips. "Downright disobedience and a refusal to participate in society. My parents have two other daughters to marry off. In the end, I believe they were quite happy to see the back of me and my brother, who is the third of four sons."

"That is something of an accomplishment," Allegra agreed. "I don't think our father would agree to such an arrangement, do you, Carenza?"

"Your father probably cares about you," Miss Cartwright said. "Mine was not interested in his daughters. He considered us a burden."

"That's . . . sad," Carenza said.

Miss Cartwright's expression turned icy. "I consider it a blessing, my lady, as it allowed me to do the work I knew I was destined for."

"And by all accounts you do it very well," Carenza hastened to reassure her. "Mr. Laurent thinks very highly of you indeed."

"Very highly," Allegra repeated as Miss Cartwright's color rose. "He sings your praises on every occasion he can."

"Mr. Laurent has been a generous benefactor to our school and mission," Miss Cartwright conceded.

"He's very handsome, too, isn't he?" Allegra said.

Carenza shot her a look. "That's hardly relevant to our current discussion, sister. Perhaps you should move on to your next question."

Precisely at eleven, Miss Cartwright rose to her feet. She'd refused their offer of refreshments but had agreed to take a batch of Cook's scones back to the school for the boys' tea.

"I'll just fetch you the scones," Carenza said after shaking Miss Cartwright's hand. "Would you care to accompany me in my carriage? I have business near Grosvenor Square this morning, and I'm more than happy to drop you back to the school."

"That would be most kind of you." Miss Cartwright looked out at the sullen gray skies. "I forgot my umbrella, and I fear it is about to rain."

Five minutes into their journey, Miss Cartwright cleared her throat and looked across at Carenza. "I would appreciate your advice, ma'am."

"Mine?" Carenza was startled. "Yes, of course. How may I help you?"

"Your sister implied that Mr. Laurent's interest in me is more than his desire to do good works. I refute that claim entirely. I have never encouraged any familiarity from him or from any other benefactor of our school."

"I'm sure you haven't, Miss Cartwright."

"Then should I say something to him? He is doing an admirable job as our treasurer." For the first time she looked remarkably unsure of herself.

"Mr. Laurent would never use his position to pressure or persuade you to do anything against your inclinations, Miss Cartwright," Carenza said gently. "He does admire you, but he also respects your work. I am certain he won't make demands you are unwilling to meet."

Miss Cartwright nodded. "Thank you. I will resist the temptation to mention his behavior to him." She looked out the window, indicating the conversation was at an end.

The traffic was busy, and the carriage moved slowly between the brewery carts, hackney cabs, street hawkers, and pedestrians.

Miss Cartwright turned to Carenza. "Would it be convenient for you to let me off at Grosvenor Square rather than the school itself?"

"Yes, of course," Carenza said.

When they finally turned into the square, Carenza rapped on the roof with her umbrella, and the carriage drew to a stop.

Moments later, her coachman appeared at the door. "Are you alighting here, my lady?"

"Miss Cartwright is leaving us, Owens," Carenza explained. "You can continue on to the usual street once she's gone."

"Thank you, Lady Carenza," Miss Cartwright said before Owens helped her from the carriage.

Carenza leaned out of the window. "Here, take my umbrella."

Miss Cartwright paused. "If you and Lady Allegra do decide to invest in our school, we would be honored to accept your help."

Carenza smiled. "Good morning, Miss Cartwright."

She closed the door and sat back. Julian might not appreciate Miss Cartwright confiding in her, but she couldn't have picked a better person to reveal her concerns to. Julian's interest in Miss Cartwright didn't surprise Carenza. He had always appreciated an intelligent woman. She had no intention of mentioning the conversation to him and simply hoped she had alleviated Miss Cartwright's concerns.

As the carriage drew to a stop at the back of Mrs. Mountjoy's house, Carenza gathered her skirts, made sure she had her reticule, and descended the step with Owens's assistance.

"I'll only be an hour," she said. "You can wait for me in the nearest inn."

"Yes, my lady."

She made sure to keep out of the way of the turning carriage and went into Mrs. Mountjoy's garden. Just as she reached the back door, someone else came through the gate. She looked over her shoulder and went still as Miss Cartwright stared at her with equal surprise.

"What . . . are you doing here?" Miss Cartwright asked.

As Carenza tried to think of a response, Mrs. Mountjoy appeared at the back door.

Carenza felt somewhat relieved when Mrs. Mountjoy greeted them both and said, "She's here for the same reason you are, Miss Cartwright. To help my girls. Won't you both come into my parlor and have a cup of tea?"

Five minutes later, they were sitting opposite each other in the cozy parlor. "I should've realized you knew of Mrs. Mountjoy's good works," Miss Cartwright said after sipping her tea. "Did Mr. Laurent tell you?"

"Yes, he did," Carenza said. "If I'd known you were coming here . . ."

"You wouldn't have dropped me off in Grosvenor Square." Miss Cartwright put down her cup. "It's quite all right, Lady Carenza. I just thought it would be easier for your coachman if he didn't have to navigate these smaller streets." She paused. "It wasn't an attempt to disguise my intended purpose. I have no shame in supporting and visiting Mrs. Mountjoy."

"I'm glad to hear it," Mrs. Mountjoy said. "Mr. Laurent did mention that he'd taken you to visit the Cartwrights, Lady Carenza. So I'm not surprised you both turned up on the same day." She looked over at Miss Cartwright. "Lady Carenza is thinking of taking one of my girls into her household."

"That's correct." Carenza nodded. "We were supposed to be considering who would be the best candidate today."

"I'd highly recommend Bridget," Miss Cartwright said. "She's as bright as a button and very keen to learn."

"I'd agree," Mrs. Mountjoy said.

The door opened again, and Julian came in. His startled gaze flew from Miss Cartwright to Carenza and back again.

"Ladies." He bowed. "What an unexpected pleasure."

"Mr. Laurent." Mrs. Mountjoy rose to greet him, her expression far calmer than Carenza's would've been if she'd had to deal with such a scenario. "I am blessed to have so many visitors in one morning. How may I assist you?"

"I was just passing by, ma'am," Julian replied with remarkable aplomb. "I will not stay if you are busy."

"Oh, please join us," Carenza said, and patted the seat beside her. "We were just discussing whether Bridget would be a good choice for my new kitchen maid."

"I think she would be an admirable choice," Julian said. "What do you think, Miss Cartwright?"

"I suspect my opinion is irrelevant, sir. Mrs. Mountjoy knows her best."

Carenza was pleased to see the younger woman betrayed no agitation at Julian's appearance. In truth, she appeared as disinterested as ever. Was that what made her appealing to Julian? Her lack of interest in a man who was normally surrounded by women who doted on him? To her surprise, the idea of his marrying Miss Cartwright did not appeal.

"Perhaps I might interview Bridget, ma'am?" Carenza suggested. "And then you could bring her to Tavistock Square to see how she likes it."

"That's an excellent suggestion," Mrs. Mountjoy said.

"And, in the meantime, if Miss Cartwright doesn't object, I could take her home in my carriage," Julian said. "It is starting to rain quite heavily."

Miss Cartwright took a letter out of her reticule and handed it to Mrs. Mountjoy. "I only came to deliver this, ma'am. If Mr. Laurent is willing to drive me home, I will gratefully accept."

She stood up to leave. Before Julian escorted her to the door, he looked over at Carenza, his eyebrows raised in an intimidating manner. Obviously, he expected her to remain at Mrs. Mountjoy's until he returned, but her frustration at the way matters had turned out left her reluctant to offer him that reassurance, so she ignored him.

Mrs. Mountjoy waited until the door closed behind two

of her guests before sitting down quite heavily on the couch. "That was worthy of a Drury Lane farce. The look on Mr. Laurent's face when he first came in . . ."

"I quite agree," Carenza said. "You handled it very well, ma'am."

"As the wife of a physician, I am used to dealing with difficult moments, Lady Carenza." Mrs. Mountjoy poured Carenza a second cup of tea. "You don't have to interview Bridget. She has no idea that I'm looking for a position for her."

"We do have a vacancy in the summer," Carenza said. "If you truly think she would suit, I'd be more than willing to speak to her about the position."

"Then I'll go and fetch her." Mrs. Mountjoy gave Carenza an approving smile. "I suspect she'll be thrilled."

Julian seated himself opposite Miss Cartwright and waited until she settled her skirts before telling his coachman to proceed. He made no effort to initiate any conversation until it dawned on him that if he didn't speak, she'd be happy to pass the entire journey in silence.

"Mrs. Mountjoy is an estimable woman," he said.

"Yes, indeed."

"I remember her husband very well."

She nodded and continued to look out the window, her hands clasped tightly together on her lap.

"I do so admire women who do good works," Julian persevered.

"I admire anyone who lives by their Bible, sir."

He smiled. "If you know my reputation, you must consider me something of a sinner, then, Miss Cartwright."

"With respect, I have no knowledge of you outside your work with our school, where you perform an exemplary job."

"And, I assume, you have no desire to know more about me."

She looked him right in the eye. "Not at all, sir."

"I see."

She returned her gaze to the window. "We're almost there. You don't need to come in with me, Mr. Laurent. I'm perfectly capable."

"I'm well aware of that, Miss Cartwright." He thumped on the roof as they came alongside the high walls of the institution and the coachman stopped. "Do you require an umbrella?"

"I have one." She brandished it like a weapon as she struggled with the latch on the door.

"Be careful—" Julian made the mistake of leaning forward to help her just as his coachman released the latch from the outside. With a gasp, Miss Cartwright fell out into his servant's arms, and Julian's forehead received a blow from the sharp end of the umbrella.

Miss Cartwright and his coachman didn't appear to notice as they sorted themselves out and shut the carriage door. Julian sat alone in the silence, one hand pressed to his temple. When he drew it away, his fingers were covered in blood. With a curse, he found his handkerchief and pressed it over the throbbing wound. He sat back as a vague dizzy feeling engulfed him and ordered himself sternly not to faint.

He realized they were back at Mrs. Mountjoy's only when his coachman opened the door and gawped at him.

"What happened to you, sir?"

"Umbrella," Julian said as he got out. "You can go home, Bert."

"But what about your head?"

"I'll ask Mrs. Mountjoy to help me," Julian said. "Now, please go." He headed toward Mrs. Mountjoy's front door.

Bridget opened the door to him and immediately started screeching, which wasn't helpful. "Mrs. Mountjoy! He's bloody bleeding!"

There was a flurry of activity in the hall behind her, and Carenza and Mrs. Mountjoy appeared.

"Well, don't let him drip blood over my newly cleaned doorstep!" Mrs. Mountjoy said. "Let him in. Take him to the kitchen, and I'll fetch my supplies."

Julian blinked as he took an unsteady step forward. "There's no need to fuss."

"What happened?" Carenza demanded as she took his arm and marched him down the hall toward the kitchen.

"What do you think?"

She made him sit on a chair. "Were you attacked?"

"In a manner of speaking."

"Were you robbed?"

"Only of my dignity."

Carenza placed her hands on either arm of the chair and stared into his eyes. "What. Happened?"

"I had an unfortunate collision with an umbrella."

Her expression changed. "Someone hit you? Not Miss Cartwright."

He looked at her.

"You didn't attempt to—"

"Damnation, Carenza! What do you take me for?"

She raised her eyebrows.

"I don't go around forcing myself on innocents!" He briefly closed his eyes, but that made things even worse. "As she got out of the carriage, the end of her umbrella caught my head."

"That doesn't make much more sense than your first answer, but I'll allow it because you are obviously suffering." Carenza gently raised his chin, angling his face toward the light. "Head wounds always look worse than they are because of the blood."

"That's correct." Mrs. Mountjoy spoke as she came to look down at Julian. "I'll clean out the wound, and then we'll see if we need to call a physician." She washed her hands and rolled up her sleeves in a rather ominous fashion.

"You are a physician," Julian grumbled.

"Not according to the law," Mrs. Mountjoy said. "Women aren't supposed to be capable of such advanced thinking."

His breath hissed out as she cleaned the wound with rather too much vigor for his liking.

"It's a remarkably small cut," she announced.

"You sound disappointed, ma'am."

"I was quite enjoying the thought of stitching the wound. I've not had much practice recently."

"That's hardly a good advertisement for your skills, Mrs. Mountjoy," Julian grumbled. "I have a terrible headache."

"I'm not surprised." Carenza gently stroked his hair. "Perhaps I should take him home in my carriage?"

"That's an excellent idea," Mrs. Mountjoy said. "And make sure you put him straight to bed."

Twenty minutes later, Carenza descended from her carriage and approached the front door of Julian's town house. She'd visited the house only once, when he'd first moved in and held a party to celebrate. Even though she was a widow, it still wasn't acceptable for ladies to visit unmarried men at home without a chaperone.

She knocked on the door and waited until the butler opened it.

"May I help you, Lady Smythe-Harding? If you are after Mr. Laurent, I regret to inform you that he isn't home."

"I know exactly where he is," Carenza pointed at her carriage. "He's in there. I'll just go and fetch him."

The butler followed her to the carriage and peered inside. Julian was propped in the corner, his eyes half-closed, his clothes ruined.

"Mr. Laurent! What happened!"

He opened one eye fully and regarded his butler. "Don't shout. I'm perfectly fine. I just had a little run in with an umbrella."

"Can you get out of the carriage yourself, Mr. Laurent, or do you require our assistance?" Carenza asked.

"I'm perfectly capable," Julian said as he levered himself out of the seat. "A change of clothes and a short nap will cure all my ills."

He staggered slightly as his booted feet hit the cobbled street, and Carenza and the butler rushed to steady him. His frosty glare persuaded the butler to stand back, but Carenza wasn't deterred.

"Lean on me, sir." She glanced over at the butler. "Can you direct me to Mr. Laurent's bedchamber? I will make sure he is settled and relay the physician's instructions to you."

"Yes, my lady." The butler hovered behind them as they went up the stairs. "I'll go and find Mr. Proctor, sir."

Carenza went into Julian's bedchamber and found it just as elegant as she'd imagined. She steered him toward a chair beside the marble fireplace, made sure he was seated, and stood back.

"I wish you could undress me and put me to bed," he murmured as he looked up at her.

"And scandalize your staff?" She raised her eyebrows. "I thought we were all about discretion."

"You could kiss everything better."

Carenza snorted. "In your current state you are of no use to me at all, Mr. Laurent."

He sighed. "I fear you are right."

She glanced around before bending to kiss him very carefully on the mouth. "I do want you."

"Don't say that."

"But it's the truth." She smiled at him. "I'll have to find another way to satisfy my . . . needs."

He scowled at her and then winced. "Don't you dare."

"I wasn't thinking of taking another lover," she said. "I am perfectly capable of taking care of myself."

"Carenza . . . you are driving me mad."

"Good." She kissed him again. "And now I must go before I scandalize your entire street by leaving my carriage outside your door. Let me know when you have recovered sufficiently to be visited."

He caught hold of her hand. "You don't seriously believe I behaved badly with Miss Cartwright, do you?"

"Of course not. My annoyance at your injury is purely selfish."

A tall, thin man in a black coat came into the room and drew a sharp breath. "Mr. Laurent! Your cravat and shirt are ruined."

"I'm glad to see you getting your priorities in order, Proctor." Julian looked at Carenza. "Note how he doesn't bemoan my horrific injuries first."

"The bandage Mrs. Mountjoy put on you masks your wounds," Carenza said. "And you're still upright and talking." She smiled at the valet. "May I suggest you get Mr. Laurent into bed as soon as possible, give him some laudanum, and let him sleep until he feels more the thing?"

"Yes, my lady." Proctor bowed. "I'll keep an eye on him, don't you worry."

Carenza left the room, her anxiety for Julian assuaged by the obvious competency of his staff. She paused in the hall to reissue Mrs. Mountjoy's instructions to the butler as to when to call his physician if things got worse, and then returned to her carriage.

Carenza sat back and blew out her breath. Her day had not proceeded quite as she had anticipated, and now she would have to wait until Julian was well enough to continue their liaison. A smile curved her lips. Who would've imagined that the process of acquiring a lover—and actually managing to have sex—would be so complicated?

Chapter 14

"How did you get a black eye?" Aragon asked as he followed Julian into their box at the theater. "I thought you were considered a competent boxer."

"I am."

Julian took a moment to look around the growing audience and hoped his appearance wouldn't cause as much comment as he feared. His guests hadn't yet arrived. As expected, his mother had declined his invitation to attend, insisting that she preferred to rent her own box when necessary.

"Then what happened?"

Julian had forgotten how dogged his brother could be when he latched on to something. "All I can say is beware of ladies attempting to open umbrellas in closed carriages."

"Ouch." Aragon made a face.

"Indeed."

"Who was the lady?" Aragon chose the best seat in the box and sat down. For once, Julian didn't mind, because he'd already decided to sit out of the sight of any but the most determined viewer. "Anyone I know?"

"No," Julian said. "And, as she was unaware that she had caused me any injury, I'll keep her name to myself."

"That's probably best," Aragon agreed. "You don't want to appear any more foolish than you already do."

The door to the box opened, and Allegra came in followed by Carenza, Mrs. Sheraton, and Mrs. Cooper.

Julian bowed. "Good evening, ladies." He waited for a moment as they all studied him intently, then he raised his hand to touch the scar on his forehead. "As you can see, I am quite well."

"Apart from that black eye," Mrs. Sheraton said.

Julian shrugged. "A mere nothing."

"Lover's quarrel?" She looked over at Carenza.

"I told you what happened, Olivia." Carenza approached Julian and smiled at him. "Good evening, sir. I am glad to see you in good health."

His gaze drifted down from her face to her bosom, which was magnificently displayed in a gown of cream patterned muslin edged with gold lace. The sudden burst of lust that ran through him reminded him that he hadn't had the pleasure of bedding her for far too long and that he wanted her very badly.

"Good evening, my lady." He brought her gloved hand to his lips and deliberately bit her knuckles. Her eyes widened, and she uttered a little gasp that did nothing to suppress his desire. "Always a pleasure."

"Not often enough," she murmured. "But we persevere."

He turned to greet Lady Allegra, who winked at him and immediately went over to speak to Aragon. Mrs. Cooper looked rather miserable.

"Is Mr. Cooper coming?" Julian asked.

"No, he's still at work," Mrs. Cooper said. "He sent his apologies."

"Perhaps he'll be able to come next time," Julian said.

"I doubt it," Mrs. Cooper said flatly. "His work is too important for him to indulge in such frivolity."

Julian was far too adroit to involve himself in a matrimonial dispute and merely smiled. He pulled out a chair for

Mrs. Cooper next to Lady Allegra and Aragon in the front row, then steered Carenza toward the seat next to his in the second row with Mrs. Sheraton settling on the other side of him. The loud conversations in the theater dimmed when the director of the opera came out to announce that they were ready to begin. Some of the candles were extinguished, leaving the stage illuminated in the darkness.

He loved opera, but tonight his interests would be focused in his own box and not on the stage. He angled his chair away from Mrs. Sheraton's until his knee brushed against Carenza's. She stiffened as he placed his hand on her thigh, his fingers tightening as he caressed her through the thin fabric of her dress and petticoat. He slid one arm along the back of her chair, his fingertips brushing the back of her neck and the lace of her bodice as he leaned in close.

"I burn for you," he breathed against her skin.

She shivered, her fingers closing over his hand on her thigh, whether to embrace his ardor or to forestall it, he wasn't yet sure.

He winced as Mrs. Sheraton jabbed him in the ribs with her fan and hissed. "If you intend to become amorous, might I ask that you find somewhere else to cling to each other? I was rather hoping to enjoy the opera."

"I do beg your pardon," Julian murmured.

He took Carenza's hand and led her out of the box, noticing only Allegra's startled face before he shut the door behind them. He pulled Carenza into a small anteroom behind the box, where refreshments would be served at the interval. After locking the door, he practically flattened Carenza against the wall.

"This is becoming a habit," he whispered as he rucked up her skirts. "But I cannot wait any longer."

As her fingers were already frantically undoing his breeches, he guessed she had no objection to being taken against the wall and acted accordingly. The moment she released his cock he lifted her up and over it. She stifled a scream against his shoulder as she sank fully onto him and immediately climaxed.

He stayed still, his cock desperate to join her, resisting temptation until she'd finished. Then he took advantage of her suddenly weakened state to fuck her as roughly as he could. He came fast and groaned through his teeth, aware that they were not really alone and that anyone who came in would know exactly what they'd been doing.

Her grip on his hair relaxed, and he set her down on her feet, steadying her as she rocked toward him. He wanted to gather her up in his arms, take her to his carriage and then to his bed, and emerge only after they'd worn each other out. His cock filled again and he reluctantly pulled free of her.

She leaned her forehead against his shoulder, her breasts heaving as he found his handkerchief, cleaned himself off, and then pressed the folded cotton gently between her legs. She drew a shuddering breath.

"I'll go to the retiring room and set myself to rights."

"Yes."

She left him leaning against the wall, listening vaguely to the sounds of the soprano on the stage as he calculated when his guests would be expecting refreshments at the interval. A sense of dissatisfaction enveloped him. He wanted more than quick, hurried couplings in inconvenient places. He wanted a large bed equipped with a naked Carenza and no interruptions for a week. He wanted to make her scream and not stifle her cries in case they were heard.

"You are behaving like a lovesick youth," he scolded himself out loud. "Not a sophisticated, discreet, renowned lover of women."

"Sounding a little conceited there, Mr. Laurent," Mrs. Sheraton spoke from behind him. "And what have you done with Carenza?"

"I believe she's gone to the retiring room." Julian turned to face her.

"May I make a suggestion?" Mrs. Sheraton looked at him. "I'll tell your other guests that Carenza isn't feeling well and that you have taken her home. What you do with that time is up to you as long as you get her back to Tavistock Square before Allegra notices she isn't there."

He stared at her and then nodded. "Yes, thank you."

"I'll take care of the others," Mrs. Sheraton said. "I do hope you've provided refreshments so that we don't have to mingle."

"They will be delivered promptly to this room at the interval," Julian promised.

Carenza arrived and went still as she saw Mrs. Sheraton. "Olivia . . ."

Mrs. Sheraton looked at Julian. "She does look rather flushed. You are right to take her home." She winked at Carenza. "Don't worry. I'll keep Allegra occupied until you return to Tavistock Square."

"Thank you." Carenza kissed Mrs. Sheraton's cheek. "I'll get my cloak."

Minutes later, they left the opera house and were ensconced in a hackney cab taking them back to Julian's house. He studied her in the dim light.

"I gave my staff the evening off, so we'll be quite alone."

"Oh, dear. How will we manage?" Carenza asked. "You'll have to help me disrobe."

"I had every intention of doing that anyway." His gaze flowed over her. "I haven't seen you naked for far too long."

She shifted slightly on the seat, aware of the wetness between her thighs and the throbbing of her flesh where he'd thrust into her so forcefully.

His eyes narrowed. "Don't do that."

She held his gaze and slowly licked her lips. "I'm just getting comfortable, sir. I am quite . . . sensitive."

"Was I too rough?"

"No. I rather liked it."

He groaned and looked out of the window. "This damn traffic. How long will it take to get to my bloody house?"

"We'll be there in five minutes, guv," the cabdriver shouted down to him. "Keep your powder dry."

Carenza hid a smile and looked at Julian. "If the floor were cleaner, I might consider going down on my knees, and—"

"Stop talking," Julian said through his teeth.

Luckily, for his sanity and hers, the cab soon arrived at the mews behind Julian's town house. He paid the driver and assisted Carenza down. He took her hand, marched her through the garden, and into the house. There was a single lamp burning in the kitchen, and the boot boy slept in his bed by the range. Light came from under the door to the butler's pantry, but no one came out to speak to them.

"Up the back stairs. It's quicker," Julian murmured.

She followed him up until he stopped, opened a door, and ushered her into a dark room which smelled reassuringly of him.

"Stay there."

She heard the rasp of a flint, and a candle flickered into life to reveal Julian on his knees turning his attention to the fireplace. She lit the remaining candles and discovered she was in the dressing room attached to his bedchamber. Ignoring his instructions to remain where she was, she took one of the candles and opened the door into his bedroom. The curtains were drawn, the fire was banked up for the night, and the bed was turned down, awaiting its occupant.

She took off her cloak and slippers and set them on one of the chairs beside the fireplace, her attention on the large mirror that reflected the bed and the man who was purposefully coming toward her. He stopped behind her, wrapped one arm around her waist, and yanked her hard against him.

"Do you ever listen to a thing I say to you?"

"Not if I can help it." She deliberately rubbed her bottom

against the hardness at her back. "I've never been very good at doing what I'm told."

"I'm beginning to remember that." He kissed the nape of her neck, and she shivered. "Perhaps I need to be more explicit about what I expect from you."

"And what do you expect?" Carenza asked.

"Obedience?"

He shoved his hand into her hair, dislodging half the pins, and wrapped the length around his fingers to draw her head back. The thrill that sang through her body released into a gasp as she arched against him.

"You're going to suck my cock."

"Am I?"

"Yes."

"Or. . . ?"

He looked at her in the mirror. "You can go home."

She considered him for a long moment. "Will you take my clothing off first?"

"Why?"

She enjoyed the flicker of interest in his eyes. "Because the thought of being fully naked while I pleasure you, and you are still dressed, excites me."

His breathing hitched. "Carenza—"

"You are supposed to be *my* lover, aren't you?" She slowly blinked at him. "But I promise I will be very amenable to your commands once you do as I ask."

His fingers tightened momentarily in her hair, and he cursed under his breath before unbuttoning the back of her gown. She helped him by stepping out of her dress and petticoats while he dealt with her stays and shift. When she was naked, she turned to face him. His expression was hard to read.

"Leave your stockings on."

"As you wish." She sank gracefully onto her knees. "May I begin?"

He nodded and moved the candelabra so they were bathed in its light.

His satin breeches were stretched tightly across the front where his cock strained to be freed. Carenza took her time unbuttoning his placket and pushing his shirt out of the way. She breathed in the hot, feral scent of his arousal and wrapped her fingers around the base of his thick shaft.

"No. Just your mouth. Put your hands behind your back."

The bite in his voice made everything inside her turn molten with the intense desire to please him. She licked his crown, which was already wet, and then carefully sucked the first few inches of his cock into her mouth.

"Take more."

She leaned in and swallowed him deeper, resisting the urge to gag as the head of his cock touched the back of her throat.

"That's better." He rolled his hips, pushing himself even farther in, and she closed her eyes to experience the sensation more clearly. "Now suck me hard."

She obliged, and his hand cupped the back of her head, holding her exactly where he wanted her. She forgot about everything but the feel of him and the way her body welcomed each demanding thrust.

"Play with your nipples."

She eagerly did as he commanded, aware that his cock was moving faster between her lips as he neared his climax, and that she no longer cared how deep he went as long as he never stopped.

"That's . . ." His hand flexed against her skull as the full length of his cock twitched, and he slammed into her, releasing a hot wave of come down her throat. She swallowed as fast as she could, unable to move as he had her locked against him.

Eventually, he loosened his grip, and she eased back, kissing his thigh as she looked up at him. He traced the edge of her mouth with his finger, and she licked her lips, catching the tip of his thumb, sucking it to make him shudder. She smiled, and his gaze narrowed.

"Did I please you, Mr. Laurent?"

He sat down in the nearest chair. "Come here."

"Why?"

"Because I haven't finished with you, yet."

She rose from her knees and walked over to him, aware of the steady throb of her own desire and her need for him to do something about it.

He pointed at his lap, and she raised an eyebrow. "I don't think you're ready for the next round, sir."

"Oh, this isn't for me." He paused. "Although, I have to admit I've been fantasizing about this since you first started arguing every point with me."

"What are your intentions?"

He wrapped an arm around her waist and tipped her over his lap.

"Oh."

He set his palm on her buttocks and spread his fingers wide. "You don't listen. You deliberately and wantonly entice me in the most inappropriate of circumstances, and then you demand I perform for you."

She settled herself more comfortably over his lap, the satin of his breeches soft against her skin.

"You have nothing to say?" he asked. "No apologies?"

The slap of his hand on her flesh was sharp but not unpleasant. Carenza considered the tingling sensation and how wonderfully it concentrated her attention.

"I'm not apologizing for anything," she said. "You understood the rules when you agreed to become my lover."

His hand came down again on her other buttock, and he settled into a relentless rhythm that made her squirm and roll her hips. Yes, it stung, but it also did something very peculiar to her level of desire, which was now concentrating in her already swollen clit.

"That's . . ." She breathed hard as she started to tremble.

He paused, his fingers sliding between her legs. "You're soaking," he said roughly as he pinched her clit.

She came, her breathing a jumbled mess, her heart racing. "Then do something about it," she gasped.

"You'll wait until I'm ready," he said. "Or until you beg."

"You . . . bastard." Carenza tried to roll off his lap, but he easily prevented her.

He stood up with her in his arms and dropped her in the middle of his bed. She gasped, and he quickly followed her down. One of his hands trapped both her wrists as he straddled her. There was a glint in his blue eyes that made her nervous but was also extremely arousing.

He ripped off his cravat and tied it around her wrists before securing the other end to the headboard.

"Just to keep you quiet for a moment, ma'am."

She kicked out at him, but he easily avoided her foot. She went still as he leaned in and kissed her hard.

"I'd gag you, but I might need your mouth to pleasure my cock."

"You—" She tried to bite him.

He laughed and sat back, stripping off his coat and waistcoat and then pulling his shirt over his head.

She sighed with pleasure as his lean torso was revealed, her gaze lowering to where his cock was already pushing against the confines of his open breeches.

"You can sigh all you like, madam, but you're not getting fucked until I decide whether you deserve it."

"And what might I have to do to earn that honor?" Carenza inquired.

He raised an eyebrow as he shucked off his breeches and stockings. "I've already told you. You beg."

"Untie me, and I'll think about it."

"No."

"I can pleasure you far better with the use of my hands."

"But this isn't about my pleasure, is it?" He kissed her nipple. "As you keep reminding me, it's all about you."

The flash of pure frustration in Carenza's eyes, along with a dash of murder, was almost worth all his frustrations—the nights when he'd had to stroke his cock to completion while thinking of her, the opportunities he'd turned down simply because his body didn't seem to want anyone but her. It was enough to drive a man to drink, and he felt he deserved a little revenge.

Having the woman he desired sprawled naked on his bed with her hands tied to his headboard was just as delightful as he'd imagined. He ran his fingers down over her breasts, traced the curve of her hips, and returned to her face where she was now scowling.

"Is something wrong?" he asked as he lightly caressed her.

"You know what I want, Julian," Carenza said with far too much composure for his liking.

"I know what you like." He kissed her hard nipple and then licked it until she shuddered. "I'm just not willing to give it to you yet."

In truth, he didn't want to give in to his *own* desires to treat her exactly as she wanted because he enjoyed it too much. He might lose his much-vaunted control, and then where would they be? In heaven? In hell? He wasn't sure he wanted to find out.

Carenza moved restlessly against the sheets, one of her thighs falling open to expose her most intimate secrets. Julian couldn't look away from the swell of her clit and the wetness tangled with her damp hair. He wanted to lick it all off and fill her again. He reminded himself to stay in control and not let Carenza goad him into behaviors he might later regret. She looked at him from under her lashes and breathed his name.

Damnation.

He lowered his head and sucked her clit into his mouth,

making her scream. He raised his head to look at her. "That's better."

When she growled, he cocked an eyebrow.

"Do I have to tie your ankles as well?"

She considered him, her gaze sultry, the hint of release already flushing her cheeks, and he realized he'd made a tactical error. She was willing to try whatever he suggested, and, if he did tie her up and had the freedom to roam over her body, he might never let her go.

"Alas, I have nothing to bind you with." He caressed her ankle.

"You could use my stockings."

"I think not." He let his fingers drift from her ankle up to her knee and beyond. "You're very wet."

"I wonder why."

He cupped her mound, and she shivered as he thumbed her clit. "I'm beginning to reconsider the gag." He thrust three fingers gently inside her in a slow, shallow rhythm that he knew would frustrate her greatly.

"You like me arguing with you."

"Whatever gave you that idea? I prefer my women to be silently in awe of my lovemaking skills."

"If that's the case, they'd probably fall asleep."

He stopped moving, and she made a face.

"I'll withdraw that remark if you'll just get on with it and prove what a spectacular lover you are supposed to be."

He added another finger and continued his slow thrust and withdrawal until she was writhing against the sheets in a most satisfactory manner.

"Was there something you wished to say to me, Carenza?" He brushed his thumb against her clit with just enough pressure to pleasure her but not enough to let her come. "I am more than willing to listen to you beg."

"Fine." She glared at him. "You win."

"I always do, ma'am, but that's not what I want to hear

from you right now." He smiled sympathetically at her. "I know that you have impeccable manners when you choose to use them."

He allowed his gaze to sweep over the curve of her hips, the gentle roundness of her stomach, and her glorious bosom, as if he really could get up and leave her. Did she not realize the power she had over him? Was it too late for him to pretend that his emotions, damn them, were not already fully engaged?

She worried her lower lip, her eyes locked on his, and seemed to come to a decision. "Please fuck me, Julian."

His wave of relief at her words was quickly followed by a roar of purely male satisfaction. He fell on her like a starving man, the hard length of his cock pressing deep as she climaxed with an almighty scream. He shut out everything but the feel of her gripping his cock as he kept thrusting, pushing her to new heights and himself to a level of physical satisfaction he'd never known before. There was no finesse, no consideration of his partner, just a mutual fight to reach completion that allowed for no surrender.

He came eventually, he had to, but not before he'd made Carenza climax half a dozen times, her words reduced simply to screaming his name and God's—not that he compared himself to the Almighty, but he certainly felt like a king.

He rolled off her and buried his face in the pillow, his body so replete he wanted to sleep for a week and then wake up and do it all again. She sighed and turned on her side, one of her arms coming across his waist.

"You've worn me out." Julian kissed the top of her head.

"Good, because I will be sore for days," Carenza grumbled. "How I'm supposed to get up, get dressed, and go back home, I don't know."

"You could stay," Julian offered.

"Here?" She sighed. "You know that's not possible."

"Who would know?"

"We were seen leaving the theater together, Julian. If it gets out that I never went home, people will talk."

A niggling sense of disquiet made him come up on one elbow and look down at her. "Am I that distasteful to you?"

"*What?*"

"That the mere idea of society thinking we are lovers makes you afraid to be seen in my company?"

She eased away from him. "That's not fair. We agreed—"

"We agreed to be lovers."

"And to be *discreet*." Carenza sat up, her arms crossed over her bosom.

"Which brings me back to my original question." Julian wasn't quite sure why he was continuing to argue, but he didn't seem able to stop. "I'm not ashamed of being your lover."

"And I'm not ashamed of you!" Carenza moved to the side of the bed, reclaimed her stockings, and began to roll them back on her legs, her movements jerky. "Why are you being so unpleasant?"

"I'm merely . . ."

She looked over at him. "I'm trying to protect *your* reputation, you idiot."

"Mine?" Julian raised his eyebrows. "What foolery is this?"

She left the bed, wincing as her feet hit the floor, and hurried over to the pile of clothes by the fire. He pulled on his breeches and joined her.

"If you're so intent on leaving, let me at least help you dress. We wouldn't want anyone thinking you'd been ravished as you left my house."

"There's no need to be sarcastic." She put on her shift and stepped into her petticoats, presenting him with her back to lace up her stays.

"Oh, I don't know, it's better than completely losing my temper over your nonsensical behavior." He yanked her laces hard and tied them off in a neat bow.

She turned to face him. "I don't think I've ever seen you lose your temper."

"And you never will."

She cupped his chin. "My dearest Julian, please think for a moment. If anyone finds out I was the lady who placed the advertisement, my reputation—as you've repeatedly reminded me—will be in ruins. I would hate to damage you by association." She went up on tiptoe and kissed him. "That's all."

He wanted to argue, but what could he say? The mere idea that anyone needed to protect him was ludicrous, and she knew it.

"You know I am right," Carenza said. "Now, will you call a hackney cab so that I can go home? I don't want Allegra to worry."

"My coachman will take you," he countered. "There is nothing to identify my carriage. I'll walk you down to the mews if you give me a moment to dress."

Her quick smile as she turned away wasn't reassuring. He had a sense that he'd erred, but he didn't know how, and he wasn't in any fit state to inquire without probably making things worse.

"I need to put up my hair." Carenza started searching the floor. "The pins have gone everywhere."

Carenza sat back in Julian's carriage and took a trembling breath. He'd offered to come with her, but she'd told him she was fine and that he should go back to bed. But she wasn't fine. He knew her well enough to sense her distress, but she wasn't in the right mood to discuss her emotions with the person who was currently causing most of them.

Julian was infuriating sometimes, and he brought out the worst in her—all the feelings Hector had deliberately provoked and then ridiculed to make her feel worthless. Hector had called her jealous and envious, and he'd laughed when she'd honestly tried to discuss how his behavior upset her. She'd been brought up in a house full of love, with parents who clearly adored each other but who weren't above the occasional disagreement. Living with a man who didn't respect her opinions had been devastating.

Originally, Hector had encouraged her to enjoy his lovemaking and to participate to the fullest extent. But after a while he'd started to criticize her, saying she was too eager and unbecomingly carnal for a wife. When she restrained herself, he told her she was dull, and that he needed other women to make up for her lack of skill because she was incapable of loving him properly.

She'd never told anyone how bewildered she'd felt and had learned to hide her fears of inadequacy behind a screen of ladylike behavior that Hector did approve of. She'd no longer asked him to explain himself or became upset when he started a new affair, and so he'd left her alone, allowing her to maintain the pretense that all was well.

Carenza reminded herself that she'd chosen Julian to be her lover and that the terms of their agreement had been dictated by her. If she chose to indulge her more risqué side in his bed, then he had the choice to end their relationship if he found her too much.

That was all well and good, but why was she still so upset? One thing being married to Hector had taught her was to be ruthlessly honest with herself, and she sensed she was hiding from a vital truth. She'd told herself she'd chosen Julian because she believed that as a rake, he'd be willing to fulfill her needs without any emotions being involved. But was that the lie? Had she chosen him for the simple reason that she trusted him? And, if that was true, why did it matter, and why were her feelings so intimately engaged?

Chapter 15

"Good morning, brother." Aragon came into Julian's bedroom with the newspapers in his hand.

"You again? What in God's name makes you get up so early?" Julian complained.

"My horses." Aragon gave him a reproachful stare. "I have to exercise them before it gets busy in the park."

"How admirable." Julian, who at least had finished his breakfast and was almost awake, held out his hand. "Are those my newspapers?"

"Yes. I picked them up from the butler as I came in and said I'd save him a trip up the stairs." Aragon hesitated. "There's something I wanted to ask you about in there."

"In the newspapers?"

Aragon paced Julian's bedroom, his expression unusually worried. He bent down to pick up something.

"Have you lost an earring?"

"I don't tend to wear them, Aragon."

"Must belong to one of your paramours, then." Aragon walked over to Julian and dropped the earring in his hand. It was one of Carenza's emerald-and-diamond pair.

"Thank you. I'll make sure it is reunited with its owner." Julian waited tensely to see if his brother would put two and two together about the events of the past evening.

"Right, you are." Aragon pointed at the newspaper.

"There's a whole column of gossip about you in there. Mother drew it to my attention over breakfast this morning. She insisted that as the head of the household I ask you what is going on."

"If there is gossip about me in the society pages, I doubt it is true," Julian said as Aragon found the offending page for him. "You are aware that they make things up?"

"I'm not stupid," Aragon said. "But even I didn't like the tone of this piece."

Julian located his name and began to read. "'It has come to the notice of this correspondent that a certain gentleman Mr. L___nt—'"

"That's you," Aragon said helpfully.

"'Has been engaged in various nefarious schemes not befitting a gentleman of birth and that several of his acquaintances are now expressing concern as to his motives and objectives.'" Julian looked over at his brother. "What in God's name are they on about?"

He carried on reading. "'This gentleman has been observed frequenting several establishments where young minds and hearts might be corrupted or led away from the path of hard work and righteousness. Why he is visiting these places is open to conjecture, but one does have to wonder if they have anything to do with his recently found wealth and his well-known reputation as a lady's man.'"

Julian set the newspaper aside and looked at his brother. "What exactly are they accusing me of? Setting up schools to funnel children into my own brothels and financially benefiting off them?"

"Is that what you're doing?" Aragon sat back. "Good Lord, Julian, *why*?"

"Of course I'm not," Julian snapped.

"Well, that's a relief. I'll tell Mother she has nothing to worry about." Aragon paused. "Why do they think you are doing that?"

"Because someone wants to blacken my reputation," Julian said grimly. "And I'm fairly certain I know who it is."

Aragon stood up, his expression suddenly as formidable as their father's. "Then perhaps we should pay that person a visit."

"Not quite yet." Julian got out of bed and rang the bell. "I need to understand exactly what is going on first."

"Fair enough." Aragon nodded.

Julian glanced at his brother as Proctor came in. "You don't have to wait for me, Aragon. You have done your part and I thank you for that."

"I think I'll stay." Aragon sat back down again and opened the paper. "If you don't mind."

"I will be visiting several places this morning to warn them of what might come." Julian pulled off his nightshirt, washed quickly, and put on the clean shirt Proctor handed him.

"Jolly good," Aragon said.

Realizing he wasn't going to shake off his brother, Julian resigned himself to Aragon's presence. In truth, having his big brother by his side might prove useful in the long run. Writing dangerous nonsense in a newspaper about him was one thing. Writing about a peer of the realm like his brother was quite another. Men had been imprisoned for less. It was also something of a revelation that Aragon wanted to help him and wasn't there merely as their mother's mouthpiece.

Julian gave Proctor his orders. "Please ask my groom to bring round my carriage and ask Mr. Benson to join us in the hall so that I can brief him on my activities. We will be out for most of the morning. Tell Cook not to worry about luncheon."

"Yes, sir."

Julian turned to Aragon. "Do you need to send a note to Mother as to your whereabouts?"

"Not particularly," Aragon said as he carefully ripped out

the offending article and handed it to Julian. "Will we be visiting the newspaper offices as well?"

Olivia came into the drawing room of Tavistock Square with a large parcel under her arm that she placed on the table beside Carenza.

"We have more applicants for the position of your lover."

Carenza gazed at the stack of letters. "How on *earth*?"

"I assume some of the regional newspapers reprinted the story in their own editions and this is the result," Olivia said. "Mr. Cox is not very pleased about it because some of the letters are addressed directly to him."

"Has he continued to threaten you with exposure?" Carenza asked.

"Not yet." Olivia sat down. "Perhaps Mr. Laurent's promise to deal with the matter has been effective after all."

Allegra cleared her throat. "You do realize this means Father might have seen the story in his local newspaper, Carenza?"

"He'll never connect it with us," Carenza said.

"Doesn't that depend on what the new articles revealed? We don't know what details Mr. Cox might have let slip to a new journalist."

"There's one way of seeing if the news has reached Norfolk yet." Olivia pointed at the letters. "We can tell where they are from by the return addresses."

"As if anyone writing to offer their stud services to a lady would volunteer their real name and location," Carenza said.

"You'd be surprised," Olivia said. "Some of the men are very open about where they live and exactly who they are."

"You've been reading the letters?" Carenza asked.

"Why not?" Olivia shrugged. "I'm always bored, and I've discovered some very interesting people."

Allegra fixed her with an anxious stare. "I do hope you haven't been answering them."

"I have entered into correspondence with some of the gentlemen," Olivia admitted. "I thought I'd already mentioned that."

"But isn't that rather dangerous?" Allegra asked.

"Far less dangerous than meeting a man in person, dearest," Olivia said. "Which is, by the way, what your own sister recently did."

"Only because you made me," Carenza said.

"That's not quite true, is it?" Olivia met Carenza's pointed stare with one of her own. "You didn't have to go. No one forced you."

"Olivia's right," Allegra said.

Olivia didn't take her attention away from Carenza. "It's far easier to blame me than admit your own culpability in this endeavor. Although why I am surprised, I do not know, because you constantly allow others to dictate the course of your life, don't you, Carenza?"

"That's hardly fair," Carenza said.

"I disagree." Olivia raised her chin. "You let Hector walk all over you."

"I was not responsible for Hector's behavior," Carenza snapped. "And I will not be blamed for his choices, including his flirtation with you, which, by the way, hurt me immeasurably."

"I flirted with him to make you *do* something!" Olivia said. "I thought—"

"You flirted with him because you wanted to," Carenza said firmly. "Please do not try to justify your behavior by yet again holding me responsible for your conduct. I am no more responsible for your choices than for Hector's."

Olivia shot to her feet. "I think I should go."

"Yes. Perhaps you should." Carenza rose as well. "Good morning, ma'am."

Olivia left, slamming the door behind her.

Allegra looked at Carenza. "Good Lord, what on earth just happened? You never argue with anyone."

"Perhaps it is time that I started," Carenza said. "Olivia loves to complain I am too biddable while simultaneously demanding I do whatever she says."

"I admire you for standing up to her," Allegra said. "I have often mentioned she can be a little condescending toward you."

Carenza walked over to the window to see that Olivia's carriage was just pulling away. Allegra joined her.

"The thing is . . . ," Allegra said carefully. "Although you did the right thing, I am worried about whether it was the right thing to do at this present moment."

"You mean when Olivia holds my reputation in her hands because of the stupid advertisement?" Carenza asked.

"Yes," Allegra said. "That."

"Miss Cartwright." Julian bowed. "May I introduce you to my brother, the Earl of Landon?"

"A pleasure, I'm sure." Aragon stepped forward and shook Miss Cartwright's hand with great enthusiasm. "What a wonderful establishment. Reminds me very much of my days at Harrow."

"Indeed." Her startled gaze fixed on Aragon, Miss Cartwright stepped back and almost collided with her brother.

"You should both be bloody proud of yourselves," Aragon continued. "And Julian's your treasurer! You couldn't have a better man for the job."

"Perhaps Mr. Cartwright could show you around the classrooms, brother," Julian suggested. "While I have a quick word with Miss Cartwright."

"Or Miss Cartwright can take me." Aragon offered her his arm. "I'd prefer that."

Julian was surprised when Miss Cartwright agreed, leaving him alone with Mr. Cartwright.

"How may I help you today, sir?" Mr. Cartwright asked as he led Julian into the office.

"You'll forgive me if I dispense with the usual small talk, sir, I wanted to warn you that there has been some press interest in my activities here and, as you might imagine, none of it portrays me or this place in a good light."

"That's unfortunate, but it's not the first time our motives have been challenged," Mr. Cartwright said. "We've been called all kinds of names from those who cannot believe good people exist in this world to help others."

"That's ridiculously unfair." Julian grimaced. "I hate to bring such unpleasantness to you again."

"It is of no matter," Mr. Cartwright said. "If the press turns up, I'll be happy to let them in, educate them as to our mission, and explain your part in it. I often find that attempts to shame us end up working in our favor and increase donations."

"I hope you are right."

Mr. Cartwright smiled. "We're tougher than we look, sir—especially Jane. The slightest hint that she's not working in the best interests of her charges brings out the tiger in her."

"I'm glad to hear it," Julian said. "The article intimated I was using your school and Mrs. Mountjoy's place to make money for nefarious purposes."

"You mean selling the children for prostitution?" Mr. Cartwright shook his head. "We've heard that one before."

"I will be consulting a lawyer as to the best way to defend myself against such insinuations," Julian said. "I'll obviously keep you informed."

Mr. Cartwright went to open the office door. "If I might offer you some advice, Mr. Laurent? I wouldn't bother taking this matter to court. Such rumors die down when left alone. If you defend yourself too vigorously, it stirs the pot, and everyone begins to wonder whether there's some truth in the insinuations after all."

"I'll bear that in mind," Julian said. "Now, we must be off to Mrs. Mountjoy's."

They walked back to the entrance hall where they were soon joined by Aragon and a slightly bewildered-looking Miss Cartwright.

"All settled?" Aragon looked at Julian.

"I believe so." Julian bowed to the Cartwrights. "Thank you, both, for your time, and please let me know if anything untoward happens."

"That's the spirit." Aragon took Miss Cartwright's hand and kissed it. "My mother wouldn't like you, but you're just the kind of woman I'd love to bring home as my wife." He studied her approvingly. "You don't gabble on and make me feel like a fool. I appreciate that."

Julian took a steadying breath. "Aragon . . ."

"I'm coming, brother." Aragon shook Mr. Cartwright's hand and winked at Miss Cartwright. "I'll be back."

Julian shepherded him out to the carriage, and they got in. Aragon waved vigorously at Miss Cartwright, who was watching them leave, her cheeks bright red.

"What a woman!" Aragon exclaimed as they pulled onto Whitechapel Road. "Knew exactly how to put me in my place."

"I thought you were only interested in women who understood horses," Julian said.

Aragon looked pleased with himself. "Miss Cartwright is very knowledgeable about horses. Grew up in the countryside and could ride before she could walk."

Despite his worries, Julian regarded his brother with some fascination. "She told you that?"

"Yes, we had a long chat. I liked her immensely. So less intimidating than the ladies at the balls Mother makes me attend. I promised I'd go back and see her as soon as we've resolved this current matter."

"And what did she say to that?"

Aragon raised his eyebrows. "She said she would look forward to it. What else would she have said?"

To Julian's relief, Mrs. Mountjoy received the news about the article as calmly as the Cartwrights. After showing them around—Aragon had been curious about the accommodations after his tour of the Cartwrights'—Mrs. Mountjoy invited them into her parlor and asked Bridget to fetch them tea.

"I've heard it all before, Mr. Laurent—the insinuations that I'm saving these girls only for my own despicable purposes, that I'm selling them into brothels, or worse." She poured them all some tea.

"Doesn't it bother you, ma'am?" Aragon spoke up. "I would be furious to have my good intentions twisted in such a vile way." He glanced at Julian. "And I deeply resent the implication that my brother would involve himself in such sordid matters."

"Your belief in your brother does you credit, my lord."

Aragon blushed. "I wouldn't go that far. He's damnably annoying most of the time. Got to protect the family name and all that nonsense, so my mother says."

"I intend to visit the newspaper offices and see if I can find out who wrote the piece," Julian said.

"And then what?" Mrs. Mountjoy looked at him. "Do you intend to take them to court? I wouldn't recommend it."

"I'd prefer to deal with the person in my own way," Julian said.

Aragon nudged him. "I'll stand as your second if it comes to a duel."

Mrs. Mountjoy barely restrained from rolling her eyes.

"Thank you, but I have no intention of calling out Walcott," Julian said firmly.

"Walcott?" Mrs. Mountjoy set down her cup. "You think Percival Walcott is behind all this?"

"He's failed to beat me in court, so I suspect he's willing to try to blacken my reputation using any means necessary," Julian said.

"He's a most unpleasant man," Mrs. Mountjoy agreed.

"You know him?" Aragon raised his eyebrows.

"I danced with him at my coming-out ball. He trod on my toes and then commented loudly to his friends that despite my dowry, I was far too plain to be married to anyone."

Aragon stared at her. "You had a ball?"

"Yes." She smiled at him.

"Did you ever dance with me?"

"Quite possibly."

Aragon slapped his thigh. "I thought you looked familiar! But I didn't want to say anything in present company, in case we'd met at a brothel or something." He laughed heartily.

Mrs. Mountjoy didn't take offense. "An easy mistake to make, sir."

"I don't think you're plain," Aragon blithely continued. "In fact, you're a very handsome woman, Mrs. Mountjoy."

"Thank you." She looked over at Julian who shrugged. "Your brother is quite an original."

"Yes," Aragon said. "Because I was the heir, I was kept in separate quarters. I had to learn all about the estate and how to be an earl. I hated every moment of it."

Julian studied his brother. He'd never thought about the way they'd been brought up from his brother's point of view before. All he'd known was that he and Anton weren't important enough to receive attention and Aragon was.

Aragon tapped his head. "I'm not the one with the brains in the family. A lot of knowledge had to be beaten into me, and it still didn't stick."

"I think your heart is in the right place, sir," Mrs. Mountjoy said. "And that is the most important thing."

"That's a good point, and to be truthful, because I'm an

earl, it doesn't seem to matter that I'm a noddlecock," Aragon said cheerfully as they stood up to leave. "Mother says I can leave all that nonsense to her."

They left the Mountjoy house and returned to the carriage. Aragon looked over at Julian and grinned. "I'd never have thought you'd have such a rum lot of acquaintances, brother. I'm having a wonderful time. I can't wait to tell Mother."

"Aragon . . . may I offer you some advice?" Julian asked.

"Usually you just tell me things without asking permission, so this must be important. Fire away."

"I think you should take control of the estate."

"Why? When Mother does it so much better?"

"Because it's yours." Julian leaned forward. "If you truly wish to marry a woman who suits you and not Mother, then it's imperative that you control your own life and inheritance."

"Oh, you're back to that, are you." Aragon considered him. "I suppose you have a point. I should look at the books more often."

"I'd highly recommend it."

"You don't think Mother is fleecing me, do you?"

"Not at all, but you might wish to attend the next meeting with your land agent." Aragon looked doubtful and Julian continued. "Just as an observer until you understand what is going on. You could ask for a private meeting with the man. I'd also think about finding your own secretary."

"That's rather a lot of thinking all at once for me," Aragon said. "Where are we going next?"

"The newspaper office. I doubt they'll tell me who wrote that damned article, but you never know who might be willing to let something slip if I offer a good enough bribe."

Carenza returned to the drawing room after a visit to her milliner to find Allegra seated at the desk, her back to the door.

"Would you like tea?" Carenza inquired.

Allegra jumped and turned to look at her sister, one hand pressed to her bosom. "You startled me!"

"So I see." Carenza walked to the desk and peered over her sister's shoulder. "What were you so engrossed in?" She sighed. "Don't tell me you've been reading those terrible letters, too."

"I was merely attempting to sort them into some kind of order, Carenza." Allegra tried to look virtuous and failed miserably. "But I must confess that I did become diverted by some of the contents."

"You're as bad as Olivia."

"I am not. I'm the one who told you not to place the advertisement in the first place!" Allegra took off her spectacles. "I did, however, establish that some of the correspondence comes from Norfolk, which means Father might have read about you in his morning newspaper."

"Unless someone specifically mentions me by name, I doubt he'll make the connection," Carenza said. "And, even if he did, he might think it highly amusing."

"He might, but Dorian won't."

"Dorian's opinion doesn't matter. He's our brother, not our father," Carenza countered. "He might be the most straitlaced man in Norfolk, but I still think he'd support me."

"In public, maybe, but in private?" Allegra shuddered. "He'd be mortified. You know how hard he tries to pretend that he's nothing like our parents. Perhaps it would be better to write and tell them what you did, so that there will be no surprises."

"And invite trouble on my head?" Carenza went to ring the bell. "I'm sure that if we leave well alone, nothing will come of it."

"I wish I shared your confidence, sister." Allegra joined her beside the fire.

"You are not to write to them and drop unhelpful hints," Carenza said. "I know what you are like."

"I just hate keeping things from anybody. It doesn't sit well with my conscience."

"Do you want to go back to Norfolk and sit in the parlor with Dorian reading improving Bible verses to you while Father snores in his chair?" Carenza asked. "Because if you don't have me to chaperone you in London, that's where you'll end up."

"Then I will stay quiet." Allegra adopted a martyred air.

"I promise that if anything bad does happen, I will publicly proclaim your innocence to the entire world," Carenza said.

"And tell me I was right all along?"

Carenza gave her a speaking look as the butler came into the drawing room.

"Good afternoon, my lady." He bowed. "The Earl of Landon and Mr. Laurent are asking if you are at home."

"Please send them up, and bring some refreshments," Carenza said.

Julian came in first, his expression unreadable, his manners as perfect as ever when he bowed and kissed her hand. "Lady Carenza."

"Mr. Laurent." Carenza regarded him carefully.

Was he still cross about her refusal to stay at his town house? It seemed unlikely. He was a pragmatic man who maintained a cool distance between himself and the rest of the world. On reflection, he must have realized that she was right to maintain their distance as well.

"Lady Carenza." Aragon bowed. "You're looking very beautiful today, ma'am—not quite as pretty as Miss Cartwright, but far more elegant."

"Miss Cartwright?" Carenza looked from Aragon to his brother.

"Yes, Julian's taken me with him this morning, and I've met so many interesting people."

"Why—?"

"Aragon, could you help Lady Allegra with the tea while I have a quick chat with Lady Carenza?"

"Yes, of course." Aragon went over to Allegra, who had sat down beside the tray of tea and cakes the butler had just brought in. "I'm quite peckish."

Julian moved over to the far window, and Carenza followed him.

"Aragon brought my attention to an article in the morning paper about me," Julian said quietly. "Whoever wrote it knew about my involvement with the Cartwrights and Mrs. Mountjoy and insinuated that I was involved in child prostitution and damaging young lives."

"That's horrible." Carenza instinctively reached out to touch him but quickly withdrew her hand when he gave her a somewhat cool look. "I assume you went to warn them?"

"Yes. Although they were both far more sanguine about such accusations than me. In truth, they told me not to pursue the culprit and to allow the matter to drop."

"And do you intend to do that?"

"Of course not." He paused. "I fear it is yet another attempt by Walcott to blacken my reputation."

"I would agree." Carenza nodded.

"The trouble is that unless Walcott admits to writing that article himself, there is very little I can do legally to hold him to account."

"I'm so sorry." She held his gaze. "You don't deserve this."

"Thank you, but I didn't come here for sympathy. I came to warn you."

Carenza's breath caught. "Am I mentioned in the article?"

"No, but if I've been seen at the Cartwrights', and particularly at Mrs. Mountjoy's, then it's possible you've been seen there, too."

"Then Mrs. Mountjoy's is no longer a safe place for us to meet," Carenza said.

"Exactly."

"Which is remarkably frustrating."

He didn't reply. His gaze had gone beyond her to the pile of letters on the desk.

"What are those?"

Carenza moved hastily to stand between him and the offending evidence. "Nothing that should concern you. I was just about to put them on the fire."

"What has happened?"

"As I said, nothing—"

"Carenza," he interrupted sharply.

"As you've probably guessed, they are replies to the advertisement. It appears that the story has spread, somewhat, around the country."

Julian briefly closed his eyes. "Good God, woman."

"Don't you start." Carenza stepped close to him. "I've already argued with Olivia and worried Allegra. I don't need your recriminations."

"You argued with Mrs. Sheraton?"

"Yes. She made some assertions about my lack of backbone, and I told her she was wrong and that she shouldn't have flirted with my husband."

"Ah, a comprehensive airing of your opinions."

"You could say that." Carenza raised her chin. "She can be incredibly dismissive of me sometimes, and I'd just had enough."

"Are you talking about Olivia?" Allegra approached Julian with a cup of tea in her hand. "The trouble with Olivia is that she is more than happy to tell everyone what *she* thinks and yet is not amenable to being told when her own conduct is reprehensible." She smiled fondly at Carenza. "I was glad to see you standing up for yourself."

Carenza went to sit down, and Julian followed her. A growing knot of anxiety settled low in her stomach as she considered all the implications of the latest news. Not only was she in danger of being exposed as the lady who put an advertisement in a newspaper for a lover, but her relationship with Julian might become common knowledge as well.

His fingers closed around her clenched fist, buried in the folds of her skirt, and teased it free. She yearned to turn her head, bury her face against his chest, and let the long-held tears come. Nothing had gone right since she'd placed that ridiculous advertisement.

"Aragon," Allegra said. "Would you mind coming down to the stables with me? My mare has strained her right forelock, and I'd value your opinion on how to treat her."

"I'd be delighted." Aragon set his tea to one side and glanced over at Julian as he stood up. "Don't leave without me."

"I wouldn't dare," Julian said.

Allegra paused beside Carenza. "I can guarantee we'll be at least half an hour, sister."

Julian caught her eye. "Thank you."

She nodded and left the room.

Julian waited until the door closed behind Allegra and Aragon and took possession of Carenza's other hand as well.

"Please don't upset yourself."

"But I feel responsible for all of this," Carenza said.

"Not all of it."

She tried to smile, but he could see the anxiety in her eyes. "I should've known you wouldn't absolve me of all the blame."

"What are friends for?" He leaned in and gently kissed her cheek. "I promise you I will do my best to avert a scandal for either of us."

"But you have done nothing wrong." Carenza looked at him. "And you are not responsible for sorting out my terrible blunders."

"As you well know, society doesn't always allow facts to hinder their enjoyment of salacious gossip," Julian said.

"And, as our fortunes are inextricably linked at this moment, I suspect we'll need to support each other."

"I'll defend you to my dying breath."

"Thank you, but let's hope it doesn't come to that." He hesitated. "I need you to be honest with me. If anything changes, I need to know about it immediately."

She nodded, her expression formal. "Of course."

"Thank you."

"We are a family used to scandal and being the subject of gossip," Carenza said. "I learned from my parents to rise above it—in public at least. You should hear my father's private opinion of some of his friends' behavior toward my mother. But he is always a gentleman when he comes to London."

"I must admit my first instinct was to visit my solicitor, but wiser counsel than mine has advised me not to pursue that route," Julian admitted. "I'm fairly certain Walcott is behind these rumors, but how he obtained the information about my activities I do not know."

"It wouldn't be hard to pay someone to follow you about," Carenza said. "You are one of the most recognizable rakes in town."

He noticed she was still holding on to his hand and that for once he didn't mind.

"That's true. I think after I leave you, a visit to Mr. Cox is in order. I need to make sure that he understands our prior arrangement."

"Do you think he's the source of the leaks?"

"It's highly likely."

"Or perhaps it's his daughter, who is employed by Olivia. She might have been seen at the inn and offered bribes," Carenza said slowly. "She might even have spoken to Olivia about the matter."

"You don't think Mrs. Sheraton is in on it?" Julian raised an eyebrow.

"She is enjoying the scandal far too much for my liking, and she is the one who brought the letters here this morning." Carenza made a face. "It probably wasn't the best of times to argue with her."

"I don't think she'd hurt you out of spite," Julian said. "Do you?"

She met his gaze. "I honestly don't know anymore. She's been behaving rather oddly lately. Both Allegra and I have noticed it."

Julian made a mental note to visit Mrs. Sheraton, but he wasn't foolish enough to mention it to Carenza.

"I hate all this uncertainty," Carenza said. "I feel as if my life has been paused, and I don't like it."

He could only agree. As a man who liked to be in control, the actions of others threatening his reputation and people he cared about was infuriating.

"Do you have any friends in common with Mr. Walcott?" Carenza asked.

"Hardly. Everyone was forced to pick sides after Percival took me to court."

"He's pleasant enough to Aragon, isn't he?" Carenza visibly brightened. "Perhaps—"

Julian spoke over her. "I'm not sure my brother has the ability to dissemble."

"I think you'd be surprised what he'd do for you." Carenza was watching him closely. "Surely it wouldn't hurt to ask?"

"I'll consider it." He brought her hand to his lips and kissed it. "I'm more invested in finding somewhere we can be alone."

She blushed rather prettily. "I agree. I thought you were organizing a house party at your country estate?"

"I am." He stood up and bowed to her. "I can assure you that your presence is a given."

"I'm glad to hear it." She paused. "I miss you."

He pretended to groan. "Don't make things . . . hard for me."

Her gaze dropped to his breeches. "It's difficult not to."

"I'm leaving." He gave her a serious stare. "I'll collect Aragon on my way."

Five minutes into their carriage journey, Aragon cleared his throat. "I've been thinking."

Julian raised an encouraging eyebrow.

"About Walcott," Aragon said. "He's always been very pleasant to me." He paused. "Seemed to think we were kindred spirits or something."

"He assumes you were as put out about me inheriting a fortune as he was."

"Why would I be?" Aragon looked genuinely surprised. "I was delighted. When Mother complained, I told her I wouldn't have to continue your allowance or take care of you in your dotage."

"How astute of you."

"And you're my brother," Aragon continued. "And I always want the best for you." He paused. "I've always thought it unfair that the oldest son gets the lot, you know."

"Have you?" It was Julian's turn to be surprised.

"Good Lord, yes. Now, back to Walcott. I could talk to him for you." Aragon looked inquiringly at his brother. "Ask him what's going on and whatnot."

"I think you'd have to be less . . . direct than that."

"How so?"

"In order to gain his trust, I suspect he'd have to believe you agreed with him about me—and that any schemes he was running to discredit me would have your backing."

Aragon frowned and went quiet, his gaze falling to his boots. "You mean I'd have to deceive him as to my true intent?"

"Yes."

When Aragon didn't speak, Julian hastened to continue. The thought of his brother inadvertently blundering into the potential scandal of Carenza's advertisement was horrifying.

"It's all right. I don't expect you to—"

"Like a spy?"

"I suppose so." Julian regarded his brother somewhat dubiously. "It is of no matter, brother."

"If I pretended to agree with Walcott, he might boast about his plans for you," Aragon said. "And then I could tell you, and we could face him together and force him to desist or lose his own reputation."

"Yes, but—"

"I'll do it!" Aragon slapped his thigh. "Can't have that weasel undermining my brother's reputation." They were rapidly approaching Landon House. Aragon put on his hat as the carriage slowed and made ready to leave. "Don't worry, Julian. I'll report back as soon as I've spoken to him."

"Aragon, please don't. . . ." Julian spoke to empty air as his brother leapt out of the carriage and slammed the door behind him.

Julian sat back, his mind in a whirl. He'd never expected Aragon to initiate a conversation about Walcott. Had Lady Allegra put him up to it, or had it sprung from his genuine concern for his little brother? Julian had the unnerving sensation that things were spiraling out of his control again, and he didn't like it one bit.

Chapter 16

"Stop fussing, Carenza." Allegra pulled on her gloves and turned to her sister. "The carriage will be here in a moment, and we'll be on our way."

Even as she spoke, the front door opened and the coachman, who had known them since they were little girls, came in. "Good morning, ladies. All the luggage is stowed and your maid has gone ahead in the gig, so she'll be there to greet you when you arrive."

"Thank you, Owens." Carenza turned to the butler. "We'll see you in a week."

He bowed. "Wishing you both a safe journey, my lady."

They went out to the carriage. It was a fine, sunny morning, which boded well for their travel plans to Epping Forest, where Julian had his country property. As he wasn't the heir, he'd had the luxury of choosing a country house that he liked rather than one he had to put up with. Carenza hadn't visited yet and was keen to see what he'd done to the place.

The journey should take around three hours, and they had already decided not to stop on the way, unless Owens needed to change his horses. Allegra settled herself opposite Carenza. Allegra had brought her sewing basket, an improving novel of sermons, and her Pomeranian, Jester, who now resided on her lap, panting happily.

Carenza, who could neither read nor sew when the carriage was in motion, resigned herself to being lectured by her sister, who always enjoyed having a captive audience.

"I hope you've brought something interesting to read," Carenza remarked as they pulled away.

"Yes, indeed." Allegra patted her dog. "Dorian sent it to me. It's a collection of sermons from a preacher called John Wesley." She picked up the book. "It's called *Sermons on Several Occasions.*"

"It sounds riveting," Carenza said. "I'll probably be asleep before we leave London."

Carenza did fall asleep and only awakened when the carriage took a sharp left turn. She sat up and looked out the window. They drove through a set of high stone gateposts and continued up an elm tree–lined drive. She searched for a view of the house between the trees and formal gardens, but caught a glimpse only of a slate roof until they made a final sweeping turn and drew up in front of the house.

"Oh," Allegra said. "It's rather like a fairy castle."

Carenza allowed Owens to assist her from the carriage and stared up at the structure. The building was clad in honey-colored stone and had huge, mullioned windows. To the right of the door was a tower that spiraled upward with strategically placed arrow slits rather than windows. There was ivy growing up the side of the tower and on the main house.

"Rapunzel, Rapunzel, let down your hair," Allegra quoted as she looked upward. "Perhaps Julian means to imprison you in this tower, Carenza, and keep you forever."

"Hardly." Julian's voice came from behind them. "I can barely get her to listen to anything I say. It would be a struggle indeed to shut her up in a tower." He smiled as he came toward them. He wore his less formal country wear with the same panache as his city clothes. "Welcome to Dovington House."

"It's very nice." Carenza allowed him to kiss her gloved hand.

"I like it." He escorted them into the house, and they paused to view the features of the grand hall. It rose two stories, showcasing the large diamond-paned window at the front of the building. Julian explained, "It was a hunting lodge that once belonged to the Tylney-Long estate in Wanstead. I heard it was being sold off, made an offer, and here we are."

"It's very pleasant," Allegra acknowledged as she stripped off her gloves. "Now, could you direct me to my room? I am in dire need of a change of clothes."

"Yes, of course." Julian turned to a woman who had just entered the hall. "Lady Allegra, may I introduce you to my housekeeper, Mrs. Glebe? She'll take very good care of you." He paused. "Tea will be served in the drawing room when you come down."

"Thank you." Allegra smiled at Mrs. Glebe and followed her up the stairs.

Julian took Carenza's hand. "Shall I escort you to your room?"

"Yes, please." Carenza set her hand on Julian's arm and let him guide her through the hall to a second staircase concealed within the turret.

"Oh, you *are* going to lock me up," Carenza said as they began to climb the stairs. She received a chuckle in return.

"I wouldn't dare. This floor can also be accessed from the main staircase. I prefer to use this one because it is more direct." He pointed out two doors on the corridor. "My bedroom is at the end of the hall and yours is . . . right here."

He opened the nearest door and stood back to let Carenza enter first. It was rather grand in a faded way, with pink silk wall hangings depicting oriental birds, and had very dainty faux-bamboo furniture. There was a large, gilded, four-poster bed that occupied most of the interior wall.

"I inherited most of this furniture from the previous owners." Julian remained with his back against the door, watching her circle the room. "I rather liked it."

"It's beautiful," Carenza agreed. "I can't wait to sleep in that bed."

"I can't wait to join you—unless you'd prefer to come to me?" Julian strolled over to take her hand. "Rather conveniently, my room is connected to yours through that dressing room."

"Mayhap we could try both beds and see which we prefer?" Carenza suggested.

He kissed her forehead. "So practical. We are quite safe here. My servants are very discreet."

She momentarily thought of all the other women he'd, no doubt, entertained here. "I suppose they've had lots of practice."

He eased back slightly to look down at her. "You're the first woman I've brought to Dovington."

"I doubt that," Carenza said tartly. "I'm sure you've done plenty of frolicking in these corridors."

"Frolicking?" His lips twitched. "I rather thought we'd be fu—"

She placed a hand over his mouth, and he smiled with delight. "I'd forgotten what a prude you are."

"Hardly." She mock-scowled at him. "Perhaps you might leave me to refresh myself after my journey. I am rather crumpled and slightly cross."

He nodded. "I'll ring for your maid. Come down when you are ready to meet the other guests."

Carenza was finally in his house. As Julian went down the stairs, the impulse to whistle like a schoolboy almost overcame him; fortunately, he remembered his current status as a sophisticated rake. He went into the drawing room and discovered Aragon and Simon, along with Viscount Chartwell, whom he'd invited mainly for Allegra's benefit, chatting amicably together by the fire.

"Lady Carenza and Lady Allegra have arrived safely," Julian said. "I'm sure they'll be down to greet you all soon."

"Excellent," Aragon said. "By the way, Mother will be here around six. She had some commitments to fulfill today that couldn't be avoided."

"Mother?" Julian looked at his brother.

"Yes." Aragon raised his eyebrows. "What of it?"

Julian turned to his secretary.

"I wrote the invitations, but I wasn't aware that Lady Landon had been invited, sir," Simon said. "I do apologize if I was in error."

"Well, of course she was invited." Aragon looked between Julian and Simon. "She's family, and for some reason she hasn't been here before." He smiled. "I thought it was time to remedy that. We wouldn't want her to think she wasn't welcome, now, would we?"

"Of course not," Julian said. "If you'll excuse me, I'll just go and inform my housekeeper that we have an extra guest."

"Jolly good," Aragon said. "Now, I'm off to your stables to see if my horses have settled in half as well as I have." He laughed heartily and strode away, leaving Julian with nothing useful to say.

He didn't have far to look for Mrs. Glebe, because she appeared in the drawing room with Lady Allegra. After Allegra went to greet the others, Julian quietly asked Mrs. Glebe to prepare a bedroom as far away from his suite as possible to receive his mother. He apologized for the inconvenience. Mrs. Glebe was delighted to oblige him and assured him it was of no consequence.

As Mrs. Glebe left, Carenza came into the drawing room. She'd changed into a dove-gray afternoon dress and had a paisley shawl draped over her elbows.

She walked over to him and paused. "What's wrong?"

"Aragon invited my mother."

"Good Lord."

"Exactly." He slowly exhaled. "My only hope is that she is

too busy preventing Aragon from making a connection with you to notice that you and I have already made one."

"Mrs. Sheraton and Lady Brenton," the footman announced.

Julian and Carenza shared a horrified look.

"You invited *Olivia*?" Carenza whispered.

"Of course I did."

"But we are at odds," Carenza whispered. "And why has she turned up with your mistress?"

"You are my mistress," Julian murmured, his joy in the day diminishing by the second. His plans for a few days of frolicking *and* fucking were rapidly going up in smoke. "What on earth was Olivia thinking asking Lady Brenton to accompany her?"

"She probably wanted to get back at me," Carenza said. She turned stiffly toward Mrs. Sheraton as she approached them with a bright smile.

"Olivia," Carenza said in a cool tone, "how lovely to see you."

Mrs. Sheraton curtsied and turned her dazzling smile and her considerable charm on Julian. "Thank you for inviting me. I hope you don't mind that I brought Lady Brenton. She was very keen to see what you've done with this place since her last visit."

Julian tried not to look at Carenza, who had gone very still beside him. Before he could speak, Carenza said, "Olivia, I know you are annoyed with me, but this isn't helpful. Lady Brenton is not our friend."

"That's not what I've heard," Olivia said. "In fact, she had some very interesting stories about Mr. Laurent that I'm sure she'd love to share with you."

There was something in her voice that made Julian pay attention. Was she trying to convey a warning to him? And if so, what exactly was she worried about?

"I hope you didn't allow Walcott to escort you," Julian said, one eye on Lady Brenton, who was rapidly approaching.

"No." Mrs. Sheraton grinned at him. "I'm not quite that awful."

Carenza muttered something under her breath, and Julian nudged her in the ribs. "Why don't you go and get yourself some refreshments while I welcome our new guest?"

The look Carenza gave him wasn't a friendly one, but she walked away without comment.

Before Julian could ask what Mrs. Sheraton was plotting, Lady Brenton joined them, looking very pleased with herself.

"Julian, how kind of you to invite me to your house." She proffered her hand, and he kissed it. "Olivia assured me that I would receive a very *warm* welcome here, indeed." Lady Brenton batted her eyelashes at Julian.

"Mrs. Sheraton is correct," Julian replied and couldn't resist a little sarcasm. "I recently had all the windows repaired or replaced. It has made a huge difference to the comfort of my guests. Now, please help yourselves to refreshments while I consult with my housekeeper."

Julian knew he shouldn't be the one yielding ground in his own house, but things were rapidly spiraling out of control. He had the fleeting urge to leave them all to it and head back to London for the peace and quiet he'd craved. But Carenza would never forgive him if he did.

He had to go into the kitchen to find Mrs. Glebe and ask her to prepare yet another room. She said she'd put Lady Brenton next to his mother and then gently reminded him it was the last decent bedroom and that any more guests would have to sleep in the nursery or in the attics. He apologized again, ignoring the glare the cook was giving him and her muttered comment about how was she supposed to divide the fish between his ever-expanding guest list?

Aragon came in through the back door and caught him staring blindly at the window.

"Everything all right?" Aragon paused beside him.

"Mrs. Sheraton brought my old mistress with her."

"Lady Brenton?"

"Yes."

Aragon patted his shoulder. "This should prove a very entertaining house party, brother. I'm so glad you invited me." He started for the door and then looked back over his shoulder. "I'll do my best to make Mother behave herself."

"Thank you."

"Least I can do, seeing as I'm the one who told her all about your new country house." Aragon scratched his ear. "I probably should've kept it to myself, eh?"

"No. I was planning on inviting her at some point." Julian walked out of the kitchen with him. "You are quite right that I should've done so earlier." He was almost dreading entering his own drawing room. . . . Another painful thought occurred to him. "I don't suppose you invited the Cartwrights, did you?" Julian asked as they paused in the open doorway.

"Well, actually . . ." Aragon glanced at him. "I did, but apparently they can't leave the boys to fend for themselves even for a day."

"Well, thank God for that. Any other surprises to spring on me?"

"No." Aragon looked thoughtful. "Not that I can think of." He winked at Julian and went off in Lady Brenton's direction.

One of his footmen stopped in front of Julian. "This is for you, sir."

"Thank you." Julian read the note, turned on his heel, and made his way up the turret stairs to his bedchamber. He went inside, stood against the door, and briefly closed his eyes.

"Please lock the door."

His eyes flared open. Carenza lounged on his pillows dressed only in her shift.

"What in God's name are you doing?" he asked, his pulse beginning to pound.

She opened her eyes wide. "Waiting for you. There are two hours before dinner and your mother's arrival. Don't you think we should put them to good use?"

He took a deep breath. His cock was already hardening, and the urge to have her overwhelmed his good sense. He shrugged out of his coat and began ripping off his cravat as he strode toward the bed.

She helped him with his shirt and breeches and then he was on top of her. He grabbed hold of her wrists and drew them over her head.

"I'm not in the mood to be kind."

"Good, because I'm seriously considering murdering you right at this minute." She glared at him. "How *could* you invite all these people who delight in getting in our way?"

She hooked her heel around his hip, opening herself to him, and he obliged with a long, hard thrust that made her gasp and grab his shoulder. He eased his hips back and slammed home again, and this time he didn't stop pounding into her, the relief of the contact forcing all other considerations from his mind. He came fast, and she barely managed to join him.

Her frown when he eased out of her was magnificent. "You selfish beast."

He smiled as he kissed his way down over her rounded stomach and set his teeth on her clit.

"Oh . . ." She climaxed immediately.

He scissored two fingers inside her, raising himself up on one elbow so that he could see her flushed face as she writhed against the pillows. She had the audacity to scowl at him, which amused him greatly. Without removing his fingers, he leaned to one side and opened the drawer beside his bed, where he'd had the forethought to leave a bottle of oil.

He shifted his thumb until it brushed over her arsehole. "Would you like my cock here?"

"I—" Her breath hitched. "Yes."

"Yes what?"

"Yes, please, Mr. Laurent."

"I'm not sure I like your tone." He eased the tip of his finger inside her. "You should be more . . . needy, more desperate, more grateful."

"Grateful? I'm the one who lured you up here to have your way with me."

"But I like it when you beg." He unstoppered the oil and applied it to his index finger. "Hands and knees, I think."

He flipped her over, kneeling behind her, spreading her thighs wide so that she was open to him. He slid his oiled finger in, and she shuddered and arched her hips. He carefully added a second, giving her time to adjust to the pressure. His cock was already hard again, but she wasn't quite ready to take him—yet.

"More," she gasped.

"As you wish." Three fingers now, and he was able to move them back and forth, widening and preparing her with every subtle twist. "I wish I had a dildo to fuck you with while my cock fucks your arse, but I was not prepared." He paused. "Perhaps you might fuck yourself?"

He watched in approval as she did exactly what he suggested, the heel of her right hand pressed tightly against her clit while her fingers pumped inside her other channel. He oiled his cock and pressed the head against her now slick arse. A small undulation of his hips and he was in her tight passage. He pushed deeper, his hips now aligned with hers, his fingers drifting upward to her breasts, where her hard nipples awaited his caresses.

"Harder," she said.

He wrapped his hand in her long hair, drawing her head back to expose her throat.

"Don't worry. I'll attend to you properly," he promised. "You won't be able to sit down comfortably tonight to eat your dinner without squirming and remembering me pounding into you so hard that you screamed."

He suited his words to his actions, forgetting all caution to give her what she craved and what he needed, a blessed release from a chaotic day. The need to come gathered at the base of his spine, and he redoubled his efforts, flesh slapping against flesh, his grip on her hip sure to leave a bruise—not that either of them would care.

He roared as he climaxed, and she screamed as predicted, her whole body straining back against him like a bow. He resisted the urge to flop over her like a beached whale and eased back.

"Stay there."

His words were met with a muffled groan. He went into the dressing room, washed himself, and brought a wet cloth back to the bed. He took his time cleaning Carenza's most intimate parts, using the roughness of the cloth to instigate another climax that made her shudder and curse his name.

He sat beside her on the bed, stroking her shoulder. Her golden hair was a wild tangle, her mouth swollen from his kisses, her cheeks ruddy. He wanted her again, but the chime of the clock reminded him that their idyll must end.

"Shall I carry you back to your own bed?" he offered.

"Only if you wish to damage your back." Carenza opened one eye to study him. "I'm quite capable of walking." She paused. "I think."

"I could toss you over my shoulder like a bale of hay," Julian suggested.

She made a face. "As if you've ever worked in a field."

He lowered his shoulder, wrapped one arm around her waist, and pulled her from the bed, making her shriek with laughter. After marching straight through the dressing rooms and into her bedchamber, he deposited her on the bed.

"My lady."

A small gasp behind him made him go still.

Carenza looked past him and smiled. "Bea, you're early. I thought you'd be attending to Allegra first."

Julian bowed. "I'll leave you to it, then."

He walked out, trying hard not to smile as Carenza continued to talk to her maid as if nothing untoward had happened. He admired her calmness as he picked up her garments and left them in her dressing room. When he reached for his shirt he remembered Carenza hadn't been the only one who was naked. He hoped poor Bea had closed her eyes.

Chapter 17

Julian made sure he was the first person down before dinner so that he could greet the rest of his guests. His valet had informed him that his mother had arrived and was comfortably settled in her room. He was beginning to regret not bringing his butler and more of his staff, but he hadn't expected a full house—just a few intimate friends who would happily overlook any indiscretions in their midst. It was how he preferred to live his life, but it seemed fate was against him.

"Julian." Aragon bounded in. He'd changed into evening attire but still had a few wisps of hay stuck to his lapel. "A word."

Julian raised an inquiring eyebrow.

"Lady Carenza." Aragon looked at him expectantly.

"What about her?"

Aragon took a quick look around the room before he leaned closer to Julian. "I don't think she's the one for me."

"Mother will be pleased."

"I'm not worried about Mother. What do you think?"

"I hate to disappoint you, but I have no opinion on your choice of bride. That decision is entirely up to you."

"I thought you'd be disappointed in me."

"Not at all. Thinking matters through and concluding you will not suit shows great maturity, brother. I'm proud of you."

Aragon rolled his eyes. "Now you sound like Mother."

"Good Lord, I hope not." Julian paused. "Might I ask what persuaded you that Lady Carenza was not the woman for you?"

Aragon looked anywhere but at Julian. "Oh, you know, things . . ."

"Such as?"

"She's rather bossy."

"Indeed." Julian fondly remembered her earlier commands when she'd been naked in his bed. "I suppose you've had enough of that with Mother."

"Enough of what?" Their mother entered the drawing room. She wore a dark blue silk gown with a black lace trimming and feathers in her hair.

He went over to take her gloved hand and kissed it. "Your excellent advice, of course," Julian said.

"I was just telling him that I'm no longer considering Lady Carenza as a bride," Aragon said helpfully as he kissed his mother's cheek.

"Well, things would have ended much sooner if you hadn't kept up your acquaintance with her, Julian. Her family are not good ton."

"I say, that's jolly unfair," Aragon protested. "They're both lovely girls. Grew up with them, like them a lot."

Julian met his brother's gaze. "I agree." He turned to his mother. "Did you have a safe journey from London?"

"Yes, this place is conveniently close." Lady Isobel looked around the drawing room. "It's quite pleasant here."

"I'm glad you approve."

"I didn't say that. I'll reserve judgment until I've seen the whole house." Her cool gaze raked over him. "Who else have you invited?"

Julian was just about to answer when Carenza and her sister came in together, both of them in shades of blue.

"Oh." His mother pursed her lips. "I thought we were done with the Musgroves."

"Not in my house." Julian left her and went over to the new arrivals. "Good evening, Lady Carenza, Lady Allegra."

He smiled as he kissed their hands, then turned his attention to Carenza, who looked like a very well-satisfied woman. He wondered if anyone else would notice. He almost wished they would . . .

Allegra went off to speak to Aragon, leaving Julian with Carenza. The bodice of her evening gown was low enough for him to see the swell of her breasts and a slight bruise where he'd bitten her throat.

"You're looking very well this evening, my lady."

Her smile was a delight. "I am enjoying the country air, sir. I find it most invigorating."

"I quite agree." He looked up as more guests appeared. "Will you excuse me?"

"Of course," she said. "I'll go and speak to your mother. She always looks so pleased to see me."

Julian was still smiling as he went to greet Maude Cooper and her husband, Gerald, who had once been a good friend of his. He'd heard from Carenza that the marriage was not a happy one, and he'd hoped that some time together in the countryside with a group of trusted friends would help repair some of the damage such long-term separations caused. To his dismay, the animosity between the couple was almost palpable. Maude looked ready to burst into tears, and Gerald's face was red.

"Thank you for the invitation." Mr. Cooper bowed very correctly to Julian. "It is a relief to get away from London."

"And a chance for you to reconnect with your charming wife," Julian said. "She has missed you quite dreadfully."

Gerald's laugh was short. "Not that I've noticed. She seems to have managed perfectly well without me."

"Excuse me," Maude said, her voice trembling. "I need to speak to Carenza."

She slipped away, leaving Julian staring at Gerald.

"Would you rather she'd fallen apart and insisted you came home?" Julian asked, his tone mild, his question more pointed. "Surely her ability to keep your family together without you is to be celebrated and appreciated rather than used against her?"

"I . . ." Gerald sighed. "I hadn't thought of it like that."

"You've been absent for almost five years," Julian said.

"Not by choice."

"And your wife didn't have any choice, either, did she? Yet she did her duty just the same." Julian held the man's defensive gaze. "You are better than this, my friend."

"Good evening, Julian." Lady Brenton interrupted their conversation seemingly without a qualm. "What a lovely house you have."

Gerald bowed and walked away, leaving Julian with an unsettled feeling. He'd attempted to make his friend see reason, but what right did he have to meddle in someone else's marriage? He dragged his gaze down to the beautiful woman in front of him.

"Good evening, Lady Brenton. How is your husband?"

"He's quite well, thank you. He sends his regards." She looked around the room, her gaze avid. "I'm trying to work out which one of these ladies has taken my place."

"Perhaps you are irreplaceable."

Her smile was complacent. "If you wish to resume our relationship, please just say so."

"I do not."

She pouted. "So the rumors are true. You have moved on. Now, who on earth is it?"

He bowed. "I hope you have an enjoyable stay, my lady. If you will excuse me."

His mother frowned as he went past, but he didn't stop to hear her criticisms of his choice of guests. She'd invited herself and would just have to put up with it. He made sure to welcome Viscount Chartwell, who was talking to Allegra, and then found himself face-to-face with Mrs. Sheraton. She wore black, which she favored because it suited her, and dark red rubies around her throat and in her hair.

She batted her eyelashes at him. "I suppose I should have mentioned that Carenza and I are at odds before accepting your kind invitation."

"I'm more interested in why you thought it a good idea to bring Lady Brenton with you."

She studied his face. "I think she is involved with Walcott."

"I already knew they've become friends."

"No, I think it is more than that."

"They're lovers?"

Mrs. Sheraton rolled her eyes. "Typical of a man to jump straight to the physical. How about co-conspirators?" He stared at her, and she smiled. "My thoughts were that if you had the opportunity to speak privately to Lady Brenton, she might admit her part in this plot to ruin your reputation."

"Why on earth would she choose to unmask herself to me—the very person she hates enough to want to destroy?" Julian asked.

"Because love and hate are very closely aligned, Mr. Laurent. Isn't it obvious?"

"She's not capable of love."

"That's rather harsh, wouldn't you say?" She met his gaze. "Everyone loves someone."

"Lady Brenton loves only herself."

"Then you'll have to find a way to use that against her, sir. You're a clever man; you'll think of something." She inclined her head. "Now, I really must go and make my peace with Carenza. She's been studiously ignoring me for the past half hour." She walked away.

Carenza wasn't particularly surprised when Olivia marched up and demanded her attention. Her friend had never been one to avoid an argument—in truth, she relished them. Usually, Carenza capitulated before the first blow was struck, but on this occasion, she wasn't quite so willing to fold her cards easily.

"Mrs. Sheraton."

"Good evening, Carenza. I suppose you're wondering why I brought Lady Brenton with me."

"No, I'm wondering why you came at all."

Olivia blinked. "Good Lord, I really did offend you."

"Yes, you did." Carenza smiled. "Now, are you going to apologize, or shall we simply avoid each other for the next few days? I don't want to spoil Julian's house party."

"You know I never apologize."

"Then we have nothing more to say to each other." Carenza half turned away.

"Wait." Olivia frowned. "What about Lady Brenton?"

"I'm sure you've spoken to Julian about your intentions. He is your host and the one most personally affected by your odd decision." Carenza paused. "I know you can be unkind, Olivia, but I never thought you would be callous enough to bring a man's ex-mistress to his own home."

Carenza turned and walked away. She didn't care what Olivia thought of her, but she had to protect Julian. She glanced over to find him watching her, his light blue eyes full of some kind of emotion she didn't want to examine too closely. He was her friend, he was her lover, and he deserved to be defended.

The housekeeper came in to announce that dinner would be served. Julian took his mother's arm, but as it was supposed to be an informal occasion, everyone else simply filed in after them. Allegra was chatting away quite happily to Viscount Chartwell as he pulled out a chair for her. Carenza paused on the threshold, wondering where to sit. With the arrival of Julian's mother and Lady Brenton, the numbers were not quite even.

"Lady Carenza." Aragon waved at her. "Come and sit beside me."

Carenza walked over and was soon settled in the seat next to him. Olivia, who was opposite her, winked before she turned to talk to Lady Brenton. Had her friend told Lady Brenton that Carenza was Julian's new lover? Did that explain her presence?

Carenza looked longingly toward the door. So much for a few quiet days with Julian. The visit had become a nightmarish landscape filled with potential dangers to navigate. Should she have allowed Olivia to explain why she'd brought Lady Brenton, beyond the obvious? It did seem unlike her friend to be so petty.

Carenza noticed the footmen were being very careful about the distribution of the soup. In such a small establishment, the arrival of unexpected guests, especially at such short notice, must have put a huge strain on the kitchen. She declined the soup, noting the footman's relief, and turned her attention to Julian. He sat at the head of the table, his head inclined toward his mother, who was speaking at some length.

He looked far calmer than she would in such circumstances, but that was his way, was it not? To keep that cool distance between himself and the concerns of the world. He'd never allow the presence of his mother or of Lady Brenton to openly annoy him and would navigate the week with the same steady calmness and outward goodwill.

Was she the only one who knew he had a temper at all? She moved slightly on her seat, aware of the throbbing between her legs and exactly who had got her in such a state. Despite all the potential problems, she still wanted to be in his bed.

He caught her eye, a question in his gaze, and she smiled before she hurriedly looked away. She didn't have the face for keeping secrets. Anyone who saw them in close proximity would soon guess that she was enamored of him. Carenza took a deep breath.

She was in love with him, and that wasn't part of the plan at all.

"Lady Carenza?"

She jumped and turned to face Aragon. "I do beg your pardon. I was woolgathering."

"Happens to me all the time." He smiled at her. "That's why I need my mother to hold the reins."

"I think you underestimate yourself, sir."

"Funnily enough, that's exactly what Julian said," Aragon said. "He told me it was high time to take control of my own estates."

"He does have a rather annoying tendency to be right about such things." She returned his smile. "And I know he has your best interests at heart."

"My mother told me not to trust him, but she was wrong to do so, because he's a good man." For once Aragon sounded serious. "I've come to appreciate his advice."

"Good for you," Carenza said. "I often disagree with him, but, again, he is usually right."

"He's very fond of you."

"Yes, we've been friends for years," Carenza agreed. "How could we not all be friends when our families grew up together?"

"I consider you my friend," Aragon said.

Carenza smiled at him. "Likewise."

"I know I've been following you around like a lost lamb recently, but on reflection, I don't think we would suit." He paused and studied her face. "Please don't cry."

"I will bravely hold back my tears." Carenza pretended to sigh. "And shed them privately in the sanctuary of my bedchamber."

"You don't mind at all, do you?"

"I'd rather we were friends."

"Then so be it." He grinned at her. "I've always thought you more suited to Julian anyway. You both have a wicked sense of humor."

Carenza picked up her wineglass and hoped Aragon hadn't

noticed she was blushing. He wasn't known as a particularly observant man, so his remarks were probably innocent. In truth, if he had noticed her connection with Julian, she was in trouble.

There was a tinkling laugh from the other side of the table. Lady Brenton looked at Aragon and then at Carenza. "I doubt Julian would consider Lady Carenza as more than a friend either, my lord. He does have rather exacting tastes."

"Good point, ma'am," Aragon nodded enthusiastically. "Julian is renowned for the beauty of his mistresses." He turned to Carenza. "Not that I'd include you among those ladies. You're far more than just a pretty face; you're an excellent rider."

"Thank you," Carenza murmured.

Lady Brenton looked rather put out.

"I've always thought Mr. Laurent would make an excellent lover," Olivia said. "In fact, now that you're done with him, Cressida, I might proposition him myself."

"You're certainly beautiful enough," Aragon told Olivia.

Carenza tried not to glare at Olivia, who was being her usual provocative self.

"Do you care to ride?" Aragon asked. "How is your seat?"

"I fear I'm not as accomplished a rider as Carenza, my lord," Olivia said. "I prefer to limit my physical activities to my bedchamber."

Aragon's eyebrows went up. "Do you, by God." He leaned forward, his gaze fixed on Olivia. He was just about to speak when his mother cleared her throat.

"Aragon, you know perfectly well it is rude to talk across the table."

"Oh! Sorry, Mother." He sat back. "I'll speak to Mrs. Sheraton after dinner."

Lady Landon's expression said otherwise. Carenza guessed she would keep Aragon tethered to her side in the drawing room and not allow him to speak to anyone. Lady Brenton turned to Olivia. She spoke quietly, but Carenza could hear every word.

"Is Lord Landon wealthy, Olivia?"

"Not as wealthy as Mr. Laurent, but he does have the title," Olivia said. "And two very nice houses, one in London and the other in Norfolk."

"Indeed."

"I didn't realize that condolences were in order, Lady Brenton," Carenza said. "Are you officially a widow?"

"I am not."

"Oh, I see. You're merely contemplating adultery again. I do apologize, how foolish of me."

"It's quite all right," Lady Brenton replied. "You've never been known for your wit or intelligence, dear, so do not dwell on your shortcomings."

Carenza set her jaw. "Better to be honest than to betray your friends and family. My conscience is clear."

"Is it really?" Olivia locked gazes with her. "I've always thought that still waters run deep and that you're not quite as angelic as you appear."

"True, no one is 'quite' that feebleminded," Lady Brenton muttered.

"I beg your pardon?" Carenza stared at Lady Brenton.

She had the audacity to smile. "I was speaking to Mrs. Sheraton, my lady. One isn't supposed to talk across the table."

"Hear, hear," Aragon said.

Carenza resisted the urge to dump the contents of her wineglass over Lady Brenton's head. She glanced despairingly at the door. It was only the first evening of the holiday. How on earth was she going to deal with Olivia at her worst *and* Lady Brenton without losing her temper? She was tired of being patronized by both of them.

Allegra caught her eye and mouthed, "Are you all right?"

Carenza nodded and returned her attention to her food,

all her pleasure at spending time with Julian destroyed by the unpleasantness of his houseguests. She slowly stopped chewing. But why should she let them ruin it for her? What if she ignored them and simply enjoyed Julian instead?

Eventually, Lady Isobel—apparently taking it upon herself to act as Julian's hostess—rose to her feet. "The ladies will withdraw to the drawing room and leave the gentlemen to their port."

Carenza stood and followed Olivia and Lady Brenton into the very pretty drawing room. She sat down next to Maude, who appeared to be struggling to smile.

"What's wrong?" Carenza whispered to Maude.

Lady Isobel took her place behind the tea tray and started ordering everyone around.

"Gerald and I had an awful argument," Maude said. "He's considering returning to France."

"If he truly is considering such a step, I'd tell him good riddance," Carenza said.

Maude blinked at her. "I beg your pardon?"

"If he is intent on making you miserable, you'll be far happier if he isn't here," Carenza explained. "Why should you continue to put up with a man who doesn't value you?"

Maude looked down at her clasped hands. "I thought you'd tell me it was my duty to put up with him."

Carenza frowned. "I spent years trying to make Hector happy by diminishing myself to fit his petty requirements. It did me no good in the end. He still behaved appallingly, and even worse, he had no respect for me because I allowed him to get away with it." She looked at Maude. "If Gerald doesn't understand how hard it has been for you while he's been away, then you're better off without him."

"Those are fighting words, Carenza," said Olivia, who had come up behind her. "I never thought I'd hear you say such a thing."

"But I was not speaking to you," Carenza said. "You are intruding on a private conversation."

Olivia sat down beside Maude and said, "Oh, for goodness' sake, Carenza, will you please accept my apology and stop treating me like a pariah?"

"Why should I?" Carenza asked. "You're behaving appallingly."

Olivia sighed. "If you would just allow me to explain, I'll tell you why I brought Lady Brenton with me."

"Fine." Carenza glared at Olivia. "Tell me."

Olivia glanced around and then lowered her voice before speaking. "I believe Lady Brenton is heavily involved in this effort to blacken Julian's reputation. She's working with Percival Walcott and has been seen in Mr. Cox's inn."

"Have you told her about your part in all this?" Carenza asked.

"No." Olivia had the nerve to look offended.

"I still don't understand why you thought it a good idea to bring her here."

"Neither do I," said Maude, who had been kept well informed about events by Allegra. "It seems . . . cruel."

"I brought her to talk to Julian," Olivia continued. "I thought that if anyone could get her to confess her secrets, it would be him."

"She's hardly likely to betray Percival to the very man she wants to bring down," Carenza argued.

"But I don't think she really wants to destroy Julian," Olivia said. "She's still in love with him. He's the first man who ended a relationship with her—that's usually her claim to fame—that she leaves her lovers behind."

"So, this is all about her hurt pride?" Carenza asked.

"And Walcott's fury that Mr. Laurent inherited his money," Maude added. "Don't forget that."

Carenza turned to Olivia. "Have you told Julian?"

"Yes," Olivia replied. "He wasn't very happy with me for spoiling his house party, but I felt I had no choice. You seem to forget that I was there with you in that inn, Carenza. My reputation is at stake as well."

"You don't care about your reputation," Carenza said.

"And you care far too much about yours," Olivia fired back. "You're so afraid of being compared to your mother that you hide behind a bland exterior that must be stifling."

Carenza wanted to argue, but what could she say?

"See?" Olivia pointed a finger at her. "You know I'm right."

"It still doesn't excuse your behavior," Carenza said.

"Perhaps you both need to stop arguing and work together to prevent anyone losing their reputation," Maude said firmly. "This really is ridiculous when you both care for each other." Carenza and Olivia stared at Maude, and she shrugged. "I'm too miserable to be anything but honest this evening. The pair of you need your heads knocked together."

"She might have a point," Olivia said.

"But what can we do?" Carenza looked from Maude to Olivia. "Until someone comes out with actual accusations rather than gossip and innuendo, there is nothing to fight."

"My main concern is whether Calloway or Mr. Cox told Percival and Lady Brenton about Julian's appearance at the inn when we were interviewing the candidates for the advertisement," Olivia said. "I'm sure they'll use that information to make matters worse for Julian and inadvertently for us."

Carenza sat back. "I have to agree, and gossip does say that Calloway has been seen in Percival's company."

"Percival never stops complaining about Julian, and if Calloway is attempting to curry favor, he's bound to tell them about Julian's presence at the Wheatsheaf Inn," Olivia said.

"Then we're doomed," Carenza sighed.

"Don't be so defeatist. All we have to do is work out what Lady Brenton and Percival Walcott fear most."

"That seems quite obvious," Maude said. "Lady Brenton likes to be seen as a beautiful woman who can ensnare any man she wants with a snap of her fingers, and Percival considers himself a leader of the ton."

"If we threaten those things, then surely they will leave Julian alone?" Carenza asked. "The only thing we need to work out is how to do it."

"Oh, that's the easy part," Olivia said. "We blackmail them. And before you both tell me you would never lower yourselves to do such a thing, think about what they've been prepared to do to Julian."

By the time Julian retired to bed, he had the beginnings of a headache, his jaw was tight, and the temptation to run screaming into the night felt almost sensible. He sat down beside the fire and pressed his hands to his head. So much for his vaunted plans. Between his mother, Lady Brenton, and Mrs. Sheraton, he was beset by women who had a bone to pick with him.

He'd barely managed a word with Carenza all evening. He had a sense she'd deliberately stayed away from him, which had been both a relief and a curse. She'd never had the face for intrigue, which was why he'd deliberately left her out of his wildest schemes when they were children. He hadn't been able to hear the conversation at her end of the table, but he'd sensed she was out of sorts.

He raised his head and stared at the connecting door between their apartments. He wanted to go to her, sink to his knees, bury his head in her lap, and let her soothe his troubled spirits. And then he wanted to take her to bed and make love to her for hours.

As if he'd called her in his mind, the door opened, and Carenza peeked into the room. "Julian?"

"I'm here."

She came into the room. She was dressed for bed, her fair

hair braided down her back and a large shawl over her nightgown.

"I am beginning to feel as if I'm the one doing all the chasing, here. This is the second time I've had to come into your bedchamber to find you."

He sat back and regarded her. "You did say you wished to be in charge. Perhaps I've decided to sit here meekly until I'm called upon to perform for you." There was a snap to his words that he instantly regretted.

Carenza raised her eyebrows. "I see you are feeling sorry for yourself."

"With considerable justification."

"I had to endure Lady Brenton suggesting I was too stupid to be your mistress and Olivia making provocative and unhelpful comments throughout dinner."

"I had to talk to my mother."

For a moment their gazes clashed, and then Julian sighed. "You are right. I am out of sorts, and it is all due to my inept planning. I'm sorry I invited you into this mess."

"I'm not." She held out her hand. "Because of this."

He reluctantly got to his feet and took her hand. "What about it?"

"*This*." She went up on tiptoe and kissed him. "When we can lock the doors and be together."

"I suppose that does make up for a lot," he grudgingly acknowledged, his hand curving around her buttock and bringing her against him. "Although knowing our luck, someone will set the place on fire and we'll be discovered with flames burning the bed curtains while we're too busy fucking to notice."

"I wouldn't object."

He looked down at her. "To burning alive?"

"Don't be such a pessimist." She poked him in the ribs. "I was referring to the part where you mentioned being fucked."

"Ah. Now *that* I can help you with." He picked her up and marched over to his bed.

He stripped off her nightgown, his fingers touching the slight bruise on her throat and the stronger marks on her hips where he'd held her so tightly earlier. She parted her thighs, and he cupped her mound.

"Are you sore?"

"Yes, a little."

"Yet you still want more?" He touched her clit, which immediately started to throb under the pad of his finger. The scent of her arousal rose around him, and he slowly inhaled. "You're insatiable."

"Does it offend you?"

He looked up at her face, sensing the tension behind the question. "Not at all. Why would it? What more could a man want than a woman who wants him back?"

Her smile was wry. "I suppose that depends on the woman."

Julian frowned. "Hector was a fool."

"Or maybe it's more about what is allowed for a married woman as opposed to a mistress," Carenza mused.

"I would not make such a distinction." Julian bent to kiss her. "There is nothing that excites me more than to be desired for myself."

She swallowed hard. "Then perhaps you might disrobe so that I can have my wicked way with you?"

He removed his clothing, his gaze fixed on hers, enjoying her reactions to the gradual reveal of his body. She touched his hip, and he wanted to explode with lust as her fingers moved inwards and traveled up his shaft to the already wet tip of his cock.

"You're just as ready as I am," she murmured.

"Mmm . . ." He pushed against her hand. "I'll be careful. Shall I blow out the candles?"

"No, I want to watch you." She eased one arm behind her head and bent her leg at the knee to give him more access.

"And not do the work yourself?" He squeezed his cock and lowered himself over her, brushing the tip against her wetness until he seamlessly slid inside. "You want to watch . . . this?"

He pushed in and then withdrew completely.

A slight frown appeared between her brows. "There's no need to stop."

"I thought you wished to admire me."

"Oh, I do." She wriggled slightly on the sheets. "But in motion is best."

"I think I'll make you wait." He replaced his cock with his tongue until she was ready to come and then sat back again. "I like to watch you on the brink of an orgasm, glaring at me to finish it."

"I can do that for myself," she pointed out rather breathlessly.

"Not tonight." He held her gaze. "You'll play my game."

"All right."

He placed his hands around her waist and arranged her against a bank of pillows. He slid his knee between her thighs and pressed it against her mound, almost making her climax.

"Suck my cock." He brought his shaft to her lips and rubbed the crown against them, coating them in his wetness.

She licked him, her tongue darting out to explore the contours of his cock and dip into the very center. He groaned her name and pushed his cock deep down her throat, holding it there while he regained control of himself. He loved the way it felt to be sheathed within her mouth, her head back, her eyes closed as she held him so deeply.

He wanted to thrust hard and come hard but reminded himself that he'd offered her a different game to play and that driving her to distraction without letting her come was his aim. He eased free and cupped her bountiful breasts in both hands, his fingers on her already hard nipples. Angling his hips, he slid his cock in her cleavage and gently rocked back and forth as he massaged her breasts.

Her breathing hitched as he kissed her lips, which were sticky from his presence, and then removed his knee from her mound and kissed her other lips, which were already swollen and begging for his attention.

"Julian . . ."

He ignored her quiet plea and fingered her until she began to tighten against him. When he drew back, she made a feral noise that made him smile.

"I think I need a drink. Would you care for one?"

He got off the bed and strolled over to his dressing table, where Proctor had left him some brandy and two glasses. He poured himself a drink and turned back to the bed, where Carenza was glaring at him.

"Are you sure you won't join me?" He held up the glass. "It's very fine brandy."

She locked eyes with him. "If you don't come back to bed immediately, I will make myself come and be damned to you."

"But that's not in the spirit of the game." Julian suddenly realized he was enjoying himself for the first time since dinner.

"Unlike you, I can climax as many times as I want. One more makes no difference to our game."

He finished the brandy and returned to the bed. "You agreed that I would dictate terms tonight, yes?"

She sighed. "Yes, but—"

He climbed back on the bed, spread her thighs, and slid his aching cock home, holding still while she tried and failed to climax around him. He reached up and cupped the back of her head.

"Stop," he said softly. "Just let me fill you."

He thought she'd argue, but she went still, her body relaxing under his.

"I can feel every hot throbbing inch of you," she whispered into his ear. "You're filling me up."

He breathed deeply out through his mouth and in through his nose, as he concentrated solely on where their bodies were joined. He could feel her, too, the tightening, the waves of motion, the gradual rise of urgency that made her quiver. He became aware of other sounds around him, like the crackling fire and the tick of the clock on the mantelpiece and the idea that he never wanted to be like this with anyone else.

With that thought, his concentration fractured, and he gave a small, involuntary thrust, sending Carenza off into a roaring climax that wrung every drop of come from him and then more.

He remained on top of her and still joined, his thoughts in a jumble as several things became undeniably clear to him. He didn't just want Carenza as his mistress. He wanted her as his wife, but how he'd achieve that was currently beyond him.

Much later, Carenza woke him up with kisses and they made love again, this time in perfect harmony without a single word spoken between them. Before Julian fell back to sleep, he reminded himself to wake early enough to allow Carenza to return to her bed, and to unlock the servant's door so that Proctor could come in and attend to him.

A persistent thumping permeated Carenza's consciousness, and she opened her eyes to unfamiliar surroundings. She was still in Julian's bed, daylight was streaming through the curtains, and someone was banging on the door.

She sat up, clutching the covers to her bosom, and shook Julian's shoulder. "Wake up! There's someone at the door."

He rolled onto his back and stared up at her as if he'd never seen her before.

"There's someone trying to get in!" she repeated.

It was enough to snap him out of his sleepy trance. He rolled out of bed. "Go back to your room. I'll deal with this."

"I'm naked."

He found her nightgown on the floor and threw it at her. "Go."

She'd barely made it into the dressing room before he was opening the door and demanding to know why Aragon was shouting at him.

"Put some clothes on, man!" Aragon boomed. "We're going riding."

Julian's reply was inaudible, but Carenza had a fair idea what it might be. She put on her nightgown but remained at the half-open door as Julian's voice rose to match his brother's.

"Aragon, please listen to me. I am not going bloody riding at the crack of dawn."

"Your loss," Aragon said cheerfully. "I'll go and ask Lady Carenza. Where exactly is her room situated?"

"You'll have to ask my housekeeper. With all the extra guests arriving, she had a struggle to fit everyone in and all my plans were overset. Now, go away. I'll see you after breakfast."

"Righty-ho." Aragon went quiet for a moment. "I say, you haven't got a woman hiding under the covers of that bed of yours, have you? Because she'll be gasping for air by now."

"I do not," Julian said. "Good morning, brother."

Carenza was still smiling when she returned to her own bedchamber and almost jumped when she disturbed a young maid laying a new fire.

"Good morning, my lady!" the girl said. "You're up nice and early. I'll tell Bea, shall I? Then she can bring up some water for your bath."

Over the remaining days of the house party, Julian made a point of distancing himself from Carenza during the day, but their wild nights continued to enchant him. Every male instinct in his body was telling him to keep her close, to roar at the world in her defense, and that would never do. The thoughts were so unusual for him, that it gave him cause to doubt them. He wasn't the kind of man who demanded such things from a sexual partner, and he wasn't quite sure how Carenza would react if he did. The thought of her ending their relationship completely was anathema to him, and he hated that, too.

So, keeping away from her—at least during the day—was sensible, and when had he ever been anything less? He spent his time making sure his guests had plenty to do—walks around the estate, carriage rides to local attractions, and endless food. Even his mother cracked a smile occasionally, although never when she thought he was observing her.

On the last day, he took them to a local church that had Saxon origins and some interesting standing stones in the graveyard that spoke of even earlier times.

After Carenza went off with Allegra into the church, Mrs. Sheraton took his arm. "Have you spoken to Lady Brenton yet?" she asked.

"I speak to her every day, ma'am, as I do all my guests."

She cast him a disapproving look. "Don't be coy. You know what I mean."

"That I'm expected to persuade her to tell me her plans for my downfall?" Julian inquired. "I still have a problem with your logic on this matter."

"You could at least try," Mrs. Sheraton observed as she kicked a stone on the path. "She's still devoted to you."

"Fine," Julian said. "If it means that you will stop nagging me, I'll make an attempt."

"Thank you." She gave him a warm smile. "She's lingering in the graveyard if you wish to speak to her now. I'll make sure the others stay in the church."

Repressing an irritated sigh, Julian went through the gate into the graveyard, where Lady Brenton sat perched on a large square gravestone, her head angled to one side, her beautiful face turned to the sun. He approached her somewhat warily, but she didn't appear to notice.

It wasn't until he cleared his throat that she affected a start and pressed her hand to her bosom. "Oh! Mr. Laurent, you startled me."

"I apologize." He inclined his head. "I came to see if you wished to go into the church. It's much cooler in there."

She gave a dainty shudder. "I'm not very fond of dark and dingy churches, sir. I prefer the sunshine."

"Quite understandable," he agreed. "I've never quite seen the appeal myself."

"You and I are similar in many ways, Mr. Laurent. I always said so." She glanced at him from under her lashes. "It's a shame we parted company."

Despite his desire to find out her plans, he couldn't bring himself to lie to her. "I suspect your husband would view the matter differently."

"I was indiscreet," she said flatly. "That was my sin. He has no issue with me having lovers, as he has no interest in bedding me himself."

Julian sat on the other corner of the gravestone. "With respect, why not? You are a very beautiful woman."

"Ours was not a love match." She shrugged. "He never liked sharing my bed. Once I'd conceived the two boys, he said that was enough of that and never came near me again. And it's not as if he already had a mistress on the side whom he loves—or a man, for that matter—he simply doesn't desire anyone."

Julian tried to think of something to say but she kept speaking.

"After the boys went to school, he gave me permission to seek other men for my pleasure—which was good of him, I suppose. But I was meant to be discreet about it, and I wasn't with you."

"I'm sorry."

"Sorrier that we were caught, rather than sorry for me, I'll wager." She met his gaze.

"Then you'd be wrong. No one should be trapped in a loveless marriage."

She looked away. "Don't be nice to me."

"I'm not. I'm simply expressing an opinion I've formed over the years." He hesitated. "I bear you no ill will for what happened."

She rose to her feet, brushing off her skirts. "How good of you. I, however, cannot reciprocate. You made me look foolish."

"How so?"

She looked back at him. "By telling everyone about the hilarious circumstances when you were caught by my husband in my bed."

He frowned. "I told no one."

"Then how is it that I heard your brother recounting the story at a ball in London just a week or so ago?"

"I didn't tell him." He looked down into her eyes, seeing both anger and, surprisingly, hurt in them. "I swear it."

"Still . . ."

"He isn't the most thoughtful of men. And, anyway, I'll wager he saw me as the fool in the story, not you."

"I don't believe you. Retelling such a yarn would be very much in keeping with the rakish and charming Julian Laurent, would it not?" She raised her chin. "I don't care anymore. One day someone will bring you down, and I'll laugh along with the rest of society."

"Do you believe my downfall is imminent?"

She smiled. "How would I know? But the sooner it happens, the more I'll enjoy it."

"I did not tell anyone about our last night together," Julian repeated. "I cannot allow you to believe such a lie about me."

"I can believe what I want, sir." She eased past him. "In truth, I am sick of the lot of you."

"Cressida . . ."

She swung back toward him. "You no longer have the right to use my first name."

"Then why did you agree to come to this house party if you can't stand the sight of me?"

She shrugged. "It was Mrs. Sheraton's idea. She likes to cause mischief. I assumed she was your latest mistress and that she'd decided to show me how happy you were without me."

"And knowing that, you still came?"

"Perhaps I wished to see it for myself, so that I could finally be free of you."

"And are you?" Julian asked.

She smiled, the sunlight illuminating her face. "Not quite, but I'm getting there."

He bowed. "I'm glad to hear it. I don't deserve such consideration."

"Another way we are alike, perhaps?" Lady Brenton moved toward the gate, and he walked alongside her. "Neither of us are capable of more than a few fleeting feelings that are easily dispersed when we find our next lover. I'm trapped in my marriage, but you . . ."

He raised an eyebrow. "What about me?"

"You just have no heart, Mr. Laurent."

She turned and walked away, her head held high, and disappeared in the direction of the church. Julian didn't follow her. Their discussion had raised several interesting points. He concluded that she really would relish his downfall and was potentially involved in bringing it about. Her comments as to his character had stung, but he wasn't prepared to dwell on them while he was experiencing such profound emotions in his relationship with Carenza.

But wasn't that why Carenza had agreed to bed him in the first place? She, too, thought he had no heart to break? He went through the gate and rested his hand on the warm stone wall that surrounded the graveyard as he stared in the direction of the church. He was tired of being thought of as a rake and not a man of substance. Even his own mother treated him like a wayward child, always anticipating the next scandal.

But he wasn't that man anymore. Now, how to convince everyone else of that?

Chapter 18

After their return to London, Carenza and Allegra were settling in for a quiet afternoon reading when Olivia and Maude were ushered in by the butler.

Carenza set her book to one side and sighed. "What is it now?"

Olivia took a seat and smoothed out her skirts. "Apparently, while we were away, Percival started spreading even worse rumors about Mr. Laurent."

"Such as?" Allegra asked.

"That Miss Cartwright is his mistress and that the home was set up to house all Julian's bastards."

"All twenty of them?" Carenza shook her head. "How ridiculous. Surely no one would believe such a thing."

"Mr. Laurent is regarded as a somewhat coldhearted man, Carenza," Maude said. "And there are many people in society who don't like him and would relish the opportunity to see him brought low."

"Then how can we support the Cartwrights and Mrs. Mountjoy and draw attention away from Julian?" Allegra asked.

"We could hold a charity ball or a concert on their behalf," Carenza said. "And show society that we all support these reputable institutions."

"That's a good idea." Olivia nodded. "I'll ask my godmother to head the committee. No one will argue with a duchess. I'll visit her this evening and secure a date for our venture."

"Are you sure she will agree?" Allegra asked.

"Yes, she gets terribly bored and loves a challenge," Olivia said. "Now, what can we do about Percival, whom I'm fairly certain is the source of all these rumors?"

All the ladies fell silent.

Carenza frowned. "I hate to admit it, but I suspect we'll need a man to deal with Percival. He's not going to listen to us, and if we do get involved, he'll wonder why, and that might make things even worse."

"I agree with Carenza," Allegra said. "I wonder if Aragon might help us?"

"Aragon? He's not exactly the cleverest of men," Olivia said.

"I think you underestimate his loyalty to his brother," Carenza said. "If Aragon was . . . carefully coached"—Olivia snorted—"I think he could deal with Percival, who is an incredibly weak man."

"But what could Aragon say to discredit Percival?" Maude asked.

"Percival is incredibly thin-skinned," Olivia said slowly. "He is afraid of being overlooked and supremely conscious of his status in life; hence, his hatred of Julian 'stealing' his fortune."

"Perhaps we could threaten to reveal how he treated his great-aunt," Carenza suggested. "Julian said she'd been badly neglected by her family. Percival would hate that to come to light."

"And Aragon might know about such treatment if he visited their aunt with Julian." Olivia looked at Carenza. "Do you want to approach Aragon, or should we do it together?"

"I think we should do it together," Carenza said.

"Excellent. Then invite him here tomorrow for tea, and I'll make sure to attend."

"What about Lady Brenton?" Allegra asked. "Have you all forgotten about her?"

Olivia made a face. "I had hoped that bringing her to Mr. Laurent's house party might persuade her to confide in Julian as to Percival's plans for him."

"Why would she do that, when she's actively plotting against him?" Allegra raised her eyebrows.

"Because I thought she still cared for him and that if he was . . . kind to her, she might regret her allegiances and confess all."

"You thought Mr. Laurent should pretend to care for her again in order to secure her confidences?" Carenza stared at Olivia.

"Yes! I already told you that." Olivia glared back. "Except he refused to do so."

"That's hardly surprising. Whatever you may think of men and him in particular, Olivia, he isn't that cruel."

"He's a man," Olivia stated. "He is capable of anything."

"And did Mr. Laurent speak to Lady Brenton as you requested?" Allegra looked at Olivia.

"He did."

"And?"

"He got the impression that she is actively involved in the attempt to blacken his reputation and had no intention of stopping. She said he'd made her a laughingstock by sharing the story of the end of their affair."

Maude frowned. "I am fairly well connected in society, and I've never heard anyone mention it."

"Mr. Laurent said he hadn't told anyone," Olivia said. "But the story is obviously out, and Lady Brenton is sufficiently angry about it to want revenge. I do have some sympathy about this, but I'm also convinced that Mr. Laurent isn't the source of the gossip."

"So many lies and misdirections," Carenza said. "Sometimes I hate the society we have created."

"We haven't created it," Olivia said. "And there is no reason why we have to constantly bow to its demands."

"Easy for you to say," Allegra sniffed. "Not all of us are fabulously wealthy widows. My chances of making a good marriage are constantly hampered by society's view of my parents as undesirables."

"There you go again, accepting defeat without even trying," Olivia said.

"I am trying." Allegra glared at her. "And I do not appreciate you making light of my misfortune."

"Can we perhaps get back to the matter in hand?" Carenza asked. "We have agreed to speak to Aragon, and we are fairly certain that Lady Brenton wishes Julian ill and has no intention of stopping. What else do we have to worry about?"

"Mr. Cox? Calloway? Our identities being revealed?" Olivia raised her eyebrows. "In your desire to protect Mr. Laurent have you forgotten about our own peril?"

"The two things appear to be linked, Olivia," Carenza replied. "If we can stop Percival, I suspect we'll have nothing to fear. His only interest in the matter is because he suspects Julian is involved."

"I hope you are right." Olivia didn't look convinced as she rose. "I'll be off. Let me know when Aragon can speak to us. In the meantime, I'll speak to my godmother about organizing that charity ball."

Carenza rose also and went over to Olivia to kiss her cheek. "I'll write a note to Aragon now and let you know the arrangements as soon as possible."

Olivia left and Allegra rang for more tea.

"As per usual, Olivia takes no responsibility for her actions over the advertisement. She always attempts to shift the blame to you, sister," Allegra said. "I find her quite infuriating sometimes."

"Don't we all," Carenza said. "But I still believe her heart is in the right place."

"I agree," Maude said. "She's been very kind to me recently."

"How are matters between you and Gerald?" Carenza asked.

Maude took a deep breath. "He's going back to Brussels."

"Oh, my dear." Carenza reached out to touch Maude's arm. "I'm so sorry."

"I'm not." Maude looked at her. "You were right about what you said. He does make me anxious and miserable. We had a terrible argument where he accused me of being undutiful. I suggested that his neglect of his family, and his pompous assurance that we were less important than his glittering career, meant that he was the one not doing his part. He was furious and suggested I'd never been an adequate wife and that I'd stalled his prospects by my unwillingness to constantly uproot the boys and follow him around Europe."

"That's a horrible thing to say," Allegra exclaimed.

Maude bit her lip. "After that, there was very little left to say to each other. He informed me over breakfast this morning that he'd applied for the post in Brussels and that was that." She looked at Allegra and then back at Carenza. "In a strange way, I'm almost relieved. I'm sure once he's settled in Brussels, we'll be able to have a more civil conversation about how to go on leading separate lives."

"It's still a shame," Carenza said. "No one wishes their marriage to experience such disharmony."

"Carenza does speak from experience, Maude," Allegra said helpfully. "Hector led her a merry dance."

"I am well aware of how badly my brother treated your sister, Allegra. I had many a word with him but with no obvious effect." Maude rose to her feet. "I must be going. Gerald had an interview at the Foreign Office this morning. They might even have offered him the job on the spot. I must prepare myself for such news."

"Please come to us if you need anything. We are quite discreet." Carenza walked Maude down the stairs to her waiting carriage. "And if you need to bring the boys, you are all welcome here."

"Thank you." Maude's eyes were shining with unshed tears. "That means a lot to me."

"We are still sisters-in-law and your boys are my nephews," Carenza reminded her. "Hector's death doesn't change that."

She went back upstairs in a somewhat pensive mood to find Allegra awaiting her.

"Poor old Maude," Allegra said. "It does make me wonder whether being a spinster is a better alternative to being married to a complete fool."

Carenza went over to her writing desk and sat down. "I must admit that I never liked Gerald. He always struck me as something of a sycophant, always fawning over those he thought could smooth his path to greatness. Hector didn't like him, either. It was one of the very few things we agreed on."

She took out a fresh piece of cut paper and opened her inkwell. "Now what should I say to Aragon to make him come and see me with all haste?"

"Just say exactly that. He's very biddable," Allegra advised. "And very fond of you, too."

"We've discussed that. He's realized I'm not the right woman for him. I think he's got his eye on Olivia now."

"The poor man."

Carenza looked over at her sister. "You seem somewhat out of sorts with our friend. Has something else happened that I don't know about?"

"She's just . . . *infuriating* sometimes. This whole mess with the advertisement is totally her fault, yet she refuses to admit it."

"So you've said." Carenza returned her attention to the composition of her note. "But she's always been like that."

"You are far more tolerant of her nonsense than I am."

"Possibly because I am in a better position to understand the horror of her marriage to a man old enough to be her grandfather."

Allegra fixed her with a hard stare that reminded Carenza of their father. "You can't always make excuses for her."

"I don't." Carenza finished the short note, signed it, and got up to ring the bell. "Do you wish to be here when Aragon visits? I've asked him to come around tomorrow afternoon."

"I don't wish to be there at all," Allegra declared, her nose in the air as she got to her feet.

"Then I will make sure that you are not."

Allegra opened the door and then turned to look at Carenza. "You asked why I don't trust Olivia, but I'm not sure you'd wish to hear the truth."

"It's most unlike you to keep anything to yourself, sister," Carenza responded. "If there is something you wish to say, please say it."

Allegra took a deep breath. "I'm fairly certain she was Hector's mistress."

"Haven't we had this discussion before? She is a terrible flirt, Hector was even worse, and they were often together in my company."

"I saw them together at a house party," Allegra said in something of a rush. "My bedchamber was next door to Hector's, and I recognized Olivia's voice in his room."

"And where was I when this was supposedly going on?"

Allegra met her gaze. "You were . . . unwell. It was just before you lost the baby."

Carenza felt the words like a low blow to her stomach and gripped the back of the chair so hard her fingers hurt.

Allegra frowned. "Now I wish I hadn't told you. You look as if you're going to swoon."

"I'll be . . . all right." Carenza reminded herself to breathe as Allegra's obvious concern washed over her. "As I said, it was all a long time ago."

"I'm sorry," Allegra whispered. "I shouldn't have said anything."

Carenza turned away and concentrated on folding her letter into a neat square even though her hands were shaking.

"Carenza . . ."

"I can't talk about this right now." Carenza was surprised at how calm her voice was.

"All right." There was a pause in which Carenza devoutly hoped her sister had gone, but there was no such luck. "Can I do anything to help?"

"No, thank you."

Allegra finally left, and Carenza sealed her note and wrote Aragon's address on the front in an uneven hand quite unlike her usual script.

The butler appeared, and she handed him the note. "Please wait for a reply."

"Yes, my lady." He bowed. "Mr. Laurent has called and is asking if he might speak to you."

Julian . . .

She couldn't allow him to see her like this. She was his mistress, and such women were not supposed to bring their everyday heartbreaks and cares into the bedroom with them. If she saw him, the desire to throw herself at his chest and cry might overcome her usual calm regard.

She took a deep breath. "Please tell Mr. Laurent that I am not at home. I have a headache and I intend to retire to bed."

* * *

After hearing Carenza wasn't receiving visitors, Julian turned toward the door to leave. He paused when he heard someone calling his name.

"Mr. Laurent, wait."

Lady Allegra came down the stairs and hurried toward him. "Are you here to see Carenza?"

"That was my intention, but your butler told me she is not receiving visitors."

"Come with me." She took his hand and led him up the stairs.

"Are you quite sure that I shouldn't accept her decision, and—"

Lady Allegra shushed him as they approached the drawing room door. "She needs you."

Julian went still. "What has happened?"

"I upset her by talking about Hector and Olivia." She met his concerned stare. "I know that they were lovers."

Inwardly, Julian winced. He'd known, too, but it wasn't something he'd ever wished Carenza to know. He said, "One might ask why you felt it necessary to share that information at this late a date."

"Because Carenza keeps sticking up for Olivia! Please go and speak to her. I'll keep everyone away." Lady Allegra walked away from him.

Julian tapped lightly on the door and went in. Carenza sat at her writing desk with her back to him. She didn't turn around, so he approached her. Something about the stiffness of her posture made him realize she was crying.

"My dear girl."

Her breathing hitched and she hurriedly searched in her pocket for a handkerchief. "Julian, you startled me. I thought I told the butler not to let you in. I have a terrible headache."

He handed her his own immaculately laundered handkerchief and pulled up a chair to sit beside her.

"Your sister told me that you were upset and that you needed me."

"Allegra is so like our father. She tells her 'truth' and then runs away, leaving someone else to pick up the pieces."

"She acknowledged that she'd been the one to upset you," Julian said carefully.

Carenza slowly turned to look at him. "I suppose you knew as well."

He didn't pretend not to know what she was talking about—she deserved his honesty. "Yes."

"Why didn't you mention it?"

He held her gaze. "Because I knew it would hurt you. It was one of the reasons why Hector and I were on such bad terms before he died."

"Allegra said she had the misfortune to be in the room next to Hector's at a house party and she heard him with Olivia."

"I'm sorry, Carenza."

"It's hardly your fault, is it?" She tried to smile as she brushed at the tears on her cheeks. "This is why I told the butler to deny you entry. You agreed to be my lover, not my confidant."

"I am quite capable of being both."

"Once, I would've agreed with you, but Hector encouraged me to pour my heart out to him, only to use my own feelings against me when he fell out of love with me."

"Hector was incapable of loving anyone but himself."

"I realized that eventually, but it took me far too long." She paused. "I was glad when he died. It felt like a blessed release."

"No one could blame you for feeling like that."

"I suspect most people would," Carenza said. "When I said my vows to him, I meant every word."

"Yes, but I doubt he ever kept a promise in his life."

Carenza got up and walked over to the window, and Julian followed her. He tentatively put his hand on her shoulder.

"If you knew how Hector was, then why did Allegra's revelation upset you so badly?"

"Firstly, because Olivia hasn't been truthful with me, and secondly . . ." She hesitated. "Because she inadvertently reminded me of the darkest point in my marriage."

"Tell me."

She half turned toward him, her expression grave. "I'm not sure if—"

"*Tell me.*"

She met his gaze. "Looking back, I don't think Hector wanted me to go to that particular house party, probably because he'd made some arrangements with Olivia. I was determined to go, and, in my usual stupid fashion, I was following him around the house while he tried to leave, attempting to argue with him. He lost his temper and slapped my face." She paused. "Unfortunately, we were at the top of the stairs. I lost my balance and fell all the way down to the front hall. The last thing I remember is him stepping over me to get to his carriage."

"He didn't even stop to see if you were all right?" Julian asked, even though he was fairly sure of the answer.

"He shouted at me that it was my own damn fault and that I shouldn't be so clumsy," Carenza said. "In fact, he aimed a kick at my ribs as he went by."

"The absolute bastard," Julian said.

"I think I must have fainted because the next thing I knew I was surrounded by the servants and someone was shouting about fetching the doctor. I tried to sit up, but there was a lot of blood."

Julian waited, but she seemed to be struggling to go on. "Blood from where you hit your head?" he asked.

"Unfortunately not." She met his gaze. "I was pregnant, and later that night, I lost my child. Hector couldn't even be bothered to come back to see if either of us lived or died."

Julian stared at her so intently that her features began to

blur. It took all his concentration to keep the rage he felt on her behalf inside him.

"If I'd known that at the time, I would've beaten him to death."

"Which is exactly why I didn't tell anyone." Carenza sounded far calmer than he felt. "Can you imagine what my father would've done if he heard how Hector had treated me? I couldn't heap more scandal on his head. Hector, of course, insisted that it was all my fault, that I was too weak to bear his children, and that his dalliances outside our marriage were justified. It took me several weeks to recover from the loss of blood, and my grief often overwhelmed me, which is why I chose to remain in the country that year."

Julian stared at her until she offered him a small smile.

"That's why I know I can't have children. There was too much damage done. At least you can be assured of that."

"Do you really think that is what I'm concerned with?" Julian demanded. "That all I care about is how this matter relates to *me*?"

She raised her chin, tears shining in her eyes. "If you're going to shout, will you please leave? I really cannot deal with your anger today."

He cursed as he yanked her into his arms and held her as tightly as he could. After a moment, she relaxed against his chest, her palm flat over his fast-beating heart. He kissed the top of her head and rocked her back and forth like the child she had lost. He could no longer deny that he cared for her. The least he could do was hold her while she grieved for what had been so cruelly taken away from her.

After a while, she raised her head and looked up at him. "Thank you."

"For what? Allowing you to soak my new waistcoat in tears? Proctor will never forgive me."

She cupped his cheek. "Send him my apologies."

"As I have no intention of sharing what happened between

us with anyone, I'll only make apologies for myself." He studied her beautiful face. "Did he hit you often?"

She went still. "It hardly matters now."

"Then he did." Julian set his jaw. "I'm actually disappointed he's already dead, because I can't kill him myself."

"He's not worth it, Julian," Carenza said softly. "We both know that."

"You are a far better person than I will ever be, my dear, because I disagree. I was supposed to be his best friend, but I made very little attempt to curb his excesses until it was too late."

He wanted to say more, but their current conversation was not meant to be about him but about what Hector had done to Carenza.

"You should go," Carenza said.

He wanted to suggest he take her to bed, but he already knew she wouldn't countenance such behavior in her father's house.

"You could come with me?" he suggested. "My bed is very comfortable."

"I know it is." She smiled. "Don't tempt me when I have things to do."

"Are they as important as spending the afternoon with me?"

She visibly sought for her composure. "Unfortunately, on this occasion, yes. We've decided to organize a ball to show our support for the Cartwrights and Mrs. Mountjoy."

"We?"

"Olivia, Allegra, and myself."

Julian frowned. "What brought this on?"

She didn't react to his change of tone. "Percival is now suggesting that the Cartwrights exist solely to deal with all your bastard offspring."

"The devil they do." Julian set his jaw. "I'm of a mind to seek out Percival and make this matter very personal indeed."

"Please don't do that." Carenza touched his arm. "Will you simply allow us to help you for once?"

He hated the very idea. "If I must."

"Then good." She nodded. "Hold your fire and let us deal with Percival Walcott. I can assure you that we don't want him to get away with anything."

Chapter 19

"Ladies." Aragon strode into the drawing room and bowed. "How may I help you?"

Carenza glanced at Olivia, who nodded for her to continue. "We need your help."

"Mine?" Aragon looked absurdly pleased. "Are you certain you don't mean my brother's?"

Carenza gestured to a seat. "As this matter concerns your brother, we think you are the best person to help us."

"I'll do my best." Aragon sat down. "Does this have something to do with that pesky Walcott fellow?"

Olivia and Carenza exchanged a startled glance.

"Has Julian spoken to you about him?" Olivia asked.

"I spoke to him. I offered to go and have a word with Walcott to set matters straight, but Julian wasn't very keen on the idea." Aragon paused. "To put it bluntly, he thinks I'm too stupid to pull it off."

"I'm sure he doesn't—"

"He's got a point, though, hasn't he?" Aragon waved away Carenza's concern. "I'm not exactly known for my intelligence. But I do want to help him. If you ladies have any ideas as to how I might do that, I'm all ears."

"We think you need to convince Percival that you share a common grievance against your brother," Carenza said.

"Because Julian is now wealthier than both of us?" Aragon

nodded. "It's never bothered me, but I'm fairly certain I could pretend that it did to gain Walcott's confidence. I suggested to Julian that I should do something similar." He looked at Olivia. "Then what?"

"This is the tricky part," Olivia said. "You need to find out what Percival plans to do next."

"I can do that," Aragon said. "And not by asking, but by listening. You'd be surprised what you can pick up if you keep your mouth shut and everyone thinks you're a dullard."

"We don't think that about you." Carenza held his gaze. "It would be good to know exactly whom Percival is conspiring with and whether he's been having Julian followed."

"Followed?" Aragon frowned. "Devil take it, that's not nice."

"It's the only way Percival could've known about Julian's visits to the Cartwrights and Mrs. Mountjoy."

"And to the Wheatsheaf," Olivia added. "I'm particularly interested in how well Percival knows a Mr. Calloway and what particular interests they share."

"Calloway isn't the sort of man who anyone should befriend," Aragon said severely. "He's a disgrace to his family." He paused. "Why would he be after Julian?"

Olivia said, "He saw your brother at the Wheatsheaf Inn when the lady who placed an advertisement for a lover was holding her interviews."

There was a long silence as Aragon regarded them rather incredulously.

"I can quite imagine Calloway being there, but my brother? He hardly needs to answer an advertisement for a woman, they fling themselves at him constantly."

Carenza went to speak, but Olivia got in ahead of her. "That was my fault. I placed the advertisement as a joke, and poor Mr. Laurent was attempting to defend my honor."

"Ah, I see." Aragon looked at Olivia. "No need for you

to advertise, either, ma'am. I'd be more than happy to oblige you."

"That's very sweet of you, sir, but I have recently decided to embrace my widowhood and concentrate on good works."

Carenza rolled her eyes, and even Aragon didn't look quite convinced. He cleared his throat. "To summarize, you wish me to become Walcott's confidant and to find out his plans and whom he's associating with, yes?"

"Exactly." Olivia nodded. "We have complete faith in you."

"More than my brother does," Aragon grumbled good-naturedly. "I appreciate the vote of confidence." He stood up. "In truth, I've already made a start on gaining his trust. Walcott's usually at our club at this time of day. I'll attempt to involve him in a conversation and see how willing he is to accept me as an ally. And don't worry, I won't mention any of this to Julian or my mother. I'll report back to one of you."

He went out, leaving Olivia and Carenza staring at each other.

"I hope we haven't made a terrible mistake," Olivia said.

"I don't think so," Carenza replied. "Would you care for some tea, or do you have other errands to run? Allegra should be back for luncheon. She's at the modiste's getting a new gown for the charity ball."

Olivia took a deep breath. "Allegra wrote me a note asking me not to come today."

"I have no idea why." Carenza walked over to the bell and rang it, her back to Olivia.

"She said she'd told you about Hector."

Carenza wished she didn't have to turn around, but she knew it was important that she did. "Yes."

Olivia swallowed hard. "I know you won't believe me, but I didn't mean for it to happen."

"You had a prearranged assignation with my husband at

a house party where you knew morals were lax, and you're suggesting it all happened by accident?"

Olivia raised her chin. "I did agree to meet him, yes, but I didn't want things to go as far as they did. I also expected you to be there."

"To prevent you both from indulging in adultery? Surely you know that Hector was quite capable of fucking another woman in the bed I was supposed to share with him at such events?"

Olivia winced. "I didn't—"

"And were you aware of the reason I didn't accompany him?"

"He . . . said that you were indisposed."

"I suppose it didn't occur to you to wonder why I was so conveniently absent?"

"I'm not sure what you mean."

Carenza held her gaze. "Hector was so desperate for me to not accompany him that he ordered me to stay home. When I protested, he hit me so hard I fell down the stairs, which caused me to miscarry our child."

All the color drained from Olivia's face. "He . . . couldn't have known."

"You're *defending* him? He knew he'd hurt me, Olivia. He had to step over me to get to his waiting carriage and scolded me for being in the way. But I'm glad you enjoyed bedding him. I hope it was worth it."

Olivia's hands clenched into fists. "Firstly, I am a widow, and whom I bed is up to me. The only adulterer was Hector."

"I'm fully aware that Hector is to blame and that what happened before he arrived at the house party is hardly your fault. What hurt was your disloyalty to *me*," Carenza said. "Your friend."

"As to that, and you may choose to believe me or not"—Olivia's voice shook—"I thought to expose Hector publicly as the adulterer he was. I *thought* that when he brought me back to his room you would be there. I intended to cause a really loud scene and finally force you to condemn him in public."

"Except I wasn't there."

"And I misjudged Hector's strength and intent," Olivia said. "He had no intention of allowing me to leave without paying the price for my stupid plan." She shrugged. "I knew how to lie quietly under a man and pretend I wasn't there, but he still enjoyed hurting me."

Silence fell as Carenza struggled to understand what Olivia was telling her.

Olivia's smile was wry. "I don't expect you to feel sorry for me. I was the fool. I became yet another of Hector's conquests, and I ruined my friendship with you. I should not have interfered."

"No, you shouldn't have," Carenza said.

Olivia's face crumpled. "I'm so sorry about the baby." She turned and ran out of the room.

The butler appeared with the tea tray, looking startled.

"Thank you." Carenza took a deep breath. "Mrs. Sheraton had to leave rather suddenly."

"Do you still wish to have the tea, my lady? Cook is already preparing lunch."

"Yes, please, but could you also bring me a small glass of brandy?"

Jones, who had known her since she was a child, gave her a concerned look. "Is everything all right, my lady?"

"Everything is fine." She summoned a smile. "Please don't tell my father that I've taken to drink."

"I wouldn't dream of it, my lady." He bowed. "I'll fetch your brandy."

Carenza realized how badly she was shaking only when she tried to pour the tea and spilled it all over the tray. A moment later, Jones returned with the brandy and left. She swallowed it quickly, hoping it would calm her nerves enough to allow her to go over her conversation with Olivia again.

"Carenza?" Allegra came in, her expression concerned. "I saw Olivia leaving the house in tears. She wouldn't even speak to me. Is everything all right?"

After Carenza explained what had happened between herself and Olivia, Allegra sat carefully on the sofa, looking stunned. "Good Lord. I could murder Hector for all the hurt he's caused."

"I suspect you'll have to join a very long queue for that," Carenza said.

"More to the point, did you believe what Olivia told you?"

"Yes." Carenza looked at her sister. "She had no reason to lie to me, and it sounds just like something Hector would do."

"To force someone?" Allegra made a face. "Ugh."

"I don't know if my friendship with Olivia will survive this," Carenza said miserably.

"But isn't that just what Hector would've wanted?" Allegra asked. "He probably encouraged Olivia, because he knew she was your friend."

"Mayhap she shouldn't have taken the bait."

"This is Olivia we're talking about. She thinks she's right about everything. She probably thought she was helping you. And, let's be honest, Carenza, she ended up being hurt by Hector as well." Allegra set down her cup. "In my opinion, the blame lies completely with Hector. If you can find it in your heart to forgive Olivia, you will deny him the very thing he wanted—to split you apart."

"I'll have to think about it," Carenza countered.

"Quite understandable." Allegra nodded. "And while you're thinking, you'll still have to work with her to stop the gossip about the advertisement and the slurs against Julian. It's the only thing to do."

"I am well aware of that," Carenza said. "But whether Olivia is willing to continue is another matter entirely."

"Oh, she will," Allegra said. "She has everything to gain and nothing to lose."

Julian entered the Wheatsheaf and strode through into the pub. His gaze immediately fixed on the landlord. "Good afternoon, Mr. Cox," Julian said as he approached the bar.

"Mr. Laurent." Mr. Cox looked anywhere but at Julian. "I'm afraid I don't have much time to chat. There's a coach due in."

"I'm sure someone can handle it for you," Julian said easily. "My business won't wait."

"Then come through to my parlor."

Julian followed Mr. Cox into the house next door. A woman he hadn't seen before was making bread at the kitchen table.

"Good afternoon, ma'am." Julian took off his hat.

"Don't mind me, sir," the woman said. "I'll keep to my own business."

"You should probably leave, Betty, love," Mr. Cox said somewhat nervously. "There's no need for you to bother your head about my business with Mr. Laurent."

"I disagree," Julian said. "Surely Mrs. Cox would like to know you've been blackmailing the lady who employs your daughter?"

"What's that?" Mrs. Cox thumped the dough onto the table and stared at her husband, her floury hands on her hips. "I told you to leave Mrs. Sheraton alone!"

"Unfortunately, Mr. Cox hasn't heeded your wise counsel, ma'am," Julian said. "He's also been attempting to blackmail me simply for helping the two ladies who paid him in good faith for the use of his parlor."

"Is this true, Reginald? I told you to take care!" Mrs. Cox's face took on an alarming hue. "You'll be the one who will suffer, not those toffs!"

Mr. Cox swung around to stare at Julian. "I was going to stop, sir, but that Mr. Calloway told me he'd ruin me if I didn't persist!"

"Did he?" Julian said. "I don't suppose he was foolish enough to commit those words to paper?"

"Show him, Reginald," Mrs. Cox commanded. "Maybe he can help get you out of this mess."

The look Mr. Cox gave Julian and his wife was full of doubt.

"This one hasn't threatened to ruin you, has he?" Mrs. Cox said. "He's a proper gentleman. That Mr. Calloway is just a bad man."

Mr. Cox scurried over to the sideboard and produced a letter. He handed it to Julian, and Julian noted the Calloway seal before reading the letter's contents.

"May I keep this?" he asked.

Mrs. Cox nodded. "You can do what you like with it if you promise to get my Reggie off the hook."

"I think I can manage that." Julian put the letter in his pocket. "Thank you, ma'am." He turned to Mr. Cox. "I'll be in touch with you very shortly to confirm that all is well. In the meantime, I'd appreciate it if you kept this meeting to yourself."

"He will," Mrs. Cox said grimly as she went back to kneading her dough. "Or he'll have to answer to me."

When Julian arrived home, he went straight into Simon's office, where his secretary was busy with the accounts.

"Good afternoon, sir. You've received an invitation to a ball."

"And. . . ?"

"It's a charity ball for the Cartwrights and Mrs. Mountjoy." Simon looked at him. "Were you aware that such an event was in the offing?"

"Who is the invitation from?"

"The Duchess of Grantleigh and her committee, which includes the ladies Carenza and Allegra Musgrove and Mrs. Sheraton."

"Then accept it," Julian said. "Do you know which club Calloway's father belongs to?"

"I believe it's the same as yours, sir," Simon said. "I also have his home address if that helps."

"We'll try both." Julian turned on his heel. "Come along. I'd like a witness to my conversation with the earl about his son's blackmailing attempts."

"Blackmailing?"

Julian barely heard Simon's reply as he strode toward the front door. His secretary came after him as he climbed into his carriage and paused only to give the coachman directions before he got in and sat across from his employer.

"Would you care to tell me what's going on, sir?"

"Oh, you'll find out soon enough. I have no intention of concealing any of the younger Calloway's indiscretions from his father." Julian tapped on the roof with his cane, and the carriage moved off. "In truth, I'm quite looking forward to it."

Chapter 20

The next day Julian contemplated the many portraits of his ancestors on the drawing room walls while waiting for his mother to appear. He rarely saw any likeness to himself, because he'd inherited his looks from his mother. Was that why she disliked him? Did she hate the comparison, or simply think he couldn't be a true Laurent if he didn't look like one?

He checked the clock on the mantelpiece. She'd requested his appearance at noon, and it was almost half past the hour. If she didn't grace him with her presence in the next few minutes, he'd make his excuses and leave. He owed Mr. Cox a last visit to tell him not to worry about Jeremy Calloway anymore. Jeremy's father had been furious to find out what his son was up to and had promised to put a stop to it immediately. Julian had complete faith that he'd rein in his son—which would put an end to the speculation about the advertisement.

He didn't greatly care about Walcott's attempts to smear his reputation, but saving Carenza and Mrs. Sheraton from social ruin was an imperative. The door opened, and his mother swept in, followed by his brother. To Julian's surprise, they appeared to be having a ferocious argument, which was unheard of.

"Julian." Aragon finally acknowledged him.

"Brother." Julian bowed and then turned to their mother, one eyebrow raised. "Ma'am."

"You must stop him," his mother said. "Carenza Musgrove was bad enough, but this new woman, who runs a . . . haven for thieves, is beyond the pale."

Aragon looked at Julian over his mother's head. "We received an invitation for a charity ball this morning hosted by the Duchess of Grantleigh. I mentioned that I'd visited the Cartwrights and found them excellent and worthy people."

"Ah, I see." Julian nodded.

"Yet again, you have deliberately introduced my son to an unsuitable woman," his mother said. "One might begin to think that your motives in doing so are Machiavellian!"

"You suspect I'm angling for the earldom?" Julian blinked at her. "Why on earth would I do that, when I am very comfortably situated on my own?"

"Please don't crow about your ill-gotten wealth, Julian. It is extremely vulgar."

"I'm hardly—"

Aragon spoke over him. "Please stop this, Mother. I've already told you that none of this has anything to do with Julian."

"You don't know what he's like, Aragon." The countess turned to her oldest son. "He's always been difficult, he's never tried to fit in with our family, and—"

Aragon held up one finger. "I said stop. Can you hear yourself? Julian has always been the best of brothers. *Your* dislike of him is the issue at hand, Mother. Not his of you or me."

"I don't know what you're talking about." The countess sniffed.

"You've never liked him. You've always treated him like a pariah in his own family, and you encouraged all of us to do the same." Aragon was far from his usual affable self. "If there is any apologizing to be done, it should be coming from you."

The countess swung around toward Julian. "You see? You see what you've done? You've destroyed his affection for me."

"No," Aragon said. "You've done that entirely by yourself." He suddenly looked quite formidable. "If you can't be civil to Julian, I'd rather you left Town. This is my house, and he is my brother, and, as I've already told you, he is always welcome here."

"And I am not?" The countess drew herself up.

"Not until you remember your manners and stop blaming Julian for everything in the entire world."

The countess turned on her heel and left the room, banging the door behind her.

In the sudden silence, Julian looked over at his brother. "You didn't have to do that."

"Yes, I did."

"I've grown so used to her dislike of me that it barely registers."

"Of course it registers," Aragon said. "Once you pointed it out, I began to see it for myself, and I was ashamed of how I'd treated you."

"There is no need for you to feel like that," Julian said.

"Again, I am going to disagree with you." Aragon came over and punched Julian on the shoulder. "And, as your older brother, *and* an earl, I would appreciate it if you'd do as you are told for once."

Julian cleared his throat. "Thank you."

"You are most welcome." Aragon grinned at him. "Now, are you involved in the planning of this ball, or is it something the ladies cooked up by themselves?"

To Carenza's relief, Olivia seemed more than willing to continue working with her and Allegra on the charity ball committee. Miss Cartwright was disinclined to involve herself in anything so worldly and had only agreed because her more practically minded brother reminded her they always needed money and that if they wished to expand, it was essential. Mrs. Mountjoy was thrilled to participate and, as the daughter of a viscount, she had all the necessary skills to understand the process of delivering a ball.

Aware that Julian's reputation could take only so much damage, the ladies made plans with some haste. Having a duchess at its helm meant that most doors were open to the committee and suppliers strove to offer them the best deals available. Mrs. Mountjoy was in her element and happily took on most of the work as she had both the time and the best bargaining skills. The duchess had her own ballroom attached to her vast London house, which made things easier, and a full staff to assist the committee in every way possible.

Carenza and Allegra took on the job of dispensing the invitations and organizing the replies, which was quite a task in itself. Luckily, Allegra loved making lists, and Carenza was happy to let her have her way.

One afternoon, a few days before the ball, Aragon appeared in the drawing room without his brother and with news to impart. Carenza, delighted to be released from her sister's small tyrannies, sat down with him to hear how he'd gotten along.

"Walcott is completely convinced that I'm in agreement with him about Julian," Aragon said. "In truth, I hardly had to complain before he started on about all his little grievances. I don't think he cared about mine, just that someone agreed with him."

"That sounds like Percival," Carenza said. "He is the kind of man who sees an insult in everything."

"I got drunk with him last night," Aragon continued. "It takes only a couple of bottles to see him under the table; whereas, I can drink about ten before I even feel a bit woozy."

"How extraordinary." Carenza stared at him. "And what did Percival reveal when he was in his cups?"

"That he's out for public revenge," Aragon said simply. "I hope I did the right thing, but I mentioned the charity ball as the perfect venue for him to humiliate Julian. He was very taken by the idea and said he would consult with Lady Brenton to see what she thought."

"I knew there had to be a woman with brains behind his schemes," Allegra commented as she joined them. "I should imagine she'll be thrilled to see Julian thrown to the wolves."

"Good. Then I did do the right thing." Aragon looked relieved. "I also noticed something else. Walcott is very short of the readies. He said he'd borrowed heavily on his expectations and that it was Julian's fault he couldn't repay his debts. He also likes to gamble. Several gentlemen approached him in my hearing asking most politely when he expects to repay them."

"Gambling debts are debts of honor," Allegra mused. "Not as easy to get out of as tradesmen's bills without a complete loss of reputation."

"I wonder if it would be possible to buy some of that debt?" Aragon asked. "I did it for a friend of mine once. He'd been fleeced at a gaming hall."

"You did?"

Aragon shrugged. "Chap was a good friend of mine, couldn't let him down."

Carenza reached over and patted Aragon's hand. "You are such a good man."

"Hardly. I let my mother bully Julian for years before I saw it for what it was." He looked up. "I told her to mend her manners or she could go back to the country and prepare to move to the dower house."

"You did?" Allegra echoed Carenza's earlier comment. "Well done."

"Mother was horrible about you, Lady Carenza. And Miss Cartwright. I couldn't have that."

"Of course not," Carenza agreed. She glanced at her sister, who nodded. "I think the idea of quietly buying up Percival's gaming debts is a brilliant one. It would be excellent leverage against him. We would be happy to lend you money to accomplish such a feat."

"There's no need." Aragon waved away the offer with his usual good humor. "I might not be as rich as Julian, but I have deep pockets. I'll put out some discreet inquiries immediately."

The butler appeared at the door. "Mr. Laurent has called, my lady. Do you wish me to show him up?"

"Good Lord." Aragon shot to his feet. "Not until I'm on my way out." He hurried toward the door. "Don't tell him anything, yet. He'll probably kill me for interfering."

"Interfering in what?" Julian asked as his brother pushed past him.

"Nothing!" Aragon said. "Good day, ladies," he shouted before running down the stairs.

Julian surveyed Carenza's and Allegra's remarkably guilty faces. "Is there something I should know?"

"Absolutely not," Carenza said as she came over to kiss him. "Aragon was simply telling us how he stood up to your mother. It's about time, too."

"I suspect she overstepped the mark with her criticisms of Miss Cartwright," Allegra added helpfully. "Aragon seems very keen on her."

Julian sighed. "He has the most unfortunate habit of fixating on the same women I admire."

"Ah, so you do have a tendre for Miss Cartwright." Allegra gave Carenza a knowing look. "I thought as much."

"I simply meant that I appreciate her dedication to her cause."

Carenza smiled. "It's all right, Julian. Your admiration for Miss Cartwright is hardly a secret. She would make any gentleman an excellent wife."

He studied her expression. Was there a hint of jealousy

behind her calm words? It was difficult to tell with Carenza, who wore her mask like a professional actor. And did he want her to be jealous? Hadn't he spent his entire adult life avoiding strong emotions, choosing his partners with an eye to their lack of interest in establishing a permanent relationship with him?

Allegra stood up, as did Julian. "I have to go out. I'll tell Jones to deny any visitors for the rest of the afternoon." She smiled at her sister. "Most of the staff are having their half day off, so you won't be disturbed."

"Thank you, Allegra."

Julian didn't miss the wink Allegra gave him as she left the room and the color that flooded Carenza's cheeks. He sat down next to Carenza and took her hand.

"I do have some good news for you."

"I'll be pleased to hear it." She met his gaze, her hazel eyes warm.

"Jeremy Calloway was behind Mr. Cox's blackmail efforts against you and Mrs. Sheraton. He was foolish enough to put his threats in writing. When confronted with the evidence of his son's duplicity, the elder Calloway promised to rectify Jeremy's behavior immediately."

"That is good news," Carenza agreed. "Olivia will be delighted."

"I don't believe there was much of a connection between what Walcott's been up to and what happened at the inn, so stopping Calloway should put an end to the threats," Julian concluded. "In truth, I hardly think it's worth going to all the bother of having the ball."

"Allegra and I think it is," Carenza said. "It is equally important to us that your name is cleared."

"With respect, that is hardly your concern."

"Is it not?" Carenza raised her eyebrows. "I thought we were friends."

"We are."

"Then we have just as much right to help you as you do us." She frowned. "Unless you're suggesting we're not as capable because we are female."

"How on earth did you assume that from what I said?" Julian asked. "I already have the upper hand with Percival Walcott. He's lost in the courts. All he has left is his constant complaining."

"But he's attempting to blacken the reputations of those who are associated with you," Carenza said gently. "That's why it's important to hold the ball."

He studied her for a long moment and then nodded. "Fair enough."

"You're *agreeing* with me?"

"I am capable of conceding a point, Carenza."

"When?"

He brought her hand to his mouth and kissed it. "Did Allegra say that we won't be disturbed for the next few hours, or did I misunderstand her?"

"Oh, now I see. You're being conciliatory, because you want me to take you to bed."

"Am I succeeding?"

"Yes, but only because I am desperate to be touched."

He drew her to her feet. "How desperate?"

Her sultry smile woke a fire in his body. "Very."

"Then come along." He marched her toward the door. "It's one of those rare moments when we're both thinking alike. We can continue our argument later."

She took him into her bedchamber, and he made certain to lock all the doors from the inside. Her room was at the back of the house, looking out over the garden and the mews beyond, which meant no one could see them.

They undressed each other slowly, enjoying the need not to rush for a change. Despite the sunlight filtering through the windows, it wasn't warm and Carenza's nipples were tight. She shivered when he cupped her breast and took one nipple into his mouth.

"That's lovely."

"I can do so much more," Julian said as he used his fingers on her other breast and slid his other hand between her legs to find her wet and waiting for him. "You smell delicious."

"That's need." She groaned as his thumb brushed her clit, and she moved sensuously against his hand. "I never realized . . ."

He raised his head to look at her. "What?"

Her smile was awkward. "Nothing."

He led her over to the bed and stripped the covers away so that she could lie down on the sheets. He climbed up and straddled her, his hips pinning her to the bed. "What hadn't you realized?"

She sighed. "Trust you to never let anything go."

"It is one of my most infuriating traits," he agreed as he stroked her breasts and pinched her nipples. He'd missed her—he'd missed this. "I suspect you were about to comment that you'd never realized how good having sex could be until you'd bedded me."

"As Hector was my only other lover, that's hardly much of a compliment."

"I'm hurt." He set his teeth on her nipple, making her squeak. "Perhaps I'll make you reconsider that statement." He licked the place he'd nipped, and she groaned, her hips rolling helplessly beneath his. "Should I fuck you hard enough to make you sore? Your nipples chafing against your stays, your clit throbbing against the starch of your petticoats? We both know how much you like that." He slid three fingers inside her. "Shall I stretch you here with my cock ramming into you, without thought of your comfort, concerned only with my desires?"

"Yes," she breathed. "All of that."

He set the crown of his cock at her entrance and slid home, making them both gasp. "And there's more to play with, my darling. I could thrust into your mouth until your lips are tired from sucking me. Or take you here." He fingered the tight bud of her arse. "Hard."

She came so suddenly that it almost caught him off guard. He had to grit his teeth and hold her still until he mastered the urge to come with her.

"So very eager," he murmured as she quivered in his arms, his heartbeat mirrored in the throb of his cock. "Now, what else have you realized?"

She mock-groaned. "That you are indeed the perfect lover? And that I will miss you when you move on to someone else?"

He stared down at her beautiful, passion-filled face. How could he ever move on from her? The question made him go still. "Carenza . . ."

"What?"

"Will you marry me?"

She blinked at him. "That isn't funny."

"It wasn't meant to be."

She pushed at his chest, and he rolled off her. She immediately sat up, drew her knees to her chest, and wrapped her arms around them. "That isn't what I want, or what we agreed, and you know it."

"Is a man not allowed to change his mind?" Julian asked.

"Not about this." She was practically glaring at him. "I've explained why it is better for us to remain as lovers and friends. If you've changed your mind, then surely our agreement is null and void?"

"Is that what you want?"

She looked away from him. "I'm not the one who is trying to change the rules."

"Then perhaps I should leave." He left the bed and began to pull on his breeches. "I wouldn't wish to distress you with my inconvenient change of heart."

"Julian . . ."

He pulled his shirt over his head and tucked it into his breeches before buttoning the placket and pulling on his boots. "And if you are going to suggest that the scandal concerning your ill-advised advertisement is reason enough for turning me away, may I remind you that I have *solved* that problem, and you have no more to fear from Mr. Cox or Calloway."

"I'm not so sure that—"

"You doubt my competence?" He stared at her.

"Oh, for goodness' sake, of course not. I still think Percival and Lady Brenton have been talking to Calloway. If he's told them his suspicions about your involvement with the advertisement they might use them as further ammunition against you."

"So, you do doubt me." He made some attempt to tie his cravat, stuck the diamond pin through the mess, and put on his coat. "I can apologize only for failing to live up to your many expectations." He strode to the door. "Pray excuse me, ma'am."

He shut the door behind him. From the thud that shook the frame, he got the distinct impression that Carenza had thrown something at his head. As he went down the stairs, he was already beginning to think that he might have deserved it.

There was no one in the hall to show him out, so he picked up his hat and cane and left, his body as unsatisfied as his mind. It was the first time he'd proposed to a woman. She'd turned him down flat because of some misguided belief that he needed saving or that his offer in some way contravened their existing agreement. He walked around to the mews where he'd left his horse and mounted up.

But if she truly cared for him, wouldn't she have just said yes?

Perhaps her attraction for him began and ended with his

physical prowess and he'd never be good enough. His mother constantly reminded him of his failures to meet expectations. Perhaps she was right.

Chastising himself for his ridiculous overreaction to the answer to a stupidly impulsive question, he went home. He'd spend the rest of the day going over the accounts with his secretary. He'd try to forget his temporary insanity in the far more satisfactory world of finance. Numbers, at least, never let him down.

Chapter 21

On the evening of the charity ball, Carenza put on her new cream patterned gown, and had her maid pile her hair high on top of her head with two ringlets hanging down on either side of her face. Tickets to the ball had sold quickly, and the committee were expecting a packed ballroom. The duchess had arranged for both the Cartwrights and Mrs. Mountjoy to speak before the ball started and had high hopes that they would inspire the attendees to donate even more money to their worthy causes.

Carenza's only hope was that Julian's reputation would be enhanced from being one of the first to support such causes. Anyone who heard Miss Cartwright speak would never think ill of her or believe that her benefactors had been engaged in nefarious activities to hurt children.

She put a touch of rouge to her cheeks and lips and donned a pair of diamond-and-gold earrings and the matching necklace her parents had given her for her twenty-first birthday. She added a thin gold bracelet Julian had given her one Christmas.

Julian . . .

She hadn't spoken to him since his extraordinary proposal in her bed, and she still didn't know what to say to put things right between them. She'd panicked—there was no other way of describing her reaction—and had pushed him away both physically and emotionally. It wasn't like Julian to behave impulsively, and the fact that she might have wounded him with her abrupt dismissal of his proposal preyed on her mind. Romantic thoughts of them sharing their lives together kept intruding in her imagination. That they'd be happy together she had no doubt, but her position in society meant she was not considered his equal. The thought of him gradually realizing she'd never be totally acceptable to the ton, and him exhausting himself trying to ensure that she was, unsettled her.

But she wanted him . . . that she couldn't deny. Others might find him cool and distant but she knew the real man, his unflinching support of causes dear to his heart and his loyalty as a friend, even to those who hadn't deserved it in the slightest.

Allegra came in as the maid withdrew. She'd dressed in blue with a peacock feather in her hair and looked rather regal.

"Why are you still sitting here?" Allegra asked. "We'll be late, and the duchess will be cross."

"I'm sorry." Carenza stood, picked up her shawl and reticule from the bed, and went over to the door. "I was woolgathering."

"About Julian?" Allegra, who could be far too knowing, smirked. "Every time I've mentioned his name in the past week, you've gone off into a dream." She nudged her sister in the ribs. "You should marry him, you know."

"You know how I feel about marriage," Carenza replied as they went down the stairs.

"Don't be missish. Julian is nothing like Hector. I'm fairly certain he'd say yes if you broke that silly agreement of yours and asked."

"Why do you think that?" Carenza tried to keep her voice light, but she desperately wanted to know the answer.

"Because he's in love with you." Allegra gave her a pitying look. "It's obvious to anyone who sees how he treats you."

"He is renowned for treating ladies well."

"He's different with you." Allegra paused as the butler opened the door and the carriage arrived in the square. "Less charming, more real."

They were assisted into the coach by the footman and sat on opposite sides to prevent their skirts being creased.

Carenza cleared her throat. "What if I did ask Julian to marry me, and he was horrified at the very idea?"

Allegra regarded her curiously. "Have you?"

"*No.*"

"Then maybe you should," Allegra advised, and sat back as if that was the end of the conversation. And perhaps it was.

Julian arrived at the Grantleigh mansion just as Mrs. Mountjoy was walking up the steps. He offered her his arm, and they continued into the vast hallway where servants were still scurrying about setting things to rights for the evening ahead.

"You look rather splendid, ma'am," Julian observed as they walked into the main ballroom where a string quartet was already tuning up.

Mrs. Mountjoy was dressed in dark blue with roses on her bodice.

"And you look unhappy."

"I'm smiling, am I not?" Julian countered. "I intend to enjoy my evening immensely."

She patted his hand. "Would you like some advice?"

"Not particularly."

"You should marry Carenza Musgrove."

"What makes you think she'd be willing to marry me?"

"Good Lord." Mrs. Mountjoy stopped walking. "Did she turn you down?"

"That is none of your business," Julian replied with a lightness he was far from feeling.

"She did." Mrs. Mountjoy nodded. "That's why you're so miserable. Good for her."

"What's good about it?" Julian asked and immediately regretted it.

"It's probably the first time in your life that you've been turned down for something you want."

"Hardly."

"I like her even more now." Mrs. Mountjoy smiled as he held the door open into an anteroom at the rear of the ballroom. "I hope she leads you a merry dance."

Barely repressing his indignation, Julian smiled as he saw the Cartwrights were already in the room. Mr. Cartwright looked his usual calm self, but Miss Cartwright was frowning, her hands knotted together on her lap. She wore a plain brown dress that Julian assumed was her Sunday best.

"Good evening, Miss Cartwright," Julian greeted her. "Are you looking forward to the ball?"

She looked up at him. "I can't say that I am, sir. I never liked dancing or crowded spaces. I'm only here because my brother insisted upon it. He said that if all these people are willing to support our cause, the least I could do was show my face."

"I tend to agree with your brother," Julian said. "You are the best advocate for your cause, Miss Cartwright. Your integrity and serenity shine through. After hearing you speak, no one could believe that either you or Mr. Cartwright have anything but the best intentions toward children."

"Thank you for saying that." She hesitated. "I have often misjudged your seriousness about our cause, but organizing this ball for our benefit shows that you are indeed sincere."

"That's very good of you, but I wasn't instrumental in arranging the ball. Although, I am fully supportive of the committee's efforts."

Miss Cartwright cleared her throat. "Is your brother attending?"

"I believe so."

"Oh."

"Did you particularly wish to speak to him? I can ask him to seek you out."

"No! Thank you." She shrank back in her seat. "Please don't draw unnecessary attention upon me."

"My brother is the best of men. I sometimes wish I had his *joie de vivre*." Miss Cartwright didn't reply, and Julian was at somewhat of a loss about how to proceed. "Do you wish me to ask him to leave you alone?"

"I don't know what I want," she blurted out.

"Then perhaps you should simply go with your instincts?" Julian suggested. "If he seeks you out, he won't force his company on you if it isn't wanted."

"Miss Cartwright, if I might offer you some advice?" Mrs. Mountjoy said. "Aragon Laurent is a true gentleman. If you ask him to stop bothering you, he will." She glanced at Julian. "And if he doesn't, then I'm sure Mr. Laurent will set him straight."

"Absolutely." Julian nodded.

Miss Cartwright still looked worried, but Julian put it down to her anxiety about the upcoming event. "I have no intention of marrying." Miss Cartwright raised her chin. "I am devoted to my work."

Mrs. Mountjoy patted her hand. "Then that's all you need to say to any man who wishes to have a relationship with you. Most of them will take the hint, and, if they don't, Mr. Laurent and I will make sure they never bother you again."

The door opened, and the duchess, dressed in silver and white to match the glitter of her diamonds, strode into the room along with several members of the committee, including Mrs. Sheraton. She beamed at the Cartwrights and came across to take Mrs. Mountjoy's hand.

"Anna, how lovely to see you again. Miss Cartwright, Mr. Cartwright, Mr. Laurent, how good of you all to come."

Julian excused himself soon after her greetings and went to check on the state of the ballroom. The duchess had excelled in the preparations. Perfume from the large flower arrangement drifted across the room along with smoke from a hundred lit candles in the massive chandeliers that hung from the center of the painted ceiling. Fires had been lit in the stone fireplaces on the end walls. When the guests arrived, it would become unbearably hot and crowded—the smell of bodies overriding the sweeter scents of the flowers.

He heard a familiar voice at the top of the stairs leading up to the ballroom and watched as Allegra, who appeared to be urging her sister to hurry up, went past the doors and into the antechamber beyond. He had to admit to a certain trepidation in meeting Carenza—something he wasn't used to. But her immediate rejection of his proposal had hurt. In fairness, he'd been almost as shocked as she had when the words popped out of his mouth, but he knew they were from his heart and that he meant them. Carenza obviously didn't agree.

The duchess and her entourage came to the ballroom doors, chattering like a flock of starlings. As the clock struck the hour, voices echoed up from the entrance hall below, and Julian quietly took his place at the end of the receiving line, ready to welcome the incoming guests. He glanced along the line but caught only a glimpse of Carenza, who was behind Mr. Cartwright.

He had little time to think after that, as a stream of guests came up the stairs like a wave of breeding salmon and worked their way along the line and then into the ballroom where the string quartet played quietly on the balcony. When the bulk of the guests had passed by, the duchess decreed they should all join her in the ballroom for the speeches.

Julian waited until Carenza approached. He cupped her elbow and said, "Good evening."

"Julian." She looked her usual calm, lovely self. "How nice to see you."

"I'm hoping you have a space on your dance card for me—preferably the supper dance?"

"Of course." She smiled at him. "That would be delightful."

He let her go on ahead of him, his gaze thoughtful. If she imagined he was going to apologize for proposing to her she was quite wrong. In his heart, he knew his impulsive offer was the truest thing he'd ever said in his life, and he was determined to ensure that Carenza realized it, too.

The duchess ascended the small, raised dais at the end of the ballroom and clapped her hands to quieten the guests.

"Good evening, everyone. Thank you for attending this charity ball to aid the inspiring work of Mrs. Mountjoy and the Cartwrights to save the impoverished children of London from the worst of fates." She gestured for Miss Cartwright, who was holding her speech in her visibly shaking hands, to step forward. "Miss Cartwright has agreed to speak to you tonight. Please give her a warm welcome."

The guests obligingly clapped, and Julian sensed Miss Cartwright was ready to bolt. But she was tougher than she looked and spoke up in a clear, precise voice about the work she and her brother did, and that of Mrs. Mountjoy, and how worthy a cause it was.

Julian could only admire her single-mindedness. Any thought he'd had of her being the perfect wife for him had disappeared once he'd realized she had a true vocation in life. He doubted even Aragon could convince her otherwise. And there was the little matter of his feelings for Carenza. . . .

The applause when she finished was prolonged, and she blushed to the roots of her hair. Mrs. Mountjoy stepped up to offer her thanks, and the duchess was just about to offer some closing remarks when someone else jumped up on the dais. Jeremy Calloway.

"Forgive me for interrupting, Your Grace," Calloway spoke very loudly. "But you have been grievously deceived by a bunch of charlatans led by Julian Laurent!"

"Good God." Julian started to push his way toward the dais.

"Ask Mr. Percival Walcott," Calloway continued. "Ask Lady Brenton! They'll tell you what a liar Laurent really is, and how he isn't above using blackmail to get what he wants."

"He's right." Percival joined Calloway on the dais. "All of this is a front for the nefarious dealings of a wicked man." His gaze found Julian's in the crowd. "He's the one using these poor unsuspecting people as pawns in his game to corrupt the innocent!"

An excited murmur ran through the crowd. The duchess, who didn't appreciate being upstaged in her own house, frowned.

"This is ridiculous," she said. "If you have genuine grievances against Mr. Laurent, then take them up with the courts and not in my ballroom!"

"Ask him what he does at the Wheatsheaf Inn!" Calloway yelled. "He's conspiring with the landlord to make sure his *children* get sent to their new owners. Who do you think set up that ridiculous advertisement to lure more of us into his clutches so that he could blackmail us and the women he forces to work for him? No wonder his fortune is always increasing. It thrives on extortion and the misery of children!"

Just as Calloway finished speaking, Aragon jumped up on the dais, drew back his fist, and planted a facer on Calloway. With a scream, Calloway dropped to the floor.

"That's for speaking ill of my brother!" Aragon said. He bowed to the duchess. "Apologies, Your Grace."

Julian finally reached the front of the room, mainly because the people around him were drawing back with various expressions of amusement or horror on their faces. Julian saw Walcott, and he sorely wished he could follow his brother's example and flatten him.

Instead, he bowed to the duchess and turned to address the guests. "I can assure you that these allegations are baseless lies, and that I will be following the duchess's advice and referring all these matters to my barrister."

"Not good enough," Walcott said loudly. "I'm willing to go back to court if your perfidy is finally exposed to the world."

Julian turned to look at Percival, his gaze icy. "The Cartwrights and Mrs. Mountjoy do excellent work to help the disadvantaged children of our city. My supposed 'involvement' in their organizations amounts to nothing more than being a proud member on their boards. Anything else is a figment of your depraved imagination."

"And what about your involvement in the advertisement?" Lady Brenton shouted from the front row. "Are you more than a blackmailer? Were you secretly seeing 'your children' onto coaches without the knowledge of these fine institutions?"

"I was doing nothing of the sort."

"If anyone thinks we entrust Mr. Laurent with the future employment of the children in our care, then you are sadly mistaken." Mrs. Mountjoy spoke clearly from behind him. "Every child is escorted to their new home by me or the Cartwrights. Mr. Laurent is an honorable and admirable man, and this is simply an attempt to smear him."

Calloway, clutching a handkerchief to his nose, got up from the floor. "Then why was he at that inn handing out money to all and sundry?" He glared at Julian. "And don't deny it. I have witnesses."

"That is an entirely separate matter," Julian said. "And one I have already discussed with your father. I suggest you speak to him and refrain from commenting in public when your understanding is so limited."

"You were at the inn more than once," Calloway persisted. "I can prove it."

"Did you have something to do with that advertisement

from the lady who was looking for a lover, Laurent?" Walcott said loudly. "I think we all deserve an explanation."

"On the contrary," Julian snapped. "I think you deserve nothing but contempt for dragging the names of these good people into disrepute when the work they do is so important. Now can we proceed with the ball?"

Lady Brenton stepped forward. "Why *were* you at that inn? Were you the person who wrote the advertisement to lure more young men into your clutches so that you could blackmail them?"

A murmur ran around the ballroom, which didn't sound particularly favorable toward Julian.

Lady Brenton smiled. "Do tell. We're all agog for your answer."

"He had nothing to do with it." Carenza stepped forward from where she'd been standing with the rest of the committee. "That was me. I placed the advertisement."

Noise rose in the ballroom as her words were repeated like an outgoing wave. Julian caught the duchess's eye, took Carenza's hand, and practically dragged her through to the anteroom. He shut the door behind them and spun around.

"What in damnation are you *doing*?"

She met his gaze quite calmly. "Protecting my friend. Admitting to my own mistake."

"They'll ruin you!"

"I'm already considered déclassé. Why does it matter if they think I'm even worse?"

"Because I have spent weeks trying to prevent this very thing from happening. And now you just stand up and admit to it?" He clenched his fists to keep from shaking her. "What in God's name is wrong with you?"

He only realized he was shouting when she winced.

"I'm tired of lying. I'm tired of being used by your enemies to bring you down."

"I was in no danger of losing my reputation. Everyone out there knows what Walcott is like. No one would believe him."

"You're wrong about that." She paused. "People love to gossip, and there would've been a shadow left on your name and reputation. I couldn't allow that to happen."

"You couldn't allow it? What in God's name does it have to do with you?"

She let out a breath. "Julian, I know that you are angry with Percival and Calloway, but—"

"You're wrong." He cut her off again. "I'm angry with you."

"For caring enough to protect you?"

"But you don't care, do you, Carenza? You take what you want from me and offer nothing in return."

She went still. "That's hardly fair."

"You considered me too far above you to contemplate marriage," he said. "One might think you'd be pleased that my reputation might be as ruined as yours. Or did you decide to 'sacrifice' yourself on my behalf, because you didn't really want us to be equal? And that way you could avoid another unwanted proposal?"

"Julian . . ." Her voice was unsteady, and there were tears gathering in her eyes. "As to that, l wanted to tell you—"

"As to that, nothing." He inclined his head an icy inch. "You win, my dear. I'll keep to our bargain. I'll be your stud, because quite honestly what else am I worth to you?"

The music started up again in the ballroom behind them, as she studied him. "Perhaps *you* are angry because I have completely ruined my reputation and you can no longer pretend I would make you a suitable wife."

"That's ridiculous!" Julian said.

"Our bargain, such as it was, is null and void, sir." She curtsied, turned around, and left by the outer door into the lower hall.

She didn't even slam the door, just shut it carefully behind her.

He took several breaths. Then, his fury dying as quickly as it had risen, he flung open the door. "Carenza!"

"Julian." Aragon came toward him, his expression concerned. "Are you all right? We got rid of the agitators, and the crowd seems to be on your side. They're all gossiping about Lady Carenza instead."

"Damn her," Julian muttered.

"Actually, I thought it was rather brave," Aragon said. "You should be grateful. Her announcement saved your reputation."

"Brave, foolhardy, or entirely unnecessary?" Julian demanded.

Aragon raised his eyebrows. "Brave. If I have to pick one. She didn't have to do that for you, brother."

"I am well aware of that."

"I hope you were sufficiently grateful."

"I—" Julian paused. "I lost my temper with her."

"Ah." Aragon nodded. "That probably explains why she was crying when I saw her leave."

Julian steeled himself against that image and scowled at his brother. "Then perhaps she shouldn't have interfered. I had everything under control."

"No, you didn't," Aragon demurred. "Have you any idea how many of your peers would love to see you brought low? They were practically salivating at the thought that you were a bad man. Why do you think I punched Calloway?"

"I have no idea."

"And why do you think I've been pretending to be friends with Walcott for the past week or so?" Aragon prodded him in the chest. "For *you*."

"What?"

"The ladies asked me to find out what Percival was up to.

I was coming here to tell them he'd definitely planned something for the ball, but Mother held me up with one of her lectures about my moral turpitude, and I arrived too late to warn everybody."

"Why does everyone around me assume I'm incapable of looking after myself?" Julian asked. "I've been self-sufficient since the age of five, when it became evident that my own mother couldn't abide me."

"Because we care about you. Is that not reason enough?"

Julian stared at him. He'd just accused Carenza of being incapable of caring and now his own brother was suggesting that he was the one who wouldn't allow anyone to care for him.

"Don't be ridiculous," Julian said. He checked his reflection in the mirror. "We should get back to the ball."

"You're not serious."

Julian swung around to look at his brother. "If I don't go out there now, there will be people who think I have something to hide."

"I understand that, but what about Lady Carenza? Don't you think you should go and put things right with her first?"

"I doubt she'll want to see me right now."

"She's very fond of you, Julian," Aragon said. "Hector knew that."

"What does bloody Hector have to do with anything? He's dead!"

"I never told you this because you and Hector were such good friends, but I happened to be seated near him at the end of the night when he became engaged to Lady Carenza. He made a point of telling me why he'd chosen to marry her." Aragon looked at Julian, all the usual humor gone from his face. "Hector said he knew you were in love with her and that it would be amusing to see if he could turn Carenza's head before she realized it. He was laughing while he told me, but he was rather drunk."

Julian blinked at him.

Aragon grimaced. "I never liked Hector." He patted Julian's shoulder. "If you insist on going back to the ball, I'm coming with you. Anyone who dares insult you will have me to deal with as well."

Carenza reached home, ran up the stairs, and collapsed on the floor of her bedchamber in a storm of weeping. All she could see, all she could hear, was Julian's disdain and fury for her. After a while, she blew her nose and contemplated the roaring fire. Despite his anger, all was not lost. If his reputation was restored then the rest of it—his wrath, his accusations that she was incapable of loving anyone—meant nothing.

Except she'd never forget him saying those things. Hector had taught her to guard her heart, but had she learned the lesson too well? Was she too damaged to reach out for happiness with the man she'd always liked and had grown to love?

Her door opened, and she turned, hastily wiping her eyes, to see Allegra coming in.

"Well." Her sister sat on the chair next to the fire. "You certainly put the cat among the pigeons. I have a feeling that my chances of making a good marriage have significantly declined."

"I'm so sorry, Allegra."

Allegra shrugged. "There's always India. Anton's already there, and I hear the men are desperate for women to marry."

"Don't even think about it." Carenza reached for her sister's hand. "I can't bear the thought of you leaving me."

Allegra gave her hand a comforting squeeze. "You did the right thing, you know."

"Yes," Carenza said. "But at what cost?"

Chapter 22

The next morning, Aragon appeared in Julian's bedroom with a collection of newspapers under his arm.

"It's bad," Aragon said, dumping the papers on Julian's bed. "Lady Carenza's name is all over the papers and not just in the social sections. Her family history has been exhumed and minutely examined, and she has been found deficient in every way."

"God . . ." Julian pressed his fingers to his eyes. He hadn't slept well. The image of Carenza's face as he'd lost his temper had never left his mind. "I hope her father doesn't see them."

"I'm fairly certain he will," Aragon said as he paced around Julian's room. "Did you see that obnoxious Lady Smythe-Harding at the ball last night? She was wallowing in all the attention as she told that ridiculous story about Lady Carenza stealing her family jewels. If you hadn't ordered me to be nice to everyone, I would've had a few choice words with her myself."

"The last thing we need is to make everything worse," Julian said.

"How could we possibly do that?" Aragon stared at him. "Lady Carenza's reputation has been destroyed while yours—"

"Has been validated. I am aware of that."

"Then what are you going to do about it?" Aragon demanded. "And please don't tell me that you plan to do nothing. That poor girl sacrificed herself for you."

"I didn't ask her to do so."

"That's your defense? Good Lord, Julian. I thought you were better than this."

"Aragon, I've just woken up. Please give me at least a moment to gather my thoughts and decide on a plan of action."

"That's better." Aragon scowled at him. "I like the Musgroves. They don't deserve this."

He departed as abruptly as he'd come, leaving Julian with a sick feeling in his stomach and a pile of newspapers that barely mentioned his name but painted Carenza in such awful terms that he sometimes struggled to read them. The consensus was that she would no longer be welcome in polite society, as she was as immoral as her infamous mother.

He got out of bed, dressed as quickly as possible, and went down to breakfast. Simon was already at the table eating. He stood up as Julian came in. "Good morning, sir."

"Good morning." Julian piled his plate with food that he wasn't sure he could eat and sat down.

Simon cleared his throat. "Is there anything in particular you wish me to deal with this morning?"

Julian just looked at him.

"I heard there was a slight contretemps at the ball last night."

"Slight?"

"I understand from your brother that your reputation was questioned but that you came through it unscathed."

"That's one way of putting it." Julian drank some coffee. "Did he also mention the only reason that happened is because Lady Carenza sacrificed her own reputation for mine?"

"Yes, sir." Simon hesitated. "I must admit that despite what you told me, I thought Mrs. Sheraton was the instigator of the advertisement and that Lady Carenza was covering up for her."

"Mrs. Sheraton certainly has a lot to answer for." Julian ate a small amount of ham and nibbled on some toast.

"I suppose Lady Carenza will be returning to the country," Simon said. "I doubt she'll be received in society."

Julian winced. Not seeing her again, watching her fade away in disgrace—it was an insult to everything she was.

The butler came in. "Lady Landon is here, sir. I've put her in the front parlor and ordered some tea."

Good God, that was all he needed . . . Julian's headache returned with a vengeance and he set down his cup. "I suppose I'd better go and get it over with. If I'm not out in fifteen minutes, please interrupt our meeting and insist that I am urgently required elsewhere."

His mother was standing by the fireplace, her critical gaze trained on the painting he'd recently acquired and hung above the mantelpiece.

"My dear Mama, how may I assist you?"

She studied him, her expression tight. "I want your assurances that you will do everything in your power to keep any hint of scandal away from your brother."

"Naturally." He bowed. "Although the only scandal I am aware of concerns Lady Carenza Musgrove."

"She is a . . . connection of both of yours." She sniffed. "At least I don't have to worry about Aragon wanting to marry her anymore. All decent members of society will treat her as the pariah she is, and hopefully she'll never show her face in London again."

Julian took a moment to control his temper before he addressed her again. "Is there anything else I can help you with today, ma'am?"

"No."

"No concerns for my current well-being?"

She raised an eyebrow. "You have never sought my concern."

"It was never offered to me, even as a child."

"Oh, for goodness' sake, Julian, you weren't a likable child." She pulled on her gloves with jerky movements. "Considering the circumstances, I did my very best with you, and I do not appreciate being judged."

"What circumstances could make a mother decide that her own child was unlikable? Am I evil incarnate?"

"Now you are being melodramatic and ridiculous."

"Perhaps I'm a bastard?" Julian asked. "I'd almost believe my father foisted his illegitimate child on you except that I am your mirror image."

"My reasons are my own. You are fully grown. You should put your silly grievances behind you and treat me with the respect I deserve." She half turned toward the door.

"Or were you the one who had an affair and I'm the result of it?" Julian asked.

She went very still.

"Now, that makes far more sense. You conceived a child out of wedlock and had to beg the earl to accept me as his son. And then you took it out on me because I had the audacity to grow up not looking like a Laurent."

His mother turned her back on him and marched toward the door. "I refuse to have this conversation. You will never dare to mention this subject or I will never speak to you again."

He bowed. "I fully expect you not to be speaking to me for many reasons in the near future, so perhaps we'd better agree to part company now. Good morning, ma'am. I'll ask my butler to see you out." He walked past her and left the room, a curious feeling of lightness in his belly.

He knew the worst now, and somehow it made complete sense of everything she'd put him through. At some point he might even dredge up some sympathy for her but not quite yet. She had no control over his current existence, and he was done with pandering to her by acting like a rake.

He went into his study and wrote a note to Carenza, asking her if he might call, and sent it out immediately. Less than an hour later, it was returned unopened with the words, *Not at home*, scrawled on the front.

His butler cleared his throat. "I understand from the boy who took the note that Musgrove House is currently besieged by onlookers and members of the press, and that they are receiving no one."

"Thank you," Julian said.

He knew how to get into Musgrove House through the mews and back garden, but he had to assume those entrances would be guarded as well. It didn't sit well with him, but it looked as if he'd have to wait until Carenza decided to contact him herself. He needed to apologize for the loss of his temper and then what? He rubbed his hands over his face. There was so much he needed to say, and for the first time in his life he had no idea how to even begin.

The sound of raised voices in the hall made Carenza put down her book. Had the crowd outside somehow gained entrance into the house? Was she about to be dragged outside by her hair and made to pay for her crimes? She rose to her feet, her gaze fixed on the door.

Allegra stood up, too. "There's no need to look so noble, Carenza. You're not about to be carted off to the guillotine."

Sometimes Allegra understood her far too well. The door opened, and her father and brother came in looking particularly displeased.

"What in the devil have you been up to?" her father roared. "We were relying on you to keep Allegra's reputation intact!"

Carenza faced him down. "I defended the reputation of my friend."

"So I hear," her father said unhappily. "One might think that the reputation of your own family would be more important to you."

"Carenza did what she thought was right." Allegra came to stand beside her sister. "I am very proud of her."

"You won't feel the same when no decent gentleman will marry you," Dorian said, his body stiff with outrage. "How many times have I told you girls that you must behave with propriety and decorum?"

Carenza turned to her brother. "You make it sound as if we have something to be ashamed of. I'm not ashamed of having parents who loved each other enough to defy the stupid conventions of society."

"But you don't have to repeat their behavior!" Dorian said. "You have embarrassed our entire family—again—and made it far harder for Allegra and me to find spouses."

"I am truly sorry if I have done so, but I felt I had no choice." Carenza looked at her father, who had taken a seat beside the fire. "Surely you of all men should understand that?"

"I loved your mother. I didn't risk everything for a family friend, and I didn't advertise in the newspapers for a bloody rake to pleasure me!"

Carenza sat opposite her father. "Now that, I will apologize for unreservedly. It was a joke that for various reasons got out of hand."

"The main reason being that Mrs. Sheraton published an indiscreet version of the advertisement before we knew what she was doing," Allegra chimed in. "Once that was published, there was little we could do."

"You could've threatened to sue the newspaper that printed it," Dorian countered. "Or asked me or Father to deal with the matter for you."

"We had no idea it would cause such a stir," Allegra said.

"You knew about this?" Dorian looked at Allegra.

"Yes."

"And you did nothing to stop Carenza ruining your future matrimonial prospects?"

Allegra shrugged. "If a man is put off by such a minor scandal, then he isn't right for me anyway." She returned her brother's skeptical look. "I already knew that from society's treatment of Mama."

Carenza cast her sister a grateful look. They might argue sometimes, but they were always loyal to each other.

"Allegra did caution me against placing the advertisement, and she was right to do so. But none of us could've imagined how it would blow up and involve others."

"Was Julian Laurent supportive of this ridiculous idea?" her father asked.

"On the contrary. He was horrified," Carenza said. "He tried everything he could to stop it becoming an even bigger scandal. That's why I couldn't allow his reputation to suffer."

Her father glanced over at Dorian. "I suppose this is another fine example of women's logic at work."

"I have to agree, sir."

The earl slapped his knees and stood up. "I told the butler to start closing up the house. I suggest you both go and pack."

"We're leaving?" Allegra asked.

"I don't see any other way of managing this scandal, do you?"

"But I'll need to inform people that we are going," Allegra said desperately. "I have commitments—"

"Perhaps Allegra could stay on for a day or two and then follow us down?" Carenza, who had accepted her fate the moment her father came through the door, asked. "She's very good at managing the staff."

"I'd be happy to stay," Allegra said. "And, as my reputation is truly ruined, I won't even require a chaperone."

Julian managed two days before his patience ran out. He'd had plenty to occupy his time dealing with the repercussions of the ball, instructing his barrister in case Walcott started up again, and calming down Aragon as he loudly took exception to anyone who said a bad thing about his brother.

He waited until it was dark and took a circuitous route to the back of Tavistock Square, through the mews, and into the well-kept garden behind the house. There were a few lights on in the house, and no one stopped his progress. He tiptoed past the kitchen and up the backstairs and emerged close to the drawing room at the front of the house. He tapped lightly on the door and went in to find Allegra sitting alone by the fire.

"Lady Allegra." He bowed. "I wanted to speak to Carenza."

"You're too late for that," Allegra said. "She left two days ago with my father. I only stayed to close up the household and deal with the staff."

Julian just stared at her. "Damnation."

"My feelings exactly. Please sit down. I expected at least a few days' grace, but none was offered." Allegra sighed. "Father was most displeased, and Dorian was insufferable."

"I thought that if they did come to town, they'd probably wish to speak to me," Julian said. "In truth, I was expecting them at any moment."

"Father decided all the fault lay with Carenza because she defended you to the last," Allegra said. "She took all the blame on herself."

Julian winced.

"You know that she is in love with you?" Allegra continued. "It is obvious to anyone who knows her well."

"She . . . is remarkably good at hiding her emotions," Julian said with some caution.

"That's because Hector enjoyed baiting and belittling her. After a while, she learned to conceal her true feelings beneath an impenetrable layer of calm, and then he couldn't hurt her so badly."

Julian had nothing to say to that. He remembered what Aragon had told him about Hector's decision to marry Carenza simply to cut him out. He grew angry all over again.

"Do you think I should write to her?" Julian asked.

"I think that whatever you choose to do is up to you, but if you hurt her, you will have me to reckon with." Allegra glared at him. "I will not allow her heart to be broken again. So be very sure that you know what you want before you disturb her peace."

Julian rose to his feet. "You are a very good sister."

"I do my best." Allegra shrugged. "For what it's worth, I believe she does care for you very deeply, but that she is almost afraid to believe you might feel that way, too."

"I asked her to marry me."

"Did you?" Allegra looked startled. "And she turned you down?"

"She suggested she wasn't good enough for me."

"How ridiculous." Allegra rolled her eyes and stood up. "She is the best woman I know."

"I agree." He took her hand and kissed it. "I wish you a safe journey back to Norfolk."

"Thank you." She paused. "Will we be seeing you at your family's country home this year?"

"It's highly likely."

"Good." She smiled at him. "Just promise me that you won't make things worse."

"I promise to try to make them better."

He left and returned home to have his dinner, his thoughts racing. Allegra had indicated that he did stand a chance with Carenza, but should he wait until she contacted him? Or should he be bold, follow her back to Norfolk, and declare his undying love? He was unsure of how to proceed because the stakes were so high. Just because he'd realized almost immediately that he was taking his anger out on the wrong person, Carenza might not. She'd learned from a master manipulator how to hide her feelings. If she was at all unsure of

Julian's love, she might not grant him another opportunity to tell her how he felt.

"Mr. Laurent."

He looked up as his butler came into the dining room, closely followed by Mrs. Sheraton.

"I beg your pardon, sir, but this lady was very insistent that she should see you."

"That's quite all right," Julian said. "Perhaps you might fetch another wineglass for Mrs. Sheraton. Or would you care to dine with me, ma'am? I'm sure Cook could accommodate you."

"Just the wine, please." She sat opposite him at the table, her fingers drumming until the glass was filled and set in front of her. She looked pale, her mouth set in a hard line. "Thank you."

"How may I be of assistance, ma'am?"

"How do you think?" She glared at him. "This is all your fault."

"Hardly." He might regret some of his actions, but not all of them. "You played your part."

"I am aware of that." She took a large gulp of wine.

"Why did you do it?" Julian asked. "Place the advertisement in all its unfettered glory in the first place?"

Mrs. Sheraton looked down at her glass. "Guilt, perhaps?"

Julian just looked at her.

She sighed. "And perhaps a little bit of jealousy?"

"Carenza didn't deserve that."

She raised her chin. "I am quite aware of that, but jealousy is not always a rational thing."

"You resented her for being married to Hector?"

"God, no. It's more that she survived him and moved on with her life, whereas I . . ." She grimaced. "I remained mired in guilt at having led him on for what I thought were the most virtuous of reasons. Namely, to expose him for what he was."

"With respect, ma'am. Hector never needed to be led to anything. He just took whatever he could without caring about whom he hurt in the process. You are hardly to blame for his amoral nature."

"It's very kind of you to say so, but I still hurt my best friend."

"And Hector hurt you and I failed miserably to hold him to account despite being his best friend."

"Carenza told you about what happened?" She sighed. "Of course she did. She's in love with you."

"So everyone keeps telling me," Julian murmured. He reached for his glass and drained it.

"One cannot blame her for being cautious," Mrs. Sheraton said. "Hector—"

"Was a bad man, as my brother would say," Julian completed her sentence. "I am aware of that."

"Then what are we going to do to fix things?" Mrs. Sheraton looked at him. "Surely you have a plan."

"I must confess that I have no idea what to do."

"I don't believe that for a minute," Mrs. Sheraton said.

"It's the truth." Julian hesitated. "I'm not even sure how to approach her, let alone fix all the damage that's been caused."

Mrs. Sheraton finished her wine, and Julian poured her another glass. "I think you will have to be honest with her."

"Not a strength of mine," Julian admitted. "I've always avoided expressing my feelings."

"Having seen the way your mother behaves toward you, I'm not surprised. She treats you like a poor relation who's been foisted on the family."

"Thank you." Julian grimaced. "I was hoping I was the only one who noticed." He drank more wine. "I think I will write to Carenza and see if she responds."

"Coward." Mrs. Sheraton drained her second glass.

"Perhaps," Julian acknowledged. "But I am more than

willing to go to Norfolk and speak to her in person if she doesn't respond."

"And if she does write back and she tells you never to speak to her again?" There was a challenge in Mrs. Sheraton's gaze.

"Then I'll definitely go to Norfolk."

She held up her glass, and he clinked his against hers.

"I wish you success," Mrs. Sheraton said. "I truly believe you are made for each other. You're both so annoyingly perfect."

"Thank you." Julian went to pour more wine and realized the bottle was empty. "Would you care to join me in my study for a glass of brandy?"

"Thank you, but I think I should be getting home. I promised to tell Maude all the latest scandal."

"Which is?"

"That Carenza is ruined, and that you are a noble hero, a man of good deeds who has been unfairly smeared by the jealous Mr. Walcott." She stood up, her cheeks rather flushed. "Carenza did that for you, Mr. Laurent. And for me. She didn't even mention my name. The least you can do is pay her back in kind."

> *My dear Carenza,*
> *I can only apologize again and ask for forgiveness. I hope you are settled in Norfolk with your family. Please let me know if there is anything I can do for you.*
> *Your friend,*
> *Julian Laurent.*

Carenza read the letter twice and then left it on the dressing table. What did he expect her to do? Write back and reassure him that she was as happy as a woman could be and that there was nothing for him to worry about? That would be a lie, and Julian wasn't a fool. He must know she'd returned home in disgrace. It was a good thing that almost no one visited the Musgroves anyway, because they would certainly stay away now.

The whole country now knew her name, and her family were receiving mail from everywhere in reply to the advertisement. Carenza's father ordered that everything they received should be burned. It was only by chance that Julian's letter had gotten through to her in the first place.

She'd also had a note from Aragon telling her he'd successfully bought up a considerable portion of Walcott's debts and was poised to deliver the bad news to the gentleman himself. Aragon wrote that Olivia had decided to accompany him when he told Walcott and that he had faith that they'd never hear from the scoundrel again. He also added a postscript that his mother was leaving London and making plans to move into the dower house at his country estate.

Carenza was momentarily diverted from her misery to wonder whether Lady Landon was departing voluntarily or if Aragon had finally fully claimed his earldom and sent her packing. She hoped it was the latter. Aragon had proved to be a staunch ally to his brother after all.

She turned as her mother, Rosaria, came into her bedroom with her usual flowing grace. She looked more like Carenza's sister than the mother of three grown children, her black hair barely streaked with silver, and her figure as voluptuous as ever.

"There is no need to skulk in here on such a beautiful day, *cara mia*. You are home now and have nothing to be ashamed of."

"I'm not ashamed." Carenza turned to her mother. "I'm just worn out worrying about all the people I've hurt because of my actions."

Her mother took her arm, the lush notes of her perfume swirling around them. "You can worry just as well outside, dearest. Your father and brother are off touring the farms, collecting rent, so I am the only person you need to talk to."

"When is Allegra due home?"

"I'm not sure. I think your father plans to send the carriage back to collect her, and he wanted to give the horses time to rest between the trips." Her mother moved over to the dressing table and picked up Julian's note.

"Mother, it's rude to read other people's correspondence." Carenza tried to grab the letter but her mother held her off until she'd finished reading.

"This is hardly the letter of a lover," she said disapprovingly. "Your father wrote me poetry!"

"Now that I do find hard to believe."

"He has the soul of a romantic," her mother continued. "It was my singing that entranced him and made him fall in love with me."

They all knew the story of how the earl had attended a private operatic performance and how he'd fallen instantly and passionately in love with the singer and defied everyone to make Rosaria his wife. He'd never faltered in his devotion to her. He still sought her out in a room, and when she sang for him, he never took his eyes off her. It was exceedingly romantic.

"Do you love him?"

"Yes," Carenza said. Her mother had extracted the full story of Carenza's affair with Julian as soon as she'd arrived home.

"Then will you reply to him in encouraging terms?"

"I'm not sure." Carenza looked at her mother. "Perhaps he is better off without me."

Rosaria snorted. "I doubt that. You are a prize."

"I'm a doubly disgraced woman who advertised for a lover in the newspapers," Carenza said. "I won't be accepted back into society, and Julian is an integral part of that world."

"Surely that is up to him to decide. If he suddenly appeared and asked for your hand in marriage, would you turn him down?"

"Yes."

"Because your sacrifice is worth more than your love for each other?" Her mother sniffed. "I tried to persuade your father to take me as his mistress rather than his wife, but he wouldn't listen to me. I'm glad he didn't listen, but I still had to make the offer."

"You're saying that I've already made my own offer? And now it is up to Julian to decide whether to ignore society or not," Carenza said slowly.

"Exactly!" Her mother looked delighted. "So, write to this man and invite him down to see you."

"And what if he says no?" Carenza asked as her mother linked arms with her and drew her out of the room and into the corridor beyond.

"Then he's not the man for you," her mother said with great certainty. "You deserve a great love in your life, Carenza, just as I did. If Julian is not the one, I will take you to Italy, where men are far less stuffy about such things, and I will find you a beautiful man to marry."

"I can't wait," Carenza said, which made her mother laugh as they went out into the garden, where the butler had set out their lunch.

Two days later, the earl sent his coachman to London to pick up Allegra and the servants who would be joining the staff at Musgrove House. Carenza sent her note to Julian with the coachman. Ever since, she'd been plagued with bad dreams where Julian laughed in her face in public, or worse, gave her the cut direct. If he replied via the coachman, she didn't expect to hear from him for a week. She did wonder if he might escort Allegra home but reminded herself not to get her hopes up. Julian still had a lot to lose by associating with her, and she wouldn't be angry with him if he chose not to come.

For once, Julian wasn't surprised to see Aragon coming through his bedroom door. He'd sent his brother a note requesting his presence.

"You're going to Musgrove House?" Aragon asked as he came in, nodding to Proctor, who was busy packing his employer's clothing.

"Yes, I received a note from Lady Carenza yesterday."

"Saying what?"

"That she'd be willing to receive me. That was all I asked for."

"Fool." Aragon rolled his eyes.

"I'd rather have the conversation in person," Julian said. "It's easier to gauge someone's sincerity when you can see their face."

"Rather." Aragon grinned at him. "You should've seen Walcott's expression yesterday when he realized he was done for."

"Walcott?" Julian looked closely at his brother.

"Here." Aragon took a sheaf of papers tied in a ribbon out of his pocket. "I think you should take care of these."

"What is it?"

"I bought up Walcott's gambling debts." Aragon grinned again. "We own him now. If he so much as looks at you strangely, we can call them in and destroy his reputation as a gentleman."

Julian untied the ribbon and looked through the scrawls on the scraps of paper and the notes from money lenders before raising his gaze to his brother's. "You did this for me?"

"Yes, of course."

"I . . . don't know how to thank you."

Aragon thumped his shoulder. "Yes, you do. Go and ask Lady Carenza to marry you. I'll even stand up with you."

Julian embraced his brother. "Thank you."

"Steady on now," Aragon said. "People will think we like each other or something."

"It will amuse you to know that Simon and I hatched a similar plan."

"To ruin Walcott?" Aragon raised his eyebrows.

"Yes, I'm now the proud owner of all the mortgages he's taken out on his family home. I was planning on paying him a visit before I left for Norfolk."

Aragon grinned. "Great minds think alike, brother. May I accompany you when you deliver the bad news? I can't wait to see his face when I turn up on his doorstep again—and demand entry into the house he doesn't really own."

Two hours later, after an exceedingly satisfactory meeting with Percival, Julian was in his curricle, driving himself out of London and toward Norfolk, where the Musgroves had their country residence. He'd thought briefly about offering to accompany Lady Allegra, but he couldn't wait for the horses to be rested, or for her to finally decide to leave.

He reached the house in the evening and was greeted at the front door by the butler who had managed the house since Julian was a boy.

"Mr. Laurent, how nice to see you." The butler took his hat and cloak. "The family are currently at dinner. Lady Carenza did mention you might be joining us. Perhaps I might show you to your room, and I'll inform his lordship of your arrival."

"Thank you." Julian followed the butler up the old shallow staircase with its exposed timbers into the more modern part of the house, where guests weren't subject to the vagaries of low medieval beams and corridors leading nowhere.

"I'll send a maid up to light the fire, sir," the butler said. "And would you wish for something to eat? I'm sure Cook could send up a tray."

"Yes, please. And may I borrow one of your footmen to help with my attire? If I am to meet the earl, I need to change my coat."

"Of course, sir."

A maid appeared almost immediately with hot water and soap for him to wash with. She lit the fire and chatted away as a footman put away Julian's clothing and took his best coat to press. Julian was surprisingly nervous—something he hadn't experienced for years. But then, he'd never been in love before, so he had to make some allowances for his heightened emotions, even if he didn't like them one bit.

He wanted to speak to Carenza but had a shrewd suspicion that the earl would insist on speaking to him first. The earl had the right to ask what the devil he was up to. How he answered that question might determine whether his suit would be acceptable or if he would be ejected from the house immediately.

When he returned with Julian's coat, the footman assisted him into it and stood back to watch Julian adjust his attire to his satisfaction with a worshipful expression on his face. "I want to be a valet, sir," he blurted.

"An admirable objective," Julian said. "Can you direct me down to the library? I wish to speak to the earl."

"Carenza, sit down. You are making me dizzy," her mother said. "Your beloved has come. Let him speak to your father, and then he will come to you, and all will be well."

"Not if Father has one of his stubborn moments." Carenza continued to pace. "You know how contrary he can be."

"It is only because he loves you, dearest, and he does need to make sure Julian understands what it means to take on a wife who is not approved of by society."

Carenza finally sat down. "I suppose there's no one better qualified to offer that advice than Father."

"Exactly."

"I wish Allegra were here," Carenza said.

"She will be here presently. If you do marry, may I suggest you do so at home? No one will judge you as harshly as they would in London."

"Please don't get ahead of yourself," Carenza pleaded. "He might simply have come down to make sure I'm all right before he moves on with his life."

Rosaria snapped her fingers. "Pah! He could've written you a note for that. He's here because he has something important to say. Let him say it."

The butler came in. "Lady Carenza, his lordship is requesting your presence in his library."

"Thank you." Carenza stood up.

Her mother laughed. "Don't look so worried."

"I am worried. What will I do if he's still angry with me?"

"Fight it out?" Rosaria shrugged. "Your father and I had some of our best nights together after an argument."

Carenza left the room, her steps slowing as she approached the library, her breathing uneven. She tapped on the door and went in. Her father rose to his feet and came over to her.

"Mr. Laurent wishes to speak with you." He patted her shoulder and left, closing the door quietly behind him.

Carenza summoned a smile. "Julian, it is so nice to see you."

"Is it?"

She studied him carefully. He was always hard to read, and on this occasion, when she really needed to understand his purpose, he was looking distinctly impenetrable.

"It's always a pleasure." She paused but he didn't speak so she went on. "Especially in these particular circumstances."

"Circumstances that you brought upon yourself despite my best efforts to protect you."

She raised her chin. Ah, it was to be a fight, then? So be it. "Yes, it was entirely my fault. If you came here for another apology, I am more than willing to offer you one."

"As you well know, the only person who needs to apologize is me. I lost my temper."

She nodded. "Quite understandably considering the circumstances."

A slight frown appeared between his brows. "Will you stop being so damned agreeable?"

"I am merely agreeing that you are right, sir. I thought all men liked that."

"I'm not bloody Hector."

"I am well aware of that." Carenza smiled sweetly as he set his jaw. "Is something amiss? You look as if you wish to lose your temper again."

He let out a slow breath. "You are the most infuriating woman I have ever met."

"I think I am offended. Surely Lady Brenton is far worse than me?"

"But I'm not in love with her."

"I'm glad to hear it." She curtsied as a strange giddy relief coursed through her. "Have we finished apologizing to each other? If so, I have some embroidery to complete."

She half turned to the door, but he caught her elbow and spun her around until she was plastered against his chest. She raised her head to look at him and went still.

"Finally," he said. "I have been waiting for you to stop talking."

"Why?"

"Because I love you, and I want you, and I can't imagine my life without you."

"Oh."

"Is that all you have to say to me?"

"You just told me to stop talking," she reminded him. "And to be truthful, I'd much rather be kissing you."

"They'll be none of that unless you agree to marry me."

Was there a tremor in his voice? She looked at him closely and saw herself reflected in his cool-blue gaze.

"You haven't actually asked me."

"I asked you weeks ago!" He was back to scowling again, which delighted her enormously.

"We both know that was a joke."

The arm around her waist tightened. "It damn well was not. I meant every word."

She cupped his chin so that he had to look at her. "But now I am truly ruined."

"So what?"

"Julian . . ."

"If I marry you, Carenza, I can no longer be a rake. So what is the point of being in society if you're not accepted there but the only person I want in my bed is you?"

"I wanted to protect you," she whispered.

"I know." His tone became intimate. "I knew it immediately. My anger was directed entirely at myself." He cleared his throat. "Will you marry me?"

She stared at him. "Yes."

"Do you love me?"

"Yes, of course I do."

"Thank God." He kissed her hard, and she joyfully reciprocated. "I have a special license in my pocket, your parents are at peace with the idea, and I can see no reason why we can't be married tomorrow if the vicar is agreeable."

"What about Allegra? She's not returned from London yet."

His frown returned. "Are you saying you won't marry me if your sister isn't present?"

Carenza sighed. Some things really weren't worth arguing about. "I'll marry you, regardless, but she won't like it."

"We'll wait for her return to have our proper wedding breakfast, will that suffice?" He hesitated. "There is one other thing you should know about me."

"That you are impossible?" Carenza asked.

"You already know that." He took her hand. "I'm not a Laurent."

She stared at him. "Your mother..."

"Had a lover."

"She's spent her whole life blaming you for her own indiscretion?" Carenza scowled. "I can't wait to see her and tell her my opinion of that!"

"I doubt she'll receive us, my darling."

"Which is probably for the best, because she would not like the things I would have to say to her!"

He led her toward the door. "Let's go and tell your family."

"Wait just one moment." She put her hand on his chest over his heart. "I have always loved you and felt safe with you. I promise that when we're married, we'll be best friends and lovers for the rest of our lives."

"Good," he said and kissed her again. "Now come along and speak to your parents."

For once, Carenza gladly complied.

Visit our website at
KensingtonBooks.com
to sign up for our newsletters, read more from your favorite authors, see books by series, view reading group guides, and more!

BOOK CLUB
BETWEEN THE CHAPTERS

Become a Part of Our
Between the Chapters Book Club
Community and Join the Conversation

Betweenthechapters.net

Submit your book review for a chance to win exclusive Between the Chapters swag you can't get anywhere else!
https://www.kensingtonbooks.com/pages/review/